The Family Fang

Kevin Wilson

W F HOWES LTD

This large print edition published in 2011 by
W F Howes Ltd
Unit 4, Rearsby Business Park, Gaddesby Lane,
Rearsby, Leicester LE7 4YH

1 3 5 7 9 10 8 6 4 2

First published in the United Kingdom in 2011
by Picador

A CIP catalogue record for this book is available
from the British Library

ISBN 978 1 40749 347 3

Typeset by Palimpsest Book Production Limited,
Falkirk, Stirlingshire
Printed and bound in Great Britain
by MPG Books Ltd, Bodmin, Cornwall

MIX
Paper from
responsible sources
FSC
www.fsc.org   FSC® C018575

for Leigh Anne

It is grotesque how they go on
loving us, we go on loving them

The effrontery, barely imaginable,
of having caused us. And of how.

Their lives: surely
we can do better than that.

        —WILLIAM MEREDITH, 'PARENTS'

'It wasn't real; it was a stage set, a stagy stage set.'

        —DOROTHY B. HUGHES, *IN A LONELY PLACE*

PROLOGUE

Crime and Punishment, 1985
Artists: Caleb and Camille Fang

Mr and Mrs Fang called it art. Their children called it mischief. 'You make a mess and then you walk away from it,' their daughter, Annie, told them. 'It's a lot more complicated than that, honey,' Mrs Fang said as she handed detailed breakdowns of the event to each member of the family. 'But there's a simplicity in what we do as well,' Mr Fang said. 'Yes, there is that, too,' his wife replied. Annie and her younger brother, Buster, said nothing. They were driving to Huntsville, two hours away, because they did not want to be recognized. Anonymity was a key element of the performances; it allowed them to set up the scenes without interruption from people who would be expecting mayhem.

As he sped down the highway, eager for expression, Mr Fang stared at his son, six years old, in the rearview mirror. 'Son,' he said. 'You want to go over your duties for today? Make sure we have everything figured out?' Buster looked at the rough sketches in pencil that his mother had drawn on his piece of paper. 'I'm going to eat big handfuls of jelly beans and laugh really loud.' Mr Fang nodded and then smiled with satisfaction. 'That's it,' he said. Mrs Fang then suggested that Buster might throw some of the jelly beans in the air, which everyone in the van agreed was a good idea. 'Annie,' Mr Fang continued, 'what's your responsibility?' Annie was looking out the window, counting the number of dead animals they had passed, already up to five. 'I'm the inside man,' she said. 'I tip off the employee.' Mr Fang smiled again. 'And then what?' he asked. Annie yawned. 'Then I get the heck out of there.' When they finally arrived at the mall, they were ready for what would come next, the strangeness they would create for such a brief moment that people would suspect it had only been a dream.

The Fangs walked into the crowded mall and dispersed, each pretending the others did not exist. Mr Fang sat in the food court and tested the focus on the tiny camera hidden in a pair of bulky eyeglasses that made him break out in a rash around his eyes whenever he wore them. Mrs Fang walked with great purpose through the mall, swinging her arms with a wild, exaggerated motion in order to create the impression that she might be slightly crazy. Buster fished pennies out of the fountains, his pockets damp and overflowing with coinage. Annie bought a temporary tattoo from a kiosk that sold absurd, worthless knickknacks and then went to the restroom to rub the design onto her bicep, a skull with a rose between its teeth. She rolled the sleeve of her T-shirt back down over her arm to cover the tattoo and then sat in one of the bathroom stalls until the alarm on her watch beeped. It was time, and all four of them walked slowly to the bulk-candy shop for the thing that would occur only if each one of them did exactly what was required.

After five minutes of wandering aimlessly through the aisles of the store, Annie tugged on the shirt of the teenage boy behind the register. 'You wanna buy something, little girl?' he asked. 'You need me to reach something for you? Because I'd be happy to do it.' He was so kind that Annie felt slightly ashamed for what she would do next. 'I'm not a tattletale,' she told him. He looked confused and then leaned closer to her. 'What's that, miss?' he asked. 'I don't mean to be a tattle-tale,' she said, 'but that woman is stealing candy.' She pointed at her mother, who was standing by a dispenser filled with jelly beans, a giant silver scoop in her hand. 'That woman?' the boy asked. Annie nodded. 'You did a good thing today, little girl,' he said and handed her a lollipop that also doubled as a whistle as he went to get the manager. Annie unwrapped the lollipop and chomped down on it, the shards of sugar scratching the inside of her mouth, as she leaned against the counter. When she was finished, she took another lollipop

3

from the display and put it in her pocket for later. When the manager and the employee returned from the back room, she walked out of the store and did not turn around, already assured of the scene that would transpire.

Having filled her fifth bag of jelly beans, Mrs Fang cautiously looked around before stowing the unsealed bag away with the others beneath her jacket. She placed the scoop back in its holder and whistled as she walked down the aisle, feigning interest in several other candies, before heading toward the entrance of the store. Just as she stepped outside, she felt a hand on her arm and heard a man's voice say, 'Excuse me, lady, but I think we've got a small problem here.' Though she would be disappointed later, she let the faint hint of a smile creep across her face.

Mr Fang watched as his wife shook her head and wore a look of disbelief as the manager pointed at the ridiculous bulges in her clothes, the contraband hidden so poorly that it added a wonderful absurdity to the proceedings. His wife then shouted, 'I'm a diabetic, for crying out loud; I can't even eat candy.' At this point, several people in the store turned toward the commotion. Mr Fang moved as close as he could to the action just as his wife screamed, 'This is unconstitutional! My father plays golf with the governor. I'll just – ' and that was when, with a slight adjustment in Mrs Fang's posture, the bags of candy spilled open.

Buster ran past his father and watched as hundreds of jelly beans fell like hailstones from his mother's clothes and click-clacked against the floor of the shop. He knelt at his mother's feet and yelled, 'Free candy!' as he shoved giant handfuls of the jelly beans, which were still spilling out of his mother, into his mouth. Two other children took up residence beside him, as if his mother was a piñata just broken open, and scrabbled for their own claim on the candy as Buster laughed with a scratchiness in his voice that made him sound like a much older person. By now, a crowd of about twenty people had gathered around the scene and his mother began to sob. 'I can't go back to jail,' she shouted, and Buster stood up from the mess of jelly beans on the floor and ran away. He realized that he had forgotten to throw the candy into the air and knew it would not go unmentioned when the family gathered to discuss the success of the event.

Thirty minutes later, the Fang children met up at the fountains and waited for their mother to extricate herself from the consequences of her ridiculous actions. She was probably being held by mall security until their father could convince them to let her off with a warning. He would show them their résumés, the clippings from the *New York Times* and *ArtForum*. He would say things like *public performance art* and *choreographed spontaneity* and *real life squared*. They would pay for the candy and most likely be banned from the mall.

5

That night, they would go home and eat dinner and imagine all the people at the mall telling their friends and family about this strange and beautiful thing that happened that afternoon.

'What if they have to go to jail?' Buster asked his sister. She seemed to consider the possibility and then shrugged. 'We'll just hitchhike back home and wait for them to escape.' Buster agreed that this was a sound plan. 'Or,' he offered, 'we could live here in the mall and Mom and Dad wouldn't know where to find us.' Annie shook her head. 'They need us,' she said. 'Nothing works without you and me.'

Buster emptied his pockets of the pennies he had taken earlier and lined them up in two equal stacks. He and his sister then took turns tossing them back into the fountains, each making wishes that they hoped were simple enough to come true.

CHAPTER 1

As soon as Annie walked onto the set, someone informed her that she would need to take her top off.

'Excuse me?' Annie said.

'Yeah,' the woman continued, 'we're gonna be shooting this one with no shirt on.'

'Who are you?' Annie asked.

'I'm Janey,' the woman said.

'No,' Annie said, feeling as if maybe she had walked onto the wrong set. 'What is your job on the movie?'

Janey frowned. 'I'm the script supervisor. We've talked several times. Remember, a few days ago I was telling you about the time my uncle tried to kiss me?'

Annie did not remember this at all. 'So, you supervise the script?' Annie asked.

Janey nodded, smiling.

'My copy of the script does not mention nudity for this scene.'

'Well,' Janey said. 'It's kind of open-ended, I think. It's a judgment call.'

'Nobody said anything when we rehearsed it,' Annie said.

Janey simply shrugged.

'And Freeman said I'm supposed to take my top off?' Annie asked.

'Oh yeah,' Janey said. 'First thing this morning, he comes over to me and says, "Tell Annie that she needs to be topless in the next shot."'

'Where is Freeman right now?'

Janey looked around. 'He said he was going to find someone to procure a very specific kind of sandwich.'

Annie walked into an empty stall in the bathroom and called her agent. 'They want me to get naked,' she said. 'Absolutely not,' said Tommy, her agent. 'You're nearly an A-list actress; you cannot do full frontal nudity.' Annie clarified that it wasn't full frontal but a topless scene. There was a pause on the other end of the line. 'Oh, well that's not so bad,' Tommy said.

'It wasn't in the script,' Annie said.

'Lots of things that aren't in the script turn up in movies,' said Tommy. 'I remember a story about this movie where an extra in the background has his dick hanging out of his pants.'

'Yes,' Annie replied. 'To the detriment of the movie.'

'In that case, yes,' Tommy answered.

'So, I'm going to say that I'm not going to do it.'

Her agent once again paused. In the background, she thought she could hear the sounds of a video game being played.

'That would not be a good idea. This could be an Oscar-winning role and you want to make waves?'

'You think this is an Oscar-winning role?' Annie asked.

'It depends on how strong the other contenders are next year,' he answered. 'It's looking like a thin year for women's roles, so, yeah, it could happen. Don't go by me, though. I didn't think you'd get nominated for *Date Due* and look what happened.'

'Okay,' Annie said.

'My gut feeling is to take off your top and maybe it'll only be in the director's cut,' her agent said.

'That is not my gut feeling,' Annie replied.

'Fair enough, but nobody likes a difficult actor.'

'I better go,' Annie said.

'Besides, you have a great body,' Tommy said just as Annie hung up on him.

She tried to call Lucy Wayne, who had directed her in *Date Due*, for which Annie had been nominated for an Oscar; she had played a shy, drug-addicted librarian who gets involved with skinheads, with tragic results. It was a movie that did not summarize well, Annie knew this, but it had jump-started her career. She trusted Lucy, had felt during the entire shoot that she was in capable hands; if Lucy

9

had told her to take her top off, she would not have questioned it.

Of course, Lucy did not answer her phone and Annie felt that this was the kind of situation that did not translate well to a voice mail message. Her one steady, calming influence was out of range and so she had to make do with the options that were left to her.

Her parents thought it was a great idea. 'I think you should go completely nude,' her mother said. 'Why only the top?' Annie heard her father yell in the background, 'Tell them you'll do it if the male lead takes off his pants.'

'He's right, you know,' her mother said. 'Female nudity isn't controversial anymore. Tell the director that he needs to film a penis if he wants to get a reaction.'

'Okay, I'm beginning to think that you don't understand the problem,' Annie said.

'What's the problem, honey?' her mother asked.

'I don't want to take my top off. I don't want to take my pants off. I definitely don't want Ethan to take his pants off. I want to film the scene the way we rehearsed it.'

'Well, that sounds pretty boring to me,' her mother said.

'That does not surprise me,' Annie said and once again hung up the phone thinking that she had chosen to surround herself with people who were, for lack of a better term, retarded.

A voice from the next stall said, 'If I were you, I'd tell them to give me an extra hundred thousand bucks to show my tits.'

'That's nice,' Annie said. 'Thanks for the advice.'

When she called her brother, Buster said that she should climb out the window of the bathroom and run away, which was his solution to most problems. 'Just get the hell out of there before they talk you into doing something that you don't want to do,' he said.

'I mean, I'm not crazy, right? This is weird?' Annie asked.

'It's weird,' Buster reassured her.

'No one says a thing about nudity and then, the day of the shoot, I'm supposed to take off my top?' she said.

'It's weird,' Buster said again. 'It's not totally surprising, but it's weird.'

'It's not surprising?'

'I remember hearing that on Freeman Sanders's first movie, he filmed an improvised scene where some actress gets humped by a dog, but it got cut out of the movie.'

'I never heard that,' Annie said.

'Well, I doubt it's something that Freeman would bring up in meetings with you,' Buster responded.

'So what should I do?' Annie asked.

'Get the hell out of there,' Buster shouted.

'I can't just leave, Buster. I have contractual obligations. It's a good movie, I think. It's a good part, at least. I'll just tell them I'm not going to do the scene.'

A voice from outside the stall, Freeman's voice, said, 'You're not going to do the scene?'

'Who the hell was that?' Buster asked.

'I better go,' Annie said.

When she opened the door, Freeman was leaning against a sink, eating a sandwich that looked like three sandwiches stacked on top of each other. He was wearing his standard uniform: a black suit and tie with a wrinkled white dress shirt, sunglasses, and ratty old sneakers with no socks. 'What's the problem?' he said.

'How long have you been out here?' Annie asked.

'Not long,' he said. 'The continuity girl said you were in the bathroom and people were starting to wonder if you were just scared about taking off your top or if you were in here doing coke. I thought I'd come in and find out.'

'Well, I'm not doing coke.'

'I'm a little disappointed,' he said.

'I'm not going to take my top off, Freeman,' she said.

Freeman looked around for a place to set his sandwich and, apparently realizing he was in a public restroom, opted to hold on to it. 'Okay, okay,' he said. 'I'm just the director and writer; what do I know?'

'It doesn't make any sense,' Annie yelled. 'Some guy I've never met before comes by my apartment and I just stand there with my tits out?'

'I don't have time to explain the complexities of it to you,' Freeman said. 'Basically, it's about control and Gina would want to control the situation. And this is how she would do it.'

'I'm not going to take off my top, Freeman.'

'If you don't want to be a real actor, you should keep doing superhero movies and chick flicks.'

'Go to hell,' Annie said and then pushed past him and walked out of the restroom.

She found her costar, Ethan, enunciating his lines with great exaggeration, pacing in a tight circle. 'Did you hear about this?' she asked him. He nodded. 'And?' she said. 'I have some advice,' he said. 'What I would do is think of the situation in such a way that you weren't an actress being asked to take off her top, but rather an actress playing an actress being asked to take off her top.'

'Okay,' she said, resisting the urge to punch him into unconsciousness.

'See,' he continued, 'it adds that extra layer of unreality that I think will actually make for a more complicated and interesting performance.'

Before she could respond, the first assistant director, shooting schedule in hand, walked over to them. 'How are we doing vis-à-vis you doing this next shot without a shirt on?' he asked her.

'Not happening,' Annie said.

'Well, that's disappointing,' he responded.

'I'll be in my trailer,' she said.

'Waiting on talent,' the AD shouted as Annie walked off the set.

The worst movie she'd ever been a part of, one of her first roles, was called *Pie in the Sky When You Die*, about a private detective who investigates a murder at a pie-eating contest during the county fair. When she read the script, she had assumed it was a comedy, and was shocked to learn that, with lines like 'I guess I'll be the one eating humble pie' and 'You'll find that I'm not as easy as pie' it was actually a serious crime drama. 'It's like *Murder on the Orient Express*,' the screenwriter told Annie during a read-through, 'but instead of a train, it's got pie.'

On the first day of shooting, one of the lead actors got food poisoning during the pie-eating contest and dropped out of the movie. A pig from the petting zoo broke out of its pen and destroyed a good deal of the recording equipment. Fifteen takes of a particularly difficult scene were shot with a camera that had no film in it. For Annie, it was a bizarre, unreal experience, watching something fall apart as you touched it. Halfway through the movie, the director told Annie that she would need to wear contacts that changed her blue eyes to green. 'This movie needs flashes of green, something to catch the viewer's eye,' he told her. 'But we're halfway into the movie,' Annie said. 'Right,' the director replied. 'We're only halfway into the movie.'

One of Annie's costars was Raven Kelly, who

had been a femme fatale in several classic noir movies. On the set, Raven, seventy years old, never seemed to consult the script, did crossword puzzles during rehearsals, and stole every single scene. While they were side by side getting their makeup done, Annie asked her how she could stand working on this movie. 'It's a job,' Raven had said. 'I do what will pay, whatever it is. You do your best, but sometimes the movie just isn't very good. No big loss. Still pays. I never understood artists, and I couldn't care less about craft and method and all that stuff. You stand where they tell you to stand, say your lines, and go home. It's just acting.' The makeup artists continued to apply makeup so that Annie appeared younger and Raven appeared older. 'But do you enjoy it?' Annie asked. Raven stared at Annie's reflection in the mirror. 'I don't hate it,' Raven said. 'You spend enough time with anything, that's all you can really ask for.'

Back in her trailer, the blinds closed, the sound of white noise hissing from a stress box, Annie sat on the sofa and closed her eyes. With each deep, measured breath, she imagined that various parts of her body were slowly going numb, from her fingers to her hand to her wrist to her elbow to her shoulder, until she was as close to dead as she could be. It was an old Fang family technique employed before doing something disastrous. You pretended to be dead and when you came out of it, nothing, no matter how dire, seemed important. She remembered the four of them sitting silently in the van as they each died and came back to life, those brief minutes before they threw open the doors and pressed themselves so violently into the lives of everyone in the general area.

After thirty minutes, she returned to her body and stood up. She slipped out of her T-shirt and then unhooked her bra, letting it fall to the floor. Staring at the mirror, she watched herself as she delivered the lines for the scene. 'I am not my sister's keeper,' she said, avoiding the urge to cross her arms over her chest. She recited the last line of the scene, 'I'm afraid I just don't care, Dr Nesbitt,' and, still topless, pushed open the door of her trailer and walked the fifty yards back to the set, ignoring the production assistants and crew that stared as she passed by them. She found Freeman sitting in his director's chair, still eating his sandwich, and said, 'Let's get this fucking scene over with.' Freeman smiled. 'That's the spirit,' he said. 'Use that anger in the scene.'

As she stood there, naked from the waist up, while the extras and crew and her costar and just about every single person involved in the movie all stared at her, Annie told herself that it was all about control. She was controlling the situation. She was totally, without a doubt, in control.

The Sound and the Fury, March 1985
Artists: Caleb and Camille Fang

Buster was holding his drumsticks upside down but Mr and Mrs Fang thought this made it even better. The boy spastically pressed his foot on the pedal that operated the bass drum and flinched with each percussive note. Annie strummed her guitar, her fingers already aching not five minutes into the concert. For two people who had never learned to play their instruments, they were managing to perform even more poorly than expected. They shouted the lyrics of the song that Mr Fang had written for them, their voices off-key and out of sync. Though they had only learned the song a few hours before their performance, they found it easy to remember the chorus, which they sang to the astonished onlookers. 'It's a sad world. It's unforgiving,' they yelled at the top of their lungs. 'Kill all parents, so you can keep living.'

In front of them, an open guitar case held some coins and a single dollar bill. Taped to the inside of the case was a handwritten note that read: *Our Dog Needs an Operation. Please Help Us Save Him.*

The night before, Buster had carefully written down each word as his father dictated it to him. 'Misspell *operation*,' Mr Fang said. Buster had nodded and wrote it as *operashun*. Mrs Fang shook her head. 'They're supposed to be untalented, not illiterate,' she said. 'Buster, do you know how to spell *operation*?' his mother asked him. He nodded. 'Then we'll go with the correct spelling,' his father said, handing him another piece of cardboard. When it was finished, he held up the sign for his parents to inspect. 'Oh, good Lord,' said Mr Fang. 'This is almost too much.' Mrs Fang laughed and then said, 'Almost.' 'Too much of what?' asked Buster, but his parents were laughing so hard they didn't hear him.

'This is a new song we just wrote,' Annie said to the audience, which was, inexplicably, larger than when they had started. Annie and Buster had already played six songs, each one dark and unhappy and played so inexpertly that they seemed less like songs and more like the sound of children having a tantrum. 'We appreciate any change that you can spare for our little dog, Mr Cornelius. God bless.' With that, Buster began to tap his drumsticks against the hi-hat cymbal, tit-tat-tit-tat-tit, and Annie plucked a single string, producing a mournful groan that changed its tone as she moved her finger up and down the neck of the guitar but never lost its intent. 'Don't eat that bone,' she warbled and then Buster repeated the line, 'Don't eat that bone.' Annie looked into the crowd but she could not find her parents, only face after face of sympathetically cringing people too nice to walk away from these cherubic, earnest children. 'It will make you ill,' Annie sang, and Buster again echoed her. 'Don't eat that bone,' Annie said, and then, before Buster could follow her, a voice, their father's voice, yelled out, 'You're terrible!' There was an audible gasp from the crowd, so sharp that it sounded like someone had fainted, but Annie and Buster just kept playing. 'We can't afford the bill,' Annie said, her voice cracking with fake emotion.

'I mean, am I right, people?' their father said. 'It's awful, isn't it?' A woman in the front of the crowd turned around and hissed, 'Be quiet! Just be quiet.' At this moment, from the opposite direction, they heard their mother say, 'He's right. These kids are terrible. Boo! Learn to play your instruments. Boo!' Annie began to cry and Buster was frowning with such force that his entire face hurt. Though they had been expecting their parents to do this, it was the whole point of the performance, after all, it was not difficult for them to pretend to be hurt and embarrassed.

'Would you shut the hell up?' someone yelled out, though it wasn't clear if this was directed at the hecklers or the kids. 'Keep playing, children,' someone else said. 'Don't quit your day jobs,' a voice called out, one that was not their parents', and this caused another shout of encouragement from the audience. By the time Annie and Buster had finished the song, the crowd was almost equally split into two factions, those who wanted to save Mr Cornelius and those who were complete and total assholes. Mr and Mrs Fang had warned the children that this would happen. 'Even awful people can be polite for a few minutes,' their father told them. 'Any longer than that and they revert to the bastards they really are.'

With the crowd still arguing and no more songs left to play on the set list, Annie and Buster simply began to scream as loudly as they could, attacking their instruments with such violence that two strings on Annie's guitar snapped and Buster had toppled the cymbal and was now kicking it with his left foot. Money was being tossed in their direction, scattering at their feet, but it was unclear if this was from people who were being nice or people who hated them. Finally, their father shouted, 'I hope your dog dies,' and Annie, without thinking, took her guitar by the neck and pounded it into the ground, shattering it, sending shrapnel into the crowd. Buster, realizing the improvisation going on, lifted his snare drum over his head and slammed it against the bass drum, over and over. Annie and Buster then left the disarray around them and sprinted across the lawn of the park, zigging and zagging to avoid anyone who might try to follow them. When they arrived at a statue of a clamshell, they climbed inside and waited for their parents to retrieve them. 'We should have kept all that money,' Buster said. 'We earned it,' Annie answered. Buster removed a sliver of the guitar from Annie's hair and they sat in silence until their mother and father returned, their father sporting an angry black eye, the smashed glasses that held the camera hanging off his face. 'That was amazing,' said their mother. 'The camera broke,' said Mr Fang, his eye nearly swollen shut, 'so we don't have any footage,' but his wife waved him off, too happy to care. 'This is just for the four of us,' Mrs Fang said. Annie and Buster slowly climbed out of the clam and followed their parents as they walked to the station wagon. 'You two,' Mrs Fang said to her children, 'were so incredibly awful.' She stopped walking and knelt beside them, kissing Annie and Buster on their foreheads. Mr Fang nodded and placed his hands softly on their heads. 'You really were terrible,' he said, and the children, against their will, smiled. There would be no record of this except in their memories and of the few, stunned onlookers that day, and this seemed perfect to Annie and Buster. The entire family, walking into the sunset just past the horizon, held hands and sang, almost in tune, 'Kill all parents, so you can keep living.'

CHAPTER 2

B uster was standing in a field in Nebraska, the air so cold the beers he was drinking were freezing as he held them. He was surrounded by former soldiers, a year returned from Iraq, young and strangely jovial and scientifically proven to be invincible after serving multiple tours in the Middle East. There were cannon-like guns, comically large and hinting at all sorts of destruction, laid out on sheets of plastic. Buster watched as one of the men, Kenny, used a ramrod to force the ammunition down the length of the barrel of a gun that everyone referred to as *Nuke-U-Ler*. 'Okay,' Kenny said, his speech slightly slurred, beer cans scattered around his feet, 'now I just open the valve here on the propane tank and set the pressure regulator to sixty PSI.' Buster struggled to write this down in his notebook, his fingers frozen at the tips, and asked, 'Now what does PSI stand for?' Kenny looked up at Buster and frowned. 'I have no idea,' he said. Buster nodded and made a notation to look it up later.

'Open the gas valve,' Kenny continued, 'wait a

23

few seconds for it to regulate, then close the valve and open up the second valve here. That sends the propane into the combustion chamber.' Joseph, missing two fingers on his left hand, his face round and pink like a toddler's, took another swig of beer and then giggled. 'It's about to get good,' he said. Kenny closed the valves and pointed the contraption into the air. 'Squeeze the igniter button and – ' Before he could finish, the air around the men vibrated and there was a sound like nothing Buster had ever heard before, a dense, punctuated explosion. A potato, a trail of vaporous fire trailing behind it, shot into the air and then disappeared, hundreds of yards, maybe a half mile across the field. Buster felt his heart stutter in his chest and wondered, without caring to discover the answer, why something so stupid, so unnecessary and ridiculous, made him so happy. Joseph put his arm around Buster and pulled him close. 'It's awesome, isn't it?' he asked. Buster, feeling that he might cry at any moment, nodded and replied, 'Yes it is. Hell yes it is.'

Buster had come to Nebraska on assignment from a men's magazine, *Potent,* to write about these four ex-soldiers who had been, for the past year, building and testing the most high-tech potato cannons ever seen. 'It's so goddamned manly,' said the editor, who was almost seven years younger than Buster, 'we have to put it in the magazine.'

Buster had been in his one-room apartment in

24

Florida, his Internet girlfriend not returning his e-mails, nearly out of money, not working on his overdue third novel, when the editor had called him to offer the job. Even with the terrible circumstances of his life at the moment, he was loath to accept the assignment.

After two years of writing about skydiving and bacon festivals and online virtual-reality societies that were too complicated for him to even play, Buster was on the verge of quitting his job. The experience of these unique events never lived up to his expectations and then Buster was forced to write articles that made these things seem not just amusing but also life-changing. Driving dune buggies through the desert was something that Buster desired without ever having considered it before the opportunity arose, but once his hands were on the steering wheel, he realized how technical and complicated it was to have the kind of fun that wasn't readily available. As he struggled to handle the vehicle, his instructor patiently explaining how to accelerate and steer, he found himself wishing he were back home, reading a book about detectives that drive around in dune buggies and solve mysteries on the beach. Once he flipped the dune buggy and was kicked off the course, he went back to his hotel room and wrote the article in less than an hour and then smoked pot until he fell asleep.

He had assumed the same thing would happen with the potato gun story, a few hours of boring explanations of how the cannons were built and what principles they operated on before he watched them fire off a few rounds of potatoes. Then he'd be stuck in the middle of nowhere in the middle of winter until he could get a flight back home. Even as he boarded the plane, holding a barbecue sandwich and a hastily purchased copy of *World Music Monthly,* which he had no desire to read, he knew he was making a mistake.

Once his plane touched down in Nebraska, the four subjects of his article were unexpectedly waiting for him at the baggage terminal. They were identically dressed in Nebraska Cornhuskers baseball caps, black wool coats, tin cloth pants, and Red Wing boots. They were tall and sturdy and handsome. One of them was, strangely, holding Buster's suitcase in his hand. 'This yours?' the man asked as Buster, his arms held up as if to show that he was unarmed, approached them. 'Yeah,' said Buster, 'but you guys didn't need to meet me here. I was going to rent a car. You gave my editor the directions last week.' The man holding Buster's suitcase turned and started walking toward the exit. 'Wanted to be hospitable,' the man said over his shoulder.

In the car, surrounded on all sides by ex-soldiers, Buster resisted the idea that he was being kidnapped. He reached into his jacket, too thin for this weather, and produced a notepad and a pen. 'What's that for?' one of the men asked. 'Notes,' said Buster. 'For the article. I thought I'd get your names and maybe ask a few questions.' 'They're easy names to remember,' said the driver, 'I doubt you'll need to write it down.' Buster put his notepad back in his pocket.

'I'm Kenny,' said the driver and then gestured to the man in the passenger seat, 'and that's David,' and finally waved his hand over his head as if to indicate the backseat, 'and on either side of you is Joseph and Arden.' Joseph held out his hand and Buster shook it. 'So,' Joseph said, 'you like guns?' Buster shook his head. 'Oh, no, not really,' he said and he could feel the air in the van become heavier, 'I mean I've never fired a gun before. I don't really care much for violence.' Arden sighed and looked at the window. 'I don't know many people who care for it,' he said. 'What about potato guns?' Joseph asked. 'You ever make one when you were a kid, fill it with hairspray and shoot at the neighbor's dog?' 'Nope,' Buster said, 'sorry.' He could feel the article slipping away from him, imagined going on the Internet and fabricating the entire thing. 'And the war?' asked David. 'I'm not a fan,' Buster replied. He looked down at his shoes, black leather sneakers with complicated stitching, his toes already slightly numb inside of them. He thought about reaching over Joseph, pushing open the door, and jumping out. 'Well, you ever been to Nebraska before?' asked Arden. 'I've flown over it a few times,' Buster said, 'I would imagine.' For the rest of the ride to Buster's hotel, there was the all-encompassing sound of five men not talking, the radio broken and filled with static, the car's engine going just a little faster than it had before.

While the other three waited in the still-running car, Joseph helped Buster carry his suitcase to his room. 'Don't worry about them,' Joseph said. 'They're just a little nervous. We're unemployed and we build spud guns and we just don't want to look like a bunch of losers when you write the article. I keep telling them, it's your job to make us look cool, isn't that right?' Buster realized he was putting the key card into the lock upside down, but once he had rectified the problem, the door still would not open. 'Isn't that right?' Joseph asked again. 'Yeah, of course,' said Buster. He imagined the three other men downstairs, restless and regretting their decision to allow some outsider to witness the bizarre thing that everyone would soon know existed.

After nearly a dozen tries to gain entry into his room using the key card, Buster finally pushed inside and went straight to the minibar. He retrieved a tiny bottle of gin and killed it in one swallow. He grabbed another bottle and downed its contents as well. Out of the corner of his eye, Buster saw Joseph unpacking his suitcase for him, placing his shirts and pants and underwear in various drawers of the dresser. 'You didn't pack enough warm clothes,' Joseph said. 'There's some long underwear in there, I think,' replied Buster, working hard to get drunk. 'Jesus Christ, Buster,' Joseph said, almost shouting, 'you'll freeze your ass off.' Buster was about to suggest that he forgo the potato-gun demonstration. He would order a hamburger from room service and watch soft-core cable TV and empty the contents of the minibar. He would go back to Florida long enough to get kicked out of his apartment and then he would move in with his parents. And then he thought about a year with his mother and father, sitting at the dinner table while they devised more and more elaborate events that he could not understand if he was a part of or not, waiting for something to explode in the name of art. 'Well, what should I do?' Buster asked, determined to seem like a capable person. 'We'll go shopping,' Joseph said, smiling.

While Kenny and Arden and David walked at a safe distance through the Fort Western Outpost, Joseph quickly rifled through racks of clothes and other cold-weather essentials, tossing them into Buster's waiting arms. 'So you write for a living?' he asked Buster, who nodded. 'Yeah,' Buster said, 'articles mostly, freelance stuff. And I've written two novels, but nobody reads those.'

'You know,' Joseph said, handing Buster two pairs of wool socks, 'I'm thinking of becoming a writer myself.' Buster made a sound that he hoped suggested interest and encouragement, and Joseph continued. 'I've been taking a night class on Tuesdays at the community college, Creative Writing 401. I'm not that good yet, but my teacher says I show promise.' Buster again nodded. He noticed that the other three men had stepped closer to the conversation. 'He's a damn good writer,' said David, and Kenny and Arden agreed. 'You know what my favorite book is?' Joseph asked. When Buster shook his head, Joseph answered, a huge smile on his face, '*David Copperfield* by Charles Dickens.' Buster had never read the book, but he knew that he should have, so he nodded and said, 'Excellent book.' Joseph clapped his hands together loudly, as if he'd been waiting for this moment for months. 'I love that first line: *My name is David Copperfield*,' he said. 'It tells you everything you need to know. I start all my stories like that: *My name is Harlan Aden* or *I go by the name of Sam Francis* or *When he was born, his parents named him Johnny Rodgers*.'

Buster remembered the first line of *Moby-Dick* and mentioned it to Joseph. Joseph repeated the line: *Call me Ishmael*. He shook his head. 'No,' he said, 'that doesn't work for me. That's not as good as *My name is David Copperfield*.'

An older man pushing an empty shopping cart asked if he could pass by the crowd of men to reach some dress socks, but no one budged.

'See,' Kenny said, 'that makes this Ishmael guy seem like he thinks he's a big deal. He can't just tell us his name? He's got to go making demands that we address him as such?' Kenny made a face like he'd had to deal with guys like this all his life.

'And that might not even be his real name,'

offered Arden. 'He's just telling us to call him that.' The men all agreed that *Moby-Dick* sounded like a book that they had no desire to read. 'Sorry, Buster,' Joseph said. '*David Copperfield* is the winner and still champion of the world.' David walked off and came back with a packet of air-activated hand-warmers. 'I like these when it gets cold,' he said, handing them to Buster.

Back in the car, Buster having nearly maxed out his credit card on a black wool coat, tin cloth pants, Red Wing boots, and a Nebraska Cornhuskers baseball cap, they drove toward their next-to-last stop, the liquor store. 'What was your last article about?' David asked Buster, who replied, 'I had to report on the world's largest gang-bang.'

Kenny carefully flipped on his turn signal and slowly pulled onto the side of the road. He placed the car in park and then turned around in his seat. 'What, now?' he asked.

'You guys ever heard of Hester Bangs?' Buster asked. All four of the men nodded emphatically. 'I was there when she broke the record for the biggest gang-bang. She had sex with six hundred and fifty guys in one day.'

'You didn't,' Joseph began, his face bright red from embarrassment, 'I mean, you didn't have sex with her, did you?'

'Oh, god, no,' Buster answered. Buster remembered the two-hour argument on the phone with his editor when he refused to take part in the

31

actual orgy. 'It's called Gonzo Journalism,' said his editor, 'I'm looking it up on the Internet right now.'

'So,' Kenny said, 'you basically watched this woman fuck six hundred and fifty guys?'

'Yeah,' answered Buster.

'And you got paid to do that?' continued Kenny.

'Yeah,' Buster again answered.

'Well,' Arden said, 'that sounds like just about the greatest thing I've ever heard of.'

'It wasn't that great, actually,' said Buster.

'What, now?' Kenny asked.

'I mean, yeah, it sounds great, I guess, but I pretty much sat around while a bunch of hairy, out-of-shape guys with their dicks hanging down waited in a line to fuck this woman who looked pretty bored about the whole thing. I interviewed some of the guys and several of them told me that they had told their wives that they were going golfing or to see a movie that day. One guy bragged about how his girlfriend had threatened to break up with him if he went through with it and, as he told me this, he got really sad and said, "And she was a pretty awesome girl." After every time a guy pulled out of Hester, she would look over at some guy who was sitting at a desk with three different clocks and tons of permission forms and an adding machine, and she would ask how many guys were left to fuck.'

Arden said, 'That sounds like just about the worst thing I've ever heard of.'

'And,' Buster continued, finding that he could not stop talking about it now that he had started, 'there was this table with food laid out for all the people on set and these naked guys would be standing over the table, constructing these sad little sandwiches and eating handfuls of M&Ms.'

'Jesus Christ,' said David, shaking his head.

'And then you had to write about it, which I bet sucked,' Joseph said.

'Yeah,' Buster said, pleased that Joseph understood the strangeness of writing about things you despise, 'and so I wrote this bizarre article about how Hester Bangs wasn't an actress, wasn't even a porn star, that she was more like a professional athlete. She was like a marathoner, and that, as disturbing as it was to witness, I had so much admiration for her ability to do it.'

Kenny nodded in agreement. 'That sounds like a good article.'

'Well,' Buster finished, 'three weeks after it comes out, some other porn star breaks the record by more than two hundred guys.'

Everyone in the car laughed so loudly that they almost didn't hear the policeman tapping on the window.

As soon as he saw the cop, Buster had the overwhelming feeling that he needed to hide his contraband, the small detail being that he had nothing illegal on his person. Kenny rolled down the window and the officer ducked his head inside the car. 'Parked on the side of the road, boys,' he said, 'not a smart idea.'

'Okay, sir,' Kenny said, 'we're just about to get moving.'

The officer stared at Buster in the backseat, his eyes flickering with the disorientation of not knowing someone in his town.

'Friend of yours?' he asked, pointing at Buster.

'Yeah,' said Joseph.

'Army?' asked the cop.

'Special Forces,' said Arden, placing a hushing finger to his lips.

'Huh,' said the cop, 'real Black Ops shit?'

Despite a lifetime spent lying without effort, Buster could only manage a weak nod in agreement.

'Okay, move it out, then,' the cop said, flicking his wrist and pointing toward the horizon.

'Special Forces,' Buster whispered to himself, everyone giddy with anticipation.

At the liquor store, Buster, emboldened by the feeling that he had made friends for the first time in years, used almost the absolute last of the cash in his wallet to buy all the alcohol the soldiers wanted. He felt warm and authentic inside his new clothes and thought, handing over all he owned to the liquor-store clerk, that he could live here forever.

Now it was Buster's turn. He leaned over a massive air cannon mounted on a tripod, which the soldiers referred to as *Air Force One*. Instead of potatoes, the gun used two-liter soda bottles as ammunition. 'See, we don't like to call them spud guns,' said David, who seemed, as the night progressed, to become more tightly wound. 'Some shoot ping-pong balls and some shoot soda bottles and some shoot tennis balls that you fill with pennies. The best term would be pneumatic or combustion artillery.' Joseph shook his head. 'I call them spud guns,' he said. Arden said, 'I only ever have called them spud guns.' 'Yeah, whatever,' replied David, 'but I'm just trying to say that, for the article, the best term is still pneumatic or combustion artillery.'

Kenny walked Buster through the steps one more time, and, though it was complicated and would result in serious injury if not performed correctly, Buster felt as though he understood each maneuver intuitively. He loaded the cannon and then turned on the air compressor until it reached the correct PSI. 'Okay,' said Joseph, 'we're not going to pretend that this is better than sex or anything, but you're going to be very happy after you do this.'

Buster wanted to be very happy; in his desperate moments of self-absorption, he felt that the earth was powered by the intensity of his emotions. When he mentioned this to a psychiatrist, the doctor said, 'Well, if that's the case, don't you think you should be out doing something a bit more, I don't know, worthwhile?'

He depressed the chamber-release trigger and

there was a resonant thoomp followed by a soft, sustained shushing sound like air escaping from an expertly slashed tire. Someone handed him a pair of binoculars, and Buster watched the trajectory of the bottle until it landed almost three hundred yards away. He was surprised to find that, long after he had fired the cannon, the happiness he derived from it had not abated. 'Does this ever get old?' Buster asked, and all four of the men answered, without hesitation, 'No.'

Two sacks of potatoes emptied, the men stood in a circle and occasionally mentioned that someone should go buy some more beer without anyone volunteering to do so.

Through his alcoholic impairment, Buster began to formulate the basic premise of his article, ex-soldiers building fake weapons to alternately forget and remember their wartime experiences. All he needed were facts to support this idea. 'How often do you do this?' Buster asked. The men looked at him like it should have been obvious. 'Every goddamned night,' Kenny said, 'unless there's something good on TV, which is pretty much never.'

'We don't have jobs, Buster,' said Joseph. 'We're living with our parents and we don't have girl-friends. We just drink and blow shit up.'

'You're making it sound like it's a bad thing,' Arden said to Joseph.

'Well I don't mean to,' said Joseph, and looked at Buster. 'It only sounds that way when I say it out loud.'

'So,' Buster began, unsure of the correct way to phrase his question, 'does all of this, shooting off potato guns, ever remind you of your time over in Iraq?' As soon as he finished his question, everyone around him seemed, momentarily, incredibly sober. 'Are you asking if we have flashbacks or something?' asked David. 'Well,' Buster continued, beginning to realize that he had been better off shooting potatoes into the atmosphere, 'I just wonder if shooting these spud guns makes you think about your time in the army.' Joseph laughed softly. 'Everything makes me think about the army. I wake up and I go to the bathroom and I think about how, in Iraq, there were just pools of piss and shit in the streets. And then I get dressed and I think about how, when I would put on my uniform, I was already sweating before I buttoned my shirt. And then I eat breakfast and think about how every single goddamn thing I ate over there had sand in it. It's hard not to think about it.'

'I thought maybe these spud guns were a way to get back some of the excitement of being over there,' Buster weakly offered, feeling the article slip away from him.

'In Iraq, I filled out reports regarding the air quality in Baghdad,' Arden replied.

'It was boring as hell,' said Kenny, 'until it wasn't, and then it was fucking terrifying.'

'But you had guns, right?' Buster asked.

'Well, we all had weapons. I had a 9 mm Beretta and an M4 carbine,' Joseph continued, 'but other than training, target practice, I never fired my weapon while I was over there.'

'You didn't shoot anyone in Iraq?'

'No,' Joseph answered, 'thank God.' Buster looked around at the other men, who all smiled and shook their heads. 'What did you guys do?' he asked. Joseph and Kenny helped set up Tactical Operations Centers. David was a logistical adviser to the Iraqi army. 'Accounting, mostly,' he said.

'What about your fingers?' Buster asked, pointing to the missing digits on Joseph's left hand. 'Hell, Buster, I didn't lose them in Iraq,' he said. 'I was testing out accelerants for a new spud gun, and I exploded them off my hand.'

'Oh,' said Buster.

'You sound disappointed,' said Kenny.

'No, I'm not,' Buster answered quickly.

'We're just bored,' said Joseph. 'That's the simplest answer. It's like, no matter where you are or what you're doing, you have to try like hell to keep from getting bored to death.'

Kenny killed his last beer and bent over to pick up another potato gun, smaller than the others, a silver canister attached to the gun by a tube, the barrel outfitted with a scope. 'Like this, for instance,' Kenny said, holding the gun out for Buster to inspect. 'Look down the barrel of this one,' he continued, but Buster hesitated, looking around at the other men. 'It's okay,' said Joseph, holding up his disfigured hand, 'it's totally safe.'

Buster leaned over the barrel but couldn't see

anything of note. 'What am I looking at?' he asked. 'It's rifled,' said Kenny, 'like a real weapon.' Buster slid his fingers inside the barrel and felt the grooves inside the PVC. 'What does that do?' he asked. 'Accuracy,' said Kenny. 'You can hit a damn target from fifty yards away. Here, Joseph, show him.'

Kenny handed the gun to Joseph and then picked up an empty beer can. He began to walk away from the crowd, counting off each measured step until he was at a fair distance from them. Like a waiter holding a tray of food, he held the beer can in his open palm, just over his head. 'This seems like the worst kind of idea,' said Buster, but Joseph reassured him. 'I wouldn't do it if I couldn't do it,' he told Buster. Arden tore open a new bag of potatoes and handed one to Joseph, who began to delicately force the vegetable down the sharpened barrel, leaving behind a sheared-off portion of potato. 'See,' said Joseph, 'we've got a little ball of ammunition in there now.' He turned on the gas, filled the chamber with the correct amount, and then took aim through the scope. When the trigger was pulled, Buster saw only the flare of ignited gas that trailed the potato. Once he heard the sound of aluminum compacting, he noticed Kenny, still in full possession of his hand, picking the demolished beer can off the ground and holding it up for the rest of them to see. 'That was incredible,' Buster said, punching Joseph's shoulder. 'Not bad, huh?' said Joseph, who seemed embarrassed or excited or both.

'Me next,' said Arden, who grabbed one of the last full cans of beer and started jogging out to where Kenny was standing. Arden placed the can on top of his head, William Tell–style, and waited for Joseph to aim and fire. 'Should we take bets?' asked David, but the odds seemed so lopsided that they didn't feel it would be worth the trouble. 'No point putting it off any longer,' Joseph said, and then fired the potato gun. And missed. 'C'mon, now,' yelled Arden, 'that was off by a mile.' Kenny sidled up to Buster, holding the beer can that Joseph had obliterated with the potato gun. The can looked like a piece of shrapnel pulled from an unlucky body, jagged edges and splattered with warm pieces of potato. The webbing between Kenny's thumb and forefinger was bleeding, but he did not seem to care. 'I wish we had a video camera,' he said. 'These are the kind of things you want to remember.'

Joseph reloaded and missed again. And again. 'I guess I'm trying to aim a little high because I'm afraid that I'm going to shoot him in the face,' he said. 'You should ignore that fear,' said Kenny, who began to urinate in full view of everyone. Joseph once again shoved a potato down the barrel of the gun, his face now serious and pale. The temperature seemed to have dropped twenty degrees in the last half hour. Joseph took an extraordinarily long time to sight the target

40

through the scope and then fired, the concussive sound reverberating in the cold air, a sound that Buster thought he would never grow tired of hearing. The can atop Arden's head exploded in a mushroom cloud of beer, sending the target almost twenty yards beyond Arden, who was soaking wet and covered in chunks of potato. He walked back to the other men, his teeth chattering, reeking of beer and French fries. Buster handed him the beer he was drinking and Arden finished it in one gulp. David picked up another beer and offered it to Buster. 'Should we keep pushing our luck?' he asked.

Buster considered the beer and then looked at Joseph. 'I don't know,' Buster said. 'It would make for a good article,' Kenny said, 'either way.' Though Buster could not reject the truth of this statement, he found that he could not will his legs to move. Joseph took the gun off of his shoulder and offered it to Buster. 'You can shoot me, instead,' he said, 'that would be a good story too.' Buster began to laugh but he realized that Joseph was serious. 'It's okay,' Joseph said. 'I'm pretty sure you can do it.'

'It's a rifled barrel,' said Arden, 'it's pretty damn accurate.' It dawned on Buster that they were all spectacularly drunk and yet operating at a fairly high level of awareness. Their judgment was impaired, admittedly, but Buster felt himself believing that there was logic to their actions. Buster assessed the situation. It was a distinct possibility that he would hurt someone, but he could not be hurt; he felt immune to whatever disaster might try to attach itself to him. 'I'm invincible,' he said, and everyone else nodded in agreement. Buster grabbed the beer and began to walk away from the other men. 'Don't miss,' he shouted over his shoulder, and Joseph replied, 'I won't.'

Buster was shaking so hard that it was impossible to balance the can on his head. 'Give me a second,' he yelled. He closed his eyes, forced his lungs to take in deep, sustained breaths, and felt his body begin to go numb. He imagined that the doctors had just taken him off of life support and he was dying in slow increments. Finally, he was dead, and then he took another breath and, all of a sudden, he wasn't. When he opened his eyes, he was ready for whatever would come next.

It was beginning to grow dark, but he could clearly see Joseph bring the gun into position. Buster closed his eyes, held his breath, and, before he realized that the gun had been fired, a gust of heat and wind passed over him and deconstructed the beer can atop his head, the sound of something irrevocably giving up its shape and becoming, in an instant, something new.

The soldiers shouted and exchanged high fives and, when Buster returned, took turns roughly embracing him, as if they had just rescued him from a cave-in or pulled him out of a dark well. 'If I was any happier,' Kenny said, 'I would combust.' Buster pulled free of their arms and

42

snatched the last unopened beer from the cooler. 'Again,' he said and, without waiting for an answer, ran into the growing dark without fear, every single part of his body overwhelmed with the task of being alive.

When Buster awoke from unconsciousness, he saw, with some degree of difficulty, Joseph's face hovering over him. 'Oh god,' Joseph wailed, 'I thought for sure that you were dead.' Buster could not turn his head and his vision went in and out of focus. 'What's going on?' he asked. 'I shot you, goddamn it,' Joseph yelled, 'I shot you in the face, Buster.' He heard Kenny shout, 'We're driving you to the hospital, Buster, okay?'

'What?' Buster asked. He understood that people were shouting but he could hardly hear them. 'It's pretty bad,' Joseph said. 'My face?' Buster asked, still confused. He moved to touch the right side of his face, which was numb and on fire at the same time, but Joseph grabbed his wrist to stop him. 'You probably shouldn't do that,' he said. 'Is something wrong with it?' Buster asked. 'It's still there,' Joseph said, 'but it's not . . . correct.' Buster made the decision, which took some degree of concentration, to go back to sleep, but Joseph would not allow this. 'You are definitely concussed,' he told Buster. 'Just listen to my voice and try to stay awake.'

There was an awkward silence and then Joseph said, 'I wrote this story last week for my class. It was about this guy who had just come back from Iraq, but it's not supposed to be me. It's an entirely different person. This guy lives in Mississippi. So, he's back in his hometown after being away for almost ten years, and he's having a drink at this bar. When he goes to play some pinball, an old friend from high school comes up to him and they start to talk.' Joseph paused and then squeezed Buster's hand. 'Are you still awake?' he asked. Buster tried to nod, but couldn't and so he said, 'I'm awake. I'm listening.'

'Good. Okay,' Joseph continued, 'so they're catching up and getting drunk and the bar's starting to close. The main character tells this guy about how he's trying to get a job and make some money so he can move out of his parents' house and get his own place. Well, this guy tells the main character that he'll give him five hundred bucks if he'll do something for him. How does that sound so far?' Buster wondered if he was dying, if, when Joseph reached the end of his story, he would be dead. 'It sounds pretty good,' he answered.

'The guy has this dog that he loves and now his ex-wife has the dog and won't give it back to him. So he asks the main character to steal the dog and bring it to him and he'll give him five hundred bucks. That's the conflict. So the main character thinks about it and he goes back and forth and finally, two days later, he calls the guy and tells him he'll do it.'

'Uh-oh,' Buster said.

'I know,' Joseph said, 'bad idea. So he breaks into the ex-wife's house one night and steals the dog but something goes wrong. The dog thinks he's an intruder, which he is, and starts to attack him, takes a big chunk out of his arm. Well, he manages to get the dog outside and into the car, but when he gets home, he realizes that the dog is dead, that he crushed the dog's windpipe or something, I wasn't too specific. Anyways, the dog is dead.'

'We're almost there,' Kenny shouted.

'So the main character takes a shovel and buries the dog in his parents' backyard. When he's done, he walks to the bus station, buys a ticket, and gets on a bus without knowing where it's headed. So he's on the bus, his arm is bleeding like hell but he's trying not to let anyone notice, and he hopes that wherever he ends up next will be a good place. That's the end.'

'I like it,' Buster said.

Joseph smiled. 'I'm still working on it.'

'It's really good, Joseph,' Buster said.

'I still can't figure out if it's a happy ending or a sad ending,' Joseph said.

'We're here,' Kenny said, the car coming to an abrupt stop.

'It's happy and sad,' Buster said, drifting off. 'Most endings are happy and sad at the same time.'

'You're going to be okay,' Joseph said.

'I am?' Buster asked.

'You're indestructible,' Joseph said.

'I'm invincible,' Buster corrected.

'You're impervious to pain,' Joseph continued.

'I'm immortal,' Buster said and then passed out, hoping that wherever he ended up next would be a good place.

A Modest Proposal, July 1988
Artists: Caleb and Camille Fang

I t was time for a vacation, so they all got fake IDs. The Fangs had just recently received a prestigious grant, more than three hundred thousand dollars, and they were going to celebrate, the counterfeit IDs spread out on the table. Mr and Mrs Fang were Ronnie Payne and Grace Truman. The children were allowed to choose their own names. Annie was Clara Bow, and Buster was Nick Fury. In exchange for this staging of real life, their parents had promised Annie and Buster that there would be no art during the four days they would be at the beach, nothing but a normal family getting sunburned and buying trinkets made out of seashells and eating food that was either deep fried or dipped in chocolate or both.

Inside the airport, Mr and Mrs Fang read magazines about people who were supposedly famous but whom they had never heard of, forcing down banal information about miracle diets and movies they would never see – all in the interests of establishing their characters. Ronnie owned a string of Pizza Huts and had been married and divorced three times. Grace was a nurse who had met Ronnie in rehab and they had been living together for the past nine months. Were they in love? Probably. 'Are you going to tell me what you're going to say?' Mr Fang asked his wife. 'It's a surprise,' Mrs Fang said. 'I think I know what you'll say,' he said, and his wife smiled. 'I bet you think you do,' she answered.

Annie sat alone in an empty aisle of chairs and sketched various people in the airport. She held a fistful of colored pencils like a bouquet of flowers and softly scratched an image into the sheet of paper in the notebook on her lap. Ten yards away, a man with a huge, hooked nose and a pair of oversize sunglasses slouched in his chair and took surreptitious pulls from a silver flask in his jacket pocket. Annie smiled as she emphasized the already outlandish features of this man, turning her drawing into something not quite caricature and not quite portraiture. As she studied him for more details, he suddenly looked in her direction and she felt her face grow hot. She winced and returned her gaze to the notebook, running a lightning bolt of pencil marks across the image she had just drawn until it was unrecognizable, no evidence of her interest. She returned the notebook and pencils to her book bag and rehearsed her story. Nearly penniless, her mother had left

Clara with her grandmother and moved to Florida to find a job. After six months, Clara was finally going to live with her mother again. 'It's a brand-new start for us,' Annie would say to the flight attendant or neighboring passenger when asked. If she did it right, and she always did, someone would slip her a twenty-dollar bill and tell her to take care of herself. When they finally got to Florida, Annie imagined that she would take the twenty dollars and bet it on jai alai while she drank a Shirley Temple so large it took three straws to reach the bottom of the glass.

Buster had found that a plausible backstory took too long to establish and provided too many opportunities to be found out. So he had begun to create obviously false stories that, in turn, established a kind of backstory of its own, that of a bizarre child who should be avoided. As he sat in the airport bar and drank glass after glass of lemon-lime soda and ate handfuls of peanuts and pretzels, he had decided that, should someone ask, he was not a real child but a robot built and designed by a scientific genius. A childless couple had ordered him and he was now being delivered to them in Florida. Beep-bop-boop. Buster wasn't even sure what the happening was going to be this time. His parents had only told him that he would have to pretend that they were not his real parents, to travel separately on the plane, and, when the event occurred, to react according to the general mood of the audience. 'The less you know, the better,' his father said. 'It'll be a surprise,' his mother told him, 'you like surprises don't you?' Buster shook his head. He did not.

On the plane, Annie and Buster were each chaperoned by a different stewardess into aisle seats on either side of the first row so they were now just a few feet apart from each other and pretending they had never before met. The children watched their parents stroll down the aisle, hand in hand. Buster could not help but stare as they passed and Mr Fang winked as they made their way to their seats in the middle of the plane. Buster asked a stewardess for peanuts and, when she brought him three packages, he asked for one more. The stewardess turned away from Buster to get another packet of peanuts and rolled her eyes. Annie saw this and felt her body go tense, one degree shy of anger. When the stewardess returned with her brother's peanuts, Annie tugged on her sleeve and asked for five packets of peanuts, her eyes like slits, hoping for trouble that would overshadow whatever would happen later on the flight. The woman seemed unnerved by Annie's nearly imperceptible quivering and hurried away to find more peanuts. As soon as she received her bounty, Annie turned to Buster and dumped them in his lap. 'Thank you,' Buster said. 'You're welcome, kid,' Annie said.

Everyone settled in, the stewardess having explained what to do in case of an emergency landing, Annie and Buster hoped that whatever their parents had planned would not end with the two of them floating in the ocean, holding on to their seat cushions, waiting for help that may or may not arrive.

More than an hour into the flight, the children turned to watch Mr Fang walk down the aisle and place his hand on the elbow of one of the stewardesses. Annie and Buster strained to listen to their father but they could not make out what he was saying. He held something out toward the stewardess and her eyes grew wide and she placed her hand over her mouth. She looked like she was going to cry. Mr Fang gestured toward the front of the plane and the stewardess nodded, leading him toward the intercom system. Annie wondered how on earth they would avoid jail time if their parents tried to hijack the plane. When he passed by their seats, Buster resisted the urge to grab his father's hand, to say, 'Dad?' and ruin the entire event. Annie sketched a drawing of two people, a boy and a girl, jumping out of a plane, parachutes deployed, nothing below them but the emptiness of the blank paper.

'Ladies and gentlemen,' the stewardess said, 'we have a very important message and we need all of you to listen very carefully. This man here, Mr Ronnie Payne, needs to say something.' There was the hum of silence over the intercom and then the children heard their father's voice say, 'I don't want to take up much of your time, folks. I'm over there in Row 17, Seat C, and right next to that seat is my special lady, Miss Grace Truman. Wave to everybody, honey.' Everyone on the plane turned to watch their mother's hand raised above the seats as she gave an uncertain wave to the rest of the passengers. 'Well,' their father continued, 'this little lady means a lot to me and I was going to do this when we got to Florida but I just can't wait. Grace Truman, would you marry me?' Mr Fang handed the microphone to the stewardess and walked back to Row 17. Annie and Buster wanted to run down the aisle to watch the proceedings, but they stayed in their seats, craning their necks to see what would come next. Their father knelt in the aisle beside Mrs Fang, whom the children could not see, and everything was silent except for the sound of the engines keeping the plane aloft. Annie and Buster both whispered the same word under their breath, 'Yes.'

Suddenly, Mr Fang stood and shouted, 'She says yes!' The entire airplane began to cheer and several men got out of their seats to shake their father's hand while Mrs Fang displayed the ring to an older woman in the seat next to her. The sound of corks popping echoed through the cabin and the stewardesses began to walk down the aisle with trays filled with glasses of champagne. The pilot's deep, smooth voice came over the intercom and he said, 'A toast to the happy couple.' Buster managed to swipe two flutes before anyone noticed and handed one of them to Annie. 'Why, thank you, little boy,' Annie said. 'Don't mention it,' Buster replied. They clinked glasses and downed the contents in one swallow, happily ignoring the burn as it went down their throats.

They spent the next four days dizzy from over-exposure to the sun and still giddy from the success of the marriage proposal. They read pulp novels and comic books and would sleep at odd hours. On the beach, they took turns burying one another up to their necks in the sand and then chased each other with jellyfish hanging on the ends of sticks. They stood in the ocean as waves gently broke across their legs while they ate cotton candy that held the slight tang of salt water. If told this kind of happiness was something that could be attained by everyone, the Fangs would not have believed it.

On the plane ride back home, everyone again separated and under assumed names, their father once again nudged the stewardess, showed her the ring he had purchased for his girlfriend, and asked for the use of the intercom. Once again, the stewardess was nearly moved to tears by the romantic nature of the request and led him to the front of the plane. Buster tore open his eighth bag of peanuts and arranged the nuts so as to form the word YES on his folded-down tray.

'I'm over there in Row 14, Seat A, and my girl-friend, Grace Truman, is in the next seat over.

Grace, honey, could you come up here for a second, please?' Mrs Fang shook her head, embarrassed, but Mr Fang continued to call for her until she finally stood up and walked over to her husband. When she arrived, Mr Fang dropped to a knee, opened the tiny box in his hand, and displayed the ring, her own wedding ring. Their four days in the sun had caused the tan line on her finger to disappear. 'Grace Truman,' their father said, 'would you make me the happiest man in the world and marry me?' Annie was sketching a picture of onlookers throwing handfuls of peanuts into the air as a married couple walked down the aisle of a plane while she waited for her mother to answer. 'Oh, Ronnie,' Mrs Fang said, looking like she might cry, 'I told you not to do this.' Their father looked uncomfortable to be kneeling for so long but he would not stand. 'C'mon, honey, just say yes.' Mrs Fang looked away but her husband raised the microphone to her face. 'Just say yes into this microphone and make my dreams come true.' Annie and Buster had no idea what was going on but they both had the same sick feeling that things were about to get worse. 'No, Ronnie,' Mrs Fang said. 'I will not marry you.' There were gasps from some passengers in the cabin and their mother walked back to her seat, leaving their father on his knees, still holding the ring. After a few seconds, he stuttered into the microphone, 'Well, folks, I'm sorry to take up so much of your time. I guess it just wasn't meant to be.' He then stood and walked back to his seat beside their mother and sat down, neither one of them looking at the other.

The rest of the flight was so tense and uncomfortable in the cabin that a plane crash would have been welcomed to avoid the embarrassment of what had happened.

In the car, driving home from the airport, the Fangs did not speak a single word. It had all been fake, a choreographed event, but they could not escape the dread that rattled inside their chests. It was a testament to their proficiency and talent as artists. They had affected themselves with the authenticity of the moment.

Annie and Buster imagined a world where their parents had not married, had separated and never returned to each other, a world in which, to their horror, they did not exist. Buster rested his head in Annie's lap as she stroked his hair. As they pulled into the long, winding driveway of their home in the woods, Mr Fang finally pulled his wife close to him and whispered, 'I love you, Grace Truman.' Their mother kissed him on the cheek and responded, 'I love you, Ronnie Payne.' Annie leaned over her brother's open face and kissed him softly on the forehead. 'I love you, Nick Fury,' she said. He smiled and said, 'I love you, Clara Bow.' Even after the car was parked and the ignition turned off, the Fangs sat, their seat belts still fastened, and allowed the world to turn without any help from the four of them.

CHAPTER 3

Standing next to a Whac-A-Mole game in an arcade in Los Angeles, Annie chewed on her fingernails and waited for the journalist from *Esquire* to arrive. He was fifteen minutes late and Annie began to hope that perhaps he wouldn't show and she wouldn't have to go through the awkwardness of revelation, of being interesting.

Annie slid a quarter into the game and picked up the mallet. As the plastic rodents peeked their heads out of their holes, Annie whacked them with such vigor that when they once again popped up, unfazed, she took it personally and smashed them even harder.

She was here, flashing lights and electronic blips and beeps, to promote the movie, *Sisters, Lovers,* which had premiered at Cannes and been uniformly hated. 'Self-indulgent, faux-intellectual, soft-core Cinemax tripe masquerading as cinema' had been one of the nicer reviews. The movie was a bust and, though Annie had been singled out by several critics as the only honest performance in the film, there was to be little to no promotion in advance of its release. However, there were a few

56

incidents regarding the making of the movie that had resulted in a little more fame than Annie had intended – the reason, she suspected, she was being interviewed at all.

'Here's the thing,' her publicist said to Annie on the phone earlier that week. 'You fucked up.'

'Okay,' Annie replied.

'I love you, Annie,' her publicist said, 'but my job is to grow your career, to maintain the flow of information regarding you and your interests. And you kind of fucked me over for a little while.'

'I didn't mean to,' Annie said.

'I know that. That's one of the reasons that I love you, honey. But you fucked me. Let's review, okay?'

'Please don't,' Annie said.

'Real quick,' her publicist said. 'Okay, first, you're filming this abortion of a movie and you decide, out of the blue, to take off your top and walk around the set.'

'Well, okay, but—'

'Just out in the open, tits exposed, so that any Tom, Dick, or Harry, or all three of them, can take pictures of you with their cell phone cameras. So that every celebrity Web site can post those pictures.'

'I know.'

'No big deal, but I don't hear about this until they show up on the Internet, until I'm on the phone with someone at *US Weekly* and I'm staring at your tits and reading stories about your instability on the set.'

'I'm sorry,' Annie said.

'So I put out that fire.'

'Thank you.'

'You're welcome. So I put out that fire. No big deal, people see tits all the time. No big deal.'

'Right,' Annie said.

'But. But. Then I find out you're a lesbian.'

'I'm not.'

'Doesn't matter,' her publicist said. 'That's what I hear. And I'm the last to hear. I have to hear it from your girlfriend, not you.'

'She's not my girlfriend,' Annie said. 'She's crazy.'

'And, best of all, she's your costar on this abortion of a movie, further proving those rumors of on-set instability.'

'Oh, god.'

'Luckily, you have me, and I am very, very good at this job. But I'm not a miracle worker. You have to tell me these things before they get out to the public so that I can determine how to allow this information to shape your career.'

'I will, Sally, I promise.'

'Think of me as your best friend. You tell your best friend everything, right? It's like, okay, who's really your best friend?'

'Sally, honestly, it might be you,' Annie said.

'Oh, honey, that makes me want to cry. Nevertheless, you tell me what's going on and I'll take care of you, okay?'

'Okay.'

'Now, you're going to talk to this guy from *Esquire* and he's going to write a nice article and he's not going to make a big deal about your tits or your lesbian lover, okay?'

'Okay.'

'Be charming.'

'I can do that,' Annie said.

'Be sexy.'

'I can do that,' Annie said.

'Do everything just short of sleeping with this guy.'

'Got it.'

'Just repeat after me, okay?'

'Okay.'

'Sally, I will not fuck you over again.'

'Sally,' Annie repeated, 'I will not fuck you over again.'

'Oh, I know that, honey,' her publicist said, and then the line went dead.

Annie imagined the center mole was her former costar, Minda Laughton, delicate features, crazy eyes, and a long, almost freakish neck. She brought the mallet down with such force that the machine creaked and stuttered, the mole retreating in clicks and whirrs into its hole. 'Don't even think about coming back,' Annie thought.

'So, you seem to be some kind of Whac-A-Mole pro,' said a man who had suddenly appeared by her side.

Annie turned quickly, the mallet raised in defense, and found a short, bespectacled man in a crisp, white button-up shirt and blue jeans. He was smiling, holding a tiny tape recorder, seemingly amused by Annie's presence in this arcade, the magazine's idea.

'I'm Eric,' he said. 'From *Esquire*? You really showed those moles who's boss,' he added.

Annie, for the fleeting second before she remembered Sally's warning, almost told him to go fuck himself, showing up late, watching her in an unguarded moment. Then she composed herself, let her breathing regulate, and became not herself.

'Impressive, right?' she asked, smiling, wagging the mallet like some obscene instrument.

'Very much so. I've already got the opening paragraph of the article,' he replied. 'Want to hear it?'

Annie could not think of a thing she would want less. 'I'll wait for the issue like everyone else,' she said.

'Fair enough,' he said, 'but it's really good.'

'Let's get some more quarters,' Annie said, and began to walk away. Eric knelt down and tore the strip of tickets that had emanated from the game, an afterthought.

'Don't forget these,' he said.

'Maybe I'll win you a teddy bear,' Annie said, sliding the tickets into her purse.

'That would be the best article ever.'

On one of her first interviews for *The Powers That Be*, the blockbuster comic book adaptation where she played Lady Lightning, a reporter asked her if she had been a fan of comic books growing up. 'I've never read a comic book in my life,' she responded. The reporter screwed up his face and then shook his head. 'I'm going to write down that you loved comics as a girl. You were kind of a geek growing up. Is that okay?' he asked. Annie, stunned, simply nodded her assent, and the rest of the interview proceeded in that manner. He would ask questions that she would answer, and then she would listen to the reporter tell her what her response would actually be. It had been the worst interview of her entire career, but, fifty, sixty, seventy more interviews for the movie, the same questions, no one seeming to have actually seen the movie or ever heard of her, she longed for the simplicity and ease of that earlier interview.

For the next twenty minutes, Annie proceeded to kick the shit out of this *Esquire* guy on a game called *Fatal Flying Guillotine III*. Having never played the first two installments, Annie merely punched the buttons in whatever random patterns came to her and watched the almost miraculous way her character, a giant half-bear, half-man wearing a kilt, responded to the instructions with such ferocity that there was nothing for Eric to do but watch his character, a tiny Japanese woman dressed as a Las Vegas showgirl, get mauled to death. 'You're pretty awesome at this game,' he said. She continued to pound his character into the ground. 'I think, actually, that you just really suck,' she answered, never once looking away from the screen, finding pleasure in the way her unfocused desires became crystalline and perfect in front of her eyes. 'No,' he replied, jamming the buttons, gripping the joystick so tightly it disappeared in his hand, 'I'm actually really good at this.' The Scottish bear lifted the showgirl into the air, spun around three times, and slammed her headfirst into the ground, creating a small hole in the earth. 'Could have fooled me,' she said.

They plunked more quarters into the machine, and Eric chose a badass Bruce Lee–like character who was, at all times, on fire. Annie stuck with her bear-man. Just before the first round began, Eric asked, 'Do you want to talk about *Sisters, Lovers*?' Annie froze, just long enough for Eric's character to land three quick roundhouse kicks, singeing her bear's fur. 'I suppose we have to, don't we?' she said. By the end of the first round, her character was laid out on the ground, smoldering.

'How about this,' he said. 'If I win this match, you tell me about the nudity incident on the set.'

Annie watched the two combatants, bouncing on the balls of their feet, eager for contact, as the game counted down for the next round to begin. She considered the offer. Sally would prefer that she let it die, pretend it didn't really happen, but Annie felt a slight satisfaction at the opportunity to tell her side of the story. And she was, without hesitation, falling in love with this bear-man. He would not let her down. 'Okay,' she said.

Two rounds later, Eric's character extinguished, beaten so badly that Annie would not have been surprised to find him permanently removed from the game, she smiled. 'I guess I'm just going to have to miss out on that scoop,' Eric said. He shrugged and then smiled, the question erased from his list, and Annie was touched by the gesture, the easy way the day was unfolding.

'It was a difficult movie,' Annie said, taking care not to look at Eric, unsure of exactly why she felt the need to unburden herself. 'It was an intensely difficult part to play and I knew it would be going into it, but I don't think I realized just how draining it would be to inhabit that character day after day.'

'What do you think of the reviews so far?' he asked, the tape recorder still in his shirt pocket.

'I'm not the best person to judge,' she said. 'I know that Freeman has a unique vision and that perhaps it's difficult for other people to appreciate it.'

'Did you enjoy the movie?'

'That is not a word I would ever use to describe the experience of watching one of my own movies.'

'Okay,' Eric said. They stared at each other in silence. A promo for the game unraveled on the screen, some giant, white-haired devil laughing and then beckoning the viewer to join the action.

'I took off my top because I didn't know if I could.'

'Mmm,' Eric said, nodding.

'I'd never done a nude scene and I wasn't sure that I would be able to do it. So I did it in real life and then I realized I could do it in the movie. I just, you know, forgot that other people could see me.'

'That's understandable. It must be difficult to shift back and forth between reality and fiction, especially with such an intense role. We can come back to that or leave it alone. For now, how about some Skee-Ball?'

Annie nodded. 'Annie,' she told herself, 'shut up. Shut up, shut up, shut up.'

When the pictures hit the Internet, fuzzy and low-resolution but without a doubt her, Annie's parents sent her an e-mail that read: *It's about time you started playing with the idea of celebrity and the female form as viewed object.* Her brother did not say or write a single word, seemed to disappear; perhaps that's what happens when a sibling sees you naked. Her on-and-off boyfriend, currently off, called her and, when she answered the phone, said, 'Is this a Fang thing? I mean, is it just inescapable that you'll do weird shit?'

'Daniel,' she said, 'you promised you wouldn't call.'

'I promised I wouldn't call unless it was an emergency. And this counts. You're losing your mind.'

Daniel Cartwright had written two novels that felt like movies and then started writing screenplays that felt like TV shows. He wore a cowboy hat all the time now. He'd recently sold a script for a staggering million, something about two guys who build a robot that runs for president. It was called *President 2.0* and Annie was not sure, other than the fact that he was unhinged and handsome, why she had ended up with him, and why, after she had left him, she would end up with him again.

'I'm not losing my mind,' she replied. She wondered if it was possible to blow up the Internet.

'It sure looks like it from here,' he said.

'I'm making a movie,' she said, 'a strange process that always requires some degree of weirdness.'

'I'm looking at your boobs right now,' he answered, and Annie, unable to think of a response, simply hung up the phone.

Later that day, at a dinner for the principal actors at Freeman's rented mansion, Annie showed up to find one of her naked photos plastered all over the house. Freeman walked into the hallway to greet her, taking nonchalant bites of a novelty-size candy bar that oozed caramel.

'What's this about?' she asked, tearing down one of the photos, balling it up in her hand.

'You're famous now,' he said, 'thanks to me.'

She knocked the candy bar out of his hand and walked out of the house.

'We'll look back at this and laugh,' he yelled.

She fumbled for the keys to her car, dropping them three times, starting to cry, when she saw

Minda running down the walkway toward her. Though they were the two stars of the movie, they had almost no scenes together and Annie rarely saw her co-star on set. To see Minda coming at her so quickly, her face contorted, her hands out, shouting for her to wait a second, Annie felt the sudden urge to run away from her, but found she could not move. Within seconds, Minda was holding her arm, panting for breath, nearly crying.

'It's awful, isn't it?' she wheezed.

Annie just nodded; she had her keys in her hand and wanted to unlock the car door, but Minda would not let go of her arm.

'Just awful,' she continued, her voice returning to normal. 'I told Freeman to stop it, but you know how he is. He writes these amazing roles for us, but I think he genuinely hates women.'

Annie, again, nodded. She wondered if, years from now, she would be unable to move her neck at all as a result of the repetitive, silent way that she had avoided the need for speech.

'Do you want to go somewhere?' Minda asked her.

Annie, reaching inside of herself, produced her voice and said, 'Yeah, sure.'

They ended up in a tiny bar, the patrons either unaccustomed to beautiful women wearing ridiculously expensive T-shirts or completely oblivious to them, and sat undisturbed at a corner table and sipped whiskey and ginger ale.

'What are you going to do?' Minda asked, still

holding Annie's arm, as if Annie might run away if she let go, which, Annie thought, might be true. Still, it was nice to have someone interested in her and not telling her she was losing her mind.

'I don't know,' Annie said. 'Finish the movie, I guess, and get the hell out of here. Take a break from acting.'

'Don't do that,' Minda said, genuinely alarmed.

'What? Why?' Annie asked.

'You're so good at it,' Minda said. 'I mean, you're incredible.'

'Well, I, well, I guess, well,' Annie would have gone on like this for hours but Minda took over.

'I love acting but I'm not very good at it yet. I'm operating on some fucked-up idea of what I'm supposed to be doing, but you know what to do instinctually. It's incredible to watch you.'

'But we haven't done any scenes together.'

'I watch you,' Minda said, smiling. 'I watch from a safe distance.'

'Oh,' Annie said.

'That doesn't freak you out, does it?' she asked. Annie shook her head.

'It's fine; lots of people watch me.'

'But I watch very closely,' Minda said, squeezing Annie's arm so tightly that her fingers began to tingle.

It finally dawned on Annie, Minda Laughton was hitting on her. It dawned on Annie, Minda Laughton had been in seven movies and, in four of them, she had kissed another woman. It dawned on Annie, Minda Laughton was pretty damn gorgeous, wide-open eyes and a graceful neck and a face so unmarked and smooth that it did not seem surgical but rather a kind of magic spell.

Minda leaned across the table and kissed Annie, who did not resist. When she sat back down, Minda chewed on her lip and then said, 'I made out with Freeman a few weeks ago.'

'Well, that was a terrible idea,' Annie said.

Minda laughed and then continued, 'I just didn't want you to hear about it from somebody else and think that I was just trying to make out with everybody in the movie.'

'Just me and Freeman.'

'And the continuity girl.'

'Really?'

'She was telling me about her uncle who tried to kiss her and I had a similar story and then we just started kissing. I don't think she remembers. She was pretty drunk.'

'You were not?'

'I was not,' Minda said.

'So just me, Freeman, and the continuity girl?'

'That's it. And I'll stick with you from here on out if you'd like.'

'Well, let's not get crazy here,' Annie said, feeling her feet grip the edge of something that felt important.

'Why not?' Minda said, and Annie, slightly drunk, could not think of a single reason.

★　　★　　★

Annie rolled the first of her Skee-Balls, polished hardwood, like a weapon in her hands, down the lane, bumping over the ball-hop, and into the fifty-point ring. 'Beginner's luck,' she said. Eric smiled and, on the adjoining machine, waited as the nine balls rolled into position. 'Another bet,' he said, 'since you did so well on the first one?' Annie rolled another ball down the lane, fifty points. 'And yet you still got me to answer your question,' she said.

'I'm good at my job,' he said.

'What's the question this time?' she asked, already prepared for the answer.

'Minda Laughton,' Eric replied.

'Fine,' Annie thought, 'why not?'

'Fine,' Annie said, 'why not?'

Eric picked up his first Skee-Ball and rolled it expertly down the lane, a short hop, and into the fifty-point ring. A split second later, the second ball hopped into the fifty-point ring, then a third, fourth, and fifth. Annie stared at Eric, who was trying not to smile. All nine Skee-Balls ended up in the fifty-point ring, the machine flashing and sirens blaring, tickets spitting out of the dispenser and piling at Eric's feet.

'So, you're a Skee-Ball hustler,' Annie said, miffed.

'I'm in a league,' he said.

'You're in a Skee-Ball league?'

'Yes.'

'We can still tie, you know,' Annie said, 'then I don't have to answer the question.'

69

'Fair enough,' Eric responded. 'Just seven more to go.'

Annie felt the heft of the Skee-Ball in her hand, swung her arm back with great force, and then felt a sudden and total resistance to the motion. She felt her index and middle fingers jam spectacularly, and she jerked her hand back as if electrocuted. Then she heard the sound of a child crying. She looked down and saw a little girl, perhaps six years old, lying flat out on the ground, holding her head, Annie's Skee-Ball rolling to a stop against another machine.

'Holy shit,' Eric said, his voice hushed.

'What?' Annie said. 'What happened?'

'Well,' Eric said, running over to the girl, Annie following, 'you hit this little kid in the head with your Skee-Ball. Or your fist. Maybe both.'

'Holy shit,' Annie said, her voice breaking as she spoke.

The child was on her knees now, rubbing her head, hiccupping from the force of her crying.

'It's okay,' Eric said. 'Easy now.'

Annie ran over to Eric's Skee-Ball machine and tore off the strip of tickets he had won. She hurried back to the little girl, as if she was an unstable element that might explode.

'Take these,' Annie said, and the girl began to quiet.

'And these,' Annie then said, handing her the nearly full cup of quarters.

'And this,' Annie finally said, handing the girl twenty dollars.

The girl, eyes red-rimmed, nose runny, smiled and then walked away. Annie saw a small bump already forming on the back of her head and wondered what would happen when the girl's parents saw it and came looking for answers.

'Let's get out of here,' she told Eric.

'I won that round,' Eric said.

'Fair enough. Jesus, let's just go.'

'That was something.'

'You're not going to put that in the article, are you?'

'I don't see how I could leave it out; you just knocked out a little girl.'

Annie, exasperated and terrified of retribution, began to walk quickly out of the arcade, the sun temporarily blinding her. She would answer his questions, go home, pack up her belongings, and move to Mexico. She would star in *telenovelas* and drink herself into a stupor. She would let it get worse before it got better.

Less than a week after making out with Minda in the bar and, later, in Minda's hotel room, Annie walked to the makeup trailer and, as her stylist fixed her face, noticed the cover of the latest issue of *'Razzi Magazine*. 'Co-Stars in Love,' read the headline, and there were two photos, one of Minda and one of Annie, doctored to look like they were shoulder to shoulder in a single picture. The stylist noticed Annie's look of horror. 'That's you,' she said, pointing to the magazine. 'I know,' Annie said. 'And that's Minda,' the stylist continued. 'Yes,' Annie said, 'I know.' There was a pause of perhaps ten seconds while Annie considered the ramifications of the cover. 'It says you're a couple,' the stylist said, and Annie grabbed that magazine and busted the door of the trailer open.

When she found Minda, Annie read her a few lines from the article. 'A close friend of the couple says that they are genuinely in love and have never been happier,' Annie recited. Minda smiled. 'It's sweet,' she said.

'It's not true,' Annie said.

'Well, kind of,' Minda replied, still smiling.

'Well, not really,' Annie said.

'Apples and oranges.'

'What?'

'Apples and oranges.'

'That doesn't—'

'Well, I think it's sweet.'

'And who is this *close friend*?' Annie said. 'I don't have any close friends.'

'It's me,' Minda said, her smile less a smile and more like paralysis.

'Oh, Jesus Christ.'

'I told my publicist and she told some magazines and so now it's official.'

Annie felt like she was traveling downhill in a machine whose wheels had, at that exact moment, come off, sparks shooting past her face, nothing to do but wait until things had come to a complete stop and she could get out and run away.

Once they found a restaurant far enough away from the arcade and were seated, Annie placed her hand flat on the table, palm down. Her index and middle fingers were swelling at a rapid pace and she was finding it difficult to bend them. While Eric ate a hamburger that looked like something a person who had never seen a hamburger would create if challenged to do so, Annie told him about Minda, the misunderstanding that had transpired, the closeness that inevitably occurs when two people are putting their creative selves into a singular project. She didn't tell him about the arguments and the stalking and the occasional moments when she would relent and sleep with Minda, the times that she thought she should just smother her with a pillow and rid the world of one more insane person. Unlike Minda, she kept some things to herself.

'Well,' Eric said, his plate a pool of ketchup and mustard and mushrooms and fried onions and all the other things his hamburger had been unable to contain (Annie thought, 'I could make a salad out of what fell out of your burger'), 'what I really wanted to talk about, what I find most interesting about you, is your family.'

Annie felt a bubble of air travel into her brain, a searing pain that flashed and was gone. Her family. Could she perhaps just keep talking about her tits and her lesbian stalker?

'For instance,' he continued, 'you don't go by your real last name.'

'My agent thought it would typecast me, nothing but horror films. It sounds made up anyways, don't you think?' she asked.

'A little. Is it?'

'I don't think so. It's Eastern European; it might have been shortened at some point. My father said that we were descendants of the first genuine wolf-man to cross the Atlantic and come to America. He had killed so many people in Poland or Belarus or wherever that he had to hitch a ride on a steamer to America to avoid being arrested and killed. And then he came here and, every full moon, killed a bunch of Americans. Later, he told us that his ancestor had probably created the whole story himself as an elaborate hoax and had changed his name to help sell it. That was less exciting for a kid to hear.'

'That's what I want to talk about,' Eric said, his face bright, his left eye twitching. 'You were "Child A" in all those art pieces that your parents created. You were, for all intents and purposes, the star.'

'Oh, Buster was the star, for sure. He had it much worse than me.'

She thought of Buster, tied to a lamppost, stuck in a bear trap, making out with a St Bernard, the numerous ways he'd been left in some bizarre situation and made to fend for himself.

'Still, you were placed in circumstances where you were doing some form of acting, some guerrilla-style, improvisational acting, so do you think that if you hadn't been a member of the Fangs, you would be an actress?'

'Probably not,' she answered.

'That's what I'm interested in,' Eric said. 'I have to admit, I think you're a pretty talented actress. I thought you deserved to win the Oscar for *Date Due* and you even managed to subvert the cartoonish sexuality of Lady Lightning by giving the character a postfeminist spin in the two *The Powers That Be* movies, shooting lightning bolts at Nazis and whatnot.'

'Yes, well, I think we can agree that everyone loves watching Nazis getting hit with lightning bolts.'

'Well, anyways, you're a good actress but I wrote my thesis in college on your parents' career, I've seen nearly every piece your family has created, and I really feel that your strongest work, when you were doing the most unexpected and emotionally resonant acting, was in those art pieces.'

'When I was nine years old,' Annie said. She felt like she was going to be sick. This magazine writer was expressing her worst fears, what she'd convinced herself was not at all true, that being a Fang, the conduit for her parents' vision, was perhaps the only worthwhile thing she had ever accomplished.

'I'm going to get a drink,' she said, and pushed away from the table. It was two in the afternoon, but it was the afternoon, and evening followed the

75

afternoon, and she was going to drink. She was going to drink well into the evening, she believed. She asked for and received a glass of gin, no ice, no mixers, no olive. She brought it back to the table and took a get-to-know-you sip that got the ball rolling.

'What I meant,' Eric continued, as if he had been waiting to say this all day, 'is that there is such a wealth of complexity in those performances. Underneath the initial shock of the act, there's something that, if you watch closely, becomes apparent.'

'And what's that?' she asked, another sip, so clean and medicinal it felt not unlike surgery under light anesthetic.

'There's sorrow, a sadness from knowing that you are forcing these events on unknowing people.'

How many times had he watched those videos? What had he been looking for? She had never, if she could help it, viewed a single one of the Fang pieces after it had been edited and completed, the finished product. When she remembered certain events, they were unconnected and random, a flash of color spilling out of her mother's body, a broken string on a guitar. They came back to her in waves and then receded for months or even years before they would return.

She looked up from her drink and Eric was staring at her, his face calm and radiant.

'You were always the best Fang,' he said, 'at least I think so.'

'There's no best Fang,' she said, 'we're all exactly the same.'

A few weeks earlier, just as the naked pictures fiasco had begun to subside, Annie's parents had called, ecstatic. Annie was reading a four-page note from Minda, two pages of which were a sestina that used the repeating words *Fang, blossom, locomotive, tongue, movie,* and *bi-curious.* She was happy to put the note down.

'Excellent news,' her father said, and Annie could hear her mother in the background saying, 'Excellent news.'

'What's that?' Annie said.

'We got an e-mail from the MCA in Denver. They are very interested in exhibiting one of our pieces.'

'That's great,' Annie said. 'Congratulations. Is it new?'

'It's so effing new,' Mr Fang said, 'it's only just happened.'

'Wow,' Annie said.

'I know, wow, exactly, wow,' her father said.

'Dad,' Annie said, 'I've got lines to run.'

'Well, good, okay,' Mr Fang said, and then Mrs Fang yelled from somewhere very close to the phone, 'Just tell her, honey.'

'Tell me what?'

'Well, the piece would revolve around those pictures of you that sprung up recently.'

'The naked pictures.'

'Right, those pictures. Well, the museum contacted us to see if your, um, performance was a Fang event.'

'Oh.'

'We said that you had created a very powerful critique of the media culture and the price of fame.'

'Uh-huh,' Annie said.

'You know, Child A creating an event on such a grand scale that it spanned the globe. It's a Fang experience to the nth degree. And we haven't done a Child A piece in a long time.'

'Because I'm not, you know, a child.'

'Well, I just wanted to let you know. Thought you'd find it exciting.'

'It is,' Annie said, suddenly wondering how that sestina ended.

'We love you, Annie,' her parents said, in unison.

'Yes,' Annie replied. 'Me too.'

The next morning, Annie circled her room and stared at the magazine writer, stripped down to his underwear, in her bed. His briefs were neon purple, which Annie did not find attractive or unattractive, simply a detail worthy of notice. She was not hungover, which meant she hadn't been that drunk the night before, which meant this wasn't a completely terrible idea on her part. 'Right?' she told herself, coffee brewing in the kitchen. 'This wasn't a completely terrible idea on my part.' Eric roused and seemed surprised, understandably, that Annie was standing over him, staring intently at his neon-purple ass. 'I'm making coffee,' Annie said, and hurried out of the room.

They sat across from each other at her dining-room table, which she never used. She ran her hand across the fine wood grain. It was a good table. She should eat here more often.

'So, we violated some pretty basic rules regarding interviewer-interviewee conduct,' he said. Annie had only half-listened to what he had said. What kind of wood was this? she wondered.

'But that could make for an interesting article,' he said, 'a postmodern, new-journalism method of celebrity profile.'

Annie looked over at Eric. He wasn't using a coaster for his mug of coffee. She slid one across the table and gestured toward his cup. He did not seem to understand and kept right on talking.

'How do you include such a significant detail regarding your relationship with the subject without overshadowing the rest of the article? Would you include the personal conversations along with the on-the-record comments? And once you've slept with someone, where does the line end?'

Annie wanted to smash the table in half.

'You're going to include this in the article?' she asked.

'I don't see how I could leave it out; we had sex.'

'Well, I see how you could leave it out,' Annie

said, her hand throbbing from bending her injured fingers into a fist that she was now tapping forcefully against the table, 'you just leave it out.'

'I don't think so.'

'This is not good,' Annie said, pacing back and forth.

'I'll send you the article before I turn in the final draft,' Eric said, 'to verify any quotes or differences in our recollection of the events.'

'No, I'll wait for the issue like everyone else.'

'Should I call you later or—'

'Just leave,' Annie said, cutting him off, not wanting at any cost to know what the *or* might entail.

'I really think you're incredible,' he said, but Annie was already heading to the bathroom, locking the door behind her.

Maybe she was going crazy. She didn't feel crazy, but she was sure that this was not the way that sane people behaved. She heard the front door open and then close. She pressed a washcloth against her face and imagined that she was a giant, remorseless, half-bear, half-man creature. She pounded all of her enemies into the earth, leaving bloodstains in all directions, buzzards circling overhead. She killed everything that needed to be killed, and when she was done, when all had been made, if not right, at least less wrong, she crawled into a cave, dark and deep, and hibernated for months, waiting for a new season to arrive and find her sated. She looked at her own hands; her right hand was purple, swollen, perhaps broken. She could not smash anything without breaking herself.

She walked back into the kitchen and placed the dishes in the sink. She picked up the phone and dialed Sally's office number, relieved to be shuttled to her voice mail.

'Sally,' she said, walking, as always, straight into the sun, 'I think I fucked you over again.'

The Portrait of a Lady, 1988
Artists: Caleb and Camille Fang

None of the Fangs could deny it: Buster was beautiful. As he walked to the front of the stage, his evening gown ridiculously sequined, his long, blond curls bouncing with the rhythm of his confident stride, the rest of his family began to realize that he might actually win. As Mr Fang continued to film the proceedings with his video camera, Mrs Fang clutched her daughter's hand and whispered, 'He's going to do it, Annie. Your brother is going to be Little Miss Crimson Clover.' Annie watched Buster, his face paralyzed with happiness, and immediately understood that, for her brother, this was no longer about making an artistic statement. He wanted that crown.

Two weeks earlier, Buster had outright refused. 'I'm not going to wear a dress,' he said. 'It's an evening gown,' Mrs Fang told him, 'a kind of costume.' Buster, nine years old, was not interested in the subtleties of wordplay. 'It's still a dress,' he said. Mr Fang, who had recently used a good portion of a grant from the Beuys Foundation to purchase a Panasonic VHS/S-VHS camcorder to replace the one broken by an irate zoo employee, zoomed in on his son's face, tight with repulsion. 'Artists are notoriously difficult,' Mr Fang said and then Mrs Fang looked into the camera and told him to please leave the room.

'Just get Annie to do it,' Buster offered, feeling the inescapable claustrophobia of his parents' desires. 'Annie winning a beauty pageant is not a commentary on gender and objectification and masculine influences on beauty,' Mrs Fang replied. 'Annie winning a beauty pageant is a foregone conclusion, the status quo.' Buster could not argue; his sister could win the Junior Miss category of the Crimson Clover pageant even if she was sobbing uncontrollably and shouting obscenities. She was the beautiful Fang, the one who could insert herself into a situation and gain the attention of anyone, which allowed for the other Fangs to continue their secret actions. So Buster understood that Annie was the beautiful one and Buster was, well, not the beautiful one. He was, well, something else. Whatever he was, he was not the Fang who wore a dress and competed in beauty pageants. Could he please not be that?

'Buster,' his mother continued, 'we have other projects lined up. You don't have to do anything that you don't want to do.'

'I don't want to do it,' he said.

'Okay, fine. I just want to say one thing. We're a family. We do things that are difficult because we love each other. Remember when I jumped that car with a motorcycle?'

After plastering a town in Georgia with flyers for a daredevil stunt, Mrs Fang, in special makeup to look like a ninety-year-old woman, drove a rented motorcycle off a ramp and over a parked car. She barely cleared the car and then wobbled for a few feet before crashing into a ditch, but was unhurt. There was an article in the local newspaper and it was subsequently picked up by national news organizations. Mrs Fang had never, in her entire life, ridden a motorcycle, much less jumped over a car with one. 'I could die,' she told her children, who were pretending to be her great-grandchildren, just before she hopped on the motorcycle, 'but whatever happens, just go with it.'

Of course Buster remembered. In the car on the way back home, their mother chugging whiskey straight from the bottle, she let the children peel off the latex makeup to reveal her own face, smiling and kind.

'I was terrified. I didn't want to do it when your father suggested it. I refused. And then I thought, how could I ever ask your father or one of you to do something difficult if I didn't go through with it? So I did it. And it was incredible. What you'll find, I think, is that the things you most want to avoid are the things that make you feel the greatest when you actually do them.'

'I don't want to do it,' he said.

'Fair enough, kiddo,' she said, miraculously smiling, cheerful. She stood, brushed off her pants, and walked down the hallway to her study. Annie walked into the living room where Buster was still on the floor and said, 'Man, Mom's pissed.'

'No, she's not,' Buster said, correcting her.

'Oh, yes,' Annie said.

'No, she's not,' Buster said again, less confident.

'Oh,' Annie said, softly stroking Buster's head as if he were a puppy, 'yes.'

That night, Buster's ear against the door of his parents' bedroom, he could hear snatches of their conversations, whispered transmissions, *I did* and *But maybe* and *He won't* and *Well, Jesus Christ* and *It'll be fine*. He stood up and walked into Annie's room. She was watching a silent film where a woman was trapped inside a barrel heading toward the edge of a waterfall and the hero was miles, dozens and dozens of miles, away. 'This is the best part,' she said and waved him over. Buster rested his head in her lap and she pinched his earlobe gently, rolling the flap of skin between her thumb and forefinger like she was making a wish on it.

On the TV, the barrel bobbed in the water, bouncing off of rocks, headed toward certain doom. 'Oh,' Annie said, 'this is gonna be good.' Just as the hero arrived at the edge of the falls, the barrel tumbled over and disappeared in the spray of water. At the bottom of the falls, shards of wood rose to the surface. 'Goddamn,' Annie whispered. And then, a form beneath the water, the heroine resurfaced, a look on her face like *motherfucker, I can't be killed*. She swam to the bank of the river and climbed out, shaking any last remnant of death from her body. The music slow and deliberate, the heroine marched, uncaring as to where her beau was and why he had not arrived in time, in the direction of the villain, ready to *put things right*. Annie turned off the TV. 'I can't watch anymore,' she said, 'I'm going to kick a hole in the wall if I watch anymore.'

'Is there anything you wouldn't do if Mom and Dad asked you?' Buster asked his sister.

She considered the question. 'I wouldn't kill anybody,' she said, 'and I wouldn't do something to an animal.'

'Anything else?' he asked.

'I don't know,' she said, obviously bored with the question. 'Maybe. Maybe not.'

'I don't want to be a girl,' he said.

'Well, sure,' Annie answered.

'I'm going to do it though,' he said, at that moment making his decision.

'Well, sure,' Annie answered.

He pulled away from his sister and stepped into the hallway, the burden off his shoulders and then, after just a second of lightness, resettled on him.

He pushed open the door of his parents' bedroom. His mother was wrapping rubber bands around his father's fingers, the appendages tomato-red and segmented in ways that suggested amputation. They looked surprised to see him but made no move to hide their actions.

'I'm going to do it,' he told them and Mr and Mrs Fang whooped with delight. They beckoned to him and he jumped onto the bed, worming his way in between them. 'It's going to be great,' Mrs Fang whispered to Buster, kissing his face over and over. Mr Fang snapped the rubber bands off of his hands and then clenched and unclenched his fists, a pleasant, easy feeling passing over his face. Then the Fangs draped their arms over Buster and fell asleep, Buster the only one still awake, the weight of his parents' bodies holding him in place and easing him into something that was not sleep but felt safe.

Buster made the final strides to the edge of the stage with a previously unknown confidence, his heels clacking on the slick walkway, clack-clack-clack-clack-clack, his rear swinging in time to the rhythm. When he reached his mark, he turned sideways, raised his lead shoulder, hand on hip, cocked his head, and looked out at the audience, who cheered. As he turned and walked back to the other girls, he lifted his hand just over his head, a gesture of farewell that could not be bothered to do more than acknowledge the fact that the audience was being left behind in favor of something much, much better. The other two girls looked at him, a stranger, no one they'd ever seen before, with nothing but bad intentions. Buster stared them down and then took his position in line, the final three.

Buster could hardly focus, his teeth bared as though he was about to eat a small animal. He was loving this. The glamour of the dresses and shoes and hair and fingernails, the attention from people who did not give him attention. The fact that, inside this costume, he was still Buster, which meant that, really, there was something essential inside of him that made this work at all. It was a magic trick, and he had to keep reminding himself not to reveal the secret, something so simple and easy if you knew how to look at it, which is what made it magical.

Blah-blah-blah, aren't they lovely, blah-blah-blah, done so well, blah-blah-blah, all winners tonight, blah-blah-blah, second runner-up, blah-blah-blah, someone's name that was not Buster's or not Buster's new name, Holly Woodlawn, blah-blah-blah, in the event that Little Miss Crimson Clover cannot fulfill her duties, blah-blah-blah, the new Little Miss Crimson Clover, blah-blah-blah, and then there was an explosion of applause. Well, shit, Buster had blah-blah-blah'ed the winner's name.

He turned to his rival and saw that she was crying. Had she won or lost? Had he won or lost? He looked into the audience, searching for his parents, but they were lost in the camera flashes and the spotlight that seemed to envelop everyone onstage. And then he felt someone's hands on his shoulders and something so light it almost didn't exist being placed upon his head. A bouquet of crimson clover was jammed into his hands. 'Hug me,' he heard the first runner-up bark, and he kissed her cheek and lightly placed his hand across her back. Now it was time for the inevitable, the thing that made Buster's crown art instead of artifice.

They had rehearsed for days, the different permutations of this event. Buster being dismissed immediately in the first round. Buster going out in the final ten. Buster being sent offstage when the final three were announced. Buster finding himself sashed and applauded but not crowned. And, without as much vigor, they practiced for this, the stage empty save for Buster, sparkling and shiny, the focus of everyone in the auditorium, a vacuum that pulled all the air into his own lungs.

He waved as he had seen the women do in the videos, not actually waving but instead turning, as if mechanized and fully wound. Tears began to fall down his cheeks, the heavy mascara raccooning his eyes and staining his face. He toed the edge of the stage, steady on his unsteady heels, and as he seemingly adjusted the crown, he leaned forward, out over the edge, bowing gracefully, and then snapped his body back to its original position. As planned, his wig flipped off and over his head, skittering across the stage behind him, the only sound for miles. And then there was the sound of the entire audience pulling that surfeit of air out of his lungs, necessary for them to now gasp, for some to scream, for the whole room to, as the Fangs dreamed, tear apart at the seams.

With an easy shift in his posture, slumping his shoulders, repositioning his pelvis, he became an obvious boy, the movements so natural that it echoed the way a chameleon changed color, the gradual but effortless reshading. Buster then stumbled on his high heels and ran to the crown, freed it from the tangles of the artificial curls, and returned it to its rightful place atop his head. Sprinting down the stage toward him, one of the directors of the pageant made a grab for his crown, but Buster ducked away from her and she lost her balance and tumbled off the stage. This was the familiar ending to all Fang events, the understanding that things had shifted and now you were in trouble, in danger, on your own.

'Say it,' Mrs Fang shouted to Buster, who seemed too stunned to proceed. There was a final stage to the event before they could reconvene and retreat, the scene of the crime disappearing in the horizon. Buster was to toss the crown into the audience and shout, 'A crown, golden in show, is but a wreath of thorns.' Instead, Buster was clutching the crown to his head like a piece of his skull that had come unattached. 'Drop it,' Mrs

Fang said, 'just toss that thing.' Buster leaped off the stage and ran down the center aisle, past the Fang family, out the door, and into the night. Mr Fang continued to film the confused faces of those in the audience, then zoomed in on the first runner-up, crying and hiccupping and shaking Buster's wig like a cheerleader's pom-pom. 'This is good,' Mr Fang said. 'It could have been even better,' Mrs Fang replied. 'No,' Annie said, still clapping for her beloved little brother, 'no it could not.'

The Fangs found Buster hiding under their van, conspicuously sparkling as he shifted his weight upon the uncomfortable asphalt. Mr Fang knelt down and helped his son inch out into the open air. 'What happened to the line from Milton?' Mrs Fang asked. Buster flinched at his mother's voice. 'You were supposed to throw the crown away.'

Buster looked up at his mother. 'It's my crown,' he said.

'But you don't want it,' Mrs Fang said, exasperated.

'Yes I do,' he replied. 'I won it. I'm Little Miss Crimson Clover and this is my crown.'

'Oh, Buster,' she said, pointing at the crown atop his head, 'this is what we rebel against, this idea of worth based on nothing more than appearance. This is the superficial kind of symbol that we actively work against.'

'It. Is. My. Crown,' Buster replied, almost

vibrating with righteous anger, and Mrs Fang allowed a slow smile to cross her face and unclenched her jaw. She gave in, nodded three times, and hopped into the van. 'Okay,' she said, 'you can redefine the crown if you want to.'

CHAPTER 4

Buster was in a bad way. In his hospital bed, properly angled, he groaned softly and felt a deep, structural pain travel across his entire face. Even though he was barely conscious and aggressively doped, he understood his unfortunate circumstances.

'You're awake,' someone said.

'I am?' Buster said, with some effort. He moved to touch his face, which ached and hummed in his ears.

'Oh, no,' the woman's voice now said, 'don't do that. People always want to put their dang hands all over the thing that just got fixed,' but Buster was already falling back into something that resembled sleep.

The next time he awoke, a beautiful woman was sitting beside his bed, her face warm and confident, as if she had been expecting him to rouse at just this very moment. 'Hello, Buster,' she said. 'Hi,' he said weakly. He felt like he had to urinate and then, as soon as the feeling appeared, it was gone.

'I'm Dr Ollapolly,' she said. 'I'm Buster,' he replied, but of course she already knew that.

He wished someone had maybe given him a lower dosage of morphine. She was beautiful and capable; he was doped up and possibly disfigured. Even through his haze, he thought, 'I am in a bad way.'

'Do you remember what happened, Buster?' she asked him. He considered the question. 'Potato gun?' he answered.

'Yes, you were accidentally shot in the face by a potato gun,' she told him.

'I'm invincible,' he said.

She laughed. 'Well, I'm glad to hear that, Buster, but that is not an entirely accurate statement. You are lucky, I'll give you that.'

She went on to explain the particulars of his situation. He had suffered some severe facial injuries. To begin, there was significant edema of the face predominantly on his right side, which, Buster guessed correctly, was where the potato had struck him. He had a stellate laceration ('like a star,' she told Buster) through his upper lip. His right superior canine tooth was missing. He sustained multiple complex fractures of the facial bones on his right side, including his upper orbital cavity. On the bright side, despite the eye shield he was wearing, his vision, she assured him, was intact.

'That's good,' he said.

'You're going to have a scar on your lip,' she said.

'Star-shaped,' he answered, wanting desperately to please her.

94

'Yes, a star-shaped scar,' she said.

'That's hard to say,' he answered.

'You are less one tooth,' she continued.

'Okay.'

'And after the operation to stabilize those fractures, you are looking at some recovery time before your face is totally healed.'

'You saved my life,' he said.

'I fixed you up,' she said. 'That's all.'

'I love you,' he said.

'That's fine, Mr Fang,' she replied. Before exiting the room, she smiled with great sincerity, as he imagined all doctors must do if they want their patients to recover.

He owed, according to the solicitous financial officer who snuck in one morning and informed him, somewhere in the neighborhood of twelve thousand dollars in medical fees. Did he have insurance? He did not. Things got awkward after that. Would he like to set up a billing plan? Buster did not. He pretended to fall asleep and waited for the woman to leave his room. Twelve thousand dollars? Half a face for twelve grand? For that kind of money, he wanted X-ray vision, a bionic eyeball. Jesus Christ, he'd at least like to get his missing tooth back. He thought about jumping out of the window and running away, but by then he was genuinely asleep, no longer necessary to pretend.

★　★　★

On the third day of Buster's recovery, one day before he was to be released, Joseph showed up, wheeling in Buster's luggage from the hotel. 'Hey, soldier,' Buster said, and Joseph reddened and stiffened. 'Hey, Buster,' Joseph finally said, flinching at what Buster assumed to be his own distorted, swollen face.

'You got me pretty good,' Buster said and tried to smile, but it was a facial expression that was beyond his abilities for the time being.

Joseph looked at the floor and would not respond.

'I'm kidding around,' Buster said. 'It's not your fault.'

'I wish I was dead,' Joseph said.

He dragged the luggage to the corner of the room and sat gingerly on the suitcase, opting against the seat next to Buster. Joseph rested his elbows on his knees and held his face in his hands. He looked like ominous weather, about to sputter and cry.

'I just, honest to god, wish I was dead,' he repeated.

'But I'm fine,' Buster said. 'It's no big deal.'

'Have you seen your face, Buster?' Joseph asked. Buster had not, having taken great care to avoid looking in the mirrors placed strategically around the room and over the sink in the bathroom.

'I'm being released tomorrow,' Buster said, changing the subject. 'I don't know if it's because I'm better or if it's because I don't have any money.'

Joseph said nothing, seemed unable to meet Buster's lopsided gaze.

Buster reached for his plastic sippy cup and took a few tentative sips of water, dribbling most of the liquid down the front of his gown. 'Where are the other guys?' he asked.

'They can't come,' Joseph said. 'I'm not supposed to be here either, but I wanted to tell you I was sorry and I wanted to bring your luggage from the hotel.'

'Why aren't you supposed to be here?' Buster said, confused. 'Are visiting hours over?'

'My parents talked to a lawyer and he said I'm not supposed to have any further contact with you.'

'Why?'

'In case you sue us,' Joseph said, now actually beginning to cry.

'I'm not going to sue you,' Buster said.

'That's what I told them,' Joseph responded, his breathing ragged and his voice cracking, 'but they say our relationship now has an *adversarial quality* and for as long as you can legally file charges, I can't talk to you.'

'But you're here right now,' Buster said.

'Even with all the crazy stuff that's happened,' Joseph said, smiling for the first time since he arrived in Buster's room, 'I'm glad we met each other.' Buster, twelve grand in the hole, face reconstructed and still tender, agreed.

*   *   *

97

He left the hospital with several photocopies regarding his medical status, several official notices of payment due, and his plastic sippy cup. As he waited for a taxi, he realized that he wasn't entirely sure where to go or, more important, how to get there. Because he had been unsure of the length of his trip, he had never purchased a return flight. He had maxed out his credit card. He tried to imagine the worst way to travel and, just as the taxi arrived, he understood how to proceed. He stepped into the backseat and said, 'Bus station.'

All around him, Nebraska remained flat and frigid, and Buster fought the urge to sleep until the taxi reached its destination. He stared at the ice-tinged fields, the inexplicable birds nearly frozen to the power lines, and understood that whatever he was returning to, wherever it was, would be surprised to have him back.

Standing in line at the bus station, he realized that he did not have enough money to get back to Florida. Unable to control the tremors of his hands, he laid out his cash on the counter and then asked, 'Where does this get me?' The ticket agent smiled and patiently counted out the bills. 'You can get to St Louis and still have five dollars left,' she said. 'I don't know anyone in St Louis,' he replied. 'Well,' she said, her kindness the only thing keeping Buster from breaking down, 'where do you know someone?'

'Nowhere, really,' he answered.

'What about Kansas City? Or Des Moines?' she

said, her fingers typing furiously on the keyboard, as if searching for the answer to a particularly difficult question with the help of very limited resources.

'St Louis is fine,' he said, unable to maintain his composure.

'Chuck Berry's hometown,' the ticket agent offered.

'That seals it then,' he replied, and took his ticket and five dollars in change and collapsed in a seat in the middle of an unoccupied row. He fished a pill out of his prescription bottle and swallowed it, waited for the ache spread tight across his face like cling wrap to disappear. He said, 'Meet me in St Louis,' but didn't know whom he was addressing. Joseph? Dr Ollapolly? The ticket agent? Perhaps he should extend the invitation to all three and hope one might take him up on the offer.

He fell asleep and when he awoke, perhaps an hour later, he had some one- and five-dollar bills resting on his chest and in his lap. He counted it out, seventeen dollars. It was both touching and incredibly patronizing. He lingered on the aspects of it that were touching and felt a little better. He thought this would make for a hilarious down payment on his medical bills, and instead walked to the diner across the street and ordered a milk-shake that was cold and sweet. It was one of the few things he could imagine consuming, considering that his mouth was constantly aching. He placed the straw in the gap where his missing tooth had once been. He ignored the few customers in the diner, who were trying, and failing, not to look at him and ruin their appetites.

At the pay phone in the bus station, he called Annie collect but the phone rang without promise of an answer, not even her voice mail. If she picked up, of course she would help him out, though he hated asking, admitting that he could not keep himself safe and sane. He had not spoken to her since he had inadvertently seen her breasts on the Internet. Seeing her naked wasn't the problem, though it wasn't something he'd recommend to other sensitive boys who idolized their older sisters, it was the feeling he had gotten from the picture, that his sister was falling into something disastrous and depressing. And then there was the resulting frustration, knowing that he probably couldn't help her. But none of this mattered at the moment, because she wasn't answering the phone, and so he hung up.

He considered his remaining options. They were obvious and terrifying. His parents. He kept trying to rewrite the equation so that the answer was something other than his parents but each and every time he worked his way to the end, it was always Mom and Dad, Caleb and Camille, Mr and Mrs Fang.

'Hello?' his mother said.

'Mom,' Buster replied, 'it's your child.'

'Oh, it's our child,' she said, genuinely surprised.

'Which one?' he heard his father ask, and his mother, not savvy enough to cover the receiver or perhaps not caring, said, 'B.'

'I'm in a bad way, Mom,' he said.

'Oh no,' she said. 'What's wrong, Buster?'

'I'm in Nebraska,' he said.

'Oh, that is bad,' she cried. 'Why are you in Nebraska?'

'It's a long story,' he said.

'Well, this is a collect call, so we better keep it brief.'

'Yeah, so I need your help. I got shot in the face and—'

'What?' she shouted. 'You got shot in the face?'

His father's voice came on the line. 'You got shot in the face?' he asked.

'Yeah,' Buster answered. 'But I'm okay. Well, I'm not okay but I'm not dying.'

'Who shot you in the face?' his mother asked.

'Is it a long story?' his father asked.

'It is,' Buster said. 'It's very, very long.'

'We'll come get you,' his mother said. 'We're on our way. I'm getting the atlas out right now and I'm drawing a line from Tennessee to Nebraska. Wow, that's a heck of a drive. We better leave right now. Caleb, we're leaving.'

'We're on our way, son,' Mr Fang said.

'Well, hold on,' Buster answered. 'I'm going to be in St Louis in a few hours.'

'St Louis?' his mother said. Buster imagined her

erasing the mark in the atlas and drawing a new line. 'Should you be traveling after getting shot in the face?'

'It's okay. It was a potato.'

'What was a potato?' Mr Fang asked.

'I got shot in the face with a potato,' Buster said.

'Buster,' his mother said. 'I'm so very confused right now. Is this some kind of guerrilla theater? Are you taping this? Are we being taped?'

Buster felt seismic shifts going on underneath his face. He felt dizzy and struggled to stay upright. For the next five minutes, he tried to walk his parents through the past few days, and by the time he was finished, they were all in agreement. Buster would come home and recuperate with his parents. Mr and Mrs Fang would take care of their boy. He would relax and his body would heal itself and the Fangs, all three of them, would have, according to his mother, 'so much damn fun.'

On the bus to St Louis, a man with a ukulele stood in the aisle and offered to play requests. Someone shouted out, 'Freebird,' and the man sat back down, visibly angered. Buster carefully made his way down the aisle to the bathroom. After several unsuccessful attempts to shut the door, he finally gave up and simply stared at the tiny, nearly opaque mirror. His face was grotesque. Despite all preparations for his disfigurement, he had not expected such spectacular swelling this far removed from the incident. One half of his face was nearly purple with bruising, strips of skin missing and scabbing over, everything twice the size that it should be, except for his eye, which was vise-grip closed and five times the size that it should be. The scar on his lip was less of a star and more of a wishbone or, more accurately, a horseshoe. Stars, horseshoes, wishbones. His scar was nothing but lucky symbols. Using the tube of antibiotic ointment, which would soon need to be expensively refilled, he dabbed the medicine on his cuts, which took some time and effort. When he was finished, Buster smiled at his reflection and saw that this made things worse. He returned to his seat, the aisles around him completely empty, everyone on the bus giving him a three-seat buffer in all directions. This was a kind of life he understood, a three-seat buffer whether he wanted it or not, time to think, whether he wanted to or not, traveling down the highway to some-place new, whether he wanted to or not.

Once he had arrived in St Louis, Buster wandered up and down the terminal for a few hours, walked into a diner, ordered another milkshake, and dabbed at his misaligned face with a moist towelette. 'You don't mind me asking?' said a woman in the booth next to his, pointing at his face. Buster was about to answer when he felt some-thing twitch in his brain, the long-dormant synapses that were programmed to lie without provocation, to create something better than

103

what had come before. 'I was doing a daredevil show over in Kentucky,' he answered. 'I rode a barrel over a waterfall but somebody had drilled some holes in it before the stunt and it began to sink before it even got close to the falls.' The woman shook her head and slid into his own booth, leaving her food untouched. 'That's awful,' she said. Buster nodded and then continued. 'Fighting for air, I finally went over the edge of the falls and the barrel busted open on some rocks and I got battered around in the churning water. By the time they pulled me out, half a mile down the river, everyone assumed I was dead.'

'I'm Janie Cooper,' she said, holding out her hand.

'Lance Reckless,' he answered, trying not to smile, now knowing what his face looked like to other people.

'You say that someone drilled holes in the barrel?' she asked.

He took a long, dramatic sip from his milkshake. He had decided he would live on milkshakes from here on out. 'Foul play,' he answered. 'I'm sure of it. A daredevil's life is full of danger, Janie, and not always for the reasons you'd suspect.'

She took out a pen and paper from her purse and wrote down her phone number. 'Are you in St Louis long?' she asked.

'Just for the day,' he answered.

'Well,' she said, placing the scrap of paper in his hand, 'call me tonight if you end up sticking around.'

She walked back to her table and Buster took such a long sip of his milkshake that he felt his head begin to ache from the effort.

Not ten minutes later, Mr and Mrs Fang stumbled into the bus station's diner. Mrs Fang was wearing a sling around her plastered arm, her head awkwardly bandaged. Mr Fang had two black eyes, his nostrils plugged with blood-crusted gauze, his body hobbled and bent. 'Buster,' they cried in unison. 'We asked around for an injured boy,' his father said, 'and everyone pointed us to the diner.'

As he hugged his parents, Buster noticed Janie again turn away from her food, her arm draped over the booth, watching the proceedings. 'Oh, my baby,' Mrs Fang cried. 'We thought we had lost you,' his father added. 'What the hell is going on?' Buster said. For all his talents, he knew he was powerless against his parents. There were two of them. It was not a fair fight.

Janie stood and introduced herself to Mr and Mrs Fang. 'Are you Lance's parents?' she asked.

'Who?' the Fangs responded.

'Lance is my stage name,' he told Janie.

'Did you two go over a waterfall in a barrel too?' she asked.

His parents had never in their entire lives allowed a stranger to confuse them.

'We were attacked by a bear,' they said, as if they had not even heard Janie's question.

'We were camping in the mountains in

Michigan,' Mrs Fang said, 'just my husband and myself and our son here, Buster, when a grizzly bear came upon our camp and we were forced to fight him off in order to save our own lives.'

'Lance?' Janie said. 'What is she talking about?'

'This was before the waterfall mishap,' he said weakly, but Janie was already paying for her meal, walking out of the restaurant.

'We lost her,' Mr Fang said.

'What the hell is going on?' Buster said. 'Why are you all bandaged up?'

'Oh, we thought, I guess, I don't know, that we'd play along.'

'You'd play along with the fact that I almost died?'

'*Play along* is the wrong phrase. We wanted to add our own interpretation of the event.'

'You folks eating?' the waitress asked. Mr and Mrs Fang each ordered a milkshake.

'St Louis,' Mr Fang said. 'Can't say I've ever been here.'

'I always think of the Judy Garland movie, *Meet Me in St Louis*,' Mrs Fang said.

'Wonderful movie,' Mr Fang replied.

'Little girl in the movie, can't think of her name, goes around killing people on Halloween.'

'Jesus, Mom,' Buster said.

'No, really. She says she's going to murder somebody and when the man answers the doorbell to hand out treats, she hits him in the face with a handful of flour. It's so insane. I wanted so badly for you kids to do that one year, but I thought it might be too obvious.'

'The whole movie should have been about that deranged girl,' Mr Fang said.

'I'm the most horrible,' Buster's parents shouted, 'I'm the most horrible,' apparently quoting from the movie. They looked like patients in an insane asylum who had found romance.

The waitress came by and slammed down their check. 'You people need to calm down,' she said. 'And pay your bill over there.'

'We'll take good care of you, Buster,' Mrs Fang said.

'I need good care to be taken of me,' Buster answered.

'Who better than us?' Mr Fang asked, and the family walked out of the diner without paying.

The Day of the Locust, 1989
Artists: Caleb and Camille Fang

'Sometimes I think my heart is in my tummy,' Annie said. She paused, considered what she had just said, and then repeated herself. She said it again, and again, and again, until the line felt like a foreign language, until the words were not words but sounds and the sentence was not a sentence but a song.

'Sometimes I think my heart is in my tummy,' she said, emphasizing the words *some* and *think* and *tummy* in the sentence, nodding her head in time with the cadence.

'Sometimes I think my *heart* is in my tummy,' she said.

'Sometimes *I* think my heart is in my tummy,' she said.

'Sometimes I think *my* heart is in *my* tummy,' she said.

'Sometimes . . . I think my heart is in my tummy,' she said.

'Sometimes I think my heart . . . is in my tummy,' she said.

'Sometimes I think . . . my heart . . . is in my tummy,' she said.

'Somet – ' and then a plastic cup hit her in the ear. She turned to see Buster standing in the doorway to her room.

'You say that line one more time,' he said, 'and I'm going to set the house on fire.'

'I'm rehearsing,' Annie said.

'You sound like a parrot,' Buster said, frowning.

'I'm rehearsing,' she yelled, and she threw the plastic cup back at Buster, who skulked back into his room, slamming the door shut.

'Sometimes I think my heart is in my tummy,' Annie said quietly, whispered to herself like a coded message. Her heart, in her chest, beat furiously with excitement.

Annie was to play Nellie Weaver in a low-budget film called *Knives Out*, which was about a traveling salesman, Donald Ray, who goes on a cross-country, year long trip selling steak knives to get out from under the debt brought on by his gambling. She was the main character's mentally challenged daughter. She was to have a single line in the movie.

There had been an open call in Nashville and Annie had begged her parents to take her. The Fangs had been skeptical. 'Oh, honey,' Mrs Fang said, 'an actress? That's one step away from a dancer.' Mr Fang then said, 'Which is one step away from a model.'

'I just want to try,' Annie said.

'I don't know,' Mr Fang continued. 'What happens if this movie becomes a success and you start getting recognized by everyone when we create our happenings? We'll lose the anonymity necessary to enact these events.'

This sounded like heaven to Annie. She would become Annie Fang, child star, instead of Child A, artistic prop. People would recognize her in the middle of a Fang event and they would ask for her autograph; her parents, not wanting to attract attention, would simply have to wait until all requests for photos and handshakes had been fulfilled. She could, effectively, ruin everything for her parents.

'Please?' Annie asked.

After a few days, Mr and Mrs Fang relented. In quiet discussions at night, they hashed out the various ways that they might disrupt the proceedings, to put their own stamp on the movie, if Annie was selected. 'Okay,' they finally told her. 'You can be an actor if you want to.'

For her audition, she performed a scene from *All About Eve*, her favorite movie, and as she brought the unlit cigarette, stolen from a woman's purse in the lobby, to her lips, she said, 'Slow curtain. The end,' and took a long drag. The director began to clap, smiling broadly, looking from side to side at the other people at the casting table. 'That was wild,' he told her, shaking her hand, 'just wild as hell.' When she walked into the lobby, her parents asked her how it went. 'Fasten your seat belts,' Annie said, the cigarette dangling from her lips, 'it's going to be a bumpy night.' The Fangs had no idea what the hell she was talking about.

Two weeks before she was to leave for Little Rock, Arkansas, the film's location, to shoot her scenes, the Fangs sat in the waiting room of the JCPenney portrait studio to have their annual Christmas photo taken. Annie had been in character for the past month, eating with a bib on, struggling to tie her shoes, a dumb smile always on her face, the broad strokes of retardation that she hoped would add authenticity to her performance. She held a magazine upside-down, her nose running, while the rest of her family put on their fangs. 'Honestly, Annie,' Mrs Fang said, her tongue probing the points of her new teeth, 'there's something to be said for subtlety.' Annie almost broke character, the idea of her parents, wearing custom-made veneers to look like werewolves, calling for subtle gestures. Her mother cupped Annie's face with her right hand and slipped the fangs into Annie's mouth. 'Don't lose them,' Mrs Fang said. 'They're expensive as hell.'

The fangs had been purchased from a cut-rate dentist open to interesting trades in exchange for services rendered. They had given him an antique quilt from the Civil War, which had been in Mr Fang's family for years, and had received, after their molding and fitting, four sets of fangs, snap-fit dentures that would go over their actual teeth and could be reused for years. 'Merry Christmas to all,' Mr Fang said, smiling, his canines long and pointed.

Their faces serious and somber, the Fangs walked into the studio and arranged themselves according to the instructions of the photographer, a heavily made-up woman, bug-eyed and nervous. For five minutes, the woman pointed and simply said, 'There, there, there.' Annie pretended not to understand what the woman wanted, staring dumbly at the unmanned camera. 'Go sit beside your mommy,' the photographer said. 'She's mentally handicapped,' Mrs Fang said, covering her mouth with her hand. 'Oh,' the woman replied and then said, louder and clearly enunciated, 'Go sit beside your mommy.' Annie sat down and looked into the camera, ready for her close-up.

'One, two, three, cheese,' the woman said and the Fangs, teeth bared, shouted, 'Cheese!' The woman made a soft, squeaking sound like a too-tight shoe, but was otherwise unfazed by the appearance of the fangs. 'Okay, Dad, I think you blinked,' she said, and then once again framed the family in the viewfinder of the camera.

The fake teeth were starting to ache a little, and

they kept running their tongues along the veneers in between shots. 'Can we take these off?' Buster asked once the photographer had finished the session, but Mr and Mrs Fang had already returned their fangs to the plastic storage container. 'Once we get the photos and send them out to people for the holidays, it'll get a better reaction,' Mr Fang said but he was obviously shaken by the lack of shock from the photographer. 'She was too busy doing her job,' Mrs Fang said, rubbing the tension out of her husband's shoulders. 'It's like asking a brain surgeon to notice the magic trick you are doing while he's in the middle of an operation.'

Buster said, 'We need some fake blood.' Mr Fang said, 'Maybe. That's not a bad idea.' Mrs Fang said, 'And a stuffed deer that we can pretend to be eating.' Mr Fang said, 'That could be arranged.' Annie said, 'Sometimes I think my heart is in my tummy.' No one else said a word.

Three days later, Annie received a phone call from the director's assistant. 'I have some bad news,' the man said. Annie, suddenly, as if struck by lightning, stopped acting retarded. 'What is it?' she asked. Had filming shut down? Had they run out of money?

'We're cutting your line,' the man said.

It was as if a doctor had told Annie that her leg could not be saved and would have to be amputated. Actually, for Annie, it was worse. She'd rather be missing a leg and have a speaking role in a feature film than the alternative.

'Why?' Annie asked. 'Do you think I can't do it?'

'That's not it, Annie,' the man said.

'Sometimes I think my heart is in my tummy,' Annie said.

'That's perfect, Annie, but Marshall just felt that the main character would be more tortured if he never got to talk to his daughter during his sales trip than if he got to talk to her once.'

'I disagree,' Annie said.

'Well, Marshall and the screenwriter discussed this and they've made their decision.'

'What do they want?' Mrs Fang asked Annie, who covered the mouthpiece of the phone and screamed, 'Get out of here.' Mrs Fang, stunned, turned and walked out of the living room.

'So I don't get to be in the movie?' Annie said.

'No, Annie, you're still in the movie, but you just don't have any lines. You'll be in the scenes where Donald Ray calls his family, and you'll be in the movie when it comes out.'

'I'll be an extra,' Annie said and began to cry.

'Oh, sweetheart, please don't cry,' the man said, sounding as if he might cry as well. 'Can I talk to your mom or dad?'

'They're dead,' Annie said.

'What?' the man asked.

'They're busy,' Annie said. 'They don't want to talk to you.'

'Annie,' the man said, his voice finally regaining its composure. 'I know you're mad but if you want to be an actress, you need to learn how to deal with disappointment. You've got a long career ahead of you; I'd hate to see you quit just because of this.'

Annie, no stranger to disappointment, felt the hope break down inside her body and disperse without any lingering effects. 'I know,' she said and then hung up the phone.

'What did they want?' Mr Fang asked when Annie returned to the dinner table. Annie speared a piece of broccoli and chewed it slowly, then took a long sip of water.

'Movie stuff,' Annie said. 'No big deal.'

Mrs Fang said, 'Well, it sounded like a big deal when you yelled at me.'

'It's nothing,' Annie said.

'Annie Fang, Oscar-winning actress,' Mr Fang said.

'Don't say that,' Annie said.

Buster, his plate empty, pushed away from the table and said, 'Sometimes I think my heart is in my tummy.'

Annie threw her glass at him. It missed his head by inches and shattered against the wall, and Annie ran out of the kitchen, locking herself in her bedroom. That night, she watched a video of Bette Davis in *Of Human Bondage*. In the scene where Davis berates the clubfooted medical student who loves her, Annie paused the movie and then stared into the mirror and screamed, 'You cad! You dirty swine! I never cared for you – not once.' She continued the monologue, slowly backing away from the mirror, getting smaller, retreating from view, and then she suddenly rushed toward her own reflection, screaming, 'And after you kissed me, I always used to wipe my mouth. WIPE MY MOUTH!'

The other Fangs, listening to punk rock in the living room, simply turned up the volume and pretended not to notice.

Six months later, *Knives Out* received a limited, almost nonexistent release. The few reviews it garnered offered mild praise; there were no mentions of Annie's performance. Nevertheless, when the Fangs found a theater in Atlanta that was showing the movie, Annie could not contain her excitement. 'You're going to be so proud of me,' Annie told her parents.

She had not allowed Mr or Mrs Fang to accompany her during the filming of her scenes. They had stayed behind in the motel and, once the few scenes had been shot, each only a single take to save film for more important scenes, she answered their questions with shrugs and one-word answers. The Fangs had assumed she had lost interest in acting and did not press her. However, her vibrating happiness in the car, on their way to the only theater showing the film within a three-hundred-mile radius, the Fangs wondered how much they were going to have to lie to make their daughter believe the movie was any good.

They bought popcorn and candy and sodas and settled into their seats in the sparsely populated theater. Once the lights died down and the film began to snap into coherence, the theme song for the movie played over the speakers. A twangy voice sang,

> *What I'm selling, you ain't buying.*
> *My debts are multiplying.*
> *Got my knives out, stainless steel.*
> *I'll find a way to make a deal.*

'Oh, dear Lord,' Mr Fang said and Mrs Fang pinched the hell out of his arm.

The movie proceeded with little to recommend it, a man with a trunk full of steak knives, his gambling debts weighing on him, driving down long, unwinding highways.

An hour into the movie, Buster had successfully fit thirty-nine Raisinettes in his mouth. He pointed to his distended cheeks but Annie would not look over at him. She continued to stare at the screen, smiling, her knees bouncing. Buster shrugged and, one by one, spit the raisins back into the box. Donald Ray sliced his hand open with a knife during a demonstration in a drunk woman's house and the splash of blood kept the Fangs from nodding off. The movie was so low-budget, Mr Fang wondered if the actor who played Donald Ray had actually cut open his hand for the scene. He felt his estimation of the actor rise considerably.

'Here it comes,' Annie whispered, turning to her parents. 'This is me.' Donald Ray, his hand wrapped in a makeshift bandage, picked up the hotel phone and made a collect call to his family back in Little Rock. As the phone rang, tinny and soft in the receiver, the film jumped to Donald Ray's home, the telephone shrilly ringing on the coffee table. As the camera pulled back, a woman leaned over to answer the phone. She listened for a few seconds and then said that she'd accept the charges. 'Donald Ray,' she finally said, both angry and relieved to hear from him.

'Look real close,' Annie said. Behind Donald Ray's wife, sitting on the floor and staring dully at the carpet, was Annie. 'That's you,' Buster said. 'Watch now,' Annie said. 'This is my big moment.' The Fangs watched their daughter on the big screen, her face empty of expression, seemingly unaware of the conversation going on beside her. It was, the Fangs would later admit, a fairly compelling performance. Then, suddenly, so fast that you would miss it if you weren't looking, Annie looked toward the camera and smiled. The Fangs could not believe it had happened, the moment so jarring and unsettling that it took them a few seconds to realize what they had just seen. Annie had smiled at the camera. Her teeth bared. Fanged.

'Annie?' Mr and Mrs Fang said at once. In the seat next to them, Annie was smiling, beaming, the scene ended, her character not to return for the rest of the movie. She was, the Fangs now understood, a star.

CHAPTER 5

Annie needed to get out of town. Three days after her disastrous interview, the index and middle fingers on her right hand were still bruised and aching. Annie had used half a roll of electrical tape to secure the fingers together, fashioning a splint out of a popsicle stick snapped in half. Holding up her damaged hand, she looked at herself in the mirror. The black tape on her fingers made her right hand look like a gun and she aimed and fired at her reflection. If it got worse, the tips of her fingers turning black, she'd simply add more tape. She would cover her entire body in tape, like a cocoon, and when things had calmed down, she would emerge, something new and capable and better than what had preceded it.

The phone rang. She let it ring; she already had a machine full of messages from the *Esquire* writer, wanting to come over and 'discuss the article,' which sounded to Annie like 'have more sex so I can write about it.' The answering machine would take care of it. She loved the answering machine as if it were a living thing, the way it protected her from the bad decisions she was entirely capable of making. The machine's robotic voice informed the caller that no one was home and to please leave a message. 'It's Daniel,' the caller said. 'Pick up the phone, Annie.' Annie shook her head. 'C'mon now, pick up the phone,' Daniel continued. 'I can see you, Annie. I know you're home. I'm looking right at you. Pick up the phone.' Annie turned toward the window and saw no one, wondered if Daniel was already inside the house. Had he ever returned the key she had given him when they were dating? She was losing faith in her answering machine, which had yet to cut off the message. 'Annie, I love you and I want to help you,' he continued. 'Just pick up the phone.' She gave up, reached for the receiver with her unin-jured hand, and answered the phone.

'Where are you?' she said. 'How can you see me?'

'I can't see you,' Daniel answered. 'I just said that so you'd answer the phone.'

'I'm going to hang up now,' Annie said.

'This is important, Annie,' he said. 'Remember the last time we talked?'

'Vaguely,' Annie responded.

'I said I thought you were going crazy.'

'Okay, yes, I remember that.'

'Maybe I was wrong.'

'I know you were wrong,' Annie said.

'But I think you're going crazy right now,' he continued.

'I've got a flight to catch,' Annie said. She made a mental note to book a flight after she got off the phone with Daniel.

'Just let me come over and talk to you for five minutes.'

'I can't, Daniel.'

'I care about you, Annie. I just want to talk for five minutes and then you never have to see me again.'

Annie took a long, thoughtful sip of whiskey and wondered if she had hit rock bottom yet.

'Okay,' Annie answered. 'Come on over.'

'Thank you,' Daniel said. 'I'm on your doorstep right now.'

'What?' Annie asked.

'Yeah, you never changed your pass code for the front gate. I've been here for about fifteen minutes.'

'Why didn't you just knock on the door?'

'I didn't want to freak you out,' Daniel said.

'That's nice,' Annie said, walking to the front door, her whiskey in dire need of a refill.

In the kitchen, Annie dumped eight Pop-Tarts on a platter and brought the breakfast pastries into the living room, where Daniel, his trademark Stetson now replaced by a porkpie hat, was waiting for her. Daniel lived on Pop-Tarts and sparkling water; Annie had never seen him consume anything else. Daniel, if she were blind and deaf, would be the sickly sweet smell of artificial strawberries and singed dough. He patted the cushion adjacent to him on the sofa but Annie smiled and took a seat on the rocking chair directly across from him, the coffee table an adequate barrier for their conversation. Annie rocked and rocked, an irritating squeak accompanying her actions. She felt like a tiny, narcoleptic dog should be in her lap.

'You said that you needed to talk to me,' Annie said.

'I do,' Daniel answered, Pop-Tart crumbs already covering the floor at his feet.

'About what?'

'Your career and what you're doing to it and what you're doing to yourself. I know you're not a lesbian,' Daniel said.

'Is that all you wanted to say?' Annie said.

'What happened to your hand?' he asked.

'I punched my publicist in the face,' Annie answered, holding her injured but unshaking hand out in front of her. She was impressed by the steadiness of her nerves.

'Yeah, I heard she let you go.'

'We let each other go. We decided at the exact same time. Is this what you came to talk about?' she said.

'Paramount offered me the chance to write the third *Powers That Be* movie.'

'Oh . . . congratulations.'

'Thank you.'

'I didn't know they had decided to make a third

one,' Annie said, struggling to keep her facial features from betraying her confusion.

'Well, that's why I wanted to talk to you.' Daniel took off his porkpie hat and twirled it in his hands. 'This hat belonged to Buster Keaton,' he said.

'You hate silent movies.'

'I do,' Daniel said. 'But I've got so much money now that I've run out of things to buy.'

'Daniel—'

'Okay, okay. When I agreed to write the third installment of *PTB,* they only had one request.'

'Which was?' Annie asked.

'They wanted me to write your character out of the film. They don't want you to be a part of the franchise anymore.'

Standing at what seemed to be rock bottom, staring up at the unreachable world above sea level, Annie felt the ground beneath her feet give way yet again.

'They don't want me in the movie?' Annie asked.

'They do not.'

'Did they give a reason?'

'They did.'

'Did it have to do with the naked Internet photos and my rumored mental instability?'

'It did.'

'Oh shit.'

'I'm sorry, Annie. I thought you should know.'

Annie, despite the voice screaming at her not to do it, began to tear up. She could not believe that she was crying about the lost opportunity to once again wear a ridiculous superhero costume and stand in front of a green screen for hours and say lines like 'It appears lightning *can* strike twice.' It seemed ridiculous to her, even as she was crying, but it did not stop her from sobbing, the chair uncontrollably rocking, in front of her ex-boyfriend.

'It sucks, I know,' Daniel said.

'Does it suck?' Annie said. 'Do you know?'

'I have a feeling that it sucks.'

Annie stood up, walked into the kitchen, and returned with the bottle of George Dickel. She took a hard slug from the bottle, felt a kind of resolve seep into her bones, a noir-like, hard-boiled toughness. Alcohol, she suddenly understood, would solve this problem. It would create other, more pressing problems, but for now, steadily rising into inebriation, she felt like she could handle the situation at hand. She could *deal with shit*.

'The third movie in the trilogy is never any good,' she said. '*Return of the Jedi, Godfather Part III, The Bad News Bears Go to Japan.*'

'Well,' Daniel said, 'I'm going to write it, so it's going to be pretty good, I think. Which is kind of what I want to talk to you about.'

Annie was trying to listen but she was unable to shake the image of herself dressed in a knock-off Lady Lightning outfit, sitting alone at a table at a mid-level comic book convention, drinking a diet soda and staring at her cell phone, which did not ring.

'Annie?' Daniel said. 'I want to talk to you about the movie.'

Annie imagined herself in Japan, shilling caffeinated tapioca pearls, living in a closet-size apartment, dating a washed-up sumo wrestler.

'Annie?' Daniel said again.

Annie imagined herself doing dinner theater in a converted barn, playing Myra Marlowe in *A Bad Year for Tomatoes*, getting fat on carved roast beef and macaroni and cheese from the buffet during intermission.

'I want to help you, Annie,' Daniel continued, undeterred by Annie's blank-faced analysis of her future. 'And I think I can.'

Annie smoothed the crease in her jeans as if she was petting a catatonic dog. 'You want to help me with what, Daniel?'

'I want to help you stop feeling so overwhelmed and I want to help get your career back on track.'

'Please don't tell me to check myself into a mental health facility.'

'No, I've got a better idea,' Daniel assured her.

'It would have to be,' Annie responded.

Daniel rose from the sofa, placed his half-eaten Pop-Tart on the platter, and walked over to Annie, who already began to flinch. He knelt on the floor beside her. Annie felt the awkwardness of a marriage proposal forming in the air and she shook her head vigorously as if to disrupt the possibility. Then Daniel, no ring in hand, positioned his body into a crouch, like a catcher about to relay signs to the pitcher. His face was less than a foot from her own.

'The studio wants a draft of the screenplay in a month. I've rented a cabin out in Wyoming, nothing but empty space and wolves. I want you to come with me.'

'And do what? Watch you write my character out of the movie and eat antelope jerky?'

'No, so you can just relax. You can go hiking and get away from all this bullshit and calm down a little bit. And then, maybe, if things go well, we could give this relationship another try.'

'You want me to come to Wyoming and have sex with you?' Annie said.

'That's correct,' Daniel said, smiling.

'And how will this help my career?'

'That's the other thing I wanted to talk to you about. I thought that if we worked together on the script, we could find a way to keep Lady Lightning in the movie, come up with an idea so good that the studio would have to go along with it.'

'They'd just hire another actress,' Annie said, leaning forward, their foreheads almost touching.

'Maybe not. You come with me, clear your head, weather all this bad publicity, and maybe they'll remember that you're a bankable star with a lot of talent.'

'All this if I just come to Wyoming and sleep with you?'

'That's it,' Daniel said.

'I had sex with a reporter from *Esquire*,' Annie said.

'Okay,' Daniel answered, genuinely unfazed.

'Three days ago. You can read about it in the next issue.'

'I don't care,' Daniel said. 'It's just further evidence that you need to get the hell out of here for a while.'

Wyoming, to Annie, was represented by a blank, bleak space in her imagination. It was a place she could hide. The worst that could happen would be that she would sleep with Daniel and then get eaten by a wolf. She could live with that.

After she agreed, Daniel placing the porkpie hat on Annie's head as if rewarding her for a sound decision, the two of them sat on the floor of her living room while she had another glass of whiskey and Daniel ate another Pop-Tart. Wasn't this how adults acted? Annie wondered, feeling slightly proud of herself. Daniel showed her his most recent tattoo, a typewriter surrounded by dollar signs. Annie told him to roll his sleeve back down and she tried to pretend that it had never happened. By the time he had left her house, with plans to meet again in the morning to leave for Wyoming, Annie felt improbably sober and, if not happy, at least assured that she was capable of not fucking up everything she touched.

Later that night, having made plans to meet again in the morning, touched by the soundness of her decision to leave Los Angeles, Annie fried a slab of bologna in a pan and listened to George Plimpton read an audiobook of John Cheever stories, which she had bought but never listened to after losing out on the part of Cheever's wife in a biopic that ended up never getting made. The soothing way that Plimpton's cosmopolitan, almost British, accent filled the kitchen with tales of people that Annie would want to punch in the face under most circumstances calmed her, made her feel smart and capable and not at all crazy.

She slathered mayonnaise on two slices of white bread and added the now-charred slice of bologna to complete the sandwich. She filled a glass with ice and whiskey and, spurred by the cocktail-guzzling Cheever characters, dumped some sugar into the drink. She stirred it with her finger, called it an old-fashioned, and retired to the dining room table to enjoy her meal, pausing Plimpton's voice in mid-sentence – '. . . from bacon and coffee to poultry . . .' – the word *poultry* sounding, to Annie's ears, like *poetry*.

Three bites into her meal, the phone rang and Annie, no longer needing the protection of the answering machine, answered. 'Hall-ow,' she said, the bread sticking to the roof of her mouth, the mayonnaise like caulk in the ridges and indentations of her palate. 'Annie?' the voice said.

She swallowed and then, her tongue able to move freely in her mouth, responded, 'This is Annie.'

'You sounded like you were pretending to be retarded,' the voice said.

'Daniel?' she asked.

'Buster,' her brother said.

It was always a strange sensation to hear her brother's voice, how it sounded not like an actual voice but a sound inside of her own head, that her brother was held in the cage of her ribs and only occasionally made his presence known to her. She hadn't heard from him in months, when he had specifically told her that she should, under no circumstances, take off her top. She had then, of course, taken off her top. That she had not heard from him felt like a justified punishment.

'What's going on?' Annie asked, genuinely curious as to her brother's current status. 'Did you kill someone? Do you need money?'

'I almost killed myself and I need about twelve thousand dollars, but that's not why I called.'

'Wait, what happened?'

'It's a long story that will make you very sad, so I'll hold off on telling it. The real news is that it turns out that you can go home again.'

'Buster,' Annie said, her voice impatient and sharp, 'I've been drinking all day so I'm having trouble understanding what the hell you're talking about.'

'I'm back home,' Buster said.

'In Florida?'

'Tennessee.'

'When did you move to Tennessee?'

'I'm living with Mom and Dad.'

'Oh, Buster,' Annie said. 'Oh no.'

'It's not so bad,' Buster said.

'It sounds bad,' Annie responded and then, as if he could not wait for her to finish her sentence, he said, 'It's pretty bad.' Slowly, as if he could not quite believe it, he told her the story of the potato gun and the rearranged face and his new living situation.

'A few times, they've called me Child B. They say it, and then, when I call them on it, they pretend it didn't happen. Maybe it didn't. I'm not sure. I'm pretty loose on pain pills.'

'Get out of there, Buster,' Annie said, nearly shouting.

'I can't,' he said. 'I'm stuck here for the time being.'

'You can't stay there,' Annie continued, refusing to take no for an answer. 'You need to escape.'

'I thought, actually, that you might come here,' he said. 'Keep me company. See how old age is treating Mom and Dad.'

Annie imagined her childhood bedroom unchanged since she had left, lobby cards still hanging on the walls, a half-empty bottle of rigid collodion on the dresser, an unsmoked bag of weed in a hidden compartment beneath the floorboards of the closet. She had not been home since she was twenty-three, always seeing her parents in neutral locations, places agreed upon by both parties to be free from incident. They would gather on holidays and birthdays in nondescript hotels in cities none of them had ever visited. The thought of returning seemed to be exactly the kind of thing that would, if entertained, ruin her in spectacular ways previously unimagined.

'I can't, Buster,' she finally said. 'I'm going to Wyoming.'

'Do not leave me here, Annie,' Buster replied.

'I'm in a weird place right now,' she said. 'I need to figure things out.'

'You're in a weird place right now?' Buster said, his voice rising. 'Right now, right this very minute, I'm sitting on my childhood bed, drinking Percocet-laced orange soda out of a straw that I'm holding in the gap where my tooth used to be, before it got shattered by a potato. Mom and Dad are in the living room listening to La Monte Young's *Black Record* at a ridiculously loud volume. They're wearing Lone Ranger masks, which seems to be a recurring thing for them. For the past hour, I've been reading an issue of *Guitar World* from 1995, because I'm afraid to go on the Internet and see another picture of my sister's tits.'

'I can't, Buster,' she said.

'Come get me,' Buster said.

'I just don't think I can do it.'

'I miss you, Annie.'

'I'm sorry, Buster,' she said and then hung up the phone.

★   ★   ★

132

When she was making the first *Powers That Be* movie, she talked to Buster every day on the phone, for hours at a time while she waited for someone to come to her trailer and lead her to the set. She would tell him about the bizarre things that went into making a blockbuster action movie, techniques and constructions that seemed, even to a Fang, to be overwhelming and ridiculous. 'There's a guy here,' Annie told Buster, 'and his entire job is to make sure that Adam Bomb walks correctly.'

'What's his title?' Buster asked.

'Ambulation consultant,' Annie said.

She began to look forward to their next conversation as soon as the previous one ended. Late at night, after a long day of shooting, her hair rigid and aching from being teased by a team of hairdressers, she would lie in bed and listen to Buster read from his second novel, a book about a boy who is the only person unaffected by the nuclear fallout from World War III. As she drifted in and out of sleep, she would listen to his voice, shaky and serious, read what he had written only hours earlier. 'The boy kicked a soup can, which skittered across the ravaged and broken asphalt road,' Buster read. 'When it came to a rest, a family of roaches poured out of the can, moving in all directions as if afraid that one of their own had been responsible for the disturbance. The boy resisted the urge to stomp the insects into nothingness and continued on his way.' Annie readjusted the phone and sat up, intent to hear every word precisely the way that Buster intended it. The story was terribly sad; hope was a flickering match that, at any moment, seemed destined to be extinguished. And yet Annie imagined the boy, randomly saved from the awful effects of the world, to be Buster and hoped that there would be a kind of happiness waiting for him at the end. 'It's happening for us, Buster,' she would tell him. 'Whatever comes next will be so big that we won't recognize ourselves when it's over.'

And then the movie had been the biggest block-buster in years and Buster's book had been dismissed by the critics and remaindered. When they talked after that, everything seemed filtered by the understanding that one of them had made it across the ocean, her feet solidly placed on an undiscovered country, while the other had been lost at sea.

Buster would call late at night from a hotel room, on assignment for some magazine, noticeably impaired. Annie would half-listen to him as she watched movies with the volume turned down low enough that he could not hear. 'You're a movie star now,' Buster once told her, 'and I am the brother of a movie star.'

'And I'm the sister of Buster Fang,' she replied.

'Who?' he said. 'Never heard of him.'

'Buster,' she said. 'Come on now.'

'I am,' he muttered, his words so slurred and shapeless it was only after he had slammed the phone down that she understood what he had actually said, 'the least of the Fangs.'

The next morning, Annie resisted the urge to make another drink and waited for Daniel to take her to the airport. She had hardly slept last night; she had a dream where Daniel stood in the doorway of their cabin, wearing fringed buckskins, his arm torn off by a grizzly bear. 'Big, wonderful Wyoming,' he said to her as she tried, and failed, to apply a tourniquet.

When Daniel arrived, cowboy hat returned to prominence, an unlit Marlboro hanging from his lips, sporting a pair of waterproof boots that looked like something astronauts or ice fishermen would wear, he quickly took her bags out of her hands and wedged them into the tiny trunk of his sports car. Annie found it difficult to follow him to the car, still standing on the front steps of her house, wondering, now sober, what the hell she was doing. 'Tell me again what I'm going to do in Wyoming,' she asked him.

'You're going to be my muse,' he said.

'I know this is a little late to be asking, but is there a TV?' she asked.

'No,' he said. 'It's just you and me.'

'I'm going to get a deck of cards,' she said, hurrying back inside the house.

At the airport, checked in, through security, waiting for the plane to depart, Annie listened to

Daniel discuss his initial ideas for the third install-ment of *Powers That Be*. 'No more Nazis,' he said, nodding wisely. 'Nazis are played out. I'm thinking we need to go bigger than that, raise the stakes.'

'Okay,' Annie said.

'Dinosaurs,' he said.

'What?'

'They're going to fight dinosaurs. It'll be awesome, trust me.'

'How about Nazi dinosaurs?'

Daniel frowned and then said, 'Annie, part of being someone's muse is not to make fun of their ideas.'

It occurred to Annie that, aside from Buster, no one but Daniel knew where she was going. She was heading to a remote cabin in Wyoming with her ex-boyfriend, with whom she had a volatile relationship. She would listen to Daniel talk for hours about dinosaurs and rocket launchers and the catchphrase 'Bomb them back to the Stone Age.' This seemed, suddenly, to be a big mistake.

She had no publicist but she still had an agent and a manager, people that, one would hope, would want to know of her plans. 'I better call my agent,' Annie said, 'and let him know I'm going to be out of pocket for a little while.'

'He probably knows by now,' Daniel said.

'What's that?'

'I sent word out to a few contacts in the media about our trip, how we were heading into the wild for business and pleasure.'

'What the hell are you talking about, Daniel?' Annie asked.

'I leaked some information to several key entertainment journalists about my being offered the *Powers That Be* sequel and how you were coming with me to Wyoming to work on the script. And . . .'

'Yes?'

'And I told them that we were back together,' Daniel said.

For an instant, Daniel looked exactly, every feature correct, like Minda Laughton.

'We're not back together, though,' Annie reminded him.

'Jesus, Annie, what do you think is going to happen? We're going to be in a cabin in the middle of nowhere, just the two of us.'

'We're going to work on the screenplay. The Nazi dinosaurs and whatnot.'

'Without me, Annie, honestly, you're done. Together, we're a power couple. We can rule this town.'

'Daniel, you're sounding like an evil scientist.'

'You need me, and, I know this may be hard to understand, I need you.'

'You need many, many things, Daniel, most of them pharmaceutical.'

'I hate turning this into something ugly, but if you don't come with me to Wyoming, I'll do whatever I can to ruin your career to the point that it can't be fixed.'

Annie felt the words pass through her, which rendered her body fuzzy and uncoordinated. 'I need a second,' Annie said. Daniel nodded and then told her that he was going to use the restroom. 'When I come back, we'll pretend like this never happened. We'll head to Wyoming and get back to what we do best.' Annie had no idea what it was that they did best; the two of them together seemed below average in all categories.

'Take your time,' Annie told him as he walked away from their gate. As soon as Daniel was out of sight, she hurried over to the counter, manned by two airline employees, and waited for them to acknowledge her. The two women shuffled papers, squinted at the computer screen, and then said, in unison, 'Well, that's wrong.' Annie looked over her shoulder for Daniel to reappear, feeling like ominous violin strains should be playing over the airport's sound system, a movie score for a thriller about an incredibly stupid woman and her insane ex-boyfriend.

'Can I ask you something?' Annie said, and both of the women looked up from the screen and set their mouths into thin expressions of annoyance that might, if challenged, be called a smile. 'Uh-huh?' they said in unison.

'I'm wondering about my plane ticket,' she said.

'It's in your hand there,' the woman on the right said.

'I know,' Annie continued, trying to convey the necessity for speed, 'but I wondered if I could change it.'

'You want a different seat?' the woman on the left said.

'I want a different airplane,' Annie told her.

'Say what?' they said.

'I want to get on a different flight.'

'Why?'

'It's complicated.'

'Well,' the woman on the right said, 'it's pretty complicated to switch your plane ticket.'

'Okay, fine,' Annie said, still no sign of Daniel, thank god. 'My ex-boyfriend asked me to go on a trip with him to Wyoming to try and get back together and I said yes and now I think I should have said no.'

'Ooh, this is good,' the woman on the left said.

'He's in the bathroom, and I need to get on a different flight, something leaving right now, before he finds out.'

'This is real good,' the woman on the right said.

A few keystrokes later, the women, taking turns, read off destinations while Annie considered the possibilities. She did not want to go to New York or Chicago or Dallas. 'Somewhere else,' she said.

'Better hurry,' the woman on the right said. 'Your boyfriend's been in the bathroom for a long time.'

'He's probably staring at his reflection in the mirror,' Annie said.

'I know the type,' the woman replied. 'You don't want to go to Wyoming with a man like that.'

She was escaping. It was a great escape. She took out her cell phone, afraid that it would begin to ring at any moment, and tossed it into a nearby trash can. There would be no one to tell her to do anything other than what she was doing right this minute. She was off the grid now and she felt the excitement that went along with cutting the lines of communication. She would be somewhere far away by evening and she would, well, she wasn't sure what she would do except try to turn herself invisible with substances. As the women magically moved her from one plane to another, mere minutes from leaving everything behind, Annie thought of Buster, propped up in his childhood bed, face distorted, trapped in that house while their parents tried, all the king's horses and all the king's men, to fix what was broken in him. She knew that she was falling apart and that Buster had already been disassembled and she wondered if there was any possibility that, every Fang restored under one roof, they might be good for each other. It seemed unlikely, but, standing in the airport terminal, people moving in all directions, she was willing to risk it. She was not going to Wyoming with Daniel. Wherever she ended up would be better than that.

'Do you have any flights to Nashville?' she asked.

'Got a flight leaving for Detroit in ten minutes, and then you can catch a flight to Nashville.'

'You need to decide right now,' the woman on the left said. 'I think I see your boyfriend coming.'

'Ex-boyfriend,' Annie said. 'And, I'll take it.'

A new boarding pass in her hand, she thanked

the women, who assured her that they would relay her message to Daniel – that she could not go with him – in their own unique way. 'It'll be real good,' the women said. 'He'll be crushed.'

Annie unwound the electrical tape on her hand and tossed it into the trash, flexed her fingers and found them to be without pain, and then she began running to catch her flight, pumping her arms, a movie star in a movie that did not exist. She imagined the cameraman moving alongside her, trying to keep her in the frame. She was running, however ill-conceived and doomed to failure it might be, and her character's motivation was simple and understandable. Escape. She ran through the expensively designed set, past all the extras that might slow her down, the cries of the director so faint that she could not even hear them any longer.

Untitled Project, 2007
Artists: Caleb and Camille Fang

When Annie walked off the escalator to baggage claim, she saw her brother, Buster, holding a sign that read: FANG. His face was as damaged as he had led her to believe, and she relied on her natural talent to feign a lack of surprise, feeling her stomach knot and tighten in response to the struggle to maintain her composure on the surface. Neither one of them knew what to do when she finally walked up to him and took the sign in her hands. They stared at each other for a long second, A and B, the easy way they fit together in sequence, and then Buster reached for his sister and hugged her.

'I can't believe you came back,' he said.

'I know,' Annie said. 'What the fuck is wrong with me?'

'We're in a bad way,' Buster told her and she agreed with him.

'Where are Mom and Dad?' she asked.

Buster looked away, took a deep breath, and

then said, 'They're in the van, planning. They've got an idea.'

'No,' Annie said, a familiar heat radiating through her body. 'Please, no.'

'Welcome home,' Buster said, and walked to the carousel to retrieve her luggage.

In the parking lot, Caleb and Camille were standing beside the van, waving wildly as if their arms were on fire, as Annie and Buster tentatively approached. For Annie it was more shocking to see her parents for the first time in years than it had been to see Buster's swollen face. Her parents seemed like miniature, crooked versions of themselves. Their hair had gone completely gray. Yes, they were still thin and they still possessed an electric kind of enthusiasm that was hypnotic to witness, but they were, it shouldn't have surprised her but it did, so old.

Their father was holding a clothes hanger that held a bright blue T-shirt that read: THE CLUCK TEAM just below the CHICKEN QUEEN logo, a plump, regal woman holding a drumstick.

'Annie!' Camille shouted.

'What's that?' Annie asked, pointing at the T-shirt as her mother kissed her on the cheek.

'A gift,' Caleb said, thrusting the shirt toward his daughter.

'No thank you,' Annie said.

'Hear us out,' her parents said in unison.

'Please,' Annie said, 'I just got back.' She looked

143

at her brother, who, she now realized, seemed slightly drugged, a sheepish smile on his face.

Her father slid the back door of the van open and gestured for Annie to climb inside.

'I need a drink,' Annie said.

'This is better,' Caleb said, placing his arms around both of his children. 'This is better than any drug ever made.'

Annie took a deep breath, nowhere else to run, and stepped into the van. Buster joined her and their parents smiled and then slammed the door shut.

The plan was simple enough, their parents explained. They were driving to a mall near the airport, all the necessary elements arranged in advance by Caleb and Camille. Annie and her mother would don the Chicken Queen T-shirts and take the massive stack of forged coupons. Camille handed Annie and Buster one of the sheets, a fairly professional job, a coupon that offered a free chicken sandwich, no strings attached. The coupon was good enough that a customer wouldn't think twice about it, but sloppy enough that a cashier at Chicken Queen would know it was a fake. 'How many of these did you make?' Annie asked her parents. 'One hundred,' they said. They continued to explain the event, how Annie and Camille would pass out the coupons, while Buster sat at a table in the food court next to the Chicken Queen. He would record the initial confusion when customer after customer came bearing bogus coupons. Then, when enough customers had been refused, the terror of the situation becoming apparent to the underpaid and overworked staff, Caleb would walk up to the counter to push things over the edge, to organize the angry customers, to overtake the Chicken Queen.

'It'll be a thing of beauty,' Caleb told his children.

'I don't want to do this,' Annie said.

'Yes, you do,' Caleb responded.

'I'm not well,' Annie said. 'Buster is not well.'

'This will make you better,' Camille said. 'We're a family again. This is what we do. This is what the Fangs do. We make strange and memorable things.'

'I can't do this,' Annie said, looking at Buster for help. Buster touched his eye patch and then said, 'I don't want to do this either.'

'Don't you start,' Caleb told his son.

'No,' Annie said. 'We aren't going to do this.'

'Kids,' Camille began, but then Caleb slammed his hand on the horn, a shock of anger, before he regained his composure. 'Fine,' he said. 'You're out of practice anyway. You'd fuck it up. Your mother and I will do it all. We'll do everything. We've done it for years on our own. We were just trying to include the two of you. We wanted to make you feel a part of this again.'

Annie felt her resolve slipping. 'Dad, it's not—'

'No,' Caleb said. 'We shouldn't have asked. We'll do it. We'll make this happen. Could you at least work the camera? Could you do that much for us?'

'Sure,' Buster said, looking at Annie for support. 'We'll do that.'

'You're just out of practice,' Caleb mumbled, staring straight ahead. 'You just need to relearn what all this means. Who you are.'

Their lazy children parked at a table in the food court, Caleb and Camille separated to opposite ends of the mall and laid the groundwork for the event. 'Free chicken sandwich at Chicken Queen,' Caleb shouted, waving a coupon toward a passing woman in a way that seemed vaguely obscene. 'No purchase necessary,' he said.

'No thank you,' the woman said.

'What?' Caleb asked her, the paper drooping in his hand.

'I don't want any, thank you,' the woman explained.

'It's free, though,' Caleb said, shocked at the refusal.

'I'm not hungry.'

'Are you watching your weight?' Caleb asked, genuinely curious. 'It's one of the healthiest things in the food court.'

'No,' the woman said, her voice rising. She slapped at the proffered coupon and quickly walked away from Caleb.

'Do you not understand?' Caleb said. 'It's free.'

*   *   *

Camille handed one of the coupons to a man wearing headphones, who took it without breaking stride. After he had walked a few feet, he tossed it in a trash can. Camille ran to the trash and retrieved the coupon. She caught up to the man and tapped him on the shoulder. He turned, annoyed. 'You dropped this,' she said, smiling.

'I don't want it,' he said, too loudly, his headphones still playing.

'It's good for one free sandwich at Chicken Queen,' she continued. 'No purchase necessary.'

'No thanks,' he said, walking away from her, nodding his head to a beat that Camille couldn't hear.

A family of five walked past Camille and she offered them a sheaf of coupons. 'Free chicken sandwiches for everyone,' she shouted, her face strained from smiling so much.

'We don't eat meat,' the mother said, shielding her children from the coupons.

'Oh, for crying out loud,' Camille said. She'd been standing here for thirty minutes and she'd only managed to hand out twelve coupons.

'I don't understand,' the man told Caleb, trying to back away from the coupon.

'What's not to understand?' Caleb said. 'You take this coupon, get a free chicken sandwich, bring it back to me, and I'll give you five bucks.'

'Why don't you just do it yourself?' the man asked.

'I'm an employee,' Caleb said, exasperated. 'The coupons don't apply to employees.'

'Then why don't you just go buy one yourself? It'll be cheaper than five bucks.'

'Do you not want free money?' Caleb asked.

'I guess not,' the man said, and hurried off.

'Free goddamn chicken sandwiches,' Caleb shouted.

At the food court, Annie and Buster filled each other in on the details of their lives, how they'd become untethered.

'What about the tabloids?' Buster asked. 'Do you need to wear a disguise or something?'

'I'm not that kind of a movie star,' Annie said. 'I don't get recognized all that much. Or maybe no one cares. Plus, the tabloids think I'm in Wyoming with Daniel now. I can't imagine he would notify them that I'd left him at the airport. I'm incognito.'

'Well, if you want an eye patch to go under-cover, I can loan you one of mine,' Buster offered. 'No one has come by with a coupon,' he added.

'These poor cashiers,' Annie said. 'They're not getting paid enough to deal with Caleb and Camille.'

Finally, a teenager walked up to the counter with a coupon. Buster watched the action through the viewfinder of the digital recorder their father had given him. 'Here we go,' Buster said.

The boy made his order and then, when the cashier rang it up, he presented the coupon. The cashier immediately frowned, snatched the coupon out of the boy's hands. The boy pointed to the word FREE on the coupon. The cashier called for her manager, a guy who seemed the same age as her, the same age as the customer. She showed him the coupon and he also frowned, held it up to the light as if looking for a watermark. He stared at the customer, sizing him up, and then handed the coupon back to the cashier and nodded. The cashier put the coupon in the register and then presented the boy with a chicken sandwich.

'Oh,' Annie said, seeing the thing fall apart in an entirely different way. 'Shit.'

A few minutes later, an older couple each produced coupons and the cashier accepted them without any hesitation. Three coupons, three chicken sandwiches, three customers now sitting within ten feet of Buster and Annie, eating free food courtesy of their parents.

'Should we go tell Mom and Dad?' Buster asked.

'No,' Annie said. 'Let's just stay out of it.'

Watching the people eating their chicken sandwiches, Annie realized that she hadn't eaten since the day before. She still had the coupon her father had given her, crumpled in her purse. She smoothed the coupon out on the table, took it to the Chicken Queen, and came back with a free sandwich. She slowly ate the sandwich while Buster filmed more and more people walking to the counter, each one getting the very thing they had been promised.

★   ★   ★

An hour and a half later, having finally handed out a decent number of coupons, Caleb and Camille met at the fountain in the center of the mall. 'Good Lord,' Caleb said to his wife. 'People have become so stupid that you can't control them.' Camille nodded. 'They are so resistant to any strangeness that they tune out the whole world. God, it's so damn depressing.'

'Well,' Caleb said, shucking off his Chicken Queen T-shirt, 'let's go make some art.'

There was no angry line at the Chicken Queen when they arrived. There was no sign of hostility, of frustration. There were, however, about twenty-five people in the food court eating free chicken sandwiches. Camille noticed Buster and Annie at one of the tables and held out her arms in confusion. Annie and Buster merely shrugged. 'What the hell is going on?' Caleb whispered. 'I don't know,' Camille said, visibly scared by the lack of pandemonium. 'Give me one of those goddamn coupons,' Caleb said, snatching it out of his wife's hand. 'You can't rely on anyone these days to make a proper piece of art,' he mumbled, striding with great purpose toward the Chicken Queen.

'Can I take your order?' the cashier said, typing a message on her cell phone with one hand, not even looking at Caleb.

'I want a free sandwich,' he said. 'I want it right now.'

'Okay,' the girl said, walking back to the food prep station to grab a wrapped sandwich.

'Wait,' shouted Caleb. 'Don't I need a coupon?'

'Okay,' the girl said, holding out her hand.

Caleb handed the coupon to the girl. 'I got this from some shady-looking characters at the front of the mall,' he said. 'It doesn't seem on the up-and-up.'

'No, it's good,' the cashier said. 'Here's your sandwich.'

'I think this is a fake coupon,' Caleb said.

'It's not, sir.'

'It is, though, for crying out loud. Look at it for two seconds. It's not real.'

'Do you want this sandwich or not, sir?' the girl asked.

'Let me talk to your manager.'

The manager came out. 'Something wrong with your order, sir?'

'This coupon is fake.'

'I don't think so, sir.'

'Did you even look at it?' Caleb said. He was shouting now.

'I did, sir. It's official.'

'Oh god, you people. You people. It's a fake. You've given out all these free sandwiches for counterfeit coupons.'

'Sir, please take your sandwich and step out of the line.'

'I wouldn't eat this sandwich if you paid me,' Caleb said. He was pounding his fist on the counter. People were starting to watch the event unfold.

★   ★   ★

Buster filmed the entire thing. 'Oh, shit,' he said.

'Sir, I'm going to call the police if you don't leave,' the manager said.

'You people have the tiniest responsibility. All you have to do is your job and I do the rest. I do all the hard work. All you have to do is let the thing happen.'

'Sir, leave right now.'

Camille came over to Caleb. 'Let's just leave, honey,' she said.

'I do all the goddamn work and you get to witness the beauty of it all. That's all you have to do.'

Camille pulled her husband away from the Chicken Queen. The entire food court was watching them. Caleb took the rest of the coupons from his wife and threw them into the air. No one moved to retrieve them.

Buster turned off the camera. 'That,' he said to his sister, 'was awful.'

Annie nodded. 'That was bad.'

As they waited at the van, Annie and Buster talked about the inescapable fact of their parents. They were losing it. Not just their artistic sensibility, but also their minds. Without Buster and Annie, is this what had become of them?

'I mean, they always had a radical idea of what constituted art,' Annie said, 'but this was almost silly. Did he really think he was going to lead some coup on the Chicken Queen? Did they really expect people to lose their minds over a free chicken sandwich?'

Buster nodded, still hazy with pain pills. 'They're in a bad way,' he said.

After nearly a half hour, their parents finally appeared. It looked like both of them had been crying, their faces somber and tinged red.

'I'm sorry, Dad,' Buster said, but Caleb didn't respond.

For almost the entire ride back home, they traveled in silence. Annie watched the unfamiliar scenery become familiar once again. Buster held his sister's hand, feeling safe in the tense atmosphere of the van. Finally, only a few minutes from home, Caleb began to snicker. 'Goddamn Chicken Queen,' he said. His shoulders were shaking. Then Camille began to chuckle. 'What a disaster,' she said, shaking her head.

'I'm sorry, Dad,' Buster said again. 'I'm sorry, Mom.' His parents waved him off.

'Great art is difficult,' Caleb said. After a few moments, he said, 'But I don't understand why it has to be so difficult sometimes.' He tried to smile, but to Annie and Buster, he seemed ridiculously tired. His hands trembled as they gripped the steering wheel and Annie resisted the urge to ask him if he wanted her to drive them home. Caleb took his wife's hand and kissed it. She pinched his ear and smiled. By the time they arrived at the house, their parents were already thinking of new

153

ideas to create the chaos that they believed the world deserved.

They paused before they stepped out of the van, every Fang in their place. The four of them then walked up to the house, their home, and each of them had the undeniable feeling that, now that they were together again, they could not hope to prevent the thing that would come next, whatever it would be.

CHAPTER 6

Though the swelling had gone down, his body inexplicably capable enough to repair itself, Buster continued to wear the protective eye patch. The lack of depth perception that it induced seemed to be canceled out by the pain pills in a way that made him feel as if he had extrasensory perception. Half-reading a comic book from his childhood about superpowered elephants, he tested his newfound abilities by guessing the time without looking at the clock. The numbers flickered in his head, just behind his covered eye, and he said out loud, 'Three forty-seven P.M.' He then looked over at the nightstand clock, which read 9:04 A.M. The ESP, he determined, came and went.

He pushed away the covers and tested the floorboards beneath his feet. His long underwear was baggy and unwashed, a uniform he refused to shed while he was in the house. As he walked down the hallway, the repetitive sound of a phonograph needle rubbing against the edge of a record filled the living room. His parents, still masked but sleeping, lay across the sofa. Scattered on the floor were books about fire manipulation and pyrotechnics, a fine coat of black ash across the coffee table. In the kitchen, his sister, two weeks returned to the Fang household, fried some bologna in one pan and an entire carton of eggs in another. While she moved the food around with a spatula, she took deep, serious sips from a sweating tumbler filled with vodka and tomato juice. 'Morning,' she said, and Buster responded, 'Yes.'

Buster slid two slices of bread into the toaster and, when they emerged toasted, he placed them on a plate and sat at the table, chewing softly, trying to keep the soggy scraps of dough out of the gap that used to hold his tooth. His sister walked over to the table, the spatula balancing a slice of bologna with a fried egg atop it, and deposited the meal on Buster's plate. Buster, uncertain of when he last ate, mashed the food into a paste with his fork until the food resembled some kind of cut-rate pâté. His sister returned to the table with her own plate, the size of a ride cymbal, heaped to overflowing with bologna and eggs, charred pink and sickly white and bright yellow.

'You have any plans for the day?' Buster asked Annie.

'Watch some movies,' Annie replied, taking careful sips of the Bloody Mary. 'Take it easy.'

'Me too,' Buster said. 'Take it easy.'

They had been taking it easy since they had returned. Annie had settled into her old room, stocked a full bar under her bed, and Buster would pass her as they walked back and forth through the house, their parents working on various artistic projects in which the Fang children tried not to take any interest. Buster would share his medicine with Annie and they would watch silent films and read comic books and avoid any mention of the parts of their lives that existed outside of this house. Buster and his sister might have been turning into shut-ins but, thanks to his sister's simple presence, they were now doing it together.

Their parents entered the kitchen and complained about the smell of grease in the air. 'Just breathing the scent of fried bologna will ruin my stomach,' Mr Fang said. Working as a team, the routine imprinted on their muscles, Mr and Mrs Fang assembled the makings of their breakfast: spinach leaves, orange juice, plain yogurt, bananas, blueberries, and ground flaxseed. They dumped the contents into the blender and, thirty seconds of whirring later, they came to the table with their glasses of purple-green liquid. They each took a heavy swig of the drink and then breathed deeply. Mrs Fang reached across the table and lightly tapped her children's hands. 'This is nice,' she said.

The phone rang but no one moved to answer it. There was not one person that the Fangs wanted to speak to that wasn't already sitting at the table. The machine took the call into its own hands, Mrs Fang's voice flatly saying, 'The

Fangs are dead. Leave a message after the tone and our ghosts will return your call.' Mrs Fang, the one at the table, holding her smoothie, began to titter. 'When did I leave that greeting?' she said.

Once the tone sounded, a man, seemingly thrown off by the silliness of the answering machine greeting, said, 'Urmm . . . yes, this is a call for Mr Buster Fang.' Buster immediately assumed that it was the hospital in Nebraska, looking for its money. How had they tracked him to Tennessee? he wondered. Had they placed a chip in his head when he had been unconscious? He touched the eye patch, concentrated, and tried to detect something alien inside his body.

'This is Lucas Kizza, and I teach English here at Hazzard State Community College. I recently became aware of the fact that you are back in town and I wondered if you might be interested in meeting with some of my students to discuss the creative process and perhaps even read from your work. I've been very much impressed by your two novels and I think the students would benefit from talking to you. I can't offer any financial compensation, but I hope you still might consider my offer. Thank you.'

Buster immediately looked at his parents. 'Did you set this up?' he asked. Mr and Mrs Fang held up their hands as if to defend themselves from physical attack. 'We did not,' Mr Fang said. 'I don't even know who this Kizza guy is.'

'Then how did he come to learn that I was back in town?' Buster said.

'It's a small town, Buster,' Mrs Fang answered. 'When you got here, you had a grotesquely swollen face. It attracted attention.'

When they first arrived back home, Buster, still adjusting to the high dosage of the medication he had given himself, woke in the van and demanded that they stop for fried chicken. 'Buster, I don't think solid food is a great idea yet,' his mother had told him, but Buster had leaned into the front of the van and reached for the steering wheel, saying, over and over in a strange monotone, 'Fer-ide chick-hen.' The Fangs pulled into a Kentucky Fried Chicken ten minutes later and walked inside the restaurant. Buster swayed unsteadily as his parents directed him to a table. 'What do you want?' they asked him. 'Fer-ide chick-hen,' he said, 'all-you-can-eat.' They left the table and returned a few minutes later with a breast, wing, thigh, and leg, a mound of gravy-soaked mashed potatoes, and a biscuit. Everyone in a five-table radius was staring at the Fangs by this point. Buster, oblivious, unpacked some blood-stained gauze from his mouth, picked up the chicken leg, extra crispy, and took a ravenous bite. He felt something come loose inside his mouth, his muscles stretched beyond comfort after so much time in atrophy, and he began to moan, a funeral dirge, dropping the leg back onto the tray. The barely chewed scrap of chicken fell from his mouth, stained a foamy red with Buster's blood. 'Okay,' Mr Fang said, sweeping the tray off of the table, dumping it into the trash. 'This little experiment is over. Let's go home.' Buster tried to pack the gauze back into his mouth, but his mother and father were already carrying him into the parking lot. 'I'm a monster,' Buster bellowed, and his parents did nothing to dissuade him of this belief.

'Well, I'm not going to do it,' Buster said.

'I think you should,' Annie said. Mr and Mrs Fang agreed.

Buster did not want to talk about writing. It had been years since his last novel had been published, a spectacular failure at that. His literary career was encased in ice, held in suspended animation, lost to future generations. And the thought of working on something new, in this house, surrounded by his family, seemed like the worst possible idea. His writing had become, like a stash of rare and troubling pornography, something that must be kept hidden, an obsession that other people would be mystified to discover.

Mr and Mrs Fang finished their drinks and returned to the living room to continue working on their latest project. Buster, his appetite having never appeared, gave up the pretense of eating and scraped the remaining food into the garbage. 'See you later,' he said to Annie, who looked up from her rapidly diminishing plate of food and nodded.

★   ★   ★

Two hours into a nap that he had taken for no reason other than he was bored, Buster was shaken into consciousness, his muscles aching from the effort of staying asleep for so long, by his sister. 'I found something weird,' she told him. 'How weird?' Buster asked, unconvinced that it warranted getting out of bed. Annie held up a tiny oil painting, the size of a dental dam, which featured a small child with his arm, up to his elbow, inside the mouth of a wolf. Around them were gleaming surgical instruments, flecked with blood. It was unclear whether the child was placing the items inside the wolf or pulling them out. 'There's like, I don't know, a hundred of these paintings in the back of my closet,' Annie told him. At the prospect of overwhelming weirdness, not simply an isolated case, Buster found his interest wax. 'Okay, I'm up,' he said, and he followed his sister into her bedroom. On their hands and knees, Buster and Annie moved the nearly one hundred paintings from the faint light of the closet to the middle of the bedroom, arranging them like tiles on the floor. When they had retrieved every last painting, they looked in stunned silence at the resulting disharmony that now filled the room.

A man, covered in mud and thin, lash-like wounds that dripped blood, wandered in a field of palominos.

A little girl, buried alive, played jacks by match light while her parents wailed above her grave.

An ocean of dead, decomposing geese were stacked like cordwood by men in biohazard suits.

A woman, her hair on fire, held a brush made of bone and smiled in an exact reproduction of the Mona Lisa's expression.

A young boy, his hands wrapped in barbed wire, wrestled with a tiger while the boy's classmates circled around them.

Two women, handcuffed to each other, stood over the steel teeth of a bear trap.

A family sat cross-legged on the floor of a cabin, surrounded by rabbits, and hurked entrails from the still-living animals.

'What *are* these?' Buster asked, his eyes moving from painting to painting as if they told an interconnected story.

'Maybe someone sends these to Mom and Dad. Remember that lady who kept mailing them Ziploc bags filled with teeth?'

'They're not bad,' Buster said, with some admiration. Technically, the paintings were nearly perfect, especially considering the tiny dimensions of the canvas. They were the work of an artist of some accomplishment, however unsettling the subject matter. He imagined these paintings made into animated movies and those movies being watched with great reverence by people who were steeped in psychedelic drugs. He then imagined that, if he were a better writer, he could make an entire career out of explicating the circumstances that created each one of the images on display. Instead, all he could do was stare at the paintings and feel like he and his sister had found something akin to pornography and that they should not be looking at them out in the open.

As they stood, afraid to move, the paintings surrounding them in ways that now seemed alive and threatening, the door swung open and their mother walked into the room. Whatever words were poised to be spoken aloud were replaced by a gasp so resonant that it seemed their mother had inhaled all of the oxygen in the room. Then a dark shadow passed over her expression, her eyes narrowing. 'Don't you dare look at these,' their mother said, her voice barely above a whisper. She pushed her children out of the way and hesitated for a few seconds before she began to turn over each painting so that the image was concealed. Annie and Buster stared at the ceiling as their mother removed the offending articles from their sight, a procedure that seemed as perilous as defusing a bomb or handling unsafe chemicals. Once it was finished, their mother, her breathing now unsteady, as if she was on the precipice of a long crying jag, sat on the bed and said, 'Fuck, fuck, fuck, fuck, fuck.'

Buster and Annie, unaccustomed to emotion, kept their distance. 'What's wrong, Mom?' Annie asked. 'I don't know,' their mother responded. 'What are these?' Buster then asked. 'I don't know,' their mother again responded. 'Where did they come from?' Annie asked. 'Me,' their mother said, finally looking up at Buster and Annie, 'I made them.'

Working together, the three of them moved the paintings from the floor back into the closet as Mrs Fang explained their origin.

'I used to be a painter,' she told them. 'That's how I got a scholarship to study art in college. And then I met your dad and I fell in love and, well, you know how he feels about visual art.'

Their father, on several occasions throughout their childhood, had referred to painting and photography and drawing as dead forms of art, incapable of accurately reflecting the unwieldy nature of real life. 'Art happens when things fucking move around,' he told them, 'not when you freeze them in a goddamn block of ice.' He would then take whatever item was closest to him, a glass or a tape recorder, and smash it against the wall. 'That was art,' he said, and then he would pick up the pieces of the shattered object and hold them out for his children to inspect. 'This,' he said, offering the remains of the broken thing, 'is not.'

'The thing is,' their mother continued, all the paintings safely hidden away, 'your father and I are getting older, entering the twilight of our artistic careers, I'm afraid. Still, I'm a good ten years younger than him and, god forbid, if he dies before I do, what am I going to do? It's Caleb and Camille Fang, the two of us, and that's why it works. I'll have to do something else. So, for the past few years, I've been painting these little, I don't know what to call them, scenes. If your father found out, good Lord, it would be such a betrayal to him.'

'Where do you come up with those images?' Buster asked.

His mother lightly tapped her forehead and shrugged, embarrassed. 'Somewhere in here,' she said, smiling.

Mr Fang then walked into the room, holding the phone, suspicious of any gathering in which he was not included. 'What's going on?' he asked.

'We were just talking, honey,' Mrs Fang said.

Mr Fang's eyes narrowed. 'Talking about what?' he said.

'Our feelings,' Annie said, and Mr Fang quickly lost interest. He tossed the phone toward Buster and said, 'It's that Kizza fellow. He wants to talk to you,' and then he walked out of the room.

Buster held the phone like it was a live grenade, Annie and Mrs Fang now slowly backing away from him. 'Hello?' came the faint voice of Lucas Kizza, and Buster, dazed by the images painted by his mother's hand, lifted the receiver to his lips and answered, 'Yes?'

Lucas Kizza turned out to be a powerful, insistent force, expertly wielding the necessary amount of flattery to maintain Buster's reluctant attention.

'I think *The Underground* is one of the most unheralded works of genius that I've ever read,' Kizza said, and Buster was too shocked to disagree. 'Sometimes, Mr Fang, I drive around this town and wonder how this environment might have helped to produce such an important voice.'

'This place had very little to do with it,' Buster admitted.

'I can understand that,' Kizza continued, Buster's interjections like weak volleys to be returned so emphatically that all Buster could hope for was to delay the inevitable. 'With such an artistic family, I imagine your development was only hindered by the outside world. Nevertheless, Mr Fang, I work with a group of promising students, the school's creative writing club, and I cannot help but wonder what your presence could do to encourage these students to continue their creative endeavors.'

'I'm in kind of a weird place at the moment,' Buster said.

'I imagine, if I might be frank with you, Buster, that you spend most of your time in kind of a weird place,' Kizza offered, not unkindly.

'What would I have to do?' Buster asked, giving up.

'Come to the college, talk to my students.'

'When would I have to do this?' Buster asked, feeling the improbable harden into fact.

'Tuesday, perhaps? We're having our monthly meeting at one P.M. in the school library.'

'I guess so,' Buster said. 'I guess I'll do that.'

'Wonderful,' Lucas Kizza exclaimed.

'Wonderful,' Buster repeated, just to hear what it sounded like coming out of his own mouth.

He placed the phone on the ground and then felt nausea pass like a train through his body.

'You're going?' Annie asked him.

Buster nodded.

'Are you going to wear the eye patch?' Annie asked.

'I haven't had time to think about it,' Buster answered.

'I would vote no,' Annie told him.

'I would vote yes,' his mother said.

Mrs Fang then stood and walked into the closet. She returned with two paintings and handed one to each of her children. 'I want you to have these,' she said. 'In exchange, if I die before your father, I want you to destroy the other ones.' Buster and Annie nodded and then looked at their gifts. Buster held the image of the boy fighting the tiger and Annie's portrayed the girl in her coffin. Mrs Fang placed her hands on Buster and Annie, as if to bestow some kind of blessing, and then said, 'I'm glad we talked.' Buster and Annie nodded and waited until their mother had left the room before they turned the paintings over, the objects uneasy in their hands.

Uneasy and itching in one of his father's ancient tweed suits, Buster sat on the sofa in the registrar's

167

office, the secretaries ignoring him, as he clutched a copy of his second novel. Not for a million dollars would he have claimed authorship of the book in his hands if the secretaries, popping gum and filled with petty grievances, had demanded a reason for his presence in the school.

His sister, off to watch a movie at the dollar cinema in the near-empty ghost mall on the outskirts of town, had driven him to the front of the building in their parents' second car, a rattling heap of a station wagon that took ten minutes to start. 'Have a nice day at school,' Annie told him, and then left tire marks as she peeled out of the parking lot, leaving him alone on the sidewalk. He instantly wished he had some kind of note, documentation to support his arrival, a mystical object to ward off bullies and truancy officers.

As he waited for Lucas Kizza to claim him, Buster's hands worried the pockets of the suit, searching for a diversion. In the inside pocket of his father's jacket, he found a digital recorder the size of a stick of chewing gum, some kind of spy-games invention that was either very, very expensive or very, very cheap. He pressed the play button and listened to his father's voice, serious and slow, say, 'We live on the edge . . . a shanty-town filled with gold-seekers. We are fugitives, and the law is skinny with hunger for us.' Buster, stunned by the strangeness of it, pressed repeat, turned up the volume, and held this matchstick of a device to his ear as if listening to radio static for the voice of a long-dead lover. '. . . the law is skinny with hunger for us,' the recorder said, and Buster took out a pen, opened to the title page of his novel, and scribbled the phrases down so that he could see the arrangement of the words on paper.

He had an image of a plantation, ruined with flame from a slave uprising, long since abandoned. He saw a group of people, barely adults, ragged and lean, prying open the boards that covered one of the windows and spilling into the mansion like an infestation. He saw them making weapons out of bone and wood, everything sharp points, and patrolling the grounds, the fields newly planted with marijuana, wild dogs running up and down the deep furrows in the ground. He hit the button on the recorder one more time. 'We live on the edge,' it began, and then Lucas Kizza was standing over him. 'The unexpected visits of the muse,' Lucas said, smiling, gesturing toward Buster's open book. 'One must always be prepared,' he continued. Buster, never prepared for a goddamned thing, immediately agreed.

Lucas Kizza was tall and lanky, his face baby-smooth and pale, easily mistaken for a student. Wearing a crisp white button-up shirt with the sleeves rolled up to his elbows, flat-front khakis, an argyle sweater vest, and black leather sneakers, he looked like an idealistic young teacher who had thus far, by luck or by talent, managed to avoid having his guts ripped out by the handful. Reeking of mothballs, his uncovered eye still adjusting to the light, holding the source of his creative shame like a peace offering, Buster wished only to make it through the day without crying.

The frowning members of the creative writing club were seated in a circle in one of the unused rooms within the library. The nervous, desperate energy contained within the room was palpable, and Buster felt as though he had walked into an Alcoholics Anonymous meeting. There were six men and five women, most of them in their late teens or early twenties, though there was one man who was in his forties, all of them holding notebooks, refusing to make eye contact with anyone. 'So, students, this is Buster Fang,' Lucas began. 'He's the author of *A House of Swans,* which was universally praised by the critics and won the coveted Golden Quill award. His second novel, *The Underground,* was, befitting a second novel, a more complex and divisive book. He's here to talk to us about the creative process, so I hope you'll give him your full attention.' Lucas then turned to Buster and smiled. Buster had not prepared. He had assumed that Lucas and the students would ask questions and he would patiently try to answer them. He had no speech worthy of anyone's full attention.

'Well, okay, thank you. It's nice to be here. I thought, well, rather than bore you to death with my talking, you might like to ask questions and I would be happy to answer them as best I could.'

He waited for questions and then, with a sickening realization, understood that there would be none. Lucas said, 'Perhaps you might begin your presentation and that will generate questions?' Buster nodded. Then he nodded again. Then, to negate that extra nod, he shook his head. The students stared at their shoes with even more interest. 'We are fugitives,' Buster thought. 'We are fugitives and the law is skinny with hunger for us.' He resisted the urge to say this out loud.

'I like,' Buster began, unsure of what would follow, 'well, I like to write on a computer.' One of the students wrote this statement down in his notebook and then, looking at what he had just written, frowned. 'They used to make this gum,' Buster continued, 'it had a kind of minty gel inside of it.' He looked at the students for recognition of this gum but found no sign of it on their faces. 'Anyways, I liked to chew that while I wrote. It's hard to find now, though.' He closed his eyes for a second and concentrated. 'God, I can't remember the name of that gum to save my life.'

Lucas Kizza finally interjected. 'Um, Buster, perhaps you might want to speak in more general terms about your process. For instance, because these students are only beginning to find their own voice, perhaps you can talk about what drives you to put pen to paper?'

'Well, I write on a computer, like I said,' Buster replied.

Lucas Kizza's patient smile, for the first time,

began to disappear from his face. Buster felt his only ally, the one person who seemed to think that he wasn't a total fuckup, pulling away from him. Buster dug deep. He touched the spot where his eye patch had once been and waited for the ESP to work its magic.

'Okay, I can do that,' Buster said. He looked at the students, who were almost willfully ignoring him now, and tried to say something that would bring them into his arms.

'Do you ever have a moment when you have this horrible thought and you can't get rid of it, even though you want to?' he said. A few of the students looked up.

'Like, when you were a kid, did you have this idea pop into your head where you wondered what would happen if your parents suddenly died?'

Every student in the group was now listening to Buster. A few of them nodded and leaned forward. Lucas Kizza looked worried, but Buster felt something click into place.

'You don't even want to be thinking about it, but you can't stop. You think, well, I'll inherit whatever money they have, but I probably won't be able to access it until I'm eighteen. And I'll probably have to live with my aunt and uncle who never were able to have kids and seem to hate me just because I exist. And then you realize that they live on the other side of the country so you'll have to go to a new school. And if you'd managed to make any friends where you live now, you're going to have to leave them behind and start all over again. And your new room is like the size of a closet and your aunt and uncle don't eat meat and one time they find you eating a hamburger and scream at you for an hour. And on and on and on, until, finally, you're eighteen and you can do what you want and so you move back to your old hometown and get a job, but no one knows how to act around you and most of your old friends have left for college and so you just kind of sit around in your apartment and watch TV and then you watch a movie that you had watched when you were a kid with your parents and you miss them so much and it's the first time, really, that you understand that they're gone for good.'

One of the students said, 'I think about that kind of stuff a lot.'

Buster smiled. If he had any money in his pocket, he would have given it to this guy. 'Well, that's why I write, I guess. These weird thoughts come into my head, and I don't even really want to think about it, but I can't let go of it until I take it as far as I can, until I reach some kind of ending, and then I can move on. That's what writing is like for me.'

'Well,' Lucas Kizza said, visibly relieved that Buster wasn't totally psychotic, 'that's exactly what we're trying to do here with this group, to learn how to take an idea and make it into a story. Thank you, Buster, for explaining it in such wonderful terms.'

'That's okay,' Buster said.

Another student, a girl who was wearing a tank top that said DON'T TREAD ON ME, asked if he was working on something new. Buster felt a quick twinge of embarrassment, having nothing to show for the past few years, but he nodded and said that he was indeed working on something big, but it was slow going. He wasn't sure if it was any good. He wasn't sure if he would even finish it. '. . . The edge . . . a shantytown filled with gold-seekers,' he thought, but then pushed the words away for the time being.

A young man wearing thick, black-rimmed glasses and sporting a thick beard was holding a copy of *The Underground* and said, 'I read some of this, and then I went online and I read some reviews of it and people really seemed to have problems with it.' Buster nodded. He found that he was not very fond of this kid, and the beard obscured his mouth so that it was hard to tell if he was smirking. 'Well,' the guy continued, 'I wondered how you deal with bad reviews when you spent a long time working on something that you thought was good.' Professor Kizza stepped in to remind the class that *The Underground* had also received some very favorable reviews and that there were many classics that had initially been met with resistance from the critics. Buster waved him off. 'No, that's fine. It mostly got awful reviews. At the time, it made me sick to my stomach. I wished I were dead. But that went away, after a while. And then I just felt relieved that, even if people had hated it, I made it myself. I don't know what I'm saying, really, but I guess it's like having a kid, though I don't have any kids. It's yours, you made it, and no matter what happens, you have that pride of ownership. You love it, even if it didn't amount to much.'

There were a few more questions, which Buster struggled to answer truthfully, then he read a section of *The Underground* when the main character, the boy, first comes out from the bomb shelter and sees the devastation that surrounds him. It was depressing as hell, and Buster wished he hadn't read it, but the students seemed to like how bleak it was. Lucas thanked him for coming, the students filed out of the room, and then it was just Lucas and Buster.

'I hope that was okay,' Buster said.

'It was wonderful,' Lucas replied.

'They seem like good kids.'

'Wonderful students.'

Buster noticed that Lucas was holding a stack of papers. 'These are some stories they've written, Buster,' Lucas then said. 'I know it would be a real thrill for them if you might look at them.'

'Oh,' Buster said. 'Oh.'

'You don't have to of course,' Lucas continued. 'I just thought you might be interested.'

Buster could not think of anything he'd be less interested in reading, but then he thought of how they had patiently listened to him ramble, talking about some fucking brand of gum like he was Andy Rooney, and he felt his resistance falter.

'Sure,' Buster said. 'Load me up.'

Lucas smiled and handed him the stories. He then reached into his bag and produced another story. 'I wrote this one,' Lucas said, his face reddening.

'Oh,' Buster said. 'Oh.'

'I'd be interested in hearing what you think of it.'

'Certainly,' Buster said. The story was titled 'The Endless Wordening of Dr Hauser's Living Manuscript.' Lucas informed him that it was a postmodern fantasy, a kind of punk rock fairy tale. Buster forced such a broad smile that his missing tooth showed. 'Certainly,' he repeated.

Then Lucas Kizza wrapped his arms around Buster and hugged him. Buster hugged him back. 'We live on the edge,' he thought, and then Lucas released his hold and walked out of the room.

Buster sat on the curb in front of the college, waiting for his sister to pick him up. To pass the time, he skimmed the stories of the creative writing students. One was about a wild party and the story consisted almost entirely of a detailed explanation of a drinking game called Flip 'N Chug that seemed, to Buster, to be too complicated to facilitate the simple goal of getting drunk. Another story was about a girl who finds out her boyfriend is cheating on her and so she hires a hit man to kill him during the prom. There was an inscrutable story that Buster believed was about a boy trying to talk his pregnant girlfriend into having an abortion. Something was odd about the story, the strange perspective, the old-fashioned language, the terse sentences, and then Buster realized it was an exact copy of Hemingway's 'Hills Like White Elephants,' but the title had been changed to 'Listening in on Someone's Conversation.' He considered telling Lucas about this plagiarism but wondered if perhaps there was some kind of experimental explanation for the story, a textual reappropriation. It made his head hurt trying to explain away some kid's stupid decision to plagiarize a famous story. He imagined that it was the kid who had asked him the question about his bad reviews, and felt a little superior. He read a story about another wild party, another complicated drinking game, and felt calm again.

After thirty minutes, he began to wonder if Annie had simply forgotten about him, returned to the house after the movie, and got drunk on vodka tonics. 'Come get me,' Buster whispered, hoping to create a psychic link to his sister.

To ease the sting of being forgotten, Buster leafed through the papers until he found a story called 'The Damaged Boy.' He liked the sound of that. The story, which was written in brief, itemized paragraphs, was about a boy who had, seconds after his birth, been dropped by the obstetrician. His skull, still unformed, had been dented. A broken arm followed when the boy climbed out of his crib. A dog bit off one of his fingers when he tried to feed it a piece of zwieback toast. A sled's runner sliced his leg open, the warm stream of blood spilling down the hill, melting the snow. He was hit by a car while crossing the street and broke his collarbone. The story proceeded in this way, a never-ending account of all the physical pain the boy accumulated on his path toward adulthood. It made Buster want to cry. By the end of the story, the boy, now an old man, bent and hobbled, placed his hand on the eye of a stove and found that he felt no pain. His hand, taken from the burning red eye, showed no signs of injury. His body, inside and out, had become as hard as a diamond, impervious to pain. It was a bizarre story, depressing as hell, and Buster instantly fell in love with the author. He checked the name, Suzanne Crosby, and walked back into the school to find her.

The secretaries in the registrar's office, strangely enough, seemed unwilling to tell him where Suzanne Crosby was. 'Who are you again?' one of them asked. 'I'm Buster Fang,' he said. She stared at him. 'I'm a guest of the college,' he offered weakly. 'Sorry,' she told him. 'Can you just give her a message?' he asked the woman. 'I don't want to be a party to any of this,' she said, which Buster admitted was fair enough. He was a strange man trying to find some young student. Frankly, he was surprised the police hadn't been called yet. He thanked her for her time and then walked back outside to wait for his sister. A few minutes later, a girl appeared beside him, tapping him on the shoulder. She had long, blond hair and perfect skin. Her eyes were an intense shade of blue, and she stared at him without emotion. 'Suzanne?' he asked, and she visibly blanched. 'God no,' she said. 'I'm an office aide,' she added, 'work study. I heard you talking to Mrs Palmer about Suzanne. I can take her a message.' Buster thanked her and then the girl held out her hand. 'Twenty-five bucks,' she said. Buster told her that he didn't have any money. 'You can write me a check,' she informed him. He laughed. 'I don't have any money at all,' he said. 'Fuck,' the girl said and turned to walk back into the building. And then Buster's sister pulled up to the curb. 'Wait,' Buster shouted at the girl, and he ran over to Annie.

'Where have you been?' he said. 'The car wouldn't start,' she replied. 'I had to get someone to jump-start it.' He asked her for twenty-five dollars. 'What?' she said. 'I need twenty-five dollars to give to this girl over there,' he told her, growing impatient. Annie looked at the girl, who kept staring at Annie with a puzzled look on her face. 'Buster,' Annie said, 'are you doing something really stupid here?' Buster told her it was a long story and tried to explain, but then the girl was standing beside him, pointing at Annie. 'I know you,' the girl said, smiling. 'You're really famous.'

Annie nodded, uninterested in pretending to be someone else, and asked the girl, 'Why are you asking my brother for twenty-five dollars?' The girl replied, 'He doesn't have to pay me anything if you'll let me take a picture with you.' Buster said, 'That sounds like a pretty good deal, Annie.' Annie nodded, too confused from having arrived late, and the girl handed Buster her cell phone. Buster snapped the photo and the girl took the phone back and looked at the picture with some satisfaction. It would probably end up on the Internet. 'So now you'll give Suzanne a message for me?' Buster asked. 'I'll do you one better,' the girl said to Buster. 'I'll bring Suzanne out here.'

Buster explained the situation in more detail to Annie, the car still running for fear that it wouldn't start again if shut off. 'Please, Buster,' Annie said, squeezing his arm as hard as she could, 'do not go crazy here. This is why we're together, remember? We're here to keep each other from going crazy.' Buster began to consider his circumstances, standing in front of a college, about to tell a student that he was in love with her. The more he thought about the story, which was indeed very accomplished for a nineteen-year-old, the more he tried to convince himself that it wasn't so good that he had to fall in love with the author. Perhaps he didn't have to profess his love every time someone came around and made him feel less unhappy than he had been previously. Perhaps he could just walk away from this and save himself the further complication of his life. 'There she is,' Annie said, and Buster turned to see Suzanne, utterly confused, walking toward them.

Suzanne was short and heavyset, her eyes tiny and clouded behind a pair of wire-framed glasses. She had long, strawberry-blond hair that she had pulled into a ponytail. Her pale skin was crowded with a crazy pattern of freckles and her thick fingers were covered with dozens of cheap rings. Her big toe was poking out of her busted-up sneakers. Buster was amazed to realize that he did not recognize her from the class, that she had gone undetected even in that tiny room. 'What did you want?' she asked, almost angry to be disturbed. Buster fumbled for her story and then held it up like it was a passport, an official document that would gain him some degree of access. 'I read your story,' he said. She looked startled by this fact, and Buster noticed that she instantly began to blush. 'Did Professor Kizza give that to you?' she asked. Buster nodded. 'I didn't tell him to do that,' she said. 'It's an amazing story,' Buster said, and Suzanne finally looked up from the sidewalk. 'Thank you,' she said. 'That's nice of you to say.' Buster told her that he would love to read anything else she had written and she said she would think about it. 'Let me give you my e-mail address,' he said, and he tore off the first page of Lucas Kizza's story and wrote his address on the back of the paper. Suzanne took the paper and nodded and turned to walk back to the entrance, but by then

181

about a dozen students, led by the office aide, were standing in the way. 'There she is,' the girl told them. 'She's famous.' The students walked forward, slowly, as if moving toward a cornered animal. 'Get in the car, Buster,' Annie said, and Buster ran around to the passenger side of the car and shut the door. Annie drove off as the students now stood at the curb, surrounding Suzanne Crosby. Buster looked back at the scene and waved to Suzanne. Just before the car turned onto the street, he watched Suzanne waving back.

Back home, the car rolling to a dead stop in the gravel driveway, Annie and Buster found the house empty, a note left on the kitchen counter. It read:

> *A & B,*
> *We have art to make in North Carolina. We'll be back in a few days. Don't go into our room.*
> *Love,*
> *Caleb and Camille*

The thought of going into their parents' room terrified Annie and Buster. The things that had spilled out of the room and into the common areas, the fake knives, the plastic bags of chicken livers and fake blood, scrawled notes for future art projects that all required some form of explosives, were enough to make them wary of what their parents would then deem so strange that it must be kept hidden in their room.

182

The house to themselves, unmonitored, they popped some popcorn, mixed some drinks, and it was nearly thirty minutes into a flimsy Edward G. Robinson noir that Annie turned to Buster, frowned, and then said, 'You never put your eye patch back on.' Buster touched his eye, perfectly adjusted to the light, his spatial dexterity returned to him, and resisted the urge to retrieve the patch from his room. 'I guess I don't need it,' he said, and Annie kissed him on the cheek and smiled. 'We're taking care of each other,' she said. 'We're getting better,' Buster replied, and the two siblings watched with glee as some poor sap on the TV screen walked unknowingly toward his own doom.

More Woe, 1995
Artists: Caleb and Camille Fang

On the opening night of the Hazzard County High School production of William Shakespeare's *Romeo and Juliet*, Buster was going to play Romeo. His sister, Annie, was to play Juliet. Other than Buster, no one backstage seemed to understand that this was a problem. 'Let me ask you something, Buster,' said Mr Delano, the high school drama teacher. 'Have you heard of the phrase *the show must go on*?' Buster nodded. 'Well,' Mr Delano continued, 'this is the kind of moment for which that phrase was coined.'

The original Romeo, Coby Reid, had driven his car into a tree only a few hours earlier, though no one was sure if it was on purpose or not, and no one seemed interested in knowing for certain. Since Coby was not dead but merely in the hospital with a broken collarbone and a collapsed lung and spectacular damage to his wonderful smile, the cast and crew decided that the show need not be canceled but rather recast. That

Buster, the stage manager, had memorized every line of the entire play seemed to make the decision fairly obvious. That his sister, two years his senior and in her final performance as a high school student, would be playing the role of Juliet was seen as only a minor inconvenience.

'I'm an actor, Buster,' his sister said to him when he went to her dressing room. She stared at her reflection in the mirror and carefully brushed her hair, dyed from its normal golden blond to a deep brown for the role. She looked, to Buster, as if she had been drugged or hypnotized. 'I won't be kissing you,' she continued, 'I'll be kissing Romeo, my one true love.' Buster spoke slowly, as if to a small child. 'Yes, but, I guess the point I'm trying to make is that, while you're kissing Romeo, you'll also be kissing me.' Annie nodded, bored with the conversation. 'And,' Buster continued, dumbfounded that he was forced to elaborate, 'you see, I'm your brother.' Annie nodded again. 'I understand what you're saying,' she said, 'but this is what actors do.'

'They make out with their siblings in front of a crowd of people?' Buster asked.

'They do things that are difficult in the service of their art,' Annie responded.

His parents loved the idea. When, over the loudspeaker, it was announced to the audience that the role of Romeo would be played by Buster

Fang, his mother and father forced their way back-stage, video camera in tow, and found Buster pacing in a circle, ill at ease in his tunic and stockings, rehearsing the lines he did not want to speak.

'Think of the subtext,' his father whispered to Buster, gripping him in a bear hug. 'A play about forbidden love will now have the added layer of incest.'

Buster's mother nodded. 'It's pretty brilliant,' she said.

Buster told them that no one cared about the subtext. 'Mr Delano is just desperate for someone who knows all of Romeo's lines,' he said.

His father seemed to consider this statement for a few seconds. 'Hell,' he replied. 'I know all of Romeo's lines.'

'Jesus, Dad,' Buster said. 'No one is going to ask you to play Romeo.'

Mr Fang held up his hands in surrender. 'Well, I wasn't suggesting that,' he said. He turned to his wife and said, 'Can you imagine, though? That would really be incredible.'

Mrs Fang again nodded. 'It would be incredible,' she said.

'I really need to prepare,' Buster said, closing his eyes and hoping that, when he reopened them, his parents would be gone.

'We'll see you at the *cast* party,' Mr Fang said, 'after you *break a leg*.'

'Caleb,' Mrs Fang said, giggling. 'You're awful.'

Buster kept his eyes closed and began to spin in

a tight, controlled circle, as if he was trying to fly away from the auditorium. When he opened his eyes, his parents were gone and Mr Delano, his sister, and the school principal, Mr Guess, were standing in front of him. 'This is a problem,' Mr Guess said. 'What is?' Buster asked. 'This,' Mr Guess answered, pointing at Buster with one hand and Annie with the other, before bringing both of his hands together, fingers interlocked.

'Buster knows all of Romeo's lines,' Mr Delano said.

'Is the day so young?' Buster said and attempted to smile, as if trying to sell a defective product to a suddenly wise customer.

'Mr Delano,' Mr Guess continued, ignoring Buster, 'are you familiar with the plot of this play?'

'I am, Joe, very much so.'

'Then you know that Romeo falls in love with Juliet, they kiss, they get married, have sex, and then kill themselves.'

'That's a rather cursory—'

'Romeo and Juliet kiss, correct?' Mr Guess asked.

'They do kiss,' Mr Delano conceded.

'Mr Delano,' Mr Guess continued. 'Are you aware of the fact that Buster and Annie are brother and sister?'

'Buster knows the lines, Joe. Without him, we don't have a play.'

'O, I am fortune's fool,' Buster said, desperately wanting to shut up without being able to do so.

'This is what's going to happen, Mr Delano,' Mr Guess said. 'We'll do this play but in those moments when Romeo and Juliet are to undertake any kind of romantic interaction, these two kids need to scale back the romance. Instead of a kiss, they'll shake hands or hug or something of that nature.'

'That's ridiculous,' Annie said.

'That's the deal, Ms. Fang.'

'It's stupid,' Annie said.

'Henceforth, I never will be Romeo,' Buster said, and Annie slapped his shoulder in frustration.

'We'll make it work, Joe,' Mr Delano said.

'Never cared for tragedies,' Mr Guess remarked. 'Give me a comedy of errors or a historical play.'

As Mr Guess walked away, Annie bit her thumb at the principal.

Keeping a safe distance from his sister backstage, Buster watched the brawl erupt between the two households, both alike in dignity. The swordplay was clumsy, the nerves of opening night, the entire cast still unsure of how the interaction between Annie and Buster would play out. Buster could see his parents in the audience, his father standing in the aisle, camera fixed on the action, nothing worthwhile if not recorded. In fact, the play now had the feeling of a Fang event, the threat of upheaval, Buster and Annie the harbingers of some great disturbance. And, as with those performances, Buster slowly felt the familiar sensation of giving in to the possibility that everything would soon be changed, and not for the better.

He had chosen the position of stage manager for the express purpose of staying out of the spotlight. He could supervise and coordinate, place his hands on every aspect of the performance without anyone in the audience knowing he was there. And now, thanks to Coby Reid's misplayed suicide attempt, he was Romeo, the idiot boy of Verona, so desperate for sex that he'd leave dead bodies in his wake.

Wearing an itchy, air-reducing mask, a ferocious tiger, Buster held his sister's hand and asked, in a way that he could not imagine ever being successful, if he could kiss it. Annie, thank god, rebuffed him. Buster, oh god no, then asked if he could kiss her lips. As he looked at his sister, he noticed the smirk on her face, the playfulness of this exchange. She was flirting with him and he, because William Goddamn Shakespeare decreed it, would give in to her. 'Then move not while my prayer's effect I take,' Buster said and, leaning forward, made to kiss his sister. Then, inches from her mouth, he loudly smacked his lips, kissing the air, and pulled away from Annie, the threat avoided, the audience tittering but not outraged. Annie scowled at him and then smiled, saying, Shakespeare on her side, 'Then have my lips the sin that they have took.' Buster, no other choice, said his line, 'Give me my sin again,' and, as Annie

189

quickly leaned forward to deliver the kiss, Buster feinted, moved slightly to the left, and again kissed the air, wet and loud. The audience now began to laugh outright. Annie stared at Buster without emotion, though her hands were balled into tight, damage-seeking fists, and said flatly, 'You kiss by the book.'

Once the scene finally ended, the first act closed, Buster looked in the front row at Mr Guess, who gave Buster a thumbs-up, obviously pleased. Tragedy, in Buster's hands, had become comedy.

As the curtain fell, obscuring the stage, Annie punched Buster in the face, a looping overhand right that sent Buster crashing to the ground. 'You are ruining this for me,' Annie said. 'This is my last high school play and people are laughing at us because of you.'

'Mr Guess said no kissing,' Buster reminded her, a bump already forming on his right temple.

'Who gives a shit?' Annie yelled. 'This is *Romeo and Juliet*. We are Romeo and Juliet. We are going to kiss.'

'No we aren't,' Buster said.

'Buster,' Annie continued, her voice breaking. 'Please. Do this for me.'

'I can't do it,' Buster said.

'A plague on your house,' Annie said, and stomped away from him.

'Your house is my house,' Buster said, but she was already out of earshot.

★   ★   ★

190

'O, Romeo, Romeo! Wherefore art thou Romeo?' Annie asked.

Beneath the balcony, in shadow, Buster had no answer for her.

Just before the end of act two, Buster stood next to Jimmy Patrick, rotund and balding at age sixteen, a perfect fit for Friar Laurence, as the friar counseled him that 'violent delights have violent ends' and that 'the sweetest honey is loathsome in its own deliciousness' and, finally, understandably, that Buster should 'love moderately.' The advice given, Annie walked onstage, so light a foot, and took Buster's hands in her own, gripping them tightly, squeezing the feeling out of them until they were ghosts of his own hands. Annie greeted Jimmy, who then said, 'Romeo shall thank thee, daughter, for us both.' The crowd began to laugh, a thunderclap of applause, and Buster stared at his sister's reddening face, embarrassed and angry at the same time, her eyes unblinking and watery. He had ruined it all; he understood this. And with the rudimentary tools he possessed, without any skill for fixing things, he leaned forward, pulling his sister toward him, and kissed her so forcefully that it took her half a second before she responded, two star-cross'd lovers. It was soft and sweet and, except for the fact that it was his sister, everything that Buster had ever hoped his first kiss would be.

'No, no, no, no, no,' Mr Guess screamed, jumping out of his seat and awkwardly climbing onto the stage. The audience began to boo and cheer in equal measure, though Buster wasn't sure if it was directed at the kiss or their principal, who was now pulling the Fangs apart, pushing them to opposite ends of the stage, grunting obscenities. Annie looked over at Buster and smiled. Buster only shrugged and then the curtain fell, not to rise again this night. And thus ended the story, though somewhat premature, of Juliet and her Romeo. More woe, of course, would follow.

Six months later, at the Museum of Contemporary Art in Chicago, Buster and Annie sat at an otherwise empty table and finished the glasses of wine left by people old enough to be nonplussed by free alcohol. Their parents were talking to the MCA curator and a gaggle of museum patrons. 'I wish we could have stayed at home,' Buster said and his sister, stone-cold sober after seven glasses of wine, said, 'It's like bringing those sharecroppers from *Let Us Now Praise Famous Men* to the Museum of Modern Art for Walker Evans's opening. It's like, hey guys, here's the source of your shame, framed and much larger than you remembered it.' In the main room of the exhibit, which the Fang children refused to enter, the entirety of the play flickered against a huge screen. Despite their best efforts, they could not avoid the amplified sound of their own voices, Shakespeare's lines echoing in their heads. 'Overrated melodrama,' Annie muttered. 'Why must I be a teenager in love? Give me a break,' Buster added. Teenagers killed themselves all the time, the two of them agreed. They stared at their parents and decided that the real miracle was how the two of them, A and B, had kept themselves alive this long.

Mr Delano, drunk and happy, suddenly appeared at their table and fell into an adjacent seat. 'Children,' he shouted, and then began to snicker. Annie and Buster had not seen Mr Delano since the night of the performance; he had been fired as soon as the curtain fell and he emptied his apartment and left town before the end of the next day. 'Children,' Mr Delano said again, now composed, though his face was still frighteningly red. 'How I have missed you.'

'What are you doing here, Mr Delano?' Buster asked.

'I wouldn't have missed the opening,' Mr Delano responded. 'After all, none of this would have happened if it wasn't for me.'

Annie took the glass of wine out of Mr Delano's hand and replaced it with an empty one. She pushed a plate of shrimp toast in front of him, but he seemed not to notice.

'Mr Delano,' Buster asked, 'what are you doing here?'

'Your parents invited me,' Mr Delano said. 'They said it was the least they could do after I got fired for putting on such a forward-thinking production.'

'I'm sorry you lost your job,' Annie told him. 'That wasn't right.'

'I knew what I was getting into, my dear,' Mr Delano said. 'I told your parents many times when we were preparing this whole thing that only difficult art is worthwhile, something that leaves behind scorched earth after it takes off.'

Annie and Buster felt their bodies levitate, a sickness entering their systems.

'What?' Annie asked.

'What?' Mr Delano asked, the drunken blush leaving his face.

'What do you mean,' Annie said, speaking through her gritted teeth, *'when you were preparing this whole thing?'*

Mr Delano tilted his empty glass to his lips, his face suddenly ashen. Buster and Annie scooted their chairs so that their knees were touching Mr Delano's, the sharpness of their bones digging into his skin. The Fang children, when angered, could make the coiled threat of their bodies crystal-clear.

'Your parents didn't tell you?' Mr Delano asked.

Buster and Annie shook their heads.

'This,' Mr Delano said, gesturing toward the room filled to overflowing with the Fangs' latest piece, 'was all planned well in advance. Your parents approached me when Annie was selected to play Juliet. I loved the idea. You may not believe it, but when I was a young man in New York, I was at the forefront of the avant-garde movement in American theater. I got arrested for eating broken glass and spitting blood into the audience during an

Off-Broadway performance of *A Streetcar Named Desire*. Your parents are geniuses. I was happy to help.'

'What about Coby Reid?' Buster asked. 'How did you know he'd drop out of the performance?'

'Your parents took care of him,' Mr Delano said.

Annie and Buster made simultaneous faces of shock and Mr Delano corrected himself. 'No, no, goodness no. They paid Coby five hundred dollars to drop out of the play. He simply wouldn't show up on opening night. The car crash was Coby's own bad luck.'

'They did all this to us,' Annie said, 'for art.'

'For art,' Mr Delano shouted, raising his empty glass over his head.

'They used us,' Buster said.

'No, Buster, that's unfair. Your parents withheld certain information in order to get the best performance possible from you. Think of your parents as directors; they control the circumstances and make all the independent pieces come together to create something beautiful that would otherwise not exist. They directed you so skillfully that you didn't even know they were doing it.'

'Fuck you, Mr Delano,' Annie said.

'Children,' Mr Delano cried.

'Fuck you, Mr Delano,' Buster said.

Annie and Buster, still holding wineglasses, unable to put them down, left their former drama teacher and walked into the crowd of people that surrounded their parents, pushing their way to the center.

'A and B,' Mr Fang said when he noticed the children standing in front of him. 'The stars of the evening,' Mrs Fang said. Buster and Annie, knowing each other's desires without having to speak, slammed the wineglasses against their parents' heads, shards falling to the floor, their parents' mouths gaping, perfect *O*s of confusion.

'We've always done whatever you asked us to do,' Annie said, her whole body shaking. 'We did what you said and we never asked why. We just did it. For you.'

'If you'd told us what was happening,' Buster continued, 'we still would have done it.'

'We're finished with you,' Annie said, and the Fang children walked softly into the main exhibit room as the shocked audience, unclear as to whether this was some sort of artistic performance or simple assault, made way with haste.

Their hands dripping blood, their own and their parents', granules of glass under their skin, Annie and Buster watched themselves on the screen, two children so unwilling to follow their parents' decree that they would rather end it all as spectacularly as their limited means would allow.

CHAPTER 7

When Annie awoke the next morning, Buster asleep in his room, she was in possession of a terrific happiness. Of course, she hadn't really done anything of note to warrant this happiness. She'd wasted two hours at the movie theater, sneaking mini bottles of bourbon throughout the film, but Buster had done enough for both of them. He'd left the house, misaligned face and all, met with a group of students, and talked about the thing that made him special. As a result, the two of them had ended the day happier than when they'd woken up, and she could not remember the last time that had happened. It was a small thing, perhaps, but there it was.

Annie slipped out of bed, still fully clothed from the day before, and grabbed the pile of stories that Buster had picked up at the community college. She leafed through them until she found Suzanne's story and then she walked to the other end of the house, into the kitchen, far enough away from Buster that she could get to work on the unenviable task of keeping her brother from falling in love with this strange girl. It had once been her job, to beat back any trouble that might try to find them, A & B, and she was out of practice. She skipped the alcohol this morning, sipped a tall glass of tomato juice, and felt, her parents an entire state away, that she could handle shit on her own.

The story wasn't great, a little too obvious, but she could see how it would appeal to Buster, her brother being obsessed with undeserved pain. If it came down to it, if she saw Buster slipping further away, she would have a talk with this Suzanne character, give her the Fang family history, send her on her way. As it was, Annie was already worried about this mysterious Joseph from Nebraska, for whom Buster had admitted a lingering affection. Joseph had shot Buster in the goddamn face, undeserved pain, and so Annie also wouldn't mind a minute of Mr Potato Gun's time if the opportunity ever presented itself.

Annie took Suzanne's story and placed it in the trash can, pushing it as far down as she could. She returned to her impressive glass of tomato juice, which she began to wish had vodka in it, and batted away the suspicion that she was jealous of these interlopers, who pulled Buster's attention away from anything except this house, their own unhappy circumstances. No, she decided, she was taking care of him; someone in this family had to make sound decisions, even if they weren't as fascinating in the end, the lack of any explosions,

198

no screaming or crying or psychological scarring. Then she thought of Daniel, growing an impressive beard in Wyoming, writing the most ridiculous bullshit a human could think of, and began to reconsider her judgment regarding potential love interests. She removed the story from the trash, smoothed out the pages, and left it on the table. When Buster arrived fifteen minutes later, worrying the healing scar above his lip, he noticed the story and looked at Annie. 'Did you read that?' he asked. Annie nodded. Buster frowned, embarrassed, and then said, 'Well, what did you think?' Annie took a long sip of tomato juice and replied, 'Very good.' Buster smiled. 'Very good,' he repeated, and then nodded.

Once they ate breakfast, Annie decided that it was necessary, now that some forward momentum in their lives had been achieved, to discuss their situations and figure out how to build upon yesterday's success. As she said all of this to Buster, she felt like someone in an infomercial. But then Buster agreed that it was a good idea and Annie felt like Oprah. They pushed away their plates and began to brainstorm. If there had been a dry-erase board in the kitchen, they would have used it.

For Buster: He had surely been evicted from his old apartment in Florida by now, and he owed the hospital twelve grand that he did not have. His face was still not completely healed; Annie stared at the light bruising and healing scabs that ran across the entire right half of his face, the scar above his lip, the busted blood vessels that still clouded his right eye.

Annie, feeling capable and assured, began formulating a plan of action. She imagined that she was talking not only to Buster, but also to a studio audience. 'I can pay the hospital,' she said, and Buster did not try to argue. She had money, she realized. A ton of money, she realized. A ridiculous amount of money, she realized. It was nice to see that money, for all the bad press it got, could sometimes solve your problems. 'After we get ourselves straightened out here, you'll come back to Los Angeles with me. Do you think you could write a screenplay?' Buster shook his head. He did not. 'Do you think you could write a teleplay? It's shorter.' Buster thought about it for a second and then shook his head again. Annie waved him off. 'It's fine, really. You can just get a regular job, something that will give you time to focus on your own writing. I mean, honestly, I can loan you some money and you wouldn't have to worry about work for a long while.' Buster shrugged, unable to find anything objectionable about the plan. Annie smiled. This was easy, Annie thought. She should have her own television show, doing this for any number of fucked-up people. 'And your face is healing,' she reminded him. 'A month or two and you'll be back to normal.' Buster smiled at that kindness, the gap from his missing tooth showing. She would, she made a mental note, get a dentist to fix that. It was done. Buster was taken care of, his life, for the moment, on steady ground. Was it possible that life could be this easy? Now it was her turn.

She was, for the foreseeable future, unemployed. She had lost her role in one of the biggest blockbuster series in movie history. Her tits were on the Internet. She had slept with a reporter. Her ex-boyfriend, who was fast becoming one of the most powerful people in Hollywood, probably did not care for her right now. Buster whistled when she finally finished reciting the particulars of her unpleasant situation. 'Not bad,' he said. 'Thank you,' she replied.

She thought about it for a second, staring at the table. Okay, she would get some supporting roles in smaller movies, focus on the quality of the script. Or better, yes even better, she would go back to theater. She would do a Tennessee Williams play Off-Broadway for a month or two, get back into fighting shape, and see what came next. Her tits, oh well, nothing to be done about that. She'd just be a little more careful in the future. A lesson learned. 'Don't worry about the magazine writer,' Buster offered. 'Nobody cares about freelance writers, trust me.' Annie nodded. As far as questionable people to fuck, she'd done okay, nothing she couldn't recover from. Same with Daniel, just a bad decision that she'd outlive. The point, she realized, was that, yes, she had made some substantial mistakes, as evidenced by the fact that she was living with her parents, but she could handle it. She could take the things that were broken and, if not put them back together, get rid of them with a minimum of unpleasantness.

Then there was the small matter of their drug and alcohol dependencies. 'How about this,' Buster offered. 'No pain pills unless I absolutely need them, and no alcohol for you until after five P.M.' Annie thought about this for a few seconds. Yes, she decided. That was sound reasoning. 'What next?' Annie thought. Though it was only talk, nothing yet having been accomplished, she felt better, stronger, faster. And she was not drunk. 'This,' she thought, 'could work.'

If an agenda had been prepared for this morning's meeting, they would be checking off the bulleted points headlined *Buster's problems* and *Annie's problems*. Annie began to rise from the table, ready to turn her words into actions, when Buster gestured for her to sit back down.

'I was thinking about Mom and Dad,' Buster continued. Annie had not been thinking about them, not even a little bit, but she let Buster go on talking. 'I know they, whatever, fucked us up beyond belief, but they are letting us stay here. They're taking care of us, as well as they can.' Annie could not disagree. Her parents had indeed fucked them up. They were indeed letting them live in their house. 'So,' Buster said, 'whatever project they have planned next, I think we should take part.' Annie shook her head. 'We're trying to get better, Buster,' she said. Buster, always so sweet, always trying to be good, frowned. 'Our participation in what Caleb and Camille do is bad for us,' she continued, the muscles in her hands tightening like a spasm. She felt herself growing angry and then made a conscious effort to control it before she went on. 'It's toxic. It turns us into children again, the way they just use us for what they want, and we've spent this whole morning trying to figure out a way past that.'

'You saw that Chicken Queen fiasco,' he said. 'We could have helped them. We could make sure whatever they do next actually works. We'd only do it once, to get them back on their feet, and then we'd never do it again.' Annie was not ready to commit to this, inserting herself into the craziness of her parents' desires, but she could not forget how feeble Caleb and Camille seemed at the mall, how ridiculous their efforts had been, and so Annie allowed herself to consider the possibility. 'Maybe,' she told Buster. 'Good enough,' he replied.

Having organized the particulars of their own lives, Annie and Buster began working on their environment, cleaning the house, which was no small task. Annie carried bag after bag, rattling with empty bottles of booze, to the garage. Buster removed the dozens and dozens of gauze and bandages from his night table, crusted with blood, still wet with ointment, which he'd never both- ered to throw away, had simply put aside to grow into some strange, living sculpture of his recovery. They helped each other make their beds, vacuumed the floors, and organized their meager belongings. They met in their shared bathroom and made it sparkle. It wasn't even noon and they had accomplished more than they had in the previous year.

The living room, the largest room in the house by far, was filled with old Fang projects, notes, and outlines, stacked from top to bottom with ephemera. She had no idea where anything went, how to even begin devising a filing system, and so she focused on the scattered LPs on the floor, a collection of sound that, to this day, baffled her.

Caleb and Camille liked two kinds of music – esoteric, impenetrable things like John Cage and the apocalyptic folk of Current 93, and then the dumbest, loudest music possible, punk rock. When they were little children, their parents had sung Black Flag's 'Six Pack' to them before bed as if it were a lullaby. 'I was born with a bottle in my mouth,' their mother would sing, and then their father would chime in, 'Six Pack!' At the end, before kissing Annie and Buster on their foreheads, Caleb and Camille would whisper, 'Six Pack! Six Pack! Six Pack!' and then turn off the light.

While she organized the albums in the cabinet beneath the hi-fi, she placed the James Chance and the Contortions album *Buy* on the phonograph and cued up the fifth song, which she remembered her parents often playing before they would all head out into the world to create some new form of chaos. It was not an unpleasant memory, which surprised her, the excitement of not knowing what would happen, watching her parents get more and more worked up about the thing they were making, knowing it wouldn't work without her and Buster. The strange, jangly music made its way out of the speakers and it wasn't long before Buster emerged from the hallway, tapping his foot. Annie waved him over and they stood in front of the speaker, nodding their heads, singing along, 'Contort yourself, contort yourself.' If Annie could not drink, if Buster could not over-medicate, then dancing to abrasive, atonal jazz-punk would have to do. The music screeched and spilled over the edges of normal rhythm, but Buster and Annie did not miss a step, dancing the only way they'd ever known, poorly, but with great enthusiasm. If there was a name for this dance, it would be The Fang.

The phone rang three times before either of them even heard it, was able to tease the sound out of the tangle of noise that surrounded them. Annie reached the phone in the kitchen just as the answering machine was saying, 'The Fangs are dead,' and Annie said, out of breath, 'We're not dead! Sorry, we're here. Sorry.' There was a brief silence on the other end of the line, and Annie figured the caller had been scared off, until she heard a man's composed, patient voice answer, 'Mrs Fang?'

'Yes,' Annie said.

The voice became slightly more interested. 'Camille Fang?' he said.

'Oh! No, I'm sorry,' Annie said. 'I'm Annie. I'm Mrs Fang's daughter. I'm Camille's daughter.' Was she drunk? She thought for a second. No, she definitely wasn't drunk. She tried to get it together.

'My mother is not here,' she continued.

'You're her daughter?' the man asked.

'Yes.'

'Well, this is Officer Dunham,' he said, and Annie was already prepared for what would follow. Arrests had been made. Her parents were in trouble, just enough to be a nuisance. Bail would be arranged. She felt, for a brief second, a slight admiration for her parents that, after the incident in the mall where they could hardly elicit an emotional response from anyone, they had managed to create something difficult enough to require police intervention.

'What did they do?'

'Excuse me?' the officer replied.

'Are they in trouble?'

'Yes, well, perhaps,' the officer stuttered, before attempting to regain control of the conversation. 'I'm afraid to say that your parents are currently missing, Annie,' Officer Dunham said.

'What?'

'This morning, we found your parents' van parked at the Jefferson Rest Stop on I-40 East, just before you head into North Carolina. Near as we can tell, the van has been there since the previous evening. We are . . . concerned about their whereabouts.'

Annie felt the slight betrayal of ruining whatever elaborate plan her parents had concocted, but she had no desire to get herself involved in police matters if she could avoid it. She was on the road to recovery. She came clean.

'Officer,' Annie began. 'It's all staged. My parents are artists of some sort, somewhat famous, and this is all some kind of performance to them. They aren't really missing; they just want you to think that they are. I'm sorry for the trouble.'

'We know all about your parents, Annie. I did a little research and talked to the police in your county and I'm well aware of the, um, artistic nature of your parents' actions. However, that being said, we are very seriously treating this as a missing persons case.'

'It's fake,' Annie said, wanting desperately to save this patient man the effort of finding her parents, doing exactly what they wanted him to do. She recalled the odd, unsettling feeling that occurred after Fang events, of realizing that you might not have been in control of your thoughts and actions when Caleb and Camille were involved.

'Ms. Fang, I think we should talk in person, but you need to understand that this is serious. There is a significant amount of blood around the car, there are signs of a struggle, and we have been dealing with similar incidents occurring at rest stops around this area for the past nine months. I don't want to alarm you, but there have been four incidents in East Tennessee involving rest-stop abductions, all ending in homicides. I know you think this is something your parents cooked up, but that is not the case. You need to prepare yourself for the possibility that this is very real and might not have a good outcome.'

Buster walked into the kitchen. 'Who is that?' he asked, but Annie shook her head and put a finger to her lips to quiet him.

'When was the last time you talked to your parents?' the officer asked her.

'Yesterday morning, over breakfast.'

'Did they mention where they were going?'

'No, they didn't say anything about a trip, but when my brother and I got home yesterday after-noon, they had left a note that said they were going to North Carolina.'

'Do they know anyone in North Carolina?'

'I have no idea,' Annie responded.

'Do they know anyone in Jefferson? Someone they might have met up with at the rest stop?'

'I don't know.'

'I'm going to give you my number, Ms. Fang, and I want you to call me if you hear from your parents. I want you to call me if you think of anything else that could be of help. I want you to call me if you think there's something we're missing. We'll do everything we can on our end.'

'You think they're dead, don't you?' Annie asked.

'I don't know that,' the officer said.

'But that's a possibility,' Annie continued.

'It is one of the possible scenarios, yes.'

'I wish I could make you understand,' Annie said, growing frustrated. 'This is not real. You are not dealing with anything real. It's all made up. It's what they do. They make something crazy happen and then they watch you try to deal with it.'

'I hope you're right, Ms. Fang, I really do,' Officer Dunham replied, and then hung up the phone.

Annie replaced the phone in its cradle and then took the half-empty bottle of vodka from the kitchen counter. 'Not yet,' Buster cautioned, pointing at the microwave clock. 'Sit down, Buster,' Annie said. 'What did Mom and Dad do?' Buster asked. 'Something awful,' Annie replied, taking a testing sip from the bottle, finding it sufficient, and tilting the bottle even more.

After she had explained everything to her brother, the rough outline, the what-ifs, Annie sat on the bed while Buster searched the Internet to learn more about the rest-stop killings. True enough, there had been incidents in the area, women and men cut up or shot, their bodies moved from the rest stops to garbage Dumpsters at gas stations or fast-food restaurants. The cops suspected a truck driver, someone regularly traveling the interstate from North Carolina to Tennessee. It all made sense, which made Annie even more certain that this was all part of her parents' elaborate plans.

'Oh, please. You don't think Camille and Caleb knew about these murders, knew they could take advantage of the situation?' Annie said. Her parents' deception seemed so obvious to her that she found herself stunned that the police were so clueless.

Buster, who had grown quiet, withdrawn, only shook his head.

'Don't let them do this to you, Buster,' she said, almost shouting, her anger against her parents amplified by the fact that Buster seemed to be falling for it. 'This is what they want, goddamn it. They want us to think they're dead.'

'They might be, Annie,' Buster said. He looked like he was about to cry, which only made Annie angrier. She thought about her parents' bedroom, door shut, barricaded from the rest of the house. Suddenly, with total clarity, she saw her parents hiding in their bedroom, giggling, waiting for someone to find them. She imagined them hiding under their bed, cans of food surrounding them, jugs of water, a bomb shelter to protect them from the rest of the world.

Annie pulled Buster into the hallway and the two of them paused in front of the door to their parents' bedroom. Annie leaned into the door, listening for any sound on the other end. 'Annie?' Buster asked. Annie shushed him. 'They're in here,' she said. 'They're hiding from us.' She slowly turned the doorknob and felt it turn without resistance. For the first time in forever, Annie and Buster stepped into a room they had only pictured, and even then reluctantly, in their minds. 'Okay,' Annie shouted into the open room. 'We know you're in here. Caleb? Camille?' Annie looked around the room, which was nearly empty of possessions. There was a bed, unmade, and two nightstands that held multiple glasses of water and multivitamins. There was no other furniture in the room. There was none of the chaos and disorder of the living room, not a single piece of paper out of place. 'They're not in here,' Buster said to Annie, but Annie then ran to the closet and pulled open the doors with a flourish. Nothing but clothes, a normal closet filled with shoes and shirts and pants, but no Fangs. 'Annie,' Buster said, 'this is weird.' Annie turned to him. She did not understand if he was referring to their search for Caleb and Camille or the fact that the bedroom was so lacking in weirdness. 'I thought they might be hiding in here,' she said. 'But they're hiding somewhere else.' Buster shrugged, allowed his face to register fear, and said, 'Or they're in trouble. Or worse. Annie, they really could be dead.'

Annie took her brother's hands in her own. She stared at him until he finally met her gaze. 'They are not dead, Buster. They are doing what they've always done; they are creating a situation in order to elicit an extreme emotional response from those closest to the event. They waited for us to come

211

home, for all of us to be together again, and then they dreamed up this horrible event to, I don't know what, make us feel something that they can use for their own designs.'

'Maybe,' Buster admitted.

'Definitely,' Annie replied. 'This is classic Caleb and Camille Fang. They have put us in a situation, left us in the wilderness, and they're waiting to see what will happen.'

'Well,' Buster said, regaining his composure, 'what *will* happen?'

'I'll tell you,' Annie said, feeling the certainty of her thoughts click into place. 'I'll tell you exactly what will happen, Buster.' She pressed her forehead roughly against her brother's, the warmth of his skin against hers. A and B, the Fang children.

'We're going to find them.'

A Christmas Carol, 1977
Artists: Caleb and Camille Fang

The Fangs were to be married, the union of two souls, till death do you part, I do, I do, the whole ridiculous charade.

Caleb slipped the ring on Camille's finger and repeated the minister's unenthusiastic recitation of the vows. To the left of the altar, the minister's wife, her fee for playing Mendelssohn's 'Wedding March' on the chapel's organ too expensive, filmed the proceedings on Caleb's Super 8 camera, which whirred and clicked throughout the ceremony. Caleb feared the woman was missing the subtlety of the event, ruining the shot with static, uninteresting angles. He reminded himself that next time he would figure out a way to film the marriage while also taking part in it, to maintain artistic control at all costs.

Camille, her stomach a tight, round ball of expectancy, could not remember if she was supposed to be happy or sad. She decided to act nervous, which could work for either emotion. Throughout the ceremony, she rubbed her obscenely pregnant belly, took deep, weighted breaths, and grimaced suddenly from time to time as if to suggest labor was imminent, as in right this second, as in right here in the chapel, as in, does this place do baptisms as well? Each time she brushed her fingers over the convex curve of her stomach, she noticed that the minister's wife, the upper part of her face a whirring glass eye, would purse her lips with disgust. Camille began to rub her stomach more and more often, smiling as the minister's wife expressed her sour displeasure with the proceedings like a Pavlovian response. Camille was amazed, once again, at the ease with which she could elicit outrage, when she realized that Caleb and the minister were staring at her. 'I do,' she said quickly, though they'd already gone through the vows.

'He wants to kiss you now,' the minister said to her as he gestured dismissively toward Caleb. 'Do you want to kiss him?' he asked.

'Okay,' she said. 'Why not?' and leaned toward her husband, her belly pressing against his cheap tuxedo.

The minister's wife threw a handful of confetti with such force it seemed she was trying to blind them, and Caleb and Camille turned and walked silently out of the chapel. As soon as they reached the doors, they turned around and walked back to the altar. Caleb retrieved the camera from the minister's wife, tipped the minister, and then posed with Camille for the wedding portrait, ten dollars, a single Polaroid.

'You want I should make this official?' the minister said, counting the ten one-dollar bills and then folding the money in half before handing it to his wife.

Camille bent over the pew and fished the marriage license, official and sealed, out of her purse. She signed the paper and then handed the pen to her husband. He signed it and then handed the pen to the minister's wife, who waved it off and produced her own pen. She scratched her name on the license, a witness to the events, and then handed the pen to the minister, who signed his name, shook the document as if it was wet and needed drying, and then handed the official record to Caleb.

'You're married,' the minister said.

'Yes, we are,' Camille said.

'Be good to each other,' the minister said.

'And that baby,' the minister's wife added.

'But mostly to each other,' the minister said, looking sternly at his wife, who had already turned to clean the chapel for the next scheduled wedding.

Back in the car, Caleb and Camille stared at the marriage license. *Mr George De Vries and Ms. Josephine Boss*. Camille awkwardly hiked up the skirt of her cut-rate wedding dress and slipped off the fake belly, which fell to the floorboard of the car like a sack of gunpowder, ready to explode. They removed their wedding bands and the cheap, fake-diamond engagement ring and placed them in the ashtray of the car, clinking like change.

'I can't do this anymore,' Camille said, arching her back to soothe the ache from wearing the heavy belly.

'Great art is difficult,' Caleb said.

'I'm serious, Caleb,' she said. 'No more weddings.'

'You don't want to marry me anymore?' he said, smiling, coaxing the car into first gear with some difficulty.

'Thirty-six marriages,' she said. 'It's enough.'

'Fifty,' Caleb replied. 'We agreed on fifty. *Fifty Weddings: An Exploration of Love and the Law. Thirty-six Weddings*. That sounds awful.'

Camille remembered *Thirty-Six Views of Mount Fuji,* which she had studied in her first art class. She could see the crashing waves off Kanagawa, the tiny people in their boats, completely powerless, endlessly threatened with disaster.

'I'm pregnant,' she said.

'Okay,' Caleb said without comprehension, fighting with the gearshift to keep moving forward, unfamiliar with the streets in this town.

'I'm pregnant,' she repeated.

The car came to a stop, the sound of metal gears grinding imprecisely. Someone behind them honked their horn and raced around the car, now parked in the middle of the street.

'I'm pregnant,' Camille said once more, hoping that three times would be enough for Caleb to understand.

'Well, what do we do?' Caleb said.

'I have no idea,' Camille answered.

'We have to do something,' Caleb said.

They sat in the car without speaking, the engine running, each of them unsure of every single possibility that presented itself.

'We have no money,' Caleb said.

'I know,' Camille answered.

'Hobart always says, "Children kill art." He's told me that a million times,' Caleb continued. He wanted to roll down the window, get some fresh air, but the handle was broken.

'I know,' Camille replied. 'I've heard him say it.'

'It's an unfortunate situation at the worst possible time,' Caleb said.

'I know,' Camille said, 'but I'm going to have it.'

Caleb put his hands on the wheel and stared at the empty street. Thirty yards ahead of them, the traffic light changed from green to yellow to red and back again. He felt the nausea of nonfulfillment, having carried Camille, ten years his junior, his former student, into possible ruination. He felt certain that he was a failure, every artistic endeavor ending with his own surprise at how little had come rom it. Perhaps that was how life worked, the expectation of success after each failure the engine that kept the world turning. Perhaps retrogression was an artistic endeavor in itself. Perhaps he might sink so far that he would find himself, somehow, returned to the surface.

'Okay,' Caleb finally answered.

'What?' Camille said.

'Okay,' Caleb replied. 'Let's do it.'

Camille leaned over and kissed him, softly, a more perfect kiss than any from the thirty-six weddings.

'We should get married,' Caleb said.

Camille reached into the ashtray and found the engagement ring. She put it back on her finger. 'Okay,' she said.

'Okay?' Caleb responded.

'Okay,' she said, 'I'll marry you.'

Three months later, they were married for the thirty-seventh time. Four months after that, their child was born, a girl, Annie. Less than a month later, their show, *Thirty-Seven Weddings,* opened at the Anchor Gallery in San Francisco, the walls covered with the marriage licenses, each expertly forged by Camille, and the amateur, post-ceremony portraits of the happy couple in various states of happiness. An entire wall of the gallery flickered with the looped footage of each one of the weddings, a never-ending reel of ring exchanges and bride-kissing. The final piece of the exhibit, the genuine marriage certificate, was displayed with a photo from the final wedding, Caleb and Camille surrounded by their friends and colleagues, his parents long dead and her family, having long posited that Caleb had brainwashed their daughter, declining the invitation. Hobart Waxman, Caleb's mentor, had performed the ceremony, a certified minister yet another hidden title on his résumé. 'A terrible idea,' Hobart had said after the ceremony, embracing the Fangs, 'elegantly rendered.'

A trite concept rendered so awkwardly as to erase any shred of meaning. This was the final line of the review of *Thirty-Seven Weddings* in the *San Francisco Chronicle*. Nine months after the show, Caleb still found the line invading his thoughts in the rare moments when Annie wasn't filling the tiny apartment with her cries, raging against some unspoken grievance. 'What does she want?' he asked his wife. 'Something,' Camille responded, rocking the baby in her arms. Camille's face, he noted, was glowing, a radiance that never failed to confuse Caleb. Was she happy or sad? He could not tell. He was, on the other hand, as he had told Camille endlessly since the review, not happy.

Since the review, Caleb had not begun work on any new projects. He taught his classes on postmodern art, watched the easy way that Camille cared for the baby, and read the classifieds section of the newspaper for some bizarre personal ad or horrible employment opportunity that might ignite the next idea for his work.

Desperate for expression, he came up with the idea of digging a hole to the center of the earth.

One weekend, his morning coffee working its magic on his internals, he spent nine dollars that they could not spare on a shovel. When he returned to the apartment, Camille was spooning strained peas into the baby and looked over her shoulder at Caleb, shovel in hand, explaining the piece. 'I'm just going to dig,' he said.

Camille was supportive. A hole? Yes, a hole. Interesting. It could be. Where? To the center of the earth, through the center, to the other side of the world. Like the mantle wasn't even there. How? With this shovel. A primitive tool, perfectly made. The baby marveled at the shiny blade of the shovel, her hands reaching for it. Caleb held firmly to the handle and stepped away from the baby.

'I'll just dig until it makes sense,' he said, and Camille gestured for him to kiss her. He kissed her, then stroked the soft curve of the back of the baby's head, her face streaked a mossy green, and strode out of the apartment, in possession of an implement, trying to ignore the thought that he was losing his mind.

In the park, he jammed the shovel into the earth and put his weight into the effort. A quick motion and then, where there had not been seconds earlier, there was a hole. He repeated the procedure and watched the way the ground opened up for him. If this was art, it existed on the furthest part of the spectrum, the part that touched up against yard work. 'The act is not the art,' he told himself. 'The reaction is the art.'

Standing knee-deep in a hole in the middle of a public park, Caleb tried to explain this to the policeman. Caleb looked up at the uniform towering over him, hand resting easy on his holster, and said, 'It's a hole in the earth. It's a depression. I think it means something.'

'Fill it back up and get out of here,' the cop said.

'Yes, Officer,' Caleb responded. He stepped out of the hole as if emerging from the shaft of a mine, dazed by the world he had reentered.

With each heave of dirt, tapped down with his foot, Caleb saw the made thing become unmade.

'Don't come back here,' the police officer said, 'or I'll arrest you.'

Caleb had been arrested several times and had never felt any animosity toward the police. He understood their reaction to his actions. It was a predictable element of his work; he would create disorder, and, once he achieved the desired effect, order would need to be restored. 'Have a nice day,' Caleb said and the police officer simply nodded.

Back at the apartment, the shovel hidden in the back of the closet, he confessed to Camille that he might be going crazy.

'I suspected as much,' Camille said.

'If only we had done fifty weddings,' Caleb said.

'Oh, Caleb,' Camille replied, her face full of what he suspected was pity. 'It just didn't work. That's all. We made a bomb and it didn't go off.

The wiring was faulty. We'll just make another one.'

'When?'

'Soon.'

The baby sputtered and spit, drool covering her onesie, darkening the fabric. Held loosely in Camille's arms, she reached for Caleb and he let her hands, soft and barely corporeal, worry his face. She lightly tapped his eyes and mouth and nose as if to say, 'Here, here, here,' or 'Mine, mine, mine.' He smiled.

'We made her,' Camille said.

'Ill-conceived,' Caleb thought, and then he said, 'Handcrafted by the finest artisans.'

For Caleb, Annie was Camille's project. He changed diapers, bathed her, attended to the grunt work of upkeep, but Camille understood the innate needs of the baby and addressed them with little wasted effort. The baby was crying and then, somehow, it wasn't. The baby was glassy-eyed and unfocused and then, suddenly, Camille would coax a smile to the surface of Annie's face. 'How did you do that?' Caleb would ask, and Camille would pull on her earlobe and wink at him. 'Magic,' she would say. The baby was a hummingbird inside of his cupped hands, and Caleb could not hold on tightly enough to believe that she was real. It was a form of art for which he had no innate talent.

'Let's get out of here,' Camille said.

'Where?' Caleb asked, still worried about the police officer.

'Let's go to the mall.'

'Why?'

'It's free,' Camille said.

At the mall, Christmas season in full swing, shoppers on all sides of them, the Fangs were endlessly fascinated by their surroundings. Sunlight from the skylit ceilings mixed with the buzzing fluorescents and made everything seem clean and expensive. Tinsel and pine needles and cottony snow hung in places that you could see but could not touch. Piped-in Muzak, Christmas standards, found you even in the restrooms. The mall was labyrinthine, exquisitely constructed and impossible to leave.

The Fangs rode the escalator up and then down, over and over, the baby overjoyed at rising and apprehensive about descending. A receipt, two feet long when unfurled, sat on top of a trash can and Caleb and Camille read through the items as though they were directions to a wonderful, previously unheard-of location. They watched a woman, loaded down with packages as if she was a store unto herself, purchase an Orange Julius and then immediately set it down on a bench in order to readjust her belongings. Properly aligned, she then walked away without retrieving her drink. Caleb picked it up, took a few tentative sips, and then passed it over to Camille. 'Mmm,' she said, smiling, 'orangey.' An item in their hands, they now felt a part of the community, no longer

sightseers but active participants in the goings-
on. They strolled through the mall without their
initial naïveté and, long after the drink was
finished, they continued to hold on to the cup,
passing it back and forth like a torch.

They found a line that stretched out from a
snowy village in the middle of the mall, its own
brand of Christmas music, more digital, higher-
pitched, emanating from the area. 'What's this?'
Camille asked the last person in line, a burly,
scowling man in custody of two small children.
'Santa Claus,' he said and then turned his back
on them. Caleb looked at the line, kinked and
unmoving, and then whistled. 'All this to see Santa
Claus?' he asked. One of the man's children turned
to them and said, 'You tell him what you want
and then he'll give it to you.' Camille and Caleb
nodded. They understood how it worked. 'And
then you get a picture with him,' the other child
said.

'Is it free?' Camille asked.

'What do you think?' the man snorted.

'I guess it's not free,' Caleb said.

'No harm in meeting Santa Claus,' Camille
replied. In her family's house, there was a reproduction of a Thomas Nast illustration of Santa
Claus, corpulent and red-faced and awkwardly
gripping a doll that Camille had mistaken for a
real child. Despite her parents' explanations, she
could never see Santa Claus as anything other
than a drunk man who kidnapped children. Later,

she began to think of Santa Claus as a true artist, crafting elegant toys in his remote studio, fucking elves when he got bored, uninterested in making a profit. 'We'll let Annie meet her first folkloric character. She can ask him for some nice things.'

'She can't talk,' Caleb said, wary of tradition.

'I know what she wants,' Camille said. 'I'll translate for Santa.'

Now a part of the line, they waited patiently for their turn. Annie happily played with the straw from the Orange Julius drink as they edged closer to Santa Land; stuffed reindeer, heads bowed, apparently eating snow; overflowing bags of toys; and the bellowing, disembodied 'Ho, ho, ho' of the store Santa, still unseen from their vantage point, which never failed to startle the Fangs. Caleb found himself uttering sounds in groups of three, 'Har, har, har,' and 'Hee, hee, hee,' and 'Hey, hey, hey,' and 'How, how, how,' until Camille shushed him.

Finally rewarded for their patience, the Fangs stepped beyond the velvet rope that separated the chosen from the not-yet-chosen and followed a bored teenage elf up the stairs to Santa's chair. 'Ho, ho, ho,' Santa shouted, seemingly genuinely pleased with his station in life. Caleb hung back with the elf while Camille knelt beside Santa and carefully placed Annie in his lap. 'Now what does this pretty little – ' and before he could finish his sentence, Annie unleashed a shrill, glass-shattering wail that seemed conjured by the dark arts, the image of the tiny baby and the sound emanating from her so incongruous that Caleb at first seemed unaware that his own child was the source of the chaos that enveloped Santa Land.

'Good Lord,' Santa shouted, his leg spasming as if trying to shake the baby off his person. Camille was shocked by the seismic shift in emotion that crossed Annie's face, her mouth open so wide it seemed possible that a horde of demons might fly out. She knew she should take the child into her arms and comfort her but she did not move from her position on the floor, a small part of her unwilling to come into contact with the baby until she was sure that Annie was not going to burst into flames.

The elf behind the camera, five minutes from a cigarette break, calmly stared through the viewfinder and prepared to take a photograph of the historic meeting. Caleb looked over at the scene, Santa's face a rictus of terror, the baby nearly purple with rage, another elf covering his ears with his hands, and Camille, puzzled, confused, as if listening to a foreign language in which she could discern elements of her own native tongue. Down the entire length of the waiting line, as if Annie's fit was a kind of wild-fire, other children began to scream and shake. A few parents had to drag their possessed children away, giving up their places, which caused the children to scream even more. The people who remained in line looked at Caleb and Camille and

Annie as if they had personally ruined Christmas for all time. It was, Caleb realized, amazing. 'Hurry up and take the photo,' Caleb said to the bored elf and there was a flash of bulbs, the click of the captured image, and Caleb quickly ran toward Santa, plucked the child out of the terrified old man's lap, and hugged his daughter, feeling the radiating warmth of her unhappiness now happily in his possession. Annie, her eyes red-rimmed, her lips quivering, aftershocks of the disaster, began to calm almost immediately. Camille finally joined the two of them, Santa Land temporarily shut down, grinding to a halt, not a single person in the twisting line wanting to step forward. 'It's okay,' Caleb whispered to Annie, 'you did great.'

'I want that photo,' Caleb said, turning to the elf.

'Five bucks,' the elf replied.

'We don't have any money,' Caleb said, shocked by the realization.

'Well, we don't barter.'

'Let's just leave, Caleb,' Camille said.

'I need that picture,' Caleb answered. 'I'll come back tomorrow and pay you.'

'I won't be here tomorrow,' the elf said. 'Thank god.'

'Please,' Camille said, everyone staring at them, Santa Claus shaking uncontrollably, his head in his hands.

Caleb felt the spark of inspiration and quickly handed the baby to Camille. 'Five minutes,' he said. 'I'll have your money.'

He left his wife and child and sprinted to the Glass Hut, the discarded receipt from earlier in the afternoon flapping in his hands as he ran. When he reached the entrance, he slowed, adjusted his demeanor, and slipped unnoticed into the store. He walked down the first aisle, his eyes searching the shelves filled with glass knickknacks. Finally, he came to a row of statues, two fish, green and orange, leaping out of the cold-blue sea. On the itemized receipt, he'd read: *Green and Orange Fish Statue: $14.99.*

Statue in hand, he walked to the register and placed the item on the counter. 'Oh, wonderful choice,' the woman said. 'Actually,' Caleb interjected, 'I'm returning this. My wife bought it earlier, along with several other items, and we realized that this particular piece didn't fit with the décor of the intended recipient. We'd like a refund.' He produced the receipt and pointed to the price of the statue. 'It is a lovely piece, though,' he added, his open palm waiting for the money.

The elf paid, Caleb carefully opened the commemorative photo frame and stared at his daughter's bottomless well of a mouth, her eyes pinched shut, the sound of her screams seeming to blur the space around her body. It was beautiful. It was chaotic and shocking and reverberated long after the Fangs had left Santa Land. It was, Caleb realized, talking so quickly that Camille almost couldn't understand him, art.

★   ★   ★

'It's perfect,' Caleb explained, Camille growing more and more interested as she allowed herself to consider the proposal. They sat in the food court and scribbled on napkins, Annie bouncing happily on Camille's knee, the incident seemingly forgotten.

'The wedding project failed because we were dealing with people accustomed to marriage and then we went right ahead and got married.'

'We should have decided not to get married at the last second,' Camille offered.

'Right, something that would surprise them, create a disorienting effect that we could harness. There was so much wasted potential.'

'And there weren't enough people to create the kind of event that we're talking about in a little wedding chapel.'

'Malls are perfect. Aside from college campuses and sporting events, where do you find this many people? And a mall has the most diverse makeup. You have a bunch of people, hypnotized by all this material consumption, stuck inside a big maze of a building that throws off their equilibrium.'

'This could be good,' Camille said.

'We need the Super 8 camera though,' Caleb said. He then pointed to the photo on the table. 'We have to capture not just the initial moment but the resulting fallout and the three-hundred-and-sixty-degree effect of the event.'

'But who's to say that she'll do it again?' Camille posited. She paused for a few moments, considering the ramifications of what they were discussing, and then said, 'And who's to say that we should make her do it again?'

'What?'

'Caleb, we placed our child in a situation that turned her into an earthquake.'

Caleb stared at Camille as if waiting for her to finish her argument. Stunned that she had to continue, she said, as patiently as she possibly could, 'She was terrified of Santa Claus. And we were the ones who put her in the fat man's lap. That seems like the makings of a long-term psychological problem.'

'Do you know how resilient kids are? When my cousin Jeffrey was three, he was chased by a pack of wild dogs and ended up falling into a well and was stuck there for three days. Now he sells vinyl siding. He's got a wife and kids. I doubt he even remembers it happened.'

'She's just a baby,' Camille said.

'She's an artist, just like us; she just doesn't know it yet.'

'She's a baby, Caleb.'

'She's a Fang,' he replied. 'That supersedes everything else.'

They both looked at Annie, who was watching them, smiling, a beautiful, glowing, movie star of a baby. Though the Fangs could not be sure, Annie seemed to be saying, 'Count me in.'

'There's another mall fifteen miles away,' Caleb said. He produced the nine dollars and change and

230

put it on the table. 'And another mall about an hour from there.'

Camille paused. She loved art, even if she wasn't always sure what it was. She loved her husband. She loved her baby. Was it so strange to put all of these things together and see what would happen? Hobart had said that kids kill art, but what did he know? They would prove him wrong. Kids could make art. Their kid was capable of making the most amazing art.

'Okay,' she said.

'It's going to be beautiful,' Caleb said, squeezing one of her hands so hard it tingled when he released his grip on her.

They stood, a family, and walked out of the mall, into the sunlight, seeking to rearrange the shape of their surroundings, to blow something up and watch all the tiny pieces resettle around them like falling snow.

CHAPTER 8

Buster sat in the barber's chair, staring at a list of haircut styles that he had never heard of, while the barber waited impatiently, scissors at the ready. 'I have no idea what these are,' Buster said, looking at the sign that held words like *brush cut, burr, high and tight, D.A., dipped mushroom, teddy boy, and flattop boogie*. 'Tell me what you want,' the barber said, 'and I'll make that happen to your head.'

'Short, I guess,' he replied. 'Not too short though.'

'Son,' the barber, nearly seventy years old, replied, 'everything is short, that's all I do. What kind of short?'

'Not too short,' Buster said, the smell of bay rum making him dizzy.

'Okay, tell me who you want to look like,' the barber then said.

'He wants to look like an intelligent man of considerable wealth,' his sister, sitting in the waiting area, offered.

The barber spun the chair thirty degrees and began to work. 'You're getting the *Ivy League*,' he said.

'I like the sound of that,' Buster said.

'You like football?' the barber asked.

'I don't dislike it,' Buster responded, 'but I don't keep up with it.'

'Well then, if you don't mind,' the man with the scissors said, 'I'll just cut the hair and we'll dispense with the conversation.'

Less than fifteen minutes later, Buster looked like an Ivy League graduate. He smoothed his hand from the top of his head to the base of his neck, the way the hair tapered to almost nothing.

'You look good,' Annie offered.

'Handsome man,' the barber said.

After the fifteen-dollar transaction, Buster and Annie made to leave, but the barber gestured toward Annie and asked, 'You want your hair cut, too?'

Annie touched her shoulder-length hair, looked at Buster, who actually did feel confident and composed with his new look, and shrugged. 'What do you suggest?' she asked.

'You got a nice face, soft features,' he said. 'I'll crop it, make you look like Jean Seberg in *Breathless*.'

'I like the sound of that,' Annie said, and sat down in the chair.

Buster watched the way the barber's hands moved quickly over his sister's head, pulling his fingers through her hair, the scissors snipping in a precise rhythm, never stopping, no desire to take stock of the situation. Buster admired the skill, loved any action that seemed to be purely muscle memory, disconnected from the brain, which was something he could hardly fathom. His brain always interrupted the actions of his body, interjecting questions and concerns. For instance, right now, his neck itching, watching his sister's hair pile up on the floor, he could not help but ask himself, 'How the hell are we going to find Mom and Dad, and why the hell are we wasting time getting our hair cut?'

The haircuts had been Annie's idea, yet another way in which they were capable people. If they looked the part, Annie reasoned, they would act accordingly. 'It's acting, Buster,' she said. 'You dress the part and pretty soon, you are that person.'

'What person?' Buster had asked.

'The person who solves mysteries and doesn't fuck things up,' she replied.

The last few days had left him wondering if perhaps it would be better if his parents really were dead, the certainty of grief, as opposed to the inescapable suspicion, fueled by his sister, that his parents were engaged in something that Buster could no longer bring himself to call *art*.

The police had been no help. The day after their parents had disappeared, Buster and Annie drove to see the sheriff in Jefferson County. The sheriff, a man in his mid-fifties, handsome and weathered, like a cop on TV, led them into his office and spoke in a calm, practiced tone that Buster believed had been perfected over years of relaying bad news to people predisposed to wild acts of grief. 'Now, I know this seems like a small outfit, but we do good work. We're good cops and we're going to get to the bottom of this,' he told the Fang children. Buster nodded, felt happy to be around someone who seemed in charge of things, but Annie was not satisfied. 'Our parents have done this to themselves, Sheriff,' she insisted, leaning so far out of her chair that she seemed in danger of falling over. 'I tried to explain this to one of your officers, but this is all a big hoax.' Buster watched the sheriff's neck muscles tense then go slack, gathering patience, and he addressed Buster and Annie, choosing to focus his gaze on Annie. 'I know about your parents,' he said. 'We investigate, you know, so we've read about your parents' little art things.'

'So you can see how something like this disappearance fits in with what they've been doing their whole lives,' Annie said.

'Ma'am, I don't think you understand what's going on here. Not everything is about art. You did not see the crime scene. You did not see the amount of blood next to the van.'

'Fake blood,' Annie interrupted. 'Oldest trick in the book.'

'Real blood,' the sheriff responded, clearly delighted to have real forensic evidence to prove Annie wrong. 'Human blood. B positive. Same as your father.' He rested his elbows on his desk and collected his thoughts. 'I understand that this is a unique event, but I fear that you're not allowing yourself to accept the possibility that this was not orchestrated by your parents. I think you're afraid to admit that this might be something more dangerous than a little art thing.'

Buster felt the sheriff's patience wearing thin and Buster tried to show that he understood, that he was not a difficult person to deal with. 'I read somewhere that denial is the first stage of grieving,' he said.

'Goddamn, Buster,' Annie hissed, turning on him, but the sheriff interjected, 'Well, I don't think you need to be grieving just yet. I'm just saying that you need to let us pursue this case as if a crime was committed, that your parents are in some form of danger.'

'They are hiding somewhere, laughing themselves silly, reading newspaper articles about their possible murder investigation. They're going to wait until you say they are dead and then they're going to show up and act like they were resurrected.'

'Okay, fine, ma'am. Let's just pursue your theory. In the state of Tennessee, if there is no body, a person isn't pronounced legally dead until seven years after the event. That's a long time to wait, don't you think?'

'You don't know Caleb and Camille Fang,' Annie said, but Buster could see the first instance of doubt on Annie's face.

'Second, where would your parents be hiding? We're tracking their credit cards. If they rent a hotel room or buy food or purchase gasoline, we'll know about it. How are they going to live without money for seven years?'

'I don't know,' Annie said. She seemed struck dumb by confusion, her mind racing to solve the puzzle of their parents' disappearance, and immediately Buster felt that he had betrayed his sister by aligning himself with the sheriff. 'They'll pay cash,' Buster offered.

The sheriff waved him off. 'And, ma'am? If your parents did decide to just disappear without a trace, as long as no crime was committed, then I really have no reason to track them down. Are you suggesting you'd prefer I stop expending any police resources to find them?'

'This is so damn stupid,' Annie said.

The sheriff paused, looked at Buster and Annie with what seemed like genuine empathy, and then he said, 'Let me just ask you this. I understand that you two have been living with your parents?'

'Yes,' Buster cut in, 'we've been temporarily living with Mom and Dad.'

'How long ago did you move back in with your parents?' the sheriff asked.

'Three or four weeks,' Annie said.

'So,' the sheriff continued, 'you two move back into your parents' house and then, a few weeks later, they disappear without telling you?'

'Okay,' Buster said.

'Maybe,' the sheriff said, 'and this is just one of many theories, but maybe they didn't want you two back at home, felt like they'd lost their privacy, and so they ran away without telling you. Maybe they aren't waiting seven years to be declared legally dead. Maybe they're just waiting until you two move back to wherever you came from, and then they'll come home. Maybe that's what's happened.'

Buster looked at Annie, thought she might start crying, but she showed no emotion. 'Don't cry, Annie,' Buster thought. They needed to be strong. The sheriff was wrong. Their parents were not dead. They were not trying to avoid Buster and Annie. They had devised a cunning and beautiful artistic statement about disappearing. They had done what they always did, made art out of confusion and strangeness. And then Buster realized he was crying. He touched his face and felt the tears that he was seemingly producing without effort. Goddamn, he was bawling, and both Annie and the sheriff were now staring at him.

'Buster?' Annie said, touching his shoulder, pulling him closer to her.

'Oh, Lord, son, I didn't mean any of what I said. I'm sorry. I don't think any of that is true. Your parents did not run away because of you. They were probably assaulted and then . . . well, son, I didn't mean any of that. I was just thinking out loud.'

'C'mon, Buster,' Annie said, helping Buster to

his feet. 'Thank you, Sheriff,' Annie continued, pushing Buster out the door of the office. As Buster, still crying, not able to stop, walked past the officers and secretaries, he felt that his outburst of emotion was not strange at all, that this was probably what they had been expecting when Buster and Annie first walked into the sheriff's office to discuss their parents' violent disappearance. This was what grief looked like, Buster realized. So he kept crying, soft hiccups interspersed with low moans, all the way to the parking lot, in the car, all the way back home.

'Okay,' Annie said, having returned from the barber, another step in reclaiming what was theirs, 'let's brainstorm.' She held a pen in one hand, a legal pad on the kitchen table. She kept absentmindedly raising her hand to her newly cropped hair before stopping short and wincing.

Buster wanted so badly to take a nap. He felt the strain of being a capable person, even if that only meant getting a haircut and reading articles about his missing parents that had begun to pop up on the Internet, was more than he could handle. Annie, however, seemed energized, her anger at her parents bringing her a superhuman level of clarity.

'We need to make a list of suspects,' Annie said. Buster did not understand. 'Someone is helping our parents disappear,' Annie said. 'If they planned on disappearing for seven years without any money, then they needed help from someone. And if we can figure out who that person is, we can find Caleb and Camille.' Buster nodded and began to think of people who might be helping their parents, people who had taken over the roles Annie and Buster had once played. But even when their careers were at their highest point, their kind of art and their decision to operate here in Tennessee had always kept them on the edge of the art world. Caleb had been orphaned when he was eighteen, his parents killed by a head-on collision with a garbage truck, leaving him the only remaining Fang, and Camille's family had disowned her when she married Caleb. During his entire childhood, he could not remember a single person coming over to the house for dinner or to play cards or to help the Fangs with their art. No one was allowed inside the house, his parents having an almost agoraphobic need to barricade themselves from the outside world. Caleb and Camille had Buster and Annie and made it clear that they needed no one else. So Buster and Annie struggled with the brainstorming, Buster wishing he had his own pen to hold just so he felt more involved in the process, and then the doorbell rang.

When Buster opened the front door of his parents' house, he found Suzanne Crosby standing on the porch with a garden salad and a tray of lasagna. 'Is this a bad time?' she asked. 'No,' Buster said, accepting the food, before he frowned and made some effort to clarify his previous statement. 'It is a bad time,' Buster said, 'but you should still come in.' Suzanne answered, 'I can't stay long anyway,' and then walked inside.

Buster wondered how long it had been since a non-Fang had entered the house. Months? Years? He had the initial desire to tell Suzanne about the momentousness of the event, and then realized how creepy it would sound and so he resisted the urge. He led Suzanne into the kitchen, where Annie was still staring at the paper, the pen held in such a way that she seemed ready to stab someone with it.

Buster stood in front of Suzanne, blocking her from Annie's view, and presented the food to his sister. 'Did you order food, Buster? What the hell? We're supposed to be brainstorming,' Annie said. 'No,' Buster said, 'Suzanne brought them for us.' He stepped aside and Suzanne waved at Annie, embarrassed. 'I just wanted to say that I was sorry to hear about your parents,' Suzanne said, refer-ring, Buster assumed, to the news stories, especially online, that had begun popping up, 'and so I thought I'd bring you guys some food. I didn't mean to impose.' Buster looked at his sister, pleading, and Annie looked at Suzanne for the first time and her posture relaxed. 'I'm sorry, Suzanne,' Annie said. 'We're still trying to deal with all this. Thank you for the food.'

'You're welcome,' Suzanne said.

'So let's eat,' Buster said, unwrapping the

aluminum foil from the lasagna, but Annie pushed away from the table, pen and pad in her hands, and said, 'I'm not hungry right now. I'll leave you two alone and get to work on this in my room. Thank you again, Suzanne.'

'I really loved you in *Date Due*,' Suzanne offered to Annie's retreating form, and Annie said, just before she shut the door to her room, 'That's nice.'

Now it was just Buster and Suzanne, the food on the table. 'I really should go,' Suzanne said. Buster stared at her short, thick fingers, her dark red fingernails, dozens of rings, cheap trinkets, that ran all the way up to her knuckles. He knew that Annie was waiting for him in her bedroom, The Case of the Missing Fangs still unsolved, but he liked having Suzanne in the house, having a guest. 'Have dinner with me,' he asked her. 'I don't want to eat alone.' She nodded and he retrieved plates and silverware, filled two glasses with ice and water. He filled his plate with food she had prepared and took careful bites, suddenly embarrassed about his missing tooth. 'This is good,' Buster said, and Suzanne thanked him.

'I read your book,' Suzanne said.

'When?' Buster asked.

'The day after you came to talk to our group,' she answered. 'I looked you up online and then I borrowed your book from Professor Kizza. I skipped class to read it in the park. It was so good.'

'Thank you,' Buster replied.

'It was so sad,' she said.

'I know. The more I wrote, the sadder it got.'

'But the end is hopeful,' she said. 'Kind of.'

They ate in silence for a few minutes.

'I really didn't know if I should come over here,' she said.

'Why?' Buster asked, having a decent idea of why, but wanting to hear her say it.

'I was pretty sure you were just hitting on me when you called me out of class.'

'Oh, god,' Buster said. 'I'm sorry about how weird that was.'

'It's okay. So, I read your book, and I read about you and your sister and your parents online, and I realized maybe you're just . . . lonely. And I'm lonely. And I really want to be a writer, and I think you could help me get better. So I want to be friends.'

'Okay,' Buster said.

'I'm nervous,' Suzanne said. 'I think I'm doing a good job of hiding it, but I don't do stuff like this.'

'Well, I'm glad you came over.'

'I'm sorry about your parents.'

'Thank you,' Buster said.

'I better go,' she said.

'Thank you,' Buster said again.

Before she left, Suzanne removed a large stack of papers from her backpack and placed them on the table. 'This is more of my writing,' she said. 'It's just fragments of stories and false starts, and it's not very good, but you said you wanted to read more of my work.'

'I do,' Buster said, looking at the sheer number of pages in front of him and feeling overwhelmed and slightly jealous. Even if it was terrible, goddamn, there was a lot of it.

'Bye,' Suzanne said, walking quickly out of the kitchen, and Buster stayed at the table, waving to her retreating form while she let herself out. He hoped, washing down the lasagna with a gulp of ice-cold water, that Suzanne was not crazy, was not overly prone to depression, and was instead a hopeful and kind, if somewhat eccentric, young woman who would find a way to make his life better. He put the rest of the food in the refrigerator and searched the kitchen drawers until he found a sharpened No. 2 pencil. There was, in his mind, a faint glimmer of something wonderful in his future. Suzanne. He looked toward his sister's room and thought of what waited for him, the mystery that would perhaps never reveal itself. He felt a renewed sense of purpose, the desire to finish what he and his sister had begun. He would find his mom and dad, solve the unsolved, and then he would be free to break off this section of his life and begin laying down a new road that would lead somewhere wonderful.

Shot, 1975
Artists: Hobart Waxman and Caleb Fang

Hobart would not stop talking about 'that goddamned fraud of an artist' Chris Burden, and Caleb began to grow worried, his body tensing for the inevitable moment when his mentor decided to do something about it. Burden, who a few years earlier had actually been shot in the arm with a rifle for a performance, had just completed his newest piece, 'Doomed,' where he lay motionless under a leaning sheet of glass, a clock ticking on the wall of the gallery space. He'd stayed like that for almost fifty hours, until some museum worker put a pitcher of water close to Burden, which caused Burden to finally get up, go get a hammer, and smash the clock. 'Motherfuckers should have left him there until he died,' Hobart said to Caleb, who shook his head. 'No, see, that was the point, Hobart. He wouldn't move until acted upon by the museum staff. They controlled the terms of the piece, but they didn't know it. It's pretty

245

interesting.' Hobart looked at Caleb as if everything he had taught his favorite pupil had been for nothing. 'It's horseshit, Caleb,' he said, waving his arms over his head, drawing the attention of the other diners in the cafeteria. 'What have I told you about anything that takes place in a controlled environment? It's not art. It's dead, inanimate. Who cares if you let somebody shoot you in a goddamn art gallery? There's no danger; there's no surprise. It has to take place in the world, around people who don't know that it's art. That's how it has to be.' Caleb nodded, embarrassed once again at having disappointed his idol. He vowed that he would do better, would burn away all his previous notions of art. He would teach himself to dislike what he actually liked, to approve of what he did not totally understand, in the hopes that he would come out the other side with something that resembled inspiration, something that would make him more famous than Chris Burden or even Hobart Waxman.

Caleb had gained Hobart's attention ten years ago, when Caleb was still a student at UC Davis, when he'd unveiled his senior project. He had wheeled a motorized contraption into the room and announced that he had built a device that would 'make anything you've ever lost or ruined instantaneously grow back.' Hobart had lost the pinkie finger on his left hand in a car accident some years back, and the students in the class instantly focused on his hand.

When Caleb flipped the switches, the machine began to hum, metal rubbing against metal. After only a few moments, smoke began to pour from the slits in the machine's frame, and Caleb ordered everyone to leave the classroom, that something was going wrong, but no one moved, they were transfixed by the simple machinery that Caleb had devised. A few seconds later, the machine exploded, a small screw embedded in Caleb's right cheek, his hands bright pink from contact burns, his lip bleeding profusely. No one else in the class had been harmed, and, once the smoke had been cleared from the room, Hobart asked Caleb a few questions. What was the art? The machine? The explosion? The refusal of the students to leave the room? The failure of Hobart's missing finger to grow back? Caleb replied, his Tennessee accent still so thick that the other students often had trouble understanding him, 'All of it. Everything. Every damned bit of it.' Hobart had smiled, nodded, and a few months later, Caleb was his assistant and closest confidant.

The problem was that Hobart hadn't produced anything noteworthy in years. 'It's the university,' he complained. 'It sucks the creativity right out of you.' Caleb, barely scraping by with his stipend from Hobart and his adjunct teaching jobs, was not so sure that a secure job, with benefits, would do anything other than help his art. 'Trust me, Caleb, art works best when it's born out of desperation. The only reason I stay here is that someone has to teach the children so that we aren't stuck with the same terrible art we've got now.' One night, Hobart asleep in his easy chair, Caleb sifted through the notes his mentor had been working on for weeks and found that they consisted of hundreds of representations of Hobart's signature, nothing more. It was at that moment, tracing his finger along the lines that made up Hobart's name, that Caleb realized that if something meaningful was going to happen, he would have to be the one to set it in motion.

That night, Camille in his bed, technically still his student, he outlined his plan. She wasn't even twenty-one, and yet he understood that she had a keen eye for what would and would not work, how art should be made. Three months previous, entirely on her own, she had developed a performance piece where she stole expensive items from department stores and pharmacies and then held a raffle for people to win those stolen goods. She then used the money to pay back the stores, usually a significantly higher amount than the actual price, and she would explain her transgressions to the manager. Not a single store had decided to press charges and one department store wondered if she might be interested in continuing the performance. He was ten years her senior, would be fired from his middling job if anyone discovered their relationship, and yet he found it impossible to stay away from her. She was poised, confident, the product of an affluent upbringing, everything that he wasn't. All they wanted to do was create something important, and they were beginning to understand that they might need each other to accomplish anything of value.

'This is a bad idea, Caleb,' she told him, smoking an expertly rolled joint with intense focus. 'It's got failure written all over it.'

'I don't think so,' he replied. It could work, and if it did, Hobart would be the most famous artist in the country. If it didn't, Caleb allowed, then Caleb would probably end up in jail for a very long time. 'Great art is difficult,' he said, hoping that hearing it said aloud would convince him that it was true.

When Caleb unveiled the plan to Hobart, explained the potential ramifications of such an ambitious project, the older man smiled, waved his hands as if to say that he needed no further explanation, and said, 'Yes.'

Camille would not let him do it alone. The day of the happening, she threatened to ruin the whole thing if she wasn't allowed to take part. Caleb, secretly, was relieved to have someone accompany him, an accomplice, another name in the police blotter to take attention away from his own. For the most part, however, he simply welcomed the idea of collaboration, for which he had suspected he was best suited, and so they left his apartment that morning hand in hand, a duffel bag slung over his shoulder.

They set up in Hobart's own office, his only window facing the courtyard, and waited. While Camille kept watch for Hobart, Caleb began the process of assembling the M1 Garand, his father's rifle from the war, a piece of his inheritance after his parents had died. His father had shown him how to operate the weapon, but Caleb found it difficult for his hands to obey the memory of his father's instructions. With each click of the gun assuming its rightful shape, he questioned the soundness of his decision, the ramifications of failure. By the time he had assembled the rifle, loaded the ammunition, tested the heft of the weapon in his hands, he was almost certain that he would not go through with it. And then Camille whispered, 'It's him,' and Caleb felt the drug-like rush of inspiration, of making something worthwhile, and he leaned out the window and aimed the rifle at his mentor.

He watched Hobart walking through the courtyard to the Arts Building, all of his weight on his toes, looking as if he would fall forward with the slightest touch. There was an ongoing sea of movement that swirled around the professor, each person, by their proximity to the event, now a part of the piece. He took a deep breath, held it, felt his body slip into a calm that he believed preceded sound decisions, and fired the rifle. Camille, standing just over his left shoulder, made a tiny yelp, bringing her hands to her mouth, and Caleb watched Hobart fall to the ground as if the bones had been instantaneously removed from his legs. A handful of onlookers, realizing what had just happened, began to run in all directions, the sound of confusion echoing through the courtyard, and Caleb quickly pulled away from the window. He was unsure of where he had hit Hobart, how significant the damage was, but he focused on the frustrating, time-consuming work of breaking down the rifle. Camille stowed the pieces of the rifle in the duffel bag and, before she left the office and returned to Caleb's apartment, where she would wait for him, they kissed. 'It was beautiful, really it was,' she said, and then walked confidently out of the office, down the hallway, and out of sight. Caleb sat on the floor, knowing that he needed to get moving, to get as far away from the event as possible, and willed his hands to stop shaking. He calmed himself with the knowledge that, whatever the outcome would be, he had made it happen. His hands had made the thing in front of him.

He managed to sneak into the hospital the next day, the radio and television still buzzing with the news of Hobart Waxman, shot in the right shoulder, tearing up quite a bit of necessary musculature, all in the name of art. In his pocket, the police had found a typewritten note that read, simply: *On September 22nd, 1975, I was shot by a friend*. The friend had not yet been located, but there were serious charges in the offing. On the local news, the police chief had been interviewed, saying, 'I understand that art is a necessary component of a civilized society, but you just cannot go around shooting people. That's going to be a problem.'

When Caleb met Hobart in his hospital room, tubes and machines and the antiseptic smell of delayed death, Hobart could not manage even the tiniest smile. 'I'm sorry,' Caleb said. He now realized how ill-equipped he had been, how horribly wrong it could have gone if not for dumb luck. Hobart managed to speak, a hissing radiator, 'It was beautiful, Caleb. I felt the impact and then I was on the ground. I could hear the chaos around me and I could see people's feet moving in all directions. And I thought I was going to pass out from the pain, from shock, but I kept telling myself to stay awake, to soak it in, that I might never see anything like this again. And it was beautiful.'

Caleb knew what would have to come next. He would turn himself in to the police, hand them his own typewritten letter, explaining the piece, signed by both Hobart and himself. There would be jail time, though less than a reasonable person would expect, thanks to the strangeness of the crime, and he would lose his job, having discharged a firearm on campus, and things would be very bad for an undetermined length of time. He knew all of this. He was prepared for it.

Hobart would recover. He would become one of the most talked-about artists of the decade. He would win an NEA grant the following year. The university, desperate to compete with UCLA, would present him with a distinguished chair. He would get to live off the infamy of this piece for years to come, and Caleb did not begrudge him this windfall. He had received an apprenticeship from Hobart, had learned the almost magical skills necessary to make the world reconfigure itself in order to fit your own desires. Hobart had taught him what was important. Art, if you loved it, was worth any amount of unhappiness and pain. If you had to hurt someone to achieve those ends, so be it. If the outcome was beautiful enough, strange enough, memorable enough, it did not matter. It was worth it.

CHAPTER 9

Annie and Buster stepped off the plane and walked into the terminal, safely arrived in San Francisco. There had been much discussion in regards to attire before they had begun their trip. Buster had suggested fedoras and rumpled suits, unfiltered cigarettes, tie clips. Annie thought perhaps matching black suits and Lone Ranger masks, crushed-up amphetamines, manicured fingernails. Buster, it seemed, wanted to be a detective and Annie wanted to be a superhero. They finally agreed that they needed something that would not draw attention to them, understated but still uniform in some way. Buster donned a white dress shirt, the sleeves rolled up past his elbows, a pair of dark blue jeans, and black leather sneakers. Annie wore a white V-neck T-shirt, dark blue jeans, and black leather flats. On their wrists, they wore the kind of watches that scuba divers swear by, heavy and solid and waterproof, synchronized and precise. In their pockets, a heavy wad of cash, pens that were half the size of regular pens – for surreptitious note-taking – a handful of Red Hots to keep them

254

sharp, and the address for Hobart Waxman, their best, their only, chance at finding their missing parents.

Their baggage claimed, rental-car key in hand, Annie and Buster began the trip to Hobart's house in Sebastopol, praying that the old man, nearing ninety, was sharp enough to give them the answers they needed, but dulled enough by age that he would be incapable of giving them a bum steer. While Buster navigated and Annie drove, they discussed the different ways to go about getting Hobart to give up their parents' location.

'Do we rush in, all angry and threatening, try to scare it out of him?' Buster asked, but Annie quickly vetoed that idea.

'We don't want to give him a heart attack. I say we play it cool, pretend we're just here to learn more about our parents, now that they have probably passed away. We get him talking and then, slowly, we shift the conversation to where they might be if they aren't really dead.'

'But if he really knows where they are,' Buster countered, 'he'll be suspicious of us showing up out of the blue. I've never met him and you haven't seen him in twenty years or so. He'll know we're after our parents. That's why we have to rough him up a little.'

'No,' Annie said emphatically. 'We cannot beat up a ninety-year-old man.'

'Rough him up,' Buster said, correcting her. 'Just get up in his business and make him see that we're not playing around.'

'Just, okay, just try to think of something else,' Annie said. 'How about this? One of us talks to him, keeps him busy. The other one pretends to use the restroom and then starts searching the house for clues. If we find something, then we've got him nailed. He'll have to play ball with us.'

'That's not bad,' Buster admitted. 'I like that.'

'Poor guy won't even know what hit him,' Annie said.

Two weeks of brainstorming and all that Annie and Buster had come up with was Hobart Waxman, all the while they were hoping for the telephone to ring and offer them even the smallest of clues. Right after the news of their parents' disappearance had been revealed, there was a startling amount of interest in the Fangs. All the major newspapers carried some mention of the suspected abduction. In the arts section of the *New York Times,* there had been a front-page article about Caleb and Camille. Though Annie and Buster were mentioned several times in the article, the siblings had wisely decided not to comment. The phone rang constantly for a few days and then it stopped as suddenly as it had begun. The news cycle had moved on, and all that was left was Annie and Buster and their belief that their parents were waiting to be discovered.

Annie checked in periodically with the police to see if any of their parents' credit cards had been used. They had not. Not a single withdrawal had

256

registered on their bank accounts. The two of them also searched through date books and random numbers on scraps of paper but found nothing that would bring them closer to their parents' current location. The gallery owner who had once represented their parents was now dead. They had no other family. All they had was Hobart.

Their parents did not think much of the history of artistic accomplishment thus far, had constantly rebuffed their children's suggestions of worthwhile art. Dada? Too silly. Mapplethorpe? Too serious. Sally Mann? Too exploitative. Hobart Waxman, however, he was the real deal. Even though Hobart had never visited the family in Tennessee, had never even met Buster, if there was another person with whom the Fangs would share the details of their grand disappearance, it would be him. It was not much to go on, but what else did they have? What else had their parents given them to work with?

Annie remembered the way her parents would breathlessly describe one of Hobart's most famous pieces, the one that had first brought him to prominence. It was called *The Uninvited Guest,* and in this piece Hobart would break into the mansions that littered the West Coast, giant structures with an army of servants. Once inside, he would live in these vast houses, dozens upon dozens of uninhabited rooms, without being detected for days, weeks, even months. He would sleep in closets, steal food from the kitchen, and watch television, taking pictures of himself to document the visit. In a few instances, he was discovered, arrested, and jailed for some period of time, but in most cases, he simply exhausted the possibilities, slipped out during the night, no sign that he had ever been there in the first place except for a card thanking the owners for their hospitality.

'It was so perfect,' Caleb had explained to Annie when she was still a child. 'He forced the art onto unsuspecting people; he made them a part of the piece, and they didn't even know it.'

'But if they didn't know what was going on,' Annie asked, confused, 'how would they appreciate it?'

'They're not supposed to appreciate it,' Caleb said, slightly disappointed with her. 'They're supposed to experience it.'

'I guess I don't understand,' Annie said.

'The simplest things are the hardest to understand,' Caleb agreed, pleased with Annie for reasons that she could not begin to know.

Hobart's house was at the end of a long, curving driveway, nothing but fields for miles in any direction. When they pulled up to the house, a small cottage with a barn-like studio in the backyard, they saw no car, no sign of anyone being home. 'This is even better,' Buster said as they idled in the car. 'We'll do a little sleuthing while he's away.' They stepped out of the car and Buster walked around the house to the studio, while Annie looked through one of the front windows. She knocked on the door and, when no one appeared, she tried the knob, which unlocked. Should she enter? Did this feel like a movie? Annie was not sure, though she did think that life was best when it felt like a movie, when, even if you hadn't read it, you knew there was a script that would tell you how things would end.

Inside, the house was spotless. There were a few pieces of expensive-looking modern furniture, a chair that Annie believed she had seen on a post-card in a museum. She walked over to a desk that held a notepad and a telephone, a small pile of mail. She looked through the mail, found no clues, and then tilted the notepad to look for indenta-tions in the paper from previous scribbling, but it was pristine. She picked up the phone, pressed *69 to find the last caller, but Hobart seemed not to have this service. The wastepaper basket was empty. That was it. Annie had exhausted the detect-ive skills that she had learned from movies.

She started to walk down the hallway, which led to more rooms, when she heard her brother say, 'Um, Annie?' She turned toward the kitchen, the sliding glass door open, and saw Buster, his posture very erect, his eyes wide open, and then she heard a voice from behind her brother. 'Don't move, honey, or I put a hole in your boyfriend here.' She then noticed Hobart Waxman, bent by age, standing behind Buster, one hand gripping the back of her brother's neck. 'So, Annie, he has a gun,' Buster said. This, Annie decided, was most certainly like a movie. She felt a panic begin to take over because she had seen this kind of movie before and it usually ended with unpleasantness, a struggle for a gun, an accidental discharge, police sirens in the background. 'Hobart?' Annie said, and the old man peeked around Buster and squinted at Annie. 'Wait,' Hobart said, relaxing his grip on Buster's neck, 'is that Annie Fang?'

'It is, Hobart,' Annie said.

'So is this Buster?' Hobart asked. Buster and Annie both nodded.

'Oh, hell,' Hobart said.

'Could you put away the gun?' Annie asked.

'I don't have a gun,' Hobart said. 'It's just my hand jammed up against his back.' He held up his hand, wriggling his fingers.

'It felt like a gun,' Buster said. 'You roughed me up a little.'

'I did no such thing,' Hobart said.

'I'm sorry, Hobart,' said Annie, as the two men walked into the living room. Hobart dismissed her embarrassment with a wave of his hand, embraced her, and then gave her a kiss. 'I haven't seen you since you were a baby,' he said. He turned to Buster and then said, 'She was the most beautiful child I'd ever seen.' Buster nodded, smiling, at Hobart, and then began to back away into the hallway. 'Well,' he said to Hobart, 'while you and Annie talk, I'm going to use the restroom.' Buster then, as he turned away from Hobart's gaze, winked at Annie and brought a finger to his lips as if to quiet her. Annie grabbed him as he passed her, pulling him back into the kitchen, her grip tight on his arm. 'Okay,' Buster said, still broadly smiling, 'I'll go later.'

'I saw you in that movie,' Hobart said, pointing at Annie. 'The one where you play a librarian who gets mixed up with skinheads.'

'*Date Due*,' Annie replied.

'That's it,' Hobart said, clapping his hands together.

'She got nominated for an Oscar for that,' Buster said.

'She should have won,' Hobart added.

'Thank you,' Annie answered, blushing.

'And this one,' Hobart said, gesturing toward Buster. 'I read your wonderful book about the couple who adopts those feral children. I'm terrible with titles.'

'*A House of Swans*,' Buster said.

'He won the Golden Quill for that,' Annie said.

'I saw you wrote another book but the reviews were not very good and so I didn't get around to reading it.'

The color went out of Buster's face, but he recovered, smiling, and shrugged. 'You didn't miss much,' he replied.

'It's even better than the first book,' Annie offered.

'Well, now that I've finally met you, I'll read it,' Hobart said.

'You're probably wondering why we're here,' Annie said, getting things back on track.

'I heard about your parents, of course, so I imagine you want to talk to me about them,' Hobart said.

Buster and Annie nodded.

'What would you like to know?' he asked them.

'Where are they?' Annie said.

'What?' Hobart asked, confused, the smile fading from his face.

'Where are our parents?' the Fang children asked in unison, inching closer to Hobart.

Hobart sighed deeply and then pointed toward the living room and said, 'Let's sit down and talk.'

Hobart took nearly five minutes to find a comfortable sitting position on his George Nelson–designed Kangaroo chair. Buster and Annie sat side by side opposite Hobart on a black leather sling sofa, feeling as though they were waiting for a bus that was very, very late.

'I have no idea where your parents are,' Hobart told Annie and Buster.

'We don't believe you, Hobart,' Annie replied.

'If they didn't tell you two what they're up to, what in the world makes you think that they would tell me?' he asked.

'They love you,' Annie said, the strange tremor of jealousy creeping into her voice. 'You were their mentor. They would want to tell you, the one person who would respect their artistic principles enough to never tell anyone else.'

'You two have no idea what you're talking about,' Hobart said, squinting in a way that suggested he was staring at the visible waves of craziness that were emanating from Annie and Buster. 'Your parents hated me.'

'No they don't,' Buster said, keeping his parents alive in the present tense. 'They had some kind of anxiety of influence issues with you maybe, but you were the only artist they ever respected.'

'I haven't seen or talked to them in at least ten years,' Hobart said, his face slowly showing signs of anger, his bald head turning the earliest shade of sunburn. 'I mean, for crying out loud, Buster, I've never even met you before, their only son.'

'We don't believe you,' Annie said once again. Buster leaned slightly, perhaps an inch or two, away from Annie, just enough that she noticed the separation, and then he said, 'I kind of believe him.'

'No,' Annie said, leaning toward Buster so that their shoulders were once again touching. 'We do not believe you.'

'Well, unless you want to try and beat it out of me, and I've seen what kind of a fight this one puts up,' Hobart said, pointing at Buster, 'I don't think we have anything else to talk about.'

Annie felt her hands snap into fists, even though she was telling herself, 'Stay calm, stay calm, calm down,' and then she felt Buster's own hand reach into her fist and slowly uncurl her fingers until they were straight and steady. 'I'm sorry,' Annie said. 'We're just trying to understand what's going on and I don't think either one of us is very good at finding things out on our own.'

'I am particularly bad at it,' Buster admitted.

'We don't know what to do,' Annie continued.

Hobart remained silent, his right hand worrying the collar of his shirt, and Annie felt the pinprick of embarrassment for having failed in front of an audience. And not only was she no closer to finding her parents, she had stormed into Hobart's life and upset the carefully constructed solitude of his final years. The mere mention of Caleb and Camille Fang seemed to have tripped something in Hobart's memory that had been, until now, successfully hidden from introspection. Annie wanted to run out of the house, jump into the car, and drive away from this scene, but she found it impossible to move, the weight of her failure keeping her anchored to the sofa.

'Can I offer you a little advice?' Hobart asked them, breaking the silence. When Annie and Buster nodded, he continued, 'Stop looking for them.'

'What?' Annie said.

'There are two options. The first is that they really are dead, that something awful happened to them, in which case, this wild-goose chase is merely prolonging the grieving that follows any death.'

'Hobart,' Annie interrupted. 'Do you really think Caleb and Camille are dead?'

Hobart paused, carefully choosing his response. Annie and Buster waited, feeling that the fate of their parents rested on his answer. 'I don't,' Hobart admitted. 'I'll agree with you on that much. Your parents have such a force of will, a belief in what should and should not be, that I cannot imagine a scenario where their death is something as random and as tacky as a rest-stop murder. Crashing to earth in a homemade flying machine at the air show of a state fair. I can see that. Throwing themselves into the tiger attraction at a zoo during a school field trip. Sure, of course. Setting themselves on fire in the middle of the Mall of America. Oh, yes.'

'So they're out there somewhere,' Annie said.

'That brings me to your second option.'

'What is it?' Buster asked.

'You let them stay missing,' Hobart continued. 'They are alive, and they have constructed this bizarre little stunt and they didn't even tell their son and daughter about it. They want you to think, obviously, that they really are dead. So do it.'

Annie looked over at Buster, who would not meet her gaze. The thought of giving up seemed as impossible as the prospect of actually finding her parents. But she kept imagining that moment, when she ruined what her parents had made, the looks of disbelief on their faces, and it made her heart beat faster.

'I used to tell all my students, not just Caleb and Camille, but any artist that showed some sliver of promise, that they had to devote themselves to their work. They had to remove all obstructions to making the fantastic thing that needed to exist. I would tell them that *kids kill art.*'

Annie and Buster both winced at the phrase, one they had heard their father recite any time the two of them had complicated one of the Fang projects.

'And I meant it,' Hobart continued. 'It's why I never married, never got involved with anyone at all. And your parents realized that they would have to find some way to overcome this theory of mine, some construction that would disprove it. So they intertwined their family and their art so tightly that it was impossible to untangle it. They made you two into their art. It was amazing, really. And then time passed, and maybe it's because I never really built on my earlier successes, perhaps I was just jealous of them, but I found it was impossible for me to see any Fang art without feeling this horrible sense of dread, that something irreparable was being done to the two of you. And Caleb understood this, my reserved judgments about their work; so pretty soon he stopped writing to me, cut off all communication, and kept right on with their vision. Your parents were right. They beat me by completely inverting my theory. Kids don't kill art. Art kills kids.'

Annie felt something electric travel up and down

her body. Hobart looked at her as if he felt responsible for their entire lives, a sadness she could not entirely comprehend.

'That's not fair,' Annie said, unable to stop herself from siding with her parents, no matter how much she might agree with Hobart. She did not want Hobart's pity or perhaps she didn't want it to come so easily.

'We're still alive,' Buster added, and Hobart held up his hands in surrender.

'Yes, that's true,' Hobart said, looking sadly at the two of them.

'So we just let them disappear?' Annie asked. 'We let them get away with it?'

'You're thinking about this in a way that makes you angry at your parents for not including you in this, for letting you think that they really are dead.'

'How else can we think about it?' Buster asked.

'That maybe your parents finally miscalculated,' Hobart said. 'They have, however inadvertently, untangled the threads of family and art. You two are free.'

Neither Annie nor Buster made the slightest sign of movement. Annie waited for Hobart to continue, still struggling to accept how much sense he was making.

'You don't have to follow your parents all over the country, hiding in plain sight, putting your lives on hold until their latest action can be revealed to the world. They forgot to keep you tied to them, and now you don't have to follow them. Does that not seem like a good thing?'

'It's hard to think like that,' Annie admitted.

'I imagine that's true,' Hobart said, 'after a lifetime of living otherwise.'

'I don't know if I want to think like that,' Buster said.

'What do you two really want if you do find your parents? What would be achieved?'

Annie, who had surprisingly never spent a single session with a psychiatrist, began to get the intense feeling that she was in therapy. She did not care for it in the least. And there went her fingers, long and slender, transforming themselves once again into tiny sledgehammer fists. She struggled for an answer to Hobart's question and, no acceptable reply forthcoming, she leaned back against the sofa, stumped. And then Buster said, 'We want to find them and show them that they can't do whatever they want, just because they think it's beautiful.'

'That is not worth the effort,' Hobart replied. 'I'm sorry, Buster, Annie, but even if you showed them, I don't think they would learn anything from it. Your parents, like many artists, are incapable of acknowledging this fact. Caleb and Camille have spent most of their lives assuring themselves that art is all that really matters.'

'Can you at least think of anyone who could help us?' Annie said, still struggling to maintain the pose of a capable person, of following their plan of action, regardless of whether or not it made sense any longer.

'Not a single person. Their agent, as I'm sure you know, passed away some time ago and they never bothered to look for other representation. They had very few friends, if any, in the art world; certainly no one else was doing the kind of things that they were. There was that man who wrote the book about your family, but I cannot imagine, under any circumstances, your parents communicating with him.'

The author he was talking about was Alexander Share, an art critic who had written a critical study of the Fangs' work, *Once Bitten: An Overview of the Perplexing Art of Caleb and Camille Fang*. He had convinced Caleb and Camille to agree to several long interviews over the phone and in person; Buster and Annie were not allowed to talk to him. As it became clear that Share had some real reservations about their work, Caleb and Camille shut off communication with him and tried to get the publisher to kill the book, but in the end it didn't matter. It was published, and it didn't amount to much; people had already, long before Alexander Share tried to make sense of the Fangs' work, decided the value of this kind of art. 'Criticism is like dissecting a dead frog,' Caleb said when the book was published. 'They're examining all the guts and shit and organs, when the thing that really matters, whatever it was that animated the body, has long since left. It does nothing for art.' When Annie and Buster asked why their parents had agreed to talk to Share in the first place, their mother said, 'If you don't get hung up on finding anything of worth, it's kind of fun to dig around in blood and guts for a little while.'

Hobart went on down the list of possible accomplices, no one of note. 'There were two artists who were pretty infatuated with all of you. The first one, Donald something-or-other, was basically a vandal, doing violent things to existing works of art. He was a supremely ignorant individual, but he was in awe of your parents.'

'Where is he?' Annie asked.

'He's dead,' Hobart replied. 'He fell off some sculpture he was trying to disassemble and cracked his head open.'

'Who's the other person?' Annie asked, now finding herself simply amazed at learning something new, however trivial, about her parents.

'There was a woman, a former student of mine, actually, who managed to get close to your parents. She was young and beautiful and had the potential to make things complicated.' He paused to see if they understood his meaning. Annie kept her face impassive, and Hobart said, 'Sex is what I was implying there. But she faded away after a while, once it was apparent that your parents had no interest in anything except making art. I believe I read in an alumni newsletter quite some time ago that she got married, had children, turned out to be normal. Usually, you hate when that happens, but it was the best thing for her. Conventional lives are the perfect refuge if you are a terrible artist.'

Annie remembered very clearly a surprisingly young woman who helped her parents with one of their earlier pieces. Her name was Bonnie, or perhaps Betty. She had acted as if Buster and Annie did not exist, could not acknowledge anyone but the two artists she hoped to impress. Often those who were infatuated with Caleb and Camille seemed compelled to pretend that Buster and Annie were invisible, in order to maintain the proper level of focus that her parents demanded. This was, to Annie at least, understandable.

'Anyone else?' she asked Hobart. He shook his head. It was getting late, the sky slowly, as if by magic, dimming. The old man was struggling to sit upright, his shoulders slumped and hands trembling so softly it seemed like he was holding a tiny, nervous animal in each cupped hand. 'No one ever got close to Caleb and Camille,' he finally said. 'It was just the four of you in your own little world. No one could compete with that.' The way that Hobart said this last sentence, Annie wasn't sure if he thought this was a good or bad thing. Did he think their parents had loved them or held them hostage? She was afraid to ask.

'We should leave you alone,' Annie said. 'We've bothered you enough, I think.'

'Don't leave,' Hobart said, suddenly springing

up. 'It's late. You can stay here tonight. I'll make dinner.'

Annie shook her head. Buster nudged her with his elbow but she continued to decline. 'We have to get going.'

'We haven't even had a chance to talk about my work,' Hobart said, his obvious desperation causing his body to expand, to take up enough space to make Annie and Buster feel cornered.

'We have a plane to catch,' Annie said, though they had no tickets for their return trip, no place to stay. 'Thank you for your help.'

'I didn't do a goddamn thing,' he replied, shrugging. 'I just gave you some advice that I don't think you're going to follow.'

Hobart took Annie in his arms, kissed her, and then shook Buster's hand.

'You two are great artists,' Hobart said as the two siblings walked back to their rental car. 'You can separate reality from art. A lot of us can't do that.'

'Good-bye, Hobart,' Annie said as she started the car.

'Come back sometime,' he told them.

Annie pressed her foot gently on the gas pedal and the car pulled slowly down the driveway. Through the rearview mirror, she watched Hobart shuffle back into the house, shut the door, and then the entire house went dark.

As they drove back to San Francisco, Buster asked what they were going to do next. Their options seemed so limited that it was impossible to ignore the feeling of failure. Where else could they go but back home? They had no leads, the few possibilities having closed shut after their talk with Hobart. Annie could not imagine how to continue searching. Buster was now asleep in the passenger seat, softly snoring. She accelerated, her headlights cutting through the darkness in front of her, and she knew there was nothing left to do. She could not shake the feeling that this was a contest, her parents competing against her and Buster. And, following this line of thinking, she could not help but acknowledge that her parents had won. Her parents were gone, for an indeterminate amount of time, possibly forever, and the only thing she could think to do was to go back to their house.

Too late to catch any flights, Annie parked the car in the long-term lot and reclined her seat. Just as she closed her eyes, Buster said, still half-asleep, 'What are we doing?'

'We'll go back to Tennessee in the morning,' she replied.

'What about Mom and Dad?' he asked.

'Maybe Hobart is right,' she said, finally giving voice to what she had been considering for the past few hours. 'It might be possible that they mistakenly put this distance between us without considering that we would forget about them. Maybe we're in the position of power now.' It was, in the game she had decided existed between her and Buster and her parents, the only way she could now imagine winning, to simply end the game on their own terms.

'Maybe,' Buster said, without conviction, and, before Annie could answer, he was asleep again. Annie closed her eyes, the car a thin shell that protected them from the rest of the world. She slept as soundly as she had in weeks, locked with her brother inside an object that had come to a complete and total stop.

Annie and Buster checked with the police almost daily for updates as to their parents' whereabouts, but there was still no activity on their credit cards, no reports of any strange activity from people matching their descriptions. 'The longer it takes, the harder it is,' the sheriff told them, and they fully understood what he meant.

Annie kept the house clean, prepared their meals, went on daily three-mile runs, and watched at least one old movie on the VCR, while Buster spent nearly the entire day in his room, at work on something so necessary to him that he could not explain it to Annie. She had walked into his room one time when he was writing and she saw a piece of paper, which read: *We are fugitives. We are the fugitives. We live at the edges. We live on the edge. The law is hungry for us. The law is skinny with hunger for us. A town filled with gold-seekers. A shantytown filled with gold-seekers. We live on the edge, a shantytown filled with gold-seekers. We are fugitives and the law is skinny with hunger for us. We=? The edge=?*

'Buster,' she asked, pointing at the scribbled words, 'what is this?' He shook his head. 'I'm not sure,' he said, 'but I'm going to find out.' She left him to bang away on his computer, the violent sound of his hands building something out of nothing. She was slightly jealous of how easily he could carry his art around with him. Unlike Buster, she needed screenwriters like Daniel to give her lines and directors like Freeman to tell her how to say them, and actors like Minda with whom to interact. She had always thought that Buster's solitude, writing all alone in a tiny room, had helped to undo him, but now she thought that making something with no one else's interference might be interesting. And yet it was impossible for her to imagine anything other than acting, the way she took the lines and made them believable, the way she processed direction and made the action possible, the way she looked at another actor and convinced herself that she loved them. She sat in her room, watching a movie where an actress, beautiful and predatory, stood under a streetlight, a handkerchief in her mouth, having transformed from a panther back into a woman. Annie wished she had been an actress in those days, when things were bizarre and yet no one seemed to notice or care.

Annie had only checked her e-mail once since fleeing L.A. There had been an e-mail from Daniel, which she had deleted without reading. There had been an e-mail from her agent, which had the subject line of *Rethinking our business rela-tionship*. She had deleted that without reading it. There had been nothing else but spam.

When she logged on again, she saw that she had a new message from Lucy Wayne, her director from *Date Due*. Annie had not talked to her in quite some time, had been so embarrassed by Freeman's movie and the subsequent hoopla over her personal life that she avoided contact with Lucy, afraid of being told that she had proven to be a disappointment. The subject line read: *News*. Annie clicked on the message and it read:

Hey Annie,

I have tried to call you about a hundred times. Your agent said you had gone AWOL, but he gave me your e-mail to try and reach you. I've been thinking about you, and, after I heard about your parents, I got worried. I hope you are okay, though I can't imagine that you are in a good place right now. I know how complicated your rela-tionship was with Caleb and Camille and, though we haven't talked in a while, I'd love to see you again.

The main reason I'm writing is that I've finished the screenplay for my next film, and I've been thinking about you a lot. This character, this woman I've been writing about for the past year and a half, is someone that I couldn't picture in my head without thinking of you. I guess, in a lot of ways, I wrote this character with you in mind. And I don't know what your situation is right now, how interested you are in acting, but I think you'd be perfect for the part. I'm lining up financing, though after Paramount basically killed my last movie with all their bullshit, I think I'll be going the independent route again. So there won't be much money, but I hope you'll consider it. I've attached it so you can read it if you'd like, and I'd love to get your thoughts on it and I would love it even more if the two of us could team up again. I would like to get that same feeling of excitement that I had when I was doing *Date Due,* and you played a huge role in that happening.

Write me if you can,
Lucy Wayne

Before writing and directing *Date Due,* Lucy had been a conceptual artist of some renown in the Chicago art scene, her own parents having been minimally famous photographers. Lucy would cross-stitch blankets with black thread to make strange phrases such as: *This Is the Best I Could Do for You* and *Run to the Ocean and Back Again, Barefoot* and *Clap Your Hands and Make Rain.* She would then hand out these blankets to the city's homeless, and soon Chicago was filled with these blanket-sized billboards. Lucy would then wander the city with a video camera in search of her own handiwork, the results of which would be shown at galleries. She started adding narrative, converting some of the material into several short films that she showed at various film festivals, which finally brought her fully into moviemaking. Annie remembered how awed Lucy had been when she found out that Annie was Child A. 'I was so in love with your parents,' Lucy told her. 'I wanted to be their kid.' Annie, still trying at that point to escape any connection to the Fang legacy, had only said, 'They would have torn you to pieces.'

Lucy's new script, *Favor Fire*, was about a woman who becomes a caretaker for a couple in Western Canada whose children periodically catch fire. The children are not harmed by their own combustion, but it is the woman's job to keep the house from burning down, to contain the flames. The matriarch and patriarch of the family, wealthy and intellectual and endlessly cruel, rule over the mansion and seek to find fault with everything the caretaker does. The four children, ranging in age from six to fifteen, are sweet but made lonely by their circumstances, their parents' obvious distaste for their affliction, and so they rely on the woman for entertainment and news from the outside world. Over time, as the woman grows more and more capable with her responsibilities, she develops an obsession with fire, matches, and sparks, and has to resist the temptation to goad the children into catching fire. The house – how could it not – burns to the ground at the end of the movie, the children swept up by the woman, leaving the parents behind, driving out of British Columbia and into the pristine cold of the Yukon.

Annie could not help but be moved by the strange emotions in the script, the unpleasant ways in which the woman finds herself giving in to the danger of this family. The movie, which would be filmed almost entirely in a single location, the mansion, had a claustrophobic feel, the constant threat of the fires, and she could see how the making of the movie would be difficult and some-what thrilling if it all managed to come together. Like *Date Due,* it was about someone who gives in to her worst impulses and yet somehow manages to survive the ordeal. She wondered if this was how Lucy saw her, a woman incapable of being harmed by the terrible choices she would always make. She minimized the document and wrote an e-mail to Lucy that read, simply: 'I love it. I'm in.'

Once she sent the e-mail, she allowed herself a vision of the future that did not include searching for her parents. And then, because she realized that she could, she imagined a future where her parents were already found. And then, no one to prevent this unfounded optimism, she imagined a future where her parents had never existed in the first place. Once she allowed herself this miracle, as soon as it had taken shape, it immediately burned up in the atmosphere, turned to vapor, as Annie realized that, without her parents, there would be no way into the world for her. She could not, despite every attempt to do so, figure out a way that she could arrive ahead of her parents, to outpace them. It would have to be her parents, young and still tender, entirely unaware that their children, Annie and Buster, were moving, inexorably, toward them, waiting to be named.

Lights, Camera, Action, 1985
Artists: Caleb and Camille Fang

Bonnie watched the Fangs pacing around the studio, none of them acknowledging the others' presence. They simply waited for whatever would come next. Their faces were so impassive that it seemed to Bonnie that they were not human, that they were robots programmed to perform their task without deviation, no matter how dire the circumstances, despite the inevitable disorder that would ensue. Finally, everything perfectly arranged, Caleb arose from his director's chair and stood behind the cameraman. 'Action!' he called. And now Bonnie, sweating through her nurse's outfit, trying so hard to keep her hands from shaking, wondered how she was going to keep up with this family, how she could possibly help them make something beautiful.

She had learned about the Fangs earlier that year, when she had taken Hobart Waxman's *Introduction to Meaningful Art* class. In the class, they had studied one of the earliest works by the Fangs, where Caleb Fang had taped a series of home-made, flare-like devices to his back and, while holding his nine-month-old son in the middle of a crowded mall, caught fire, the flame shooting from underneath his coat and smoke issuing from the legs of his pants, while he continued to walk through the mall with the baby in his arms. The whole event was captured on video by Camille, who was standing on the second level of the mall, hanging over the railing to focus on the unemotional faces of both Caleb and, even more amazingly, the baby, as the other shoppers tried to make sense of the event unfolding before them. 'This,' Hobart had told the class, 'is so rudimentary, so unen-cumbered by the traditions that have come before it, that it almost strains the notion of what consti-tutes art. The Fangs simply throw their own bodies into a space as if they were hand grenades and wait for the disruption to occur. They have no expectations other than to cause unrest. It is, if you are one of the few to witness it firsthand, deeply unsettling because of how little the Fangs seem to care about the psychic and sometimes physical pain that accompanies their perform-ances.' Bonnie had watched the way Caleb Fang, obviously suffering some degree of burns on his body, walked so steadily through the mall that it felt to Bonnie as if she was being hypnotized by his movements. Caleb Fang walked, on fire, and shielded his own son from the flames. It felt so unnecessary and yet so arresting that Bonnie immediately fell in love, not with art but with the Fangs.

She had received a mailing address for the Fangs from Hobart Waxman, after some degree of flirtation, her considerable beauty something she was only recently learning to utilize for her own benefit. She proceeded to write Caleb and Camille letter after letter, hoping for a response, though not knowing what she would want them to say. She told them of her own artistic desire, which was merely to be yet another component of the performances that the Fangs enacted.

There was no response from the Fangs, and Bonnie could not blame them. They had developed something perfect and why would they seek to disrupt that process by including another person, especially one with no vision of her own? She had tried for months now to think of her own performance, some unique revelation of the absurdity of life, but she had no capacity for new ideas. She could see an existing artwork and understand why it was or was not successful. But she could not take that knowledge and arrange it into something wholly original, or even a reinterpretation of that existing piece. She was, as Hobart had explained to her, as kindly as possible, simply a critic.

She watched a few other videos of the Fangs that Hobart had loaned her, the quality so grainy and inexpertly framed that it was sometimes difficult to immediately ascertain what had just happened. If only the Fangs were able to stage their events with actual lighting, a cameraman who knew what he was doing, multiple cameras to pick up all the nuances of the happening. If only the Fangs could make their art as if they were making movies, but Bonnie realized this was impossible, that you would lose the most important aspect of the performance if you were to draw attention to the fact that something was about to happen that needed to be documented.

And then she realized what she could offer the Fangs, how she could improve their work, how she could make herself essential. They could utilize the equipment of an actual film, all the people who go into making a movie pleasing to the eye, but they could still maintain the spontaneity that was so crucial to their art. It was so perfect that, for the first time, Bonnie allowed herself the small hope that she might actually be an artist after all.

Caleb had flown to Los Angeles to work alongside Bonnie while Camille and the children prepared themselves for their eventual roles. When she had met him at the airport, in her tiniest dress, her hair teased in such a way that it seemed she had fallen from a great height and landed right at Caleb's feet, he merely shook her hand and then began to outline all the things he would need in order to make his vision a reality. Bonnie struggled to find her notepad in her purse and followed at Caleb's heels as she jotted down the rapid-fire instructions that he expected her to follow exactly to his specifications. 'I have to believe that you are a capable woman,' he told her when they were finally seated in her car, driving through the city streets. 'My family is nothing if not capable, and so I will proceed with the understanding that you can do what I ask you to do.' Bonnie nodded. 'I will do whatever you want, Caleb,' she said. 'Whatever you ask me to do, I will make sure that it happens.' Caleb smiled and drummed his fingers against his thigh. 'This could be quite special, Bonnie,' he said. 'A new chapter for the Fang family.' Though he had not said it explicitly, Bonnie allowed herself to believe that she was included as part of the family.

They worked quickly to rent cameras, lights, a small studio space for one week. They hired a crew to work for three days on a short film, promising them cash up front. They hired a documentary crew to film the making of the movie. Caleb worked on a script for the film while Bonnie, having skipped classes for the past two weeks, arrived every morning at Caleb's hotel room to update him on how things were progressing. 'I want you to be in the movie,' he told her, and Bonnie felt like maybe the two of them would have sex, but Caleb never once acknowledged any physical attraction to her. He was focused on only one thing, making something amazing, and this made Bonnie want to fuck him even more.

Finally, the rest of the Fang family arrived. The children, Annie and Buster, were so emotionless that Bonnie found it difficult to be around them. Though they were eight and six years old, they seemed like tiny adults and Bonnie, who felt nothing like an adult, simply found it easier to avoid them altogether. They devised complicated games that Bonnie could not understand and would play them for hours, never once acknowledging the activity in the room until finally one of their parents would call for them and the children would immediately stop their game and walk quickly to Caleb and Camille. And Camille, well, that was complicated for Bonnie. She was very warm, constantly offering words of encouragement, and eventually Bonnie began to wonder if perhaps she could sleep with Camille instead of Caleb; she found that she no longer cared how she gained entry into the family. She just wanted to be one of them.

Finally, cameras rolling, Bonnie, who was playing the nurse, led the children into the room. Camille, playing the bedridden mother of the children, weakly propped herself up and called for the children to come closer. 'Let me see my beautiful children,' she said, and, before she had even finished the line, Caleb called out, 'Cut!' The crew worked to reset the shot and Caleb said, 'Okay, Jane, I need a little more emotion from you. You haven't seen your children in months and now here they are. Does that make sense?'

Camille nodded. 'I can do that,' she said.

Lights, camera, action.

Bonnie once again led the children into the room and Camille leaned forward and said, 'Let me see my beautiful children!'

'Cut,' Caleb shouted. 'Okay, that's maybe a little too much emotion. You are dying of cancer. So somewhere in between.'

'I got it,' Camille replied, flashing a thumbs-up sign.

Lights, camera, action.

Bonnie led the children into the room, and Caleb shouted, 'Cut!' As the regular crew scrambled around the set, the documentary crew focused on Caleb as he said, 'Okay, Bonnie, I think you're bringing those kids in a little too quickly. Their mom is dying; she's in a bad way. You're going to be hesitant to show them what has happened to their mother.'

Bonnie nodded, too nervous to speak.

Lights, camera, action.

Bonnie led the children into the room and Camille leaned forward and said, 'Let me see my beautiful children,' and Caleb shouted, 'Cut!' He pressed his index finger against his forehead, thinking, and then said, 'Jane, let's try that line without the word *beautiful*, okay? I think maybe that's laying it on a bit thick.' Camille gave the director another thumbs-up sign.

Lights, camera, action.

Bonnie led the children into the room and Camille leaned forward and said, 'Let me see my chil – ' and Caleb shouted, 'No, okay, cut. Okay, sorry, Jane, but we do need that *beautiful* in there. Sorry.'

Lights, camera, action.

Bonnie led the children into the room and Caleb shouted, 'Cut! Okay, you kids are walking a little strangely. You're not moving your arms. It's weird. Can you move your arms for me?' Buster and Annie nodded.

Lights, camera, action.

Bonnie led the children into the room and Camille leaned forward and said, 'Let me see my beautiful children,' and Caleb said, 'Cut! No, wait, I'm sorry. Did we decide to go back to the *beautiful children* line?' Camille smiled patiently and said, 'Yes, we did. *Beautiful children* is what you wanted.'

'Okay,' Caleb said, holding up his hands in apology. 'We'll get it on the next take.'

Lights, camera, action.

Bonnie led the children into the room and Camille leaned forward, and Caleb yelled, 'Cut! Okay, Jane, you're leaning a little too far forward. It looks desperate. I need a slow, gradual movement toward the children. The beautiful children.' Camille's smile became a little tighter, and she said, 'Maybe you can show me how you want me to move,' but Caleb waved her off. 'I'll know it when I see it,' he said.

Lights, camera, action.

Bonnie led the children into the room and Camille leaned forward and said, 'Let me see my beautiful children,' and Caleb, of course, yelled, 'Cut! Okay, you're not emphasizing the word *me* in that line. Let *me* see my beautiful children. You haven't seen them in months.' Camille looked confused but nodded anyway. 'I'll give it a shot,' she said.

'I've got a good feeling about this take,' Caleb shouted.

Three hours later, they did not have a single take that met with Caleb's approval. While he focused most of his anger on Camille, the dying woman in the bed whose voice was nearly hoarse from saying the same line over and over again, he did not hesitate to lecture Buster and Annie at length as to the obvious mistakes they were making in their nonspeaking roles. The children had begun to cry in between takes, and Caleb would say, 'Use that. Use that emotion in the next take.' Camille had flipped him the bird from her bed. 'Fuck you,' she said. 'Action!' he shouted.

After a while, he found fault with the lighting, the camerawork, the boom mike operator. 'Listen, guy,' one of the crew said, 'just tell us exactly what you want before we shoot, and we'll give it to you.' Caleb looked toward the documentary camera and shook his head in disbelief. 'I don't know what I want until I see it,' he said. The crew member replied, 'Well, that's not how it works.' Caleb snorted. 'Well, that is how I work, and I have dozens of prestigious awards from various film festivals to back me up.'

Lights, camera, action.

Bonnie led the children into the room and Camille leaned forward and said, 'Let me see my beautiful children.' Caleb said nothing, arms crossed, and so Bonnie guided the children to the foot of the bed so that Camille could brush her hand across Buster's face. 'Cut!' Caleb shouted. 'I want you to touch the girl's face before you touch the boy's.' Camille began to slam her fists into her pillow. 'What is wrong with you?' she shouted.

'I just want it to be perfect,' Caleb replied.

Buster and Annie began to sob loudly and Camille pulled the children into her arms. Bonnie could not tell if this was real or part of the performance. One of the crew members was trying to reason with Caleb and placed a conciliatory hand on the director's shoulder, which caused Caleb to slap the man's hand away. 'You get your hands off of me,' Caleb shouted. He gestured toward the documentary crew and said, 'Keep filming, this is the process of a genius and you need to capture all of it.' Right after he said this, Caleb grabbed the script from his chair and began to rip it into tiny pieces. 'Okay,' he said, 'no more script. We'll totally improvise this thing.' The film crew was simply standing around the set, staring at Caleb. 'Lights, camera, action,' Caleb shouted, but no one moved. He pushed the cameraman toward the camera and that's when one of the crew rushed Caleb and put him in a headlock. Another man grabbed Caleb's legs to keep him from kicking anyone, and they dragged him off the set. Five minutes later, Caleb stormed back onto the set and began to swing the director's chair like a weapon. He then grabbed the camera from the documentary film crew and summarily fired all of them. He shouted, 'That's a wrap,' and the crew quickly shuffled off the set, screaming obscenities at Caleb as they passed by. Once the set was totally empty except for the Fangs and Bonnie, the children immediately ceased crying and began to smile. Camille started to laugh and then clapped her hands slowly as Caleb took a deep bow. His nose was bleeding and his shirt was ripped so badly it was hanging off his body, but he shrugged and then said to his family, 'What do you think?' Camille nodded and replied, 'Absolutely beautiful.' Bonnie could not move, felt as if she was suffering from shock, and it wasn't until nearly ten minutes had passed that Caleb noticed that Bonnie was crying, stuttering sobs that turned into hiccups. 'Bonnie,' he said. 'You did great. You did just fine.' He motioned toward the rest of the family and they stood around Bonnie and placed their hands on her shoulders, rubbing her back. 'I was so scared,' Bonnie said. 'That's good,' Camille said. 'That's exactly how you should feel.'

They collected the equipment, retrieved every reel of film so they could edit it together later. Once things were cleared up, Caleb suggested that they go out to celebrate, and the children began to cheer. 'I think I should probably go back home,' Bonnie said. 'The hard work is over,' Caleb told her. 'Now we can relax and talk about how it went.' Bonnie could not imagine anything she would want to do less, to relive the strangeness of the past few hours. 'I don't think I can,' she said. 'I don't think I can do what you do. I'm not a real artist.'

Camille touched Bonnie's arm and said, 'It's always hard the first time. There are all these emotions and you don't know which ones to trust. You know it's not real but it feels so real that you can't help but feel uneasy. It goes away, trust me.' Bonnie shook her head. 'I can't do it,' she said. 'You have real promise, Bonnie,' Caleb said. 'You are going to be something special, I can tell. You're going to make something really bizarre and the four of us will be so happy to see it.' The entire family encircled Bonnie, hugging her until she felt like she was going to scream. And then the Fangs bounded away, their bodies electric with the pleasure of having created something worthwhile, and Bonnie watched as they disappeared down the street, a family bound so tightly they could not be separated.

CHAPTER 10

Inside the house, Buster could not shake the feeling that he and his sister were being watched. By whom he could not say. Or, rather, he could say it: Caleb and Camille. One night, Buster removed each of the air vents, looked under all the lampshades, ran his fingers lightly over the fibers of the carpet in order to check for listening devices. Annie walked into his room while he was on the floor, his fingers moving deftly over the carpet as if he was reading something in Braille. 'What are you doing, Buster?' she asked. He looked up, his ears rushing with blood, a humming in his head, and replied, 'I lost something.' 'What?' she asked, and he answered, his gaze returning to the carpet, 'I don't know.'

There was a growing certainty in Buster's heart that he and Annie were a crucial part of the happening that their parents had devised. His parents had disappeared and now it was up to Annie and Buster to decode the series of actions that would bring their parents back from the missing world, to complete the piece. How often had their parents sent them into the wilderness of a mall or public park or private party and asked them only to be prepared, to open themselves up to the infinite possibilities that their parents, god-like, would create? And how often had Buster and Annie, their reflexes so attuned to the chaos that rumbled just beneath the surface of every living and nonliving thing, been able, once the event began, to respond in just the right way to push everything into a better – stranger – place?

His fear was that he would tell Annie all of his suspicions, that they were supposed to keep looking for their parents, and she would refuse. It was a delicate thing, wanting something that might not be the same as what his sister wanted. He was unaccustomed to the position he was in, and so he continued to press his ear against the walls of the house, listening for the sound of his parents' voices.

'Have you tried reaching out to them spiritually?' Suzanne asked him as she sat in his car, the motor running, a copy of one of her stories in his hands. Buster had been meeting with her every couple of days since he had returned to Tennessee, waiting in the parking lot of the Sonic Drive-In, where she worked nights as a car hop. During her breaks, she would fly across the parking lot on her roller skates, slip into the car, the wheels on her skates still rolling, and they would discuss her stories and how to fix them. He ate the food that she brought him and they would sit, their shoulders nearly touching, as the windows fogged up around them.

'What did you say?' he asked, putting down the story.

'Well, if they're dead, then you could try to communicate with them through a séance or something. Or a Ouija board. You can get one of them at Walmart.'

'I don't think that's such a hot idea,' he replied. 'I don't believe in that stuff, so I wouldn't accept anything it told me, even if my parents were dead and trying to communicate with me.'

'I don't believe in that stuff either,' she said, 'but it means something, right? You put your hands on the little wooden arrow, and you make it move around the board and it tells you something, even if it's something that you already knew. It's you doing the talking, but maybe it's something you wouldn't say otherwise.'

'I don't think so,' Buster said, eager to change the subject.

'I guess I don't understand what's going on,' Suzanne said quietly, suddenly shy. 'You think your parents are dead?'

'Maybe.'

'But you also think they're alive.'

'Yes, maybe so.'

'And you think that maybe they're doing this on purpose?'

'Yes.'

'And you don't know how to find them, if they were alive?'

'Yeah, we tried, but we're not very good at it.'

'Well,' Suzanne said. 'It seems like you won't be satisfied until you know for sure what happened to them. And you don't have any good ideas left for finding them. So maybe you need to start doing stupid things in order to find them.'

'Go on,' Buster said, suddenly interested in her logic.

'You need to do something stupid, something unexpected, and maybe that will draw them out or get you closer to them.'

'And you want me to use a Ouija board?'

'Maybe something even more stupid,' Suzanne admitted, her eyes like slits, as if she was thinking very hard about ridiculous things, as if ridiculous things did not naturally come to her.

'That makes sense,' Buster admitted. 'That's not bad.'

'You help me,' Suzanne said, gesturing toward the story which Buster had obliterated with a red pen until it was unclear what belonged to Suzanne and what belonged to Buster. 'It'd be nice if I could help you, too.'

She kissed him on the lips, quickly, the taste of mayonnaise and ketchup on her breath, and then she rolled away from him before he could respond. He watched her, pumping her arms, swinging them like precise machinery, as she moved toward the rear lights of other cars.

Buster walked into the living room, where Annie was reading a book from their parents' limited collection, a how-to manual for overthrowing governments.

'I think I have an idea,' Buster said, immediately feeling embarrassed. He could not decide if he was embarrassed for saying this out loud or the fact that this was the first time he could remember ever saying it.

'What is your idea?' Annie said.

'We kill ourselves.'

'Terrible idea,' Annie replied.

'Not really kill ourselves. We pretend to kill ourselves. To make Mom and Dad come out of hiding.'

'What's good for the goose is good for the gander,' Annie said, then added, 'that's not a good idea, Buster.'

'Why not?'

'If they really are dead – ' she began.

'But you don't think they're dead,' he interrupted with enthusiasm.

'I don't,' Annie admitted.

'I don't either. So why don't we try this?'

'Because if we pretend to kill ourselves, we'll be fucking up our lives for the sole purpose of finding our parents, who willfully let us think that they were violently killed. Does that sound healthy to you?'

'They *want* us to do something,' Buster told her. 'I can feel it. I'm certain of this. They are hiding somewhere, waiting for us to take the next step and make this thing happen.'

'We don't do this, remember? We don't let them run our lives anymore,' Annie replied, her body now electric with anger. 'They are hurting us, Buster. And if they are hurting us on purpose, to make us do what they want, then I want them to stay disappeared forever. I don't want them near me.' As soon as she finished the last sentence, she slumped back onto the sofa, her anger replaced by a sadness that left Buster temporarily mute.

They would forever come to this impasse. Buster wanted to believe that his parents still loved them, that they had planned all of this as a way to save their children from falling apart, to make them strong. Annie, however, was certain that their parents had created something just for themselves, and that they did not care what pain they caused in service of this idea.

'I'm sorry, Buster,' Annie told him. 'I won't let them do this to us.' She returned her gaze to the book.

'This is something,' Buster said, and he immediately had no idea what he meant. So he said it again, louder, until Annie dropped the book and stared at him. 'This is something,' Buster said again, but there was no force behind it. He thought of his parents in some kind of cell, the cinder block walls leaving chalky residue on their hands. He thought of them huddled together at night, waiting for their children to unlock the clues they had hurriedly left for them, to free them from the awful thing they had themselves created. Annie stood and pulled Buster into an awkward embrace. 'It's something, goddamn it,' Buster said. 'We are in it, and it's happening, and even if we do nothing, we will still be in it.' Annie held him tightly and said, 'They fucked us up, Buster.'

'They didn't mean to,' he replied.

'But they did,' she said.

Buster sat in his room, Annie asleep next door, the air moving through the vents of the house sounding exactly like his parents' breathing. He had been working on something, a book maybe, and he said the line again, a prayer he repeated each time he dug into the story he was telling himself, 'We live on the edge, a shantytown filled with gold-seekers. We are fugitives and the law is skinny with hunger for us.' He understood now who the fugitives were, a brother and sister, twins. Orphans. Orphans, in this world, were shipped off to terror orphanages as preparation for the next stop, to fight in a pit against other children for the entertainment of the rich and powerful. The brother and sister had escaped, had set up camp along with several other orphans, at the edge of the country, hoping to stay hidden long enough to become adults and therefore undesirable to the people looking for them. Buster had started with the words, his father's own voice reading it aloud to him from the tape recorder, and he now had nearly ninety pages of something so strange that he had to remind himself to slow down, to let the words arrange themselves on the page, in order to prevent himself from smashing the story into tiny little pieces.

He knew what was happening. He was not stupid. The twins, they were him and Annie. The dead parents who had left them orphans were Caleb and Camille. The pit where the children fought was just a way for Buster to write about the violence that he sensed would be the ultimate end of all things. It would not, Buster understood, end well. But he had nowhere else to go but to the end of the story. He wrote for hours before exhaustion sent him to his bed, and he felt the satisfaction of creation, of making something that, while perhaps not yet successful, was made by his own two hands.

When he found himself unable to continue, the bend in the story obscuring what would come next, Buster would uncover the painting his mother had given him, which he kept hidden under his bed for fear that continued exposure to the image would turn the air he breathed radioactive. The boy in the painting was so intertwined with the tiger he was battling that it sometimes seemed to Buster that the two of them were embracing, were consoling each other for the inevitability of one of their deaths. The boy's hands, wrapped in barbed wire, the rusted metal digging into his knuckles, were so expertly painted, so detailed, that Buster felt his own hands ache when he stared at the painting for too long. He was not sure, if asked, how he would place himself in the painting. Was he the boy? The tiger? One of the children who watched the struggle unfold? Sometimes he imagined that he was the barbed wire, an instrument used to cut open whatever resisted its touch. Other times, he imagined that he was already inside the tiger's belly and the boy was fighting to retrieve him. His mother had chosen this particular painting for Buster. She had put it in his hands. And it was at this moment, holding the painting, sitting on the floor, the world still and frozen around him, that Buster felt he had found the thing that would bring his parents back to him and Annie.

He pushed open the door to Annie's bedroom, the floor creaking beneath him, and Annie quickly snapped upright, her eyes wide open, something spring-loaded and delicately calibrated. There was no hint of sleep in her voice when she said, 'What now, Buster?' He held out the painting for her. 'This,' he said, offering the painting like a treasure that he could not possibly keep to himself, 'is how we find them.'

When Annie returned from the kitchen, a coffee mug filled with vodka, Buster was arranging the rest of the paintings, until now hidden away in Annie's closet, on the floor of her bedroom. 'This will give me nightmares, Buster,' she told him, but Buster continued to lay out each tile, each baffling image of unrest. She took a long sip from the mug and then settled onto the bed. 'Just tell me what you're doing,' she said.

'These paintings,' Buster told her, sweeping his hand over them as if giving a benediction. 'If Mom wanted them to be such a secret, why did she keep them in this closet? Why would she make it so easy for us to find them?'

'She wasn't hiding them from us,' Annie answered. 'She was hiding them from Caleb.'

'Maybe she wasn't, though,' Buster said, growing more and more excited as he kept talking. 'This is something,' he said. 'This is the something that we've been waiting for.'

'I don't understand you, Buster. I don't understand,' she gestured toward the paintings without looking directly at them, 'any of this.'

'This is Fang art, unknown to the rest of the world. I don't think she wanted us to destroy them. I think this is how they'll come back, a way for Mom and Dad to finally reveal themselves.'

'These paintings?' Annie asked.

'A show,' Buster said. 'We get a major gallery to show these paintings, the hidden art of Camille Fang. We get as much press as we can. We give them a public forum and let them disrupt it.'

'You're not thinking this through, Buster,' she said.

'This is how we bring them back,' he continued, unflinching in the midst of Annie's doubt.

302

'No,' she said, shaking her head. 'I don't want any part of this.'

Buster looked at the paintings, the tools he felt certain his mother had left for him to utilize. He imagined them hanging on the walls of a prestigious gallery, a multitude of people bringing their faces as close as possible to the canvas in order to understand their intent. He imagined standing in the middle of the gallery, his sister beside him, and then watching as the sea of people parted and their parents revealed themselves to the world, reborn, no aspect of art beyond their control.

'Think of it this way, then,' he finally said. 'Maybe they have no plan for us, maybe we don't matter to them at all. Then these paintings are our secret weapon. It's a trap we can use.'

'Go on,' Annie said, her eyes becoming clear and focused at the mention of the words *weapon* and *trap*.

'We say that these were Mom's real idea of art, that she had labored beneath Dad's insistence of what constituted artistic expression. We say everything that would send Dad crawling up the walls. And maybe we create so much chaos in their lives that they'll have no choice but to reveal themselves publicly to set the record straight.'

'Camille will deny that she had anything to do with these paintings,' Annie continued, now seeming to admit that this *was* something, after all. 'Caleb will have to come to the gallery to see for himself. She'll come with him to try and reason with him. And we'll be waiting for them.' Annie took another sip of the vodka, letting the alcohol seep through her system, turning bad ideas into good ones. 'Yeah,' she said, smiling. 'I like that.'

Buster was content to let Annie think they were constructing their own event rather than taking part in their parents'. He believed, truly, that they were simply doing the work their parents demanded of them. If Caleb and Camille Fang had gone to so much trouble to kill themselves, to disappear, they would need someone to return them to the world of the living. Who else but Buster and Annie? A and B. Buster looked at the finished tapestry he had created from the paintings, an unbroken chain of chaos and unsettling strangeness. It looked, if you were far enough away from it, like a portrait of his parents.

It took time, the planning. Annie and Buster were unaccustomed to this aspect of their family's art, the space between conception and action. But with their parents gone, it was up to them, and Buster found himself excited about the chance to show someone, his parents, his sister, the world, that he could create weirdness with the best of them. So they started at the beginning, and Annie and Buster went about the slightly monotonous task of photographing each and every one of their mother's paintings.

They used a rectangular swatch of black velvet they had purchased at the general store in the town square. They laid the velvet on the floor in the living room, bringing each painting, one at a time, into the room and placing it neatly on the velvet. They took the lampshade off of the lamp in the living room and Buster held it over the painting while Annie took a photo of it. After about fifteen paintings – grasshoppers eating the hollowed-out remains of a dead mule, children poking a lame bird on the beach with a sharp stick – Annie opted out of the task. 'I don't think I can keep looking at this stuff, Buster,' she informed him, handing the camera to her brother. 'It makes me want to drink either more alcohol or none, and I can't imagine either possibility.'

'It's part of the process,' Buster said, staring at the painting through the viewfinder of the camera. He took the picture, checked its digital image to make sure it was acceptable, and then shuffled the painting to the side and replaced it with another, equally bizarre, painting. He had originally imagined, after his mother had claimed these paintings as her own, that she was sitting in the dimly lit closet of her daughter's childhood bedroom, painting these images while her husband was away on some errand, the sharp, crackling fear of being discovered always with her. He imagined her visiting the paintings while her husband was asleep, staring at them for signs of why she might be so obsessed with creating them. Now, however, believing these paintings to be props for a larger, more important artistic work, the Fang reappearance, he imagined his parents laughing, working to outdo each other as they tossed out ideas for the paintings, his father's hand on his mother's shoulder as she carefully moved the brush across the canvas, his father murmuring words of encouragement. He imagined the two of them staring at the finished product with great satisfaction before hiding them in the closet of Annie's bedroom until some unknown time when they could be discovered and they could perform the task for which they had always been intended.

Once they had the paintings cataloged, Annie and Buster began to whittle down the possibilities for this unveiling. Museums were out, they decided. There was too much lead-time required and the structures themselves were so big that it would complicate matters. They needed a space that would fill up, would focus entirely on the work of their mother, and would do it fast. So they concentrated on galleries, ones with which the Fangs had previously worked.

'There's the Agora Gallery in New York,' Annie suggested. This particular gallery, in Chelsea, had once shown a video (security-camera footage that the Fangs had stolen plus Mr Fang's own secretive camerawork) of one of the Fangs' earlier works: Buster left in a dressing room in a department store, walking through the store with the security guard, pointing to a random couple and saying that they were his parents, loudly insistent in the face of their denial.

They sent the gallery an e-mail, along with a few

JPEGs of the paintings, and it was only a few hours later that they received a call from the owner of the gallery, Charles Buxton. 'Is this A or B?' he asked when Buster answered the phone. 'B,' Buster said, before he caught himself and said, 'Buster.'

'Is this bullshit, Buster?' the gallery owner asked.

'Excuse me?'

'What's the deal here? Are your parents putting you up to this?'

'Our parents are gone, Mr Buxton,' Buster replied, his nerves starting to go haywire, the feeling coming over him that he would ruin the whole thing if he wasn't careful.

'I know that,' he said. 'I read about it in all the papers. And I also know that the Fang family isn't known for doing things on the up-and-up.'

'This is real,' Buster said. 'This is something my sister and I are doing, on our own, as a way to remember our mother.'

'You have any way of verifying that your mother painted these images?' Mr Buxton asked.

Buster paused. There was no signature on the paintings, nothing that would suggest that their mother was the artist behind these works. Buster began to wonder if perhaps his mother and father had found these paintings, had bought them from another artist, in service of their greater work. 'My sister and I talked to my mother about these paintings before she disappeared,' he finally said. 'She admitted that she had painted them.'

'Something's not right here,' Mr Buxton said. 'I remember your family. The show was a success, and I know that the personality of your father and mother played a large role in that, but I was interested primarily in the work. I was not interested, and I am still not interested, in being a part of the work. I don't want to be a source of derision when I find out this is all just some Fang scam. It's not worth it to me.'

'It's real,' Buster said. 'This is all very real.'

'That sounds like something your father would say, right before something really bad happened,' Mr Buxton replied. Buster heard the line go dead, the conversation morphing into a single, steady tone.

'This is very, very strange, Buster,' Suzanne told him as she stared at the painting of the boy and the tiger. 'It's really great.'

Buster felt the sickening certainty that Annie would push him down a flight of stairs if she knew that he was showing Suzanne their mother's painting, that he had told an outsider about their plan to bring their parents back from the wilderness. She was already slightly cool on the idea of Buster spending so much time with Suzanne, still relying on the old Fang tendencies to distrust anyone who wasn't family. 'Is her writing that good?' Annie had asked him when he returned home after another meeting with Suzanne.

'I think so,' Buster said. 'I think she wants it to

be, and I think I can show her how to make it good. It's not just about that. I like her. She likes me. It's an uncommon situation for me to be in.'

'Fair enough,' Annie said. 'That's nothing I want to stand in the way of.' Then, as if it weren't the entire focus of her conversation, as if it were merely an afterthought, she had said to Buster, 'Just don't tell her about the paintings, okay? That's just for us.' Buster nodded his assent.

And then, having talked about writing, his and hers, hashing out ideas, rewording lines until they were perfect, the two of them had reached a lull in the conversation. The drive-in had emptied around them without their knowledge, the entire parking lot dark. The floorboards of the car were littered with food wrappers and balled-up pages from failed attempts at storytelling. Buster was so unnerved by the quiet, the thought that Suzanne might take it as a cue to leave, that he decided he would show her the painting, tell her about his great plan for finding his parents, just to keep her in the car. If it seemed desperate, he did not care. If Annie would freak out later, he did not care. What he wanted was Suzanne beside him for ten more minutes. And then, as he opened the middle compartment to retrieve the painting, Suzanne pressed her body against his, forced her tongue into his mouth, probing the place where his missing tooth had once been. Her tongue rubbed that open spot of gum, and it made his ears burn, his tongue fuzzy.

'I want to do this,' she said, quickly slipping out of her uniform, her limbs seemingly double-jointed to have disrobed so quickly in such a cramped space, 'if you want to do it.' Buster was not used to this experience, physical desire that was actually fulfilled. In his entire life, he had kissed five women. One of them had been his sister. This was, Buster understood, a terrible percentage. He could count on one hand the number of times he'd had sex and still have enough fingers left over to make complicated shadow puppets. He wisely remained silent, forced himself not to reveal anything that would tip Suzanne off that having sex with him might be incredibly underwhelming, and simply nodded. He removed her glasses, placed them on the dashboard, and followed her into the backseat of the car, shedding his pants on the way, somehow, unintentionally, keeping his shoes on. Yes, he decided, her legs wrapped tightly around his torso, forcing him to exhale so rapidly that it sounded like he just emerged from a burning building, he wanted this.

Now, Buster's car still parked in the empty lot, his mouth aching from pressing his tongue against nearly every spot on Suzanne's body, Buster wondered why he was still showing her the painting. Was it anything other than his own need to tell another person about his parents, the idea that he had figured out something complicated and unwieldy and was utilizing it in a way that made him seem capable? Was he honestly using his mother's bizarre, violent paintings and his idea to put them on display to draw out his parents so as to appear more attractive to Suzanne? Was it working? he wondered.

'You think this is a clue?' she asked Buster.

'I think so,' he replied.

'It's got to be more than that,' Suzanne said. Buster, his body twisted awkwardly in the backseat of the car, ran his hands over her right arm, the soft hair that lifted to meet his touch. He wished that he had waited to show her the painting. He wanted her to keep touching him, the way the multitudes of rings on her fingers rubbed against his skin.

The only real girlfriend he'd ever had, another writer who had published a collection of stories at the same time as *A House of Swans* was published, had told him that his emotions were incorrectly hardwired. 'You are very sweet,' she told him after a year of dating, as they shared dessert at a restaurant, 'but it's like your family trained you to react to the world in a way that was so specific to their art that you don't know how to interact with people in the real world. You act like every conversation is just a buildup to something awful.' In response to this, he acknowledged her concerns, said he needed to use the restroom, then ran out of the restaurant, leaving her with the bill, and never saw her again. He had desires, but they were complicated by his inability to understand those desires, and so he opted out of relationships.

And now, in the backseat of his parents' car, he was tangled up with a half-naked woman, and he only wished that he had waited a little longer after having sex with her to show her a painting his mother had made. This seemed, he understood, to be a strange emotional response. Suzanne, to her credit, did not seem to care. Or, rather, she seemed to care very much, and this made Buster want her even more.

'I mean, if it was just supposed to be a clue, I don't think she would have put this much effort into it. This looks like something that a person took a lot of time to create. It looks like something that meant a lot to her. I'm not saying that you're wrong about it being a clue, but I think it's more than that, too. Isn't that what art is, right? It's about one thing, but it's really about a lot of things.'

'Okay,' Buster said. 'But it is definitely, first and foremost, a clue. And whatever it also is, whatever deep stuff it says about my mom, I'm not sure that I want to know.'

'I don't know,' Suzanne said, touching the barbed wire as if she expected it to puncture her skin, 'that even your mom could tell you what it says.'

Having heard from five more galleries, none interested in his mother's paintings, or perhaps wary of allowing potential chaos in their spaces, Buster began to realize that their parents had made a slight miscalculation in their plans. If no one would show the paintings, how would they return? Annie had gone so far as to contact Hobart for help with finding a gallery, something the old man resisted for a few back-and-forth e-mails before finally giving in to the insistence of the Fang siblings. No matter how it happened, Buster understood that some gallery, somewhere, would eventually show the paintings. The Fangs were still important enough as artists that someone would want to present an offshoot of their recognizable art. But that could take years. Buster did not think he could wait that long, could not live with the uncertainty. And he knew that Annie, if this went on much longer, would spontaneously combust.

One afternoon, a package appeared in the mailbox, and Buster felt as if every bone in his body had, for a split second, rubberized. He steadied himself, touched the address label, and saw that Annie's name was on it. Annie. Not Buster, who had spent so much time searching for his parents, but his sister, who seemed content, like an experienced assassin, to wait patiently for the perfect moment to kill her target. He brought the package into the house, into her room, and he tossed it on her bed. 'This came for you,' he said. She smiled. 'I think we've watched every movie in the house,' she said. 'I ordered some more.' Buster frowned. 'I thought maybe Mom and Dad had sent it to us,' he admitted. Now it was Annie's turn to frown. 'They're not looking for us,' she told him, 'we're looking for them.'

She opened the box and produced a stack of DVDs. Buster saw *Five Easy Pieces* and *Orpheus,* movies he remembered Annie loving, movies he did not particularly enjoy or, to be honest, understand. In the pile, Buster picked up *The Third Man,* a black-and-white image of Orson Welles on the cover. 'I never saw this,' Buster said, 'though I know I should have.' Annie brightened, swiped the DVD from his hands, and tapped it on the bed as if she was a conductor about to begin a symphony. 'This one,' she said, 'holy shit. It's got a writer as the main character. And there's an actress in it. And somebody gets killed but maybe he's not really killed. Maybe he disappeared on purpose.' Buster shook his head. 'Did you just ruin the movie for me?'

'If a movie is really amazing,' she said, 'you can't ruin it by giving the plot away. The plot is incidental to everything else.'

'So this movie is the story of our lives?' Buster asked.

'It's the story of our lives, if our lives were better and more interesting,' Annie replied. 'Let's watch it tonight.'

That evening, the two of them settled on the sofa, Buster's computer resting on the coffee table, the movie opened and they listened to the score, nothing but a zither, so chaotic and atonal that Buster had the sudden urge to turn off the movie.

They watched Joseph Cotten run all around Vienna, looking for a man, Harry Lime, who might or might not be dead. In the movie, there were shadowy, suspicious people at every turn, people who pushed Cotten into stranger and stranger places. Buster wished for shadowy, suspicious people in his own life. When Lime turned up indeed alive, Buster felt an instantaneous and shocking relief, even though he understood that it would have been better for everyone if Harry Lime had really been dead.

Atop a Ferris wheel, Orson Welles told Joseph Cotten how Italy's thirty years of war and terror and bloodshed had produced the Renaissance and Michelangelo, and how Switzerland's five hundred years of democracy and peace had produced, goddamn, only the cuckoo clock. It was the exact kind of thing that Buster could imagine his own father saying. Annie told Buster that Orson Welles had written that line himself, had added it after the script had been finished, and Buster felt that Orson Welles and his father would have been best buddies if they had ever met.

Once the movie was over, Cotten and the authorities tracking Orson Welles through the sewers beneath the city, Cotten finally shooting Welles dead, Buster turned to his sister. 'I know why you picked that movie,' he told her. Annie smiled and said, 'It fits our life in a few ways, I guess.' Buster pointed at the screen, which was now blank. 'It shows you that you have to stay vigilant to find a missing person, even when people tell you not to, that it's possible to bring them back from the dead.' Annie shook her head. 'I picked it because it shows that after you bring someone back from the dead, you get to kill them yourself.' Annie whistled the song from the movie, doing a terrible job of it, and ejected the disc from the computer. She placed the DVD back in its case and snapped the box shut.

Buster was the only person in the house, to his knowledge, when the phone rang. Annie was at the grocery store, something that had once been a chore now being an excuse to get out of the house; she also had begun to warm up to the fact that now that she had been back in town long enough, people were beginning to recognize her, to ask for her autograph. Annie admitted that it was not a bad feeling. People were polite, always kind, and none of them seemed to have seen the disaster of a movie that she had recently made. They knew her as a superhero, and that was fine with her. Sometimes the checkout girl gave Annie packs of gum for free. But now the phone was ringing and Buster was alone. He walked over to the phone, let it ring for the fifth time, and answered it, hoping the voice on the other end of the line would be a familiar one.

'Is this A or B?' the voice asked, a voice so old that Buster was unsure of whether it was a man or a woman. Buster knew immediately that it was another gallery. This was the language that they used, A and B Fang, and Buster answered, as Annie had taught him years ago when someone other than their parents tried to call them by their stage names, 'This is Buster.'

'I saw the paintings,' the person said. 'I thought I'd better give you a call.'

'Who is this?' Buster said. He thought it might be Annie, trying to lighten Buster's mood. All morning, Buster had been digging even deeper into the novel, having finally given it a name, *The Child Pit*. The twins, now captured, were kept underground, hidden within rooms connected by tunnels built underneath the structure, steel-reinforced doors, the sound of murder-ballads played over the loudspeakers. Micah and Rachel, the twins, had quickly established themselves as fierce fighters, earning the respect of the other kids. Escape was constantly plotted, without any real hope of coming to fruition. Even as he increased the inherent danger among the children, wild and dirty and struggling to keep their anger focused on the adults, not each other, Buster could not help but feel an affection for the pit, the idea that, even if their lives would not escape ruination, they would at least suffer together. And now, light-headed like a swimmer quickly surfacing after minutes underwater, Buster was finding himself overmatched by the insistent, scratchy voice on the phone. 'Dad?' he asked, confused. 'Mom?'

'What? No, this is Betsy Pringle. My husband and I ran the Anchor Gallery here in San

Francisco for many years. We're a rather experimental gallery space. Now I run the gallery with my son.'

Buster did not remember this gallery, had not sent them any e-mail. This fact, and the randomness of the call, began to steady Buster's mind, forced him to focus.

'What are you calling about?' Buster asked, drawing this person out, hoping to gain some clarity.

'The paintings. I'm calling about your mother's paintings, of course. Are you okay? Is Child A there, perhaps? Could I talk to her?'

'She's not in. I can handle this, however,' Buster replied.

'Good. That's good to hear. Now, we were, I'm sure you know, the first gallery to ever show a Fang piece. Your father had done a bit of work on his own, but we showcased the first work created jointly by your mother and father. This was before you and A were born. We'd like to take some credit for having discovered them. My husband was always a big supporter of your parents' work. And now, we'd like to be able to show the final Fang work, to bring things full circle, if you will.'

'The Anchor Gallery?' Buster asked, still trying to make sense of things. 'I don't remember contacting you.'

'Hobart talked to me,' the woman replied. 'He's an old friend, a genius. I guess your sister sent him an e-mail, asking for help, and he got in touch with me, smart man that he is. I'm looking at the paintings right now. Wonderful, wonderful work. I remember your mother had started as a painter, had won all kinds of scholarships based on her more traditional artistic pursuits. So it wasn't as shocking as you might think to see these paintings. And, I don't know what your situation is, but you seem eager to showcase your mother's work, and we happen to have a slot coming up very soon. I think this would be a good thing for everyone involved.'

Buster wished Annie was here. He had no pen or paper. He could not even remember the woman's name. He kept repeating, in his head, the word *Anchor,* so he would not forget. If this was true, he reminded himself, this would set into motion the thing he had been hoping for, the initial finger-flick that sent the marble rolling down the ramp of the inelegantly crafted Rube Goldberg device.

'I think it's a great idea,' Buster said. 'We just want to find a way to showcase the fact that my mother was a talented artist in her own right, in her own medium.'

'That's what we want as well,' Mrs Pringle replied. 'To honor her memory.' This made Buster flinch and he thought about clarifying the fact that his parents were simply missing, not dead, not officially dead, but he kept his mouth shut.

'My son wants to talk to you about the details,' she said. 'I just wanted to make the offer. I still own the place. I still make the final decisions. And I still think, though I am old and I'm not as connected to the art world as I used to be, that something strange is always better than something beautiful.'

'Something can be both,' Buster reminded her.

'Sometimes,' she admitted, and then she handed the phone over to her son.

When Annie came home from the grocery store, Buster became a tidal wave, the story washing over her with such force that, when Buster finished speaking, he was panting for breath. 'This is it, Annie,' he told her. 'It's happening.' Annie smiled, her teeth so perfect and white that it seemed to Buster as though she was in a commercial for a medically impossible formula of toothpaste. 'I wish,' she said. 'Goddamn, I just wish I could see Caleb's face when he finds out about these paintings. I would pay any amount of money to see that.' Buster wanted to tell her that their father more than likely knew about the paintings already, but he understood that they were coming at this thing from different angles, and he did not want to spoil her happiness. What did it matter, their motivations, as long as it ended with the Fangs, all four of them, in the same room?

'Let me come with you,' Suzanne asked Buster once he had told her about the gallery opening in San Francisco, only a few weeks away. The two of them were in her tiny apartment in a government-housing complex, which seemed one busted water main away from being condemned. At all hours, Buster could hear children running up and down the hallways, the walls little more than a sheet of fabric hanging on a line.

'I don't think that's a great idea,' Buster admitted. He imagined the four Fangs, Annie and Buster and Caleb and Camille, rejoined, angry and relieved and unsure of how to proceed. And then he imagined Suzanne, roller-skating around and around the four of them. Was it that he didn't want to expose her to the Fangs or was it that he didn't want to expose the Fangs to her? Was it that he simply needed to be alone when the important thing happened? He had no idea. He tried to think of all the people in his life as chemicals, the uncertainty of mixing them together, the potential for explosions and scarring. However, it seemed the most likely explanation was that he simply liked having Suzanne to himself, away from the possibility of chaos. Whatever the reason, however much he might want her close to him when his parents returned, he could not allow her to come.

'I wouldn't just tag along,' she said. 'I could be useful. You think your parents are going to reappear at the opening, right, make a big spectacle? But Annie thinks they'll come incognito and then try to disappear again? Either way, they're calling the shots. But they don't know me. I could set up a stakeout or something, be watching from a building across the street. We could have walkie-talkies, and I could use binoculars, and when I saw them, I could let you know so you'd be ready. I could be your tactical advantage,' she said, her pupils dilating with the excitement of her imagined spy games. She was, Buster realized, someone his parents would probably love, the way she so quickly adjusted to the weirdness around her.

'I just don't think it's a great idea. It's not how I want you to meet my parents,' he told her, as if there was some version of reality where Buster would bring Suzanne to his parents' house and they would all have iced tea on the porch and play cards and talk about horse racing. He could not figure out why, having found someone who seemed unfazed by his family history, he believed that she deserved something traditional and boring.

They were in her bed, the TV still playing some kung-fu movie marathon that had been on the entire time they were having sex. The room echoed with the whiplash sounds of kicks being unleashed, the constant, staccato laughter that was dubbed in English and yet sounded so foreign to his ears. Suzanne wasn't wearing her glasses and it made her eyes seem dim and unfocused. She looked disappointed, and he wondered if she was upset with him. 'You met me at a strange time. I'm glad you did, but I think everything will be better after I do this thing for my parents, for

Annie and me. There won't be this, I don't know, uncertainty hovering over me.'

Suzanne leaned closer to him and tapped him on the forehead with her finger, a sharp thwack of the tip of her finger glancing off his skin. It made him flinch, but not before registering the odd expression on her face, as though she was trying to decide what kind of person he really was. He held as still as possible, not breathing, hoping that she liked what she saw.

'I remember when you came into the room for our creative writing group,' she began. 'I kind of thought you were cute, even with the bruising on your face, and then you started to talk about some kind of ridiculous bubble gum that you liked to chew and then I saw that you were missing a tooth and you seemed so nervous that I immediately realized that you were a very weird person. And that, for some reason, made me more interested in you. And then that girl came and took me outside, and you were standing there, and then you said that you liked my story and I thought that was the nicest thing I'd ever heard. You just showed up and made me happy.'

'You make me happy, too,' he said, though he wished he had said it before she did. He wanted to say it in a way that showed her that he was not just parroting her, but Suzanne smiled at him, and he knew he'd said it well enough.

'You talk as if you think there's going to be a time in the future when things aren't completely weird. I don't know if that's going to happen, based on your life history. And I guess all I want to tell you is that it isn't really that big of a deal to me. If this is how strange your life is, that's okay with me. It's fun.'

Buster didn't know how to respond to her, was dumbfounded by her easy kindness, but also by her belief that his instability was 'fun.' She was, he began to realize, as weird as he was. Perhaps weirder. If she had been born a Fang, she might have become the focal point of the art, leaving Annie and Buster far behind, of no further use to their parents. And though being face-to-face with someone who possessed a strangeness that could outpace the Fangs should have made him hesitate, he quickly pulled her close to him and let the riotous sounds of children past their bedtimes and unafraid of the darkness, kung-fu masters punching their way through all evils, and the sound of Suzanne's breathing, so steady that he thought she might be dead asleep, lull him into a state that he imagined was what other people referred to as serenity.

Annie and Buster were carefully boxing up each painting, bubble wrap and cardboard and packing tape creating a sea of detritus in which the siblings seemed to be floating. Holding a sheet of bubble wrap in her hand, Annie twitched slightly, popping one of the plastic pods, a sound like she was snapping her fingers in discovery. Her face flushed with whatever secret knowledge she had acquired and Buster watched the darkness sweep across her face. She tried to speak, but could only stutter, which caused her to grow even angrier. Finally, the bubble wrap going off like fireworks in her tightening fist, she found her voice. 'If you think Caleb and Camille had planned all of this,' she said, gesturing toward the paintings, 'then doesn't it seem like they would want to document this?' She spread her arms as if to suggest the frame of their house, everything under this roof, and Buster instantly nodded. 'I have thought that many times,' he replied. Annie frowned, looking out the window, seeing nothing. 'I don't like that,' she said. She put down the bubble wrap and stood up, her eyes searching the room. 'If they are taping us,' she continued, 'I will kill somebody.'

Buster also stood, and the two of them moved slowly throughout the living room, starting out with their backs to each other and moving outward. Annie touched the stereo, listened for the hiss of a recording device, and then unplugged the machine. Suddenly, she thought better of this decision and turned it back on and played, at a high volume in order to drown out their voices, the first record she could produce, *Rock for Light* by Bad Brains. The sound was frenetic and intense and it made Annie's heart beat three times faster than it should, which felt necessary for the task at hand.

Buster clicked the lamp on and off, as if the

change in brightness might help focus his vision, and then hefted a paperweight that seemed incongruous to the décor, a pewter gavel. He lightly tapped it against his open palm. He shook it, expecting a rattle, and then opened the drawer of the desk and placed the object inside, shutting it in the dark.

'Mirrors,' Annie said, but there were none to be found in the living room. They both quickly turned to the entryway of the house, where there was a tall mirror that allowed the Fangs to check their appearance right before heading out of the door. Buster nodded toward Annie and placed his index finger against his lips to quiet her. He walked to the linen closet, produced a paisley sheet, and, holding it like a net used to capture a wild animal, he padded over to the mirror. He was as close as he could get to the mirror without being caught in its reflection, and he looked over at Annie, who nodded her approval. He expertly draped the sheet over the mirror, pulling the edges free so that it cascaded down the length of the glass. 'Well done,' Annie said, and Buster smiled.

They spent the next half hour cleverly obscuring every mirror in the house. When the task was finished, their actions unobserved by any outsider, they unscrewed the cordless phone, unsure of what they were looking for, having some confidence, thanks to spy movies, that they would recognize a bug if they saw it. Finding nothing suspicious, or accepting the suspicious nature of all the elements that made up the hardwiring of a phone, Buster screwed the thing closed, wondering if he had damaged something in its internals, if the phone would ever ring again and if he would care one way or the other.

'I can't believe I'm letting this happen,' Annie suddenly shouted, grinding her teeth, her hands balled up so tightly her knuckles were fish-belly white. 'This is what they want us to do. This is what they love.' She was on the edge of hysteria, about to cry, and she placed her hand on Buster's arm for balance.

'Is this going to work, Buster?' she asked him.

'It's the only thing I can think of,' he answered. 'I guess, if it's the only thing you can think of, it doesn't matter if you think it's going to work or not. What else can you do but try it?'

'I want you to say that it will work,' Annie said. Buster was not used to being in this situation, the source of certainty. 'It will work because it has to,' he said, and he watched as Annie's form sagged slightly and then stiffened, became strong again. He stood beside his sister, who seemed lost in a trance. The music that spit out of the speakers was loud enough to make the tips of each carpet fiber vibrate with the force of the bass.

He imagined that his mother and father were the orphans in his novel, hidden at the edge of civilization, waiting for the inevitable footsteps of someone who would soon wrap them in their nets and cart them off to another, stranger place.

He then imagined, shocked by the understanding that it might be true, that Annie and Buster were not tracking down their parents, but that their parents, who, in his mind, controlled even the rising and setting of the sun, were simply pulling their children closer and closer to them.

The Last Supper, 1985
Artists: Caleb and Camille Fang

They had reservations at the most expensive restaurant in Atlanta, the Fangs dressed in such finery that Buster and Annie felt like models for an unattainable lifestyle. 'If the menu is in French, how will we know what we're eating?' Annie asked her parents. 'That's part of the fun,' her mother said. Neither Annie nor Buster, itching in their new clothes, unaware of the exact nature of their parents' plans, believed they would ever totally understand what their parents meant when they said fun.

'Fang, party of four,' the hostess said as she checked the reservation against the leather appointment book. 'Right this way,' she said. The children watched as their parents, smiling, at ease in this strange situation, settled into the high-backed chairs, surrounded by people who wanted only a quiet evening. Annie and Buster felt a sickness deep in their stomachs, were certain whatever transpired would be anything but quiet.

'Are you not going to tell us?' Buster said, his hands cold and clammy, his nerves jangling around inside his body. 'No,' Mr Fang replied. 'You just have to be ready. You'll know it when it happens. And when it happens, you do whatever comes naturally.'

'Can you at least tell us if it will happen before or after the food comes?' Annie asked, desperate for some clue. 'We cannot tell you,' Mrs Fang said, smiling, sipping a glass of wine from a bottle so expensive that Annie deduced that the 'event' would be skipping out on the check, running in all directions the minute they had finished dessert. She looked at her brother, who was taking deep, controlled breaths, willing himself to die and come back to life, and so she took the opposite approach, holding her breath until the dim, candlelit room began to bend and tick and turn wavy, finally taking a breath and feeling electric, aware of every single utensil scraping against a plate.

The food arrived. 'Eat your food,' Mrs Fang said to Buster. 'I'm not hungry,' he replied, a thin strip of liver, soaked in burgundy, sitting in front of him. He looked around the restaurant for the umpteenth time and confirmed, once again, that he and his sister were the only children in the entire dining room. 'You have to eat it,' Mr Fang said. 'Is this part of the piece?' Buster asked. Mr and Mrs Fang smiled at each other, clinked their wineglasses, and said in unison, 'Eat your food.'

Buster dug his knife into the liver, the sauce

shimmering as he delicately sawed a bite away from the meat. He placed the liver in his mouth, allowed the taste of it, the overwhelming gaminess of the meat, to settle on his tongue before he swallowed, no attempt to chew. His parents stared at him, and he tried to smile, beads of sweat on his forehead. 'It's good,' he said.

More wine, no conversation, classical music coming from a source that Annie and Buster could not determine, the dinner continued. Buster, somehow, sheer force of will, had eaten the entire liver without once chewing. He had the constant, insistent need to gag, but he fought the urge. He would not ruin the evening before the evening had been ruined.

Annie thought that perhaps it was the subdued lighting in the restaurant, but Buster's skin was the most distinct shade of green, sea-foamy and pale. His tongue seemed enlarged, too big for his mouth. She ran her finger along the edge of her spoon, over and over, feeling the dull edge of the utensil dig into her fingertips, erasing the whorls of her fingerprints. Her parents, who rarely drank, disapproving of the way alcohol slowed their responses, continued to sip their wine. They seemed so happy, sharing a secret of how the world would end. It was as if Annie and Buster were not present, as if the children were watching a movie of their parents. Mr and Mrs Fang checked their watches, exchanged a glance, and then continued to drink their wine.

Buster stared at a chandelier with such intensity that he hoped the force of his desire would snap the cable and send the hulking, sparkling mass of light and glass crashing to the floor. Something had to happen. Something had to disrupt. Buster wanted only for something to happen so that he could run, could leave this building, could return to the safety of his room. He felt an insistence running electric through his body. He felt hot and cold at the same time, his joints aching. He felt, all of a sudden, a relaxation in his muscles, the slightest shift in tension, and he could not control the machinations of his own body.

Annie turned to her brother just as he sent a stream of vomit across the table, deep brown and dark red, the remains of a shredded animal. Mr and Mrs Fang gasped; Mr Fang tried to hold a saucer under Buster's chin but it was too late for that. Buster made a sound like the air had been kicked out of him, and the other patrons in the restaurant turned to face the Fangs. A waiter began to rush toward the table and then, hesitating, turned back to the kitchen. Buster's hands covered his face, and he muttered, 'I'm sorry, I'm sorry,' and Annie watched as her parents seemed incapable of action. They were watching the event with surprise, with interest. Annie pushed her chair over, rattling the glasses on the table, and took Buster in her arms. Somehow, Annie did not understand how, she lifted her brother without effort, and he wrapped his arms around her neck. She carried him through the restaurant, a blur of color around her, out the door, into the open air. She set him on the sidewalk, and she stroked his hair. 'I'm sorry,' Buster said, and Annie kissed his forehead. 'Let's get out of here,' she said.

The van was locked, and Annie searched the parking lot for some implement to pick the lock or to smash the window. She would leave her parents behind to do whatever it was that they had waited so long to enact. Buster, his color returning to him, rested against one of the tires, suddenly hungry again. And then, just as Annie had begun to wrap her coat around her arm in order to bust into the van, their parents appeared.

'I'm sorry,' Buster said, but Mr and Mrs Fang surrounded their son and embraced him. 'You have nothing to be sorry about,' Mr Fang said. 'You did great.' He lifted Buster onto his shoulder and then unlocked the van, slipping his son into the backseat. 'Did you get to perform your event?' Annie said. 'We didn't have an event,' Mrs Fang said. 'You did. You children did it for us.'

Annie, the van now on the interstate, heading home, felt heat radiating through her body, her hands clenching and unclenching. 'That was mean,' she said to her parents. Buster rested his head in her lap and she stroked his hair, sticky with sweat, cooled by the AC. 'That wasn't nice,' Annie said.

'It's no different than other times, Annie,' Mr

Fang said. 'We always tell you that something is going to happen. Even if you don't know exactly what it is, you are always a part of it. You see now, don't you? You and Buster are Fangs. You are a part of us. We put you in a situation and, without even trying, you made something happen. You created something amazing.'

'It's inside of you,' Mrs Fang said. 'It's what we do; we distort the world; we make it vibrate, and you kids did it without any help from us. No direction. No idea of what would happen, and you created such chaos. You manufactured it from somewhere inside of you.'

'You made Buster so nervous that he made himself sick,' Annie said.

'You think we're mean, but we're just trying to show you how it all works,' Mr Fang said. 'Even if we die, when it's just you and Buster, you'll be able to do this. You are true artists. Even when you don't want to make it, it manifests itself without your permission. It's in your genes. You make art. You cannot help it.'

'We're mad at you,' Annie said. 'We don't care about this.'

'You'll be mad at us sometimes,' Mrs Fang said to her children. 'We'll make you unhappy, but we do it for a reason. We do it because we love you.'

'We don't believe you,' Annie said. Buster was now asleep, twitching and yelping.

Mrs Fang turned around to face Annie, her hand resting on Annie's own hand. 'You have no idea how much we love you, Annie,' Mrs Fang said, and then she turned around again. She and Mr Fang held hands, the van traveling through the night. 'No idea,' Mrs Fang said.

CHAPTER 11

Annie stood in the middle of the gallery, surrounded on all sides by her mother's art, feeling something akin to stage fright, something more exhilarating than simple anxiety. It was a feeling like she had spent ten minutes climbing the stairs of an impossibly high diving board, and was now standing on the edge, knowing there was only one way to get back down. Or, Jesus Christ, maybe she was just flat-out crazy, hoping her dead parents would come back to life and appear at this very location to look at some paintings.

Annie was wearing a little black dress with a halter top that tied in a bow at the back of her neck. It was very much like the dress that Jean Seberg had worn in *Bonjour Tristesse,* except Seberg's dress had been designed by Givenchy and Annie had found this one at a Target in Nashville. Still, with her hair cut short like Seberg's, she felt like a movie star in the dress. She reminded herself that she was kind of a movie star, but it felt better to pretend to be a full-on movie star than to actually be kind of a movie star. Buster was wearing one of their father's tweed suits, slightly too big for him, but he said he thought it would catch their father's attention when he eventually showed up to the gallery. Annie drank a glass of wine that someone handed her, nodded and smiled each time someone approached her, and waited for something to fucking happen.

Annie had done everything possible to make this event a success. She had used every contact she had to get the word out. She offered herself up for interviews about her mother's work, talking to anyone in the hopes that each subsequent article would be the one that got her parents' attention. In the weeks before the show, there had been articles in the *New York Times*, the *San Francisco Chronicle*, the *San Francisco Examiner*, the *Los Angeles Times*, *ArtForum*, *Art in America*, *BOMB Magazine*, and essays in *Juxtapoz* and *Raw Vision* that sought to champion Camille's work as an excellent example of lowbrow art. One of Annie's main talking points was the idea that her mother's paintings showed an artist who was seeking to move beyond the limiting, outdated forms of art that the Fang family had once made, was doing something perhaps more important, more difficult, and more artistic, and it was a shame that she felt the need to hide it from the world.

As she gave these interviews, Annie pictured Caleb having conniption fits, so upset that he would steal a car, hotwire it, and jam the accelerator until he arrived in front of the gallery, knocked over the table bearing wine and cheese,

337

and started to deface the paintings with as much vigor as he could manage, which would be a lot, knowing Caleb. This was what Annie hoped for, at least, getting her parents so emotionally unsettled that they would make a mistake, would reveal themselves, would provide Annie the opportunity to publicly renounce them, once and for all and, Buster at her side, walk off into the sunset, slow curtain, the end.

An appearance by Caleb and Camille was also what Mrs Pringle's son, Chip, hoped for. It took Annie several phone conversations with Chip before she could keep herself from snickering at his name – Chip Pringle, for crying out loud – but even with her barely contained laughter, she understood that he was hoping this exhibit was mere prelude to the reappearance of Caleb and Camille Fang. He tried, several times, to get Annie to admit that this was an elaborate ruse conjured up to allow Caleb and Camille to reintroduce themselves to the world. Since this was exactly what Buster believed, and Annie, truth be told, had begun to realize that this might be exactly what her parents had planned, she let Chip believe this without ever actually confirming it. 'Art,' Chip would say, breathlessly, without ever elaborating, and Annie would simply reply, 'Art,' as if they were members of a secret club and this was their password.

While Buster circled the gallery, avoiding conversation with anyone, his eyes darting from the paintings on the wall to the activity in the room, searching for their mother and father, Annie stayed absolutely still, her sentry post one that allowed her to see the only entrance to the gallery.

Buster walked over, holding a handful of cheese cubes. 'Nothing yet,' he said. Annie looked down at the cubes of cheese resting on Buster's open palm. 'Why didn't you get a plate for those?' she asked. Buster studied his hand with evident surprise. 'I didn't even know I was holding these,' he said. 'Give me one,' she said, and she placed one of the cubes in her mouth, the cheese warm and tangy on her tongue. Buster slipped the rest of the cubes into the inside pocket of his suit coat and dusted off his hands. Annie was beginning to wish that he would retire to the exact opposite side of the gallery.

'I keep imagining how it will happen,' he whispered to her. 'An hour or so from now, the place will be as crowded as it's going to get, and we'll hear someone shout, *These paintings are fake!* And everyone will turn toward that voice, and Mom and Dad will walk right into the gallery and everything after that will be chaos. That's how I hope it will go down.'

'I think Caleb and Camille are going to break in through the bathroom window, hide in there until the place closes, and then they'll take every painting and drive back to wherever they came from,' Annie replied. As soon as she said this, she felt an instant regret, as though her dreaming up the scenario would cause it to come true. And she did not want that. She did not want her parents to sneak in, undetected. She wanted them in the gallery, surrounded by witnesses, face-to-face with Annie and Buster. Whatever came next, she could not quite imagine, but she was content to wish simply for their presence and allow whatever followed to come to her later.

'I'm going to keep walking around, scan the crowd,' Buster said, and then he pushed his way through the small crowd of people in the gallery and disappeared. Annie felt her nerves jangling around inside of her. She resorted to the old Fang technique, slowly numbing every part of her body, a forced death, and as she felt the numbness climb up the nape of her neck, slip inside her brain, she held that moment as long as she could. She let her thoughts fade out, like the final scene of *Sunset Boulevard*, the clarity of the image turning opaque, unfocused, and then slowly fading to black. After a few seconds, though it could have been hours, for all she knew, she opened her eyes, felt her body return to her, when she saw Buster moving quickly toward her, shrugging, a strange look on his face, almost sheepish. Annie stiffened, wondered what she had missed, and tried to quickly reclaim the parts of herself that she needed for what would come next. Buster was now almost beside her, and yet she still could not quite hear what he was saying, her ears still readjusting, recalibrating. 'What?' Annie asked as he touched her arm, and

Buster pointed toward the entrance and then said, 'Lucy.' Annie looked across the room and saw Lucy Wayne, a woman she hadn't seen in more than two years, smiling at her. And Annie, reborn and feeling brand-new, shining and perfectly calibrated, smiled right back.

Lucy, so short, barely five foot two, her black hair pulled into a bun, walked through the gallery toward Annie and Buster, who made no movement at all. Lucy held her hand out in a way that seemed as though she was trying to navigate through the dark, but Annie realized she was just waving, nervously, hello. Annie waved back. So did Buster. Lucy was wearing a white blouse, the first four buttons undone, with a pair of horn-rimmed glasses hanging from the V of her neckline, complemented by a black-and-white checkered skirt, and she looked, to Annie, like the coolest librarian on the face of the earth, someone who spent most of her time having sex in the stacks.

'Hey there,' Lucy said, tapping Annie on the shoulder. 'You wanted to come to this?' Annie asked, still processing Lucy's appearance in the gallery. 'This is my kind of thing,' Lucy said, gesturing toward the paintings. 'Weird shit,' Lucy said, still smiling, her dark eyes, almost black, gleaming with interest, 'is what I live for.' When Annie seemed unable to respond, Buster said, 'Well, you came to the right place. You'll meet your yearly quota for weird shit with just one wall of this stuff.' Lucy retrieved her eyeglasses, settled them on her face, and began to walk over to one of the paintings. 'Oh,' she said, holding the syllable for so long that it seemed as though she was humming, 'this is good.' Annie still did not look at her mother's paintings, could only imagine which bizarre image had sparked Lucy's interest. She finished her wine, and, as soon as she felt the awkwardness of holding an empty glass, a young man in formal wear, holding a tray, plucked it out of her hand and continued on his way. Having spent years in Hollywood, Annie was accustomed to this situation, surrounded by weirdness, being taken care of by people she did not know.

Two hours into the opening, the gallery still filled with an abnormal amount of people for an exhibit of paintings by an experimental performance artist, there was still no sign of their parents. This did not worry Annie. She said to herself, 'No worries,' and then realized she was saying it out loud.

So far, more than a dozen people, all of them right on the edge of being elderly, had come up to Annie to say how much her parents' art had moved them, had done something indefinable to the way they saw the world. Annie always smiled, always nodded, but she was amazed by these people, what kind of wiring they possessed that would cause a Fang event to occupy a pleasant place in their memories. And then she realized these people were probably talking about seeing a representation of the original Fang event in a museum, which was even more astonishing to Annie. Was this how trauma worked? she wondered. Those closest to it remained dumbfounded by the fact that those who weren't present could derive meaning from it? She felt the walls closing in on her, and she took a deep breath and refocused on keeping the world at bay. If her parents appeared – when her parents appeared – she would be ready for them. She had to resist that which others could not.

She had lost count of how many glasses of wine she had consumed. It could have been two or it could have just as easily been a dozen. The man who kept collecting her wineglasses prevented her from having a physical chart of her level of inebriation. She needed to pee, but she could not imagine abandoning her post. The thought that she would miss the moment when her parents returned was something she would not allow herself to contemplate. If she was not there to witness her parents' reappearance, would it have really happened?

She could see Lucy, standing with Buster, examining her mother's paintings, and Annie knew that she should be over there, talking to the woman who would be directing her in another movie, if all went according to plan. She and Lucy had been in touch by e-mail for the past few weeks, but she was unnerved to see her in person. Annie had purposely not mentioned the exhibit to Lucy, though she imagined that Lucy had read about it, having been a fan of the Fangs long before she ever met Annie, because she did not want Lucy to frame her within the context of the Fang family. But now, Lucy standing less than ten feet away from her, Annie found that she did not care, was happy that Lucy had come. Then, as if she could read Annie's mind, Lucy walked over to her and said, 'You haven't moved since I got here. I keep thinking you're doing some kind of performance piece here. You're a living statue or something.' Annie shook her head. 'I'm just being still,' Annie said. 'I'm just thinking.'

'Can I ask you something?' Lucy asked her, and Annie nodded. 'Buster said that the two of you are waiting for your parents, that you think they'll show up tonight,' Lucy continued. She said it without any betrayal of how she felt about this idea. Annie looked for Buster, who was now sitting on one of the benches, talking to some of the elderly Fang fans. Buster could not keep his big mouth shut. 'That is a possibility,' Annie admitted.

'But you don't know?' Lucy asked. 'I mean, they didn't tell you this?'

Annie shook her head. Lucy's eyes widened, her lip twitched in a manner that suggested either a smile or a frown that had been quickly abandoned. It seemed like Lucy wanted to say something more, but was keeping herself from saying. So Annie said what she thought Lucy wanted to say. 'I know that sounds crazy,' she admitted.

'Honestly, for Caleb and Camille Fang, it does

not sound crazy,' Lucy replied. She then looked around the room, as if checking to ensure that the Fang parents were indeed not in the gallery, and then she said, 'It seems like some heavy stuff is going on. Should I go? I think maybe you and Buster need to be alone.'

'You can stay,' Annie said. She looked down and noticed that she was holding another glass of wine. It was as if her hands were performing magic without her knowledge or consent. 'Please stay,' she said, not flinching even though she heard the desperation in her voice, her hope that Lucy might stay overriding her own embarrassment. When Lucy nodded her assent, Annie felt the strength necessary to move, and handed her glass to Lucy. 'I have to use the bathroom, but I'll be right back.'

As she walked toward the restrooms, she noticed that the crowd was beginning to thin out, that the opening had reached the point where there would be no more people to replace those who would depart. It was a critical point, knowing that someone in the gallery was the last person to arrive. Besides her parents, she reminded herself. Just before she made it to the restroom door, Chip Pringle grabbed her arm, offering the slightest bit of resistance, as if reversing her orbit, and he said, 'Still no sign of them. I don't want to ruin the element of surprise, but do you have an idea of when they might be here? Is that something you can tell me?'

'Soon,' Annie said, instantly regretting having

said it. She began to correct herself and then decided to let it stand. It seemed like the truest statement she could make, truer even than 'I don't know,' or 'they probably aren't coming,' or 'they're already here.' She freed herself from his grip, not even looking to see how he processed her comment, and pushed her way into the restroom, forgetting, for a few moments, what she was doing in there, what in the world she was doing.

When she returned to the gallery, Lucy was still standing in her spot, Annie's glass of wine now empty. Buster intercepted Annie before she made it back to her post.

'I'm worried,' he told her.

'Don't be,' Annie said.

'Worried isn't the right word, maybe,' Buster continued. 'I'm scared.'

'Don't be,' she said again. 'Either one of those things, don't be.'

'I don't think they're coming,' Buster admitted. He seemed to be shrinking inside the suit.

'They operate on the element of surprise,' Annie said. 'They won't show up until we think they won't show up.'

Buster nodded, convinced of the logic, and it made Annie want to scream, the understanding that their parents had done so much weird shit to them that it seemed plausible that Caleb and Camille could read their minds. She could feel her anger, which lived so easily inside of her, become ragged and unstable, working its way into her blood and her muscles. She knew there was little remedy except to hold on to the anger, keep it from spilling over, until it could be properly unleashed, directed toward those who deserved it, those who were, goddamn, still not fucking here.

Annie walked over to Lucy, who moved just a few inches to allow Annie to reclaim her spot. 'What's your favorite one?' Lucy asked, her neck craning to stare at one of the paintings over her right shoulder.

'None of them,' Annie responded. She wished she had a glass of wine and when she found that there was not one in her hand, she felt an intense disappointment, the shock of not seeing the thing you expected to see.

'I should probably leave,' Lucy said, not checking her watch, not trying to pretend that she still had any tangible reason to leave other than she knew it was time to go. 'I wanted to tell you something, though I don't know if this is the time. But I'm here and you're here and I haven't seen you in so long, so I want to say it. I hope it'll make you feel excited.'

'What is it?' Annie asked, wanting good news. She needed something that had the possibility of being realized. She softened for an instant, which was enough for her muscles to stop spasming, and she focused on Lucy and whatever good things she might proffer.

'I got the green light on the film. We've got the money, we're finalizing the location, and we're starting auditions for the other roles. I'm going to make this movie, Annie. You and I are going to make this movie.'

Annie smiled, reached out for Lucy, who returned the hug. 'It's happening, Annie,' Lucy said. 'Whatever else you have going on, you'll have this movie, and you'll have me to help you, whenever you need it.'

'Thank you,' Annie said. 'I want this to be good. I want to be good in it.'

'It will be,' Lucy said, disentangled herself from Annie, and began to walk away, waving good-bye. 'You will be,' she said, amending her statement.

Buster walked over to Annie and gestured to the almost-empty room. 'They're not coming,' Buster said, sucking on his teeth, as if the air was so sharp it hurt him to breathe it in.

There were ten people left in the gallery, fifteen minutes until closing, and Annie and Buster stared at the floor, unblinking, as if waiting for something to emerge from the floor beneath them. A few more people started to leave, a man and a woman, but they hesitated, watching Annie and Buster as if waiting for some sign that they should actually stay. Annie waved to them. 'Bye,' she said, and the couple nodded and left, looking very disappointed, having probably expected the same thing as Annie and Buster. After that, the others trickled out the door, leaving Annie, Buster, Chip Pringle, and his mother. Even the caterers had already left, nothing to do but turn off the lights and lock up.

Chip walked over to Annie, shaking his head. 'They didn't show,' he said to her. Annie nodded, unable to speak. 'I guess that was always a possibility,' Chip admitted. 'If you expected it to happen,' Mrs Pringle said, swaying, tipsy, radiant, 'then Caleb and Camille Fang wouldn't go through with it.' She seemed the only person in the room who was happy; she had loved the paintings for nothing but what they were, and she seemed content to let them do the work that the disappeared Fangs could not.

What else was there for Annie and Buster to do? They would return, would wait for their parents every single day of the exhibit's lifespan, until something happened, until the hidden was revealed.

Buster started to cry, shaking his head, holding up his hand as if to apologize or perhaps to ask for a second so that he could compose himself. 'They're not coming,' he said. Annie placed her hands on Buster's shoulders, facing him, breathing deeply, showing him how to breathe, how to keep the air moving in and out of his system, how to stay alive. 'The door's locked. Just finish turning off the lights when you leave,' Chip whispered, and he awkwardly escorted his mother out of their own gallery, leaving behind the kind of art that Annie and Buster were making, which was not, at all, the kind of art they desired.

Annie understood Buster's sudden collapse, should have been waiting for it to happen. The exhibit had been his idea, everything riding on this final feint. And now, after Buster and Annie had lined up everything they believed their parents required in order to return, Caleb and Camille again refused to make themselves known. It was failure, yet another failure, and even for Buster, so used to the feeling, it was simply too much to take.

'They're dead, Annie,' Buster finally said, his voice as clear and as calm as if he was reading the weather report for a country where it had never rained, and never would.

'Buster, don't say that,' Annie said. At this moment, the gallery dark and empty, no sign of their parents except for the brushstrokes that created the paintings on the walls, Annie could not tolerate, would not allow, any deviation from the singular fact that their parents were alive, were hiding, were awful people that needed to be punished.

'Maybe they've been dead from the start and we just missed the clues,' Buster said. 'We kept thinking that it had to be a ruse. It was just too much like a Fang event to be real.'

'That's right,' Annie said. 'It was too strange to be unplanned.'

'So, what if it was planned?'

'That's what I keep saying, Buster.'

'No,' Buster continued, waving her off frantically. 'What if it was planned, and the plan was for them to die?'

Annie didn't respond; she simply stared at Buster and waited for the inevitable.

'You saw how bad the chicken thing went at the mall, how sad it made them to fail in such a ridiculous way. What if they thought they couldn't make art anymore? And if they couldn't make art, then what did they have to live for? And if they had nothing to live for, why not just end it all? And if they were going to end it all, why not do it in some bizarre, mysterious way that would get people to talk about them, to remember the best of their art, one last time?'

'Please, Buster,' Annie said.

'Maybe it felt like a Fang event because it was. We just didn't understand what it really meant.'

Annie felt the sudden sickness of an uncertainty becoming certain. Had she been holding this possibility at bay for so long, with all of her strength, that it was only a matter of time before she gave in to the inevitable truth? She tried to locate the uneasy, shifting plates inside of her, the way her emotions clanged against each other and formed mountains that could not be scaled. There were stages of grief; she understood this. The first stage was denial, the next being anger. She had no idea what came next, and she had no illusions that she would ever reach it.

Back at the hotel, once Annie had deposited Buster in his room, her brother falling asleep the minute she helped him into bed, and returned to her own room, she fell onto the bed, still processing the fact that her parents would always be missing, were not capable of being resurrected. In some ways, it should have been a relief, the understanding that, no matter what they did, the line that connected them to their parents had gone slack. But Annie found herself wishing that her parents, even if they were not alive, were not dead. She wished for animation, even if there was no spark behind it that gave the actions meaning. She wanted, she supposed, the sounds of their voices but for them to speak a language that she did not understand. She rolled over, picked up the hotel phone, and dialed her parents' home phone number. The phone rang and rang and rang and then, crackling and slightly too loud, there was her mother's voice.

'The Fangs are dead. Leave a message after the tone and our ghosts will return your call.'

Annie waited, her silence filling up the answering machine back at home. Finally, everything unspoken, Annie returned the receiver to its cradle. Ten minutes later, Annie lifted the receiver once more, hit the redial button, and again listened to her mother's voice, a disembodied sound, the ghost of a ghost. 'The Fangs are dead. Leave a message after the tone and our ghosts will return your call.'

Annie hung up the phone just as her mother finished the message, not allowing the machine to record the sound of her grief, however faint. She would not call again. She had heard everything she needed to hear. Annie lay there, not thinking, not moving, not aware of anything except the sound of the air conditioner in the corner of the room, rattling like a machine that could not possibly make it through the night, though, of course, it would.

The Inferno, 1996
Artists: Caleb and Camille Fang

The Fangs, the three who still remained, were in a rut. Since Annie had left for Los Angeles to become a movie star, Caleb and Camille and Buster had spent the past six months sinking deeper and deeper into the crowded interior of the house, unsure of how to proceed. After the *Romeo and Juliet* incident, which had hastened Annie's departure, Buster wanted no part of the spotlight. He was content to observe and, even then, he would rather keep his eyes closed and simply listen. Camille insisted that it wouldn't be the same without Annie, that they were a family and it was this unity that had made the art so successful. Caleb continued to proclaim that Annie was no longer necessary, that they were entering into a new and productive phase of their career. He only needed time to figure out what it would be. So they waited, and Buster felt himself becoming invisible in the house, his parents sometimes shocked to find him in the kitchen, as if they thought that he had left along with Annie. To Buster, his parents seemed edgy, every object in the house likely to explode in their hands. They were, in short, a family in flux and they were unused to being in such a state. They *caused* flux, for crying out loud. Flux was their *thing*.

To occupy his time while his parents fretted over their next piece – he had heard the word *crossbow* whispered more than once – Buster focused on his writing. Before she left, preparing him for life without her, Annie had encouraged him to do something artistic, something that wasn't associated with Caleb and Camille. 'You need to find something, like playing the guitar or writing novels or arranging flowers,' she told him, 'so that you can see that creating something doesn't have to be as fucked up as Caleb and Camille make it seem.' Of the suggestions, writing seemed the easiest to hide from his parents. He held a fistful of pencils as if they were a bouquet for a date way out of his league. He flipped the empty pages of a notebook and imagined symbols bleeding into the paper. And then, nothing.

He was unsure of how to begin. He had no idea what to write about. What else was there but his family? Could he write about his family? That seemed like a bad idea. But he would write about *a* family. The Dang family. The parents

355

would be midgets. The brother would be older than his sister. This seemed, to Buster's nascent powers of imagination, to be enough to hide their true identities. And then he simply placed the Dangs in all manner of trouble. Inside the belly of a whale. Locked in the trunk of a car about to drive off a cliff. Falling through the sky, not a single parachute opening. All of these calamities were the result of bad parenting, Mr and Mrs Dang dragging the family into danger. And, just when it seemed the family would be saved, thanks to the calm and inventive actions of the children, one of the parents would make some critical mistake that would doom all of them. Every story ended the same, with the family spectacularly dead, only to be resurrected for the next tale. When he first read one of these stories to Annie, she had been silent and then said, 'Do you think you might want to play the guitar instead?' No, he did not. He had found something that he could do. He could create conflict. He could see it through to the end. And when it was over, he was the only one left unharmed. He was, he decided without anyone else telling him, a writer.

Buster would call Annie late at night so as not to arouse his parents' suspicion. Not that his parents would care. Annie had not been exiled. Unlike Camille's family, Mr and Mrs Fang did not disown their child because she had disappointed them. They would support her, but, if she was not going to be a part of their own work, they could not spend too much time thinking about her. They had, in fact, handed over to her a large sum of money to help her get started in California. 'It was a lot of money, Buster,' Annie had told him once on the phone, 'like *rich people* kind of money.' It reminded Buster that his parents were, technically, rich. In addition to the yearly grants and fellowships that they seemed to receive without fail, Caleb and Camille had won a MacArthur Genius grant when Buster was ten years old, a windfall so great that it was exactly like winning the lottery. His parents, however, simply kept on as if nothing had changed, perhaps occasionally buying more expensive props for their pieces. The thought that his parents had given some of that money to Annie made Buster happy, because it showed that his family, fractured as it was, might someday heal. It also showed him that, if he played his cards right, there would be a wad of cash for him when he moved on to the thing that was next.

Annie's roommate, Beatrice, a lesbian who helped run a complicated, illegal-sounding mail-order pornography company, answered the phone. 'Is Annie there?' he asked. 'She's right here,' Beatrice said. 'How come you haven't sent me the thirty dollars like I told you?'

'I don't have that kind of money,' Buster replied. How to explain that he had the money in a sealed envelope under his bed, too radioactive to deliver, its intentions seeping through the floor and into the ground, tainting the water supply.

'If you sent me that money,' she said, as she always did, 'I could send you something wonderful.'

'Is Annie there?' Buster asked again.

'Fine,' Beatrice said. 'Hang on.'

Annie answered the phone and she and Buster talked about the usual things. Annie's auditions ('I got a callback for the TV movie about a bank robbery gone wrong. I get to try and talk some sense into the stupid bank robber before the smart one catches on and beats the shit out of me'). Buster's stories ('Then they realize that one of the grenades is missing its pin. Oh, man, you can guess what happens next'). Annie's dreams of being a movie star ('I don't want to be some kind of huge movie star. I just want people to see me in a movie and remember that they saw me in some other movie and that I was good in it'). Buster's sudden dreams of being a writer ('I don't think Mom and Dad would read any of it').

'We're going to do incredible things, Buster,' Annie would always tell him. 'People will remember Caleb and Camille only as the parents of Buster and Annie Fang.'

'They still haven't performed since you left,' Buster said, unable to hide the worry in his voice.

'That can only be a good thing, Buster,' Annie said.

'It's easy for you to say that,' Buster replied. 'You're in California. I'm right here.'

'Soon you can leave too,' she said. 'Soon you can come with me to L.A. and we'll never have to go back.'

'Never?' Buster asked.

'Never ever,' Annie said.

In the supermarket, Buster's father, mid-sentence, did an awkward dance across the floor, tumbled into a display of spaghetti sauce, and sprawled on the ground, looking not unlike a murder victim as he lay there, stunned. Buster, his mother in another aisle, froze, unsure of how to proceed. They had not discussed this in advance. His father's right hand was bleeding in a way that suggested a need for stitches. People were coming to Caleb's aid, shouts were echoing through the aisles. Buster quickly slid to the floor, the knees of his jeans darkening, and began to frantically scoop handfuls of the sauce into his mouth.

'No, no no,' his father whispered, still grimacing in pain. Buster felt the shame burn across his face, and he began to rethink the situation. Now a crowd was beginning to form around them. Buster shouted, 'I saw the whole thing. We'll sue. We'll sue the pants off this place.' Buster's father grabbed him by his T-shirt and used it to awkwardly sit up. 'I just fell, Buster,' his father said. 'That's it. I just fell.' Buster hung his head, refused to look at the people surrounding the two of them, and waited for someone else to restore order. In his mouth was the tiniest grit of glass from the broken jars. He let it rest on his tongue for a few seconds and then swallowed it.

Later, in the car, Buster and his father sitting on dozens of plastic shopping bags to keep the seats clean, his father shook his head. His cut hand, not nearly as bad as it seemed when covered in tomato sauce, was wrapped in napkins. 'Pratfalls,' he said to his wife. 'B thinks we've been reduced to pratfalls.'

A few weeks after the incident in the supermarket, Buster came home from school to find his parents blasting thrash metal and dancing so furiously that it was as embarrassing to Buster as if he'd walked in on them having sex. 'Buster!' they both shouted over the music when they saw him standing in the hallway. His mother walked over and then led him into the living room. The table was covered with candy bars. This was how his parents celebrated, loud music and sugar. Buster knew something was going to happen, and he simply waited for his parents to show him how he fit into the dangerously unstable structure they had finally designed.

'Look at this,' his father said when things had calmed down. Buster sat between his parents on the sofa, eating his third candy bar, this one filled, somehow, with two different consistencies of caramel. His parents handed him an article from the *New York Times* titled 'Burning Down the House.' In the photo that accompanied the article, there was a close-up of a man holding a lit match while standing on the doorstep of a house. It seemed that the man, a performance artist named Daniel Harn, intended to burn down his house and everything in it, a statement regarding materialism and the cruelty of nature. His house, all the memories inside of it, would be reduced to ash, all in the name of art.

'We're going to burn our house down?' Buster said.

'No,' shouted his father. 'Jesus, no. I would never steal another artist's idea. Especially one this bad.'

'Buster,' his mother began, 'this Harn character is trying to create this spectacle, but it's as dull as any typical piece of art. He's telling everyone about it in advance. He's inviting an audience to come to upstate New York with the understanding that they will see his house burn down. He's telling them what to think about it before it happens.'

'That's not art,' his father continued. 'It's an art show. The work has already been done.'

'So, will we put out the fire?' Buster asked.

'That's not bad,' his mother admitted, 'but we have a better idea.'

'Much, much, much better,' his father said, sugar high, starting to laugh. Then his mother started to laugh. And they were laughing with such vigor, so genuinely moved, that Buster tried it out, to see what it felt like. He laughed and laughed and, though he did not yet know what the joke was, he hoped it would be worth the effort he'd already put into enjoying it.

During their next phone call, Buster told Annie about the proposed Fang performance, the burning house, their parents' plan.

'You don't have to do what they tell you to do,' she reminded him.

'*You* don't have to do what they tell you to do,' he replied. 'I still have to live with them. And I want to do it. At least this way, I'm part of it. They have some affection for me. If not, I'm just this guy in their house.'

'That's not how people are supposed to feel about their children.'

'I'm just taking pictures anyways,' he continued. 'I am in no danger of getting arrested.'

'Be careful,' she told him.

'It won't be the same without you,' he said.

'It will be,' she replied. 'It will be as awful as it always is.' Neither one of them spoke for a few seconds, and then Annie said, 'I am finding myself wishing I was there, all of a sudden.' She hung up the phone, as if she did not want to discuss that feeling any further, and Buster was left on the other end of the line, still holding the phone to his ear, thinking that if he listened hard enough he could still hear his sister in Los Angeles, rehearsing her lines, clearly enunciating every syllable.

Three weeks later, Buster was in Woodstock, New York, wishing he'd brought a heavier coat, holding a Leica R4 camera that he wasn't quite sure how to operate, waiting for some guy to burn down his house. He was sitting with about eighty to one hundred other people, folding chairs set up a safe distance from the house, the youngest person by far in the audience. There seemed to be a mix of New York artist types and people who just wanted to watch some kind of spectacle. There was also a crew of firemen; apparently this kind of thing required permits and the artist had obtained them. Buster could not imagine what his parents would say about an artist who filled out paperwork in order to realize his vision. His parents were no longer in sight, having disappeared twenty minutes earlier, according to the plan. Buster was simply to wait for the fire and take as many pictures as possible.

He sat down in a folding chair on the edge of the third row and began to turn the camera over and over in his hands. 'You come for the art?' he heard someone behind him ask. Buster quickly turned around to see an older man, bow-tied, nice warm coat, smiling at him. 'Or did you come to see a big fire?'

'Both,' said Buster.

'I came mostly to see this fool burn down his house,' the man said. It seemed to Buster that the man was just slightly drunk and that the man probably spent most of his time in this state. 'My sister is a big-time artist. She makes protest signs or some such nonsense. I'm afraid I don't understand contemporary art anymore,' he said. He pointed to Buster's camera. 'That,' he said, 'I understand. Photographs. Paintings. Sculpture. Even when it's not very good, I understand it. Burning down a house? Eating your own feces? Standing up for three straight days? You do that under most circumstances, you get locked up.'

Buster began to disengage himself from the conversation by turning his body away from the man as much as possible while still looking at him. Buster felt like his head might twist off his body.

'I mean, am I not right? If I punched you in the face right now, could I call that art?'

Buster held up the camera and took a picture of the man.

'Is that art?' the man asked, his face getting redder and redder, his anger puffing out his cheeks.

'This is for evidence,' Buster said. 'In case you punch me.'

'Art,' the man said, and then made a wanking motion with his hand. Buster stood and then moved to put a row of seats between himself and the man. He was cold. When was the fire going to come?

Nearly twenty minutes later, a man walked out of the house with a can of gasoline. He did not address the audience. He reached into his pocket, pulled out a book of matches, struck one, and tossed it through the open door of the house. The fire sparked immediately but it took a long time for it to begin to move through the rooms of the house. Buster could hear the popping of the heat rearranging molecules, but it wasn't nearly as spectacular as he had imagined. He realized he had pictured an explosion, not a fire. He revised his expectations. It was a house and it was on fire. What else did he want? He thought it would be polite to clap, to acknowledge the effort that went into this display, but no one else was doing it, so he simply sat in his seat and waited for his parents.

A window shattered and smoke began to pour out of the house and Buster watched as his parents, hand in hand, calmly walked out of the house, flames dancing around their hazy forms. Buster framed his parents through the viewfinder of his camera and clicked away. His father's arm was on fire and he waved in such a way that Buster wasn't sure if he was greeting the stunned onlookers or if he was trying to put out the fire. As they moved closer, it was apparent that his mother's entire back was covered in flames. They seemed unsteady, smoke-sick, but they kept walking, past the crowd, past Buster, and it appeared that they would walk all the way back home, but one of the firemen ran up to them and sprayed them down with an extinguisher. They looked like poorly made snowmen, flecked with a foamy substance. They fell to the ground, hacking the smoke out of their lungs. By the time they had regained their composure, Buster and the rest of the crowd had formed a circle around them. Aside from Buster, still snapping away, no one made a sound. They were staring at these two strange creatures while, behind them, the skeleton of the house continued to burn, the flame throwing strange shadows over everyone. Buster watched as his parents embraced, kissed, and then pushed away from the crowd, out of the grip of the firemen, and ran into the woods, toward their van, and Buster suddenly realized that they would, he was quite certain, leave him behind if he did not meet them there soon.

As if reminding the crowd of the reason for their attendance, the rear half of the house began to cave in, and Buster used this distraction to run after his parents. It was hard to see where he was going, and he was careful not to damage the camera, so expensive that his father made him name it (*Carl*), so he would treat it more carefully. He felt like he was perhaps running in the entirely wrong direction. He felt like perhaps his parents were also running in the wrong direction, smoke-drunk as they were. He knew this period of time well, the space between the event and when the family could safely reunite. However, this time, Annie was not with him. He was alone. His parents were together, but he was alone. He stopped, took a picture of the darkness, and then followed his instincts back to the van.

When he finally made it, his parents were waiting for him. They sat in the backseat of the van, the door open, each of them inspecting the angry pink marks on their bodies, rapidly swelling. They waved him over and he took a picture of them. 'Here's the deal, Buster,' his father began. 'If someone tells you something is fireproof, what they really mean is fire-lessening. It still burns like a son of a bitch.'

'It looked really great,' Buster assured them. His father nodded in agreement, but his mother offered up a weak smile. 'When you came through the woods just then,' she said to Buster, 'I thought Annie was going to be right behind you.'

Buster focused on his mother, who winced in pain as she shifted her weight. The air smelled of burned hair. 'I miss her too,' he said.

His mother gestured for him to come closer and then she hugged him. These were rare moments, and Buster did not let anything distract him from how wonderful it felt to share the same emotion with his mother, even if it was sadness. And then his mother began to sob. 'It's not the same, is it?' she asked.

'Camille,' his father said, but he did not continue when he saw the awful look on his wife's face, the look of someone holding on to the edge of a cliff, knowing they are about to let go.

'The whole reason we did this was so that we could still be a family. We could create these beautiful, fucked-up things and we could do it together. Your father and I made you and your sister and then the four of us made these things. For her to not be here, I don't know, I feel like whatever we make from here on out will be lacking. It will be missing something essential.'

Buster's father leaned in close to the both of them. 'We knew this was going to happen at some point. Either we would die or the kids would leave, but it couldn't always be the four of us. We just have to adapt. Our art will evolve. It will become something different, something better.'

'Don't say that,' his mother said.

'Not better, okay, that was a poor choice of words. But still rewarding.'

'I don't know if I can keep doing this without you two,' his mother said to Buster. 'I don't know if I want to.'

Buster hugged his mother again and then said, 'It's just temporary.'

'Is that how I should think of it?' she asked him.

'We'll go away, and then we'll come back and it'll be better because Annie and I will know more about what we can do, how we can help you guys.'

'You'll come back,' his mother said.

'We'll have to teach you all over again,' his father said.

'And then we'll make something wonderful,' Buster said.

His mother stopped crying and stroked Buster's cheek. 'I know that's not true,' she said, 'but let's pretend for now.'

CHAPTER 12

Having finally accepted their parents' death, Annie and Buster were surprised to find the process of grieving to be so ordinary, so boring. Without a funeral, which they agreed was a terrible idea, there seemed no concrete way to mourn. The notion of creating something violent and bizarre in their parents' name passed through them without any serious consideration. It seemed that their parents' disappearance from this world had left them without any options other than to simply continue their own lives, to move forward and see what kind of a world awaited them.

Annie would soon be back in L.A., resettling her life before she was asked to leave it behind again and start filming Lucy's movie. She had invited Buster to stay with her, the house more than big enough to contain the two of them, but he had already enacted plans to stay in town, hoping he was not making a huge mistake. He had, due to some begging, some false praise for Lucas Kizza's insane, rambling story, obtained an adjunct teaching position at the community college, teaching composition and technical writing. People would call him Professor Fang, which sounded so much like a supervillain that he wasn't sure he could go through with it. He would move in with Suzanne, what they had talked about for a few weeks now and had been unable to find any reason not to do so. The Fang house would be left unattended, tied up in the vagaries of the law until someone made a decision on how to proceed. Annie and Buster had some ragged desire to burn it down or to blow it up, but they were done with this kind of messy grief, with how it was really just anger masquerading as mourning. They would simply leave it behind, never return, and if they were lucky, their brains would do the careful editing necessary to omit this part of their lives from memory.

For the time being, Annie and Buster went about a revised routine. Buster wrote, and Annie rehearsed. Sometimes Buster, as he had years ago when he had still been living with his parents and Annie had been in Los Angeles, would run lines with his sister, trying his hardest to keep up with her, finding it impossible. Any attempts to find their parents, all that work, that embarrassingly earnest effort, simply ended, and the two of them were shocked to find out how much more free time they had without it.

On one of the last evenings in the house, Annie locked in her room doing some kind of jazzercise along to a videotape she had found at a thrift store, Buster heard Suzanne's car tires crunching over the gravel driveway, but he kept typing, trying to wring as many words as he could out of the story in his head. The novel seemed to be a cave of sorts, twisting, maze-like passages, but Buster focused only on finding an exit that was not the original entrance, pushing his way through the dark until he found a path that held the promise of escape. He knew that Micah and Rachel would emerge, finally, from the pit and take their places aboveground, but he had to get there, had to find the correct sequence of events that would unlock that image. He heard Suzanne's voice calling from the hallway and he finally removed his hand from the keys of the computer. Suzanne held two paper bags of food from Sonic, the bottom of the bags wet with grease and steam, and, in her other hand, a tray that held two sodas in a size so large that the cups looked like barrels. 'Dinner,' she said. He nodded, cleared off the coffee table in the living room, and they sat on the floor and tore into their burgers. Buster hadn't eaten since that morning, and he let the food, the salt and the grease and the shocking tang of condiment, serve as a reward for having written enough to be satisfied. 'Good day?' he asked Suzanne.

Suzanne had finished her burger and was carefully opening packets of mustard to dress up a corn dog. 'Not bad,' she said. 'Okay tips, no jerks, day went by fast. And I think I had an idea about the story I'm working on. I wrote it down on a napkin during my break.' Buster smiled. 'I did okay, too,' he said. She smiled and kissed his cheek. 'I knew you were doing okay,' she said. 'It made me happy at work to think that you were writing the hell out of your book.' They ate their food, took sips of soda so sweet that it tasted like liquefied candy, and Buster allowed himself the excitement of knowing that this could go on forever if he didn't fuck it up.

'I brought some music,' Suzanne said, reaching into her backpack. 'I ordered new stuff for you, off the Internet. It sounds like the crazy shit you listen to on that record player, but it's brand-new.' She produced a CD by a band called The Vengeful Virgins, the cover art consisting of hundreds and hundreds of guitar strings, wound into strange shapes. 'It's two twin brothers and they're, like, savants or something. They're four-teen years old or close to that, and they make this really weird music. It's just drums and guitar, but it sounds like animals.' Buster shrugged. He didn't want to get into a long conversation, but he only listened to his parents' music because he had never developed his own tastes. He had found it too difficult to search out other music, to constantly listen to something and wonder, 'Is this any good?' His parents had selected worth-while music and so he listened to it, but he did not say this to Suzanne. He said, 'Put it on,' and went back to the Tots that Suzanne had instructed the fry cook to fry twice so as to make them extra-crunchy.

The first song opened with the sound of a bass drum, the beat slightly off, spastic. It went on for over a minute until he heard a voice, a pitch that suggested sudden pubescence, singing, 'When the end comes, and it always comes, we will drown in our own dust. We will watch the sky as it slowly darkens and we'll be left with rot and rust. But we won't die. We won't die.' Suzanne pointed at the stereo, nudging Buster with her elbow. 'Was I right? Weird.' Buster nodded. A guitar, or something like a guitar, squealed, and then, suddenly, the drumming tightened up, became as steady as a heartbeat, and the song began to bend and twist and Buster felt like something wonderful was happening that would soon implode. By the end of the second song, he said, 'This is good,' confident of the proclamation, turning the volume up so the house began to vibrate. Suzanne kissed him again. 'I knew you would like it,' she said.

'It's a sad world,' the voice on the CD screamed, shredding his vocal cords, as a new song began without warning. 'It's unforgiving.' Buster sat up, the song tripping the hard wiring of his memories, and he placed his hands firmly on the coffee table, pressing so hard that the table began to softly vibrate. 'Kill all parents, so you can keep living,' Buster sang, in perfect time to the voice on the

CD. 'Kill all parents,' he repeated, his voice cracking, 'so you can keep living.' Suzanne touched his shoulder. 'You know this song?' she asked, and Buster could only nod.

Annie emerged from her room, dumbbells still in her hands, her expression one of such confusion that her facial features seemed scrambled, some kind of cubism. 'What the fuck is this?' she asked, one of the dumbbells pointing at the stereo. Buster held up the CD case and Annie dropped the dumbbell, shaking the floor, and snatched it out of his hand. 'Number three,' Buster said, pointing to the track list on the back cover. 'Song number three, 'K.A.P.' ' 'What's wrong?' Suzanne asked, backing away from the intensity of the Fang children.

'This is a Fang song,' Buster said, as he and his sister ran out of the room, to his computer, the Internet, a sudden interest in The Vengeful Virgins. 'What?' Suzanne asked. 'Our parents,' Annie shouted, her voice echoing throughout their parents' house, where they had somehow grown up. 'Our goddamned parents.'

As the Fang children searched every inch of the Internet, Suzanne having let herself out of the house, leaving the two of them to their own wicked devices, Buster scrolled through the Google results so quickly that Annie had to keep slapping his hand to get him to slow down. The Vengeful Virgins were signed to Light Noise, a tiny indie label based in the Northwest, one that had discovered The Leather Channel, another band Buster and Annie had never heard of, who had subsequently signed a multimillion-dollar contract with Interscope Records. The two boys who made up the band, Lucas and Linus Baltz, thirteen years old, had no real Web site, nothing but a bare-bones MySpace page with little beyond a few of their songs playing on a loop and a few pictures of the two boys, shaggy-haired, their eyes so dark they seemed black, thin and lanky, big smiles that showed slightly crooked teeth. It seemed impossible that these kids were responsible for the brain-rattling songs that Buster had heard. Though there were numerous bloggers who breathlessly championed the album, always mentioning the boys' bewildering youth, Buster could find only a few articles that had any personal information about the boys. He learned that they lived in Wayland, North Dakota, were self-taught, obsessed with the apocalypse. They were, according to the label's Web site, currently on tour.

Buster looked at the tour dates for The Vengeful Virgins. They were playing this very night in Kansas City, Missouri. Tomorrow they would be in St Louis.

It was shocking to Buster, after how hard he and his sister had forced themselves to let go of their parents, to accept their deaths, how quickly the two of them jumped right back into the frenzy and uncertainty of searching for Caleb and Camille. The plan, which Buster devised quickly, was that he and Annie would travel to St Louis, go to the show to see The Vengeful Virgins. They would figure out some way to get backstage, and then confront the kids with their knowledge of the song, and try to get them to tell Buster and Annie where their parents were. That was it. That was the whole plan. It had some holes, he admitted. If their parents had made the decision to allow these two kids in on their disappearance, then they must have known that these two boys could be trusted. So how would they get the kids to tell them what they needed to know? And what if the twins had no idea what they were talking about? What if their parents really were dead, as they had finally accepted, and this was all some strange coincidence? He tried not to think about it, focused only on the sharp, painful feeling inside of him that he was closer to the thing that he needed to know.

Annie sat on Buster's bed as he packed a duffel bag with clothes and toiletries. 'Okay, so let me ask you this,' she began. 'You think these fucking kids somehow know Caleb and Camille and they gave them this song?' Buster considered the statement and then nodded. 'So,' Annie continued, 'that means that The Vengeful Virgins probably know about the Fangs and that we made all this art.' Buster again nodded. 'So they probably know who we are, if they know enough about our parents to know that they're hiding out. So don't you think they'll recognize us when we meet them?' Buster had not considered any of this. 'Maybe,' Buster admitted. 'Definitely,' Annie corrected. 'It won't work this way. We have to be smarter than them. We have to find a way around their defenses.' He began to unpack his bag. 'I guess we're not going to St Louis,' he said, frowning.

And then, before he could return a single article of clothing to his dresser, he heard his sister laugh. He turned around to find Annie, smiling as if she knew the secrets of the world and did not care if revealing them would ruin everything, signaling for him to move closer to her. 'Caleb and Camille only care about art,' she told him. 'Nothing else matters.' Buster nodded in agreement, still puzzled as to what was coming. 'These kids, they're so young, I imagine there are still some things they couldn't resist.'

'Money?' Buster asked, still struggling to catch up to whatever his sister had already realized.

'Fame,' Annie replied.

As she continued to outline the rudimentary elements of her plan, Buster half-listened to The Vengeful Virgins still pounding through the speakers of the stereo and felt the overwhelming urge to carve his name into something, letters so large that they could be seen from space, to claim everything that was undeniably his own.

★　　★　　★

Later that night, unable to enact their plan until daylight, Buster sat on the sofa in the living room and, once again, listened to The Vengeful Virgins. He closed his eyes and let the screeching and thumping work its way into his muscles like a medically disproved balm. He imagined his parents, hiding in some basement in North Dakota, listening to these same songs, sending some strange clue as to their disappearance out into the world, traveling from city to city, until Annie and Buster discovered its existence. Or was this clue even meant for Annie and Buster? Was it their parents' own joke, some way to continue their work in anonymity? And perhaps, worst of all, something that Buster had forced out of his mind since he'd heard the song, these two boys were a replacement for Annie and Buster, the new children that Caleb and Camille Fang would use to restore their name to prominence. They had tired of Annie and Buster, their failures, the simple fact that they were no longer children, and now they had Lucas and Linus. And, as a show of this new partnership, they had given the boys a song that had once belonged only to the Fangs, knowing that they would be able to send it out farther into the world than Annie and Buster could have ever imagined.

Buster turned off the music, sat in the dark silence of his parents' house. He sucked on an ice cube, rubbed the curve of the ice against the back of his teeth. He concentrated until it seemed that his body temperature had adjusted to the cold ice in his mouth. His arms and legs were numb, nothing but his heart pumping blood to the extremities that he refused to utilize. Thirty minutes passed and then Buster suddenly came back to life, lifting off the sofa, his feet taking him back to his computer. He erased the last few pages of the novel, a mistake of imagination, and began anew. It was the only thing he could control, the world he had made, and he made it bend to his will, feeling the satisfaction of saying something was a certain way and having no one tell him differently.

There would be redemption, the twins escaping the pit, disavowing their intended future, finding a new world to call their own. And, unfortunately, it would mean that nothing would change beyond them, that children would still be enslaved to fight each other in the pit, to smash their hands into tiny pieces of grit and then live with the repercussions for years after. But what could the two children do? Better to leave it behind than try to fix what was already broken. Had this not been what Annie had been trying to tell Buster for weeks now regarding their own parents? Was he agreeing with her only for the purposes of his novel, or was this a universal truth? He typed out the scene, reread it, and realized that it was the only possibility that made any sense. When he finally pushed away from his computer, it was one in the morning and he was not in the least bit tired. He knocked on Annie's door and found her wide awake, simply staring at the wall. 'My body won't let me do anything but think about them,' she said. 'It's so fucking ridiculous.'

Buster grabbed a videotape, the first thing he could find, and the two of them, their hands trembling, watched a Buster Keaton movie where Keaton was slammed, flipped, and thrown through walls. And each time something disastrous happened, Annie and Buster watched with amazement as Keaton, his face impassive as stone, merely righted himself and kept moving along.

The next afternoon, still without sleep, Buster sat in the car with Annie in the passenger seat, engine silenced, windows rolled down, parked in front of a pay phone at a gas station in Nashville. Earlier in the day, Buster had called the club in St Louis where The Vengeful Virgins would be performing and talked to the owner, informing him that he, Will Powell, was a reporter from *Spin* magazine with an interest in talking to Lucas and Linus. Buster made it clear that there was the distinct possibility of a cover story if the boys would offer him an exclusive interview. The owner said he would pass the information along to the boys when they arrived at the club, and now Buster and Annie waited in the car, Chick-O-Stick wrappers littering the floorboards, the interior reeking of peanut butter and coconut. Buster and Annie had driven to Nashville to help obscure their intentions to Lucas and Linus. If they were involved in his parents' disappearance, he couldn't very well leave his parents' home number for them to call back. He didn't even want the area code of Coalfield to appear in the phone number, so as not to arouse suspicion. Nashville was Music City USA. Even if the Virgins weren't Grand Ole Opry material, it was where a free-lance music journalist might reside. It was only after they had entered into this complicated ruse that they realized they could have purchased a prepaid cell phone and done all of this at home. To rearrange their plans, to change the pieces of the trap they had set, seemed like a bad idea, a worse idea than waiting for hours for the pay phone to ring, understanding that it might not happen. Buster realized that, regardless of his slight attempts at reconnaissance, he needed some degree of luck for any of this to work. And with each minute that passed, Buster remembered how unlucky he was, how he seemed a beacon for all manner of ridiculous misfortune.

Buster had wanted to put up a sign on the phone, which said OUT OF ORDER, but Annie nixed the idea. 'No one uses pay phones anymore,' she said. 'I can't believe they still exist. There's no point complicating things with fake signs.' On the drive to Nashville, she came up with a set of questions for the Virgins, open-ended questions that would allow the boys to make their own case for stardom.

Buried at the bottom of the list, the ninth of ten questions, she finally asked the only question that mattered, the single question whose answer would be recorded for posterity. *How did you come to write 'K.A.P.'?* The tenth question, if it became necessary to ask it, was *If you were a tree, what kind of tree would you be?*

And then the pay phone began to ring, once, twice, before Buster jumped out of the truck and snatched the receiver from its holder. 'Hello?' he said. 'Is this the guy from *Spin* magazine?' the voice replied. 'It is,' Buster said, just as he felt someone tapping him on the shoulder. He turned to find Annie by his side, holding the questions for the interview. He took the notebook from her and she stood close to him, almost close enough to hear the conversation unfold.

'Is this Lucas or Linus?' Buster asked.

'Lucas. Linus plays the drums. He likes to stay quiet and make the sounds. I do the talking. Anything I say, he would agree with. Okay?'

'Okay. Perfect. So, the first question is, well, you have such an interesting sound, it seems wholly original, and yet I wonder if you have any influences.'

'Not really. We like speed metal, but we're not good enough to play like that. We listen to some rap music, I guess, but that has nothing to do with us. Mostly we like movies and books for ideas. We like *Mad Max* and *Dr Strangelove* and *Carnival of Souls* and Vincent Price movies. We read

Dragonlance novels and comic books about zombies and we like books about the end of the world. We like anything about the end of the world. We really like this little book called *The Underground*. Have you read that book?'

Buster felt dizzy, wished he was in St Louis so he could see Lucas's expression as he asked this question. Had he already been discovered, so early in the ruse? 'I have read that book,' he answered.

'Fucking great book. The first song on the album, I wrote that song after I read *The Underground*. Nobody else really knows about it.'

'What kind of guitar do you play?' Buster asked quickly, changing the subject. He resisted the urge to ask Lucas why, exactly, his novel was so amazing, knowing it would lead the interview further away from what he really needed to know.

'I don't know. I got it from a catalog. We don't care about instruments. The expensive ones make you feel bad for doing awful things to them. And they don't make the same kind of sounds that the cheap ones make. We like the way cheap things sound.'

Buster went through the questions, Lucas giving shorter and shorter answers, his enthusiasm for being on the cover of *Spin* magazine overridden by his own attention deficit. Buster could hear him rubbing the tips of his fingers against the strings of his guitar, making a squeaking sound like animals trapped in a pen. Annie jabbed Buster in the ribs, keeping him focused, moving him

384

toward the inevitable. Finally, with no way to avoid it, Buster summoned up the courage, in the face of constant disappointment, and tried once again to find his parents.

'How did you come to write "K.A.P."?' he asked.

There was silence on the other end of the line. Buster could hear Lucas breathing, deep and steady. Buster expected the boy to hang up, but, slowly, in a measured voice, Lucas replied, 'It just kind of came to me.'

'There wasn't any event that made you write it?' Buster asked.

'I guess not,' Lucas said. 'I just, you know, thought that people should kill their parents if they want to do anything good with their lives. This is a stupid question, I think. No offense.'

'You didn't write that song, Lucas,' Buster said.

'Yes I did.'

'I know you didn't write that song,' Buster said. 'I'm going to write an entire article about it unless you tell me.'

'I'm going to hang up.'

'Who wrote that song, Lucas? It's not even the best song on the album. I think there's, like, eight other songs that are better, much better. The writing is sloppy and I think the sentiment is a little trite. It doesn't have the depth of your other songs. That's how I know you didn't write it.'

'It's going to be our hit,' Lucas replied.

'That doesn't mean you don't have other songs that are much, much better.'

'I . . . I didn't write it,' Lucas said.

'I know that, Lucas,' Buster said. 'It doesn't sound like you.'

'Everybody loves that song and I didn't even write it,' Lucas said, his voice cracking.

'Who wrote it?'

'Somebody else,' Lucas said, and Buster resisted the urge to smash the phone against the brick wall.

'Who wrote it?'

'My dad,' Lucas finally said.

'What?' Buster said, amazed at how unsteady the earth felt beneath his feet.

'My dad wrote it. He said we could use it; it was the first song that we ever played, and so we just thought we'd put it on the album because we knew it so well.'

'Your dad?'

Annie frowned at this statement, jabbed Buster again, but he shook his head and turned slightly away from her.

'Well, my stepdad. But I call him my dad. He's been my dad for so long that I call him my real dad.'

Buster heard the sound of another voice on the phone, a woman's voice.

'My mom just came in here,' Lucas said. 'She wants to talk to you.'

Buster did not want to talk to this woman, not at all. 'Wait,' Buster said to Lucas. 'I have one more question.'

'Okay, but she really wants to talk to you.'

'Um, if you were a tree, what kind of tree would you be?'

Lucas, without hesitation, replied, 'One that just got struck by lightning,' and then handed the phone to his mother.

'Who is this?' the woman said.

'Who is this?' Buster replied.

'What are you up to, sir?' the woman said.

'Do you know Caleb Fang?' Buster asked.

'You leave him alone,' the woman said. 'I'm warning you, leave my husband alone.'

Buster, confused, his arm aching from holding the phone to his ear, replied, 'Mom?'

'Oh, god, is this Buster?' the woman said. 'No, Buster, I'm not your mother.'

'What's going on?' Buster said, his anger now properly summoned at the embarrassment of mistaking a perfect stranger for his mother.

'Leave them alone, Buster. Just let them live their lives.'

'What the fuck is going on, lady?' Buster shouted, but the woman had hung up the phone.

Buster stayed on the line, unwilling to put the receiver back in its cradle. In a few seconds, he would turn to his sister and try to explain as best he could, then wait for her to decide how to proceed. For the moment, he simply listened to the dial tone, the way the unbroken sound seemed to be pulling him into the wiring of the phone. He wondered where his fangs were, those veneers

387

from his childhood. He wished he had them on right now, teeth so sharp that they could tear through anything. He imagined the fangs digging into something soft and pulsing with life, leaving an imprint that would never, ever, go away.

CHAPTER 13

As soon as they arrived in North Dakota, Annie understood that it was the exact place you wanted to live if the apocalypse ever arrived: the clear, stingingly pure air, the absence of color, the feeling that the place had never recovered from the Ice Age and would therefore be nearly unchanged when the world was stripped of what mattered most. It was wilderness, even the largest city in the state, and Annie felt trepidation upon walking out of the airport, the sense that her parents knew the terrain, had acclimated to this barren expanse of land, whereas Annie and her brother would be torn apart by wild animals.

Yet even as they drove down the single-lane highway, static and heavy metal on the radio, Annie prepared herself for the possibility that their parents would not be here. If the woman – Caleb's other wife, if they were to believe this woman's outrageous claim – had alerted the Fangs to their children's sudden discovery, it was possible that they would keep running, move on to the next hiding spot. There was some grand reason that they had disappeared in the first place, and Annie now wondered if she and Buster were intended to play a part in it. She began to believe that her parents had created something that they would not allow to be compromised, even by their own children. Especially by their own children.

It was easy enough to find the twins' house. A cursory look online provided the address for the only Baltz, Jim and Bonnie, in Wayland, North Dakota. 'What will we do, if it's really them?' Buster asked Annie, who struggled to answer with any confidence. The options were violence or forgiveness, which meant there was only one option. Unless her parents could explain this to them in such a way that there was a third option, begrudging acceptance. 'We won't do anything,' Annie said. 'We'll wait until it comes to us, how to proceed, and then we'll do that.'

The house was nearly identical to the Fangs' house in Tennessee, a one-story ranch, undecorated, left to weather the elements with little concern for upkeep. In the long gravel driveway, a semitruck was parked. FLUXUS TRUCKING, it said on the door. IF IT EXISTS, WE SHIP IT. 'This is it,' Annie said, turning off the car, staring into the windows of the house for signs of movement, finding nothing. 'They won't be happy to see us,' Buster said, his face tight with the possibility of disappointment. 'We won't be happy to see them,' Annie said, and stepped out of the car, onto the porch, standing on a mat that bore no words of welcome. Buster took his place beside her on the porch, and, forgoing the doorbell, Annie rapped her knuckles on the doorframe, insistent, bone on wood, musical. There was silence inside the house, thirty seconds, a minute, and then Buster and Annie, together, knocked again on the door. They heard the sound of activity inside the house, footsteps on hardwood, and the knob twisted and the door opened and there, in front of them, no mistaking his presence, was their father, Caleb Fang.

'A and B,' he said, not a trace of emotion in his voice, a scientist classifying a familiar species. 'We found you,' Annie said, muscle spasms softly twitching under her skin. Caleb nodded. 'You did,' he said. 'I've been expecting you. Bonnie called me after she talked to Buster, warned me that you might be coming. I've been waiting for you. If you hadn't shown up, I think I might have been a little disappointed.'

'Where's Mom?' Buster asked, remembering the woman, Bonnie, but not able to give it any more thought at the moment. Caleb shrugged. 'Not here,' he said.

'What?' Annie said.

'She doesn't live here,' Caleb said.

Annie pushed past her father, into the house, and Buster followed her. 'We are in a position of power here, Caleb. Do you understand that?' she asked her father. Caleb nodded. 'Whatever you're doing, we can ruin it. I don't think you want us to do that, all the work you've obviously put into it. But Buster and I, we want to ruin this very badly. We want it to blow up in your face. So you are going to tell us everything we want to know.'

'That's fine, Annie,' Caleb said. 'I can tell you the basics and I think you'll be satisfied. I think you and Buster, of all people, will understand.'

'You're going to tell us everything,' Annie said. 'You and Camille are going to tell us everything, every detail, and we'll decide whether we're satisfied or not.'

'It would take a long time to explain everything,' Caleb replied.

'That's fine,' Annie said.

'Annie?' Buster said, and Annie turned to see that Buster had wandered into the living room, was holding a framed picture. Annie walked over to her brother and stared at the photo: their father, younger; that woman who had once helped create a Fang event; and the twins, maybe seven or eight years old – a family portrait.

'What is this?' Annie said.

'That's my family,' Caleb said.

'When was this taken?' Buster asked.

'Six years ago, something like that,' Caleb replied.

'Who is this?' Annie asked, pointing to the woman.

'My wife,' Caleb said.

'Dad?' Buster said.

'It's complicated,' Caleb said.

'Stop talking,' Annie said, tossing the picture to the floor. 'Don't say another word until Camille is here, until all of us are together, and then we'll talk.'

'I'll see what I can do,' he said.

Caleb went to the telephone, dialed a number, and then whispered, 'It's me.'

'Is that Mom?' Buster said, but Caleb held his hand up to silence him.

'There's a problem. We need to talk.' There was a long pause, Caleb listening intently, staring directly at Annie and Buster. 'A and B,' Caleb finally said, and then he hung up the phone.

'Was that Mom?' Buster asked, and Caleb nodded.

'We need to drive to the meeting place,' Caleb said. 'You two follow me; it's about forty-five minutes away.'

'We'll ride together,' Annie said.

'Fine,' Caleb said, taking a baseball cap from the coatrack, stepping outside, waiting for his children to follow him so he could lead them to the place they needed to go.

Annie drove, her father in the passenger seat, and Buster sat in the back, his body leaning forward into the space that separated his sister and his father. 'We really started to think that you might be dead,' Buster said to his father. Caleb laughed softly, a hiccup of breath. 'That was the idea,' he said. Annie placed The Vengeful Virgins album in the CD player and her father winced. 'Can we not listen to this?' he said. 'We like it,' Annie said, turning up the volume.

Their father directed them to a mall three towns over, only one level, the anchor stores long out of business. 'This is it,' he said, 'but when we talk, you need to call me Jim. None of this Caleb bullshit.'

'We'll try to remember,' Annie said.

'What's Mom's name?' Buster asked.

'Patricia,' Caleb said.

'Jim and Patricia Fang,' Buster said.

The three of them walked into the mall, three distinct shapes fitting themselves into a new space.

They found their mother in the food court, sitting alone at a table near a restaurant that sold corn dogs and lemonade. When she saw Buster and Annie, she frowned, then quickly reconfigured the structure of her face into a grimace of sorts. She waved them over. 'Hello, Buster,' Camille said. 'Hello, Patricia,' Buster said, and Camille immediately looked over at Caleb. 'How much do they know?' she asked her husband. 'Not a fucking thing,' Annie interjected. 'But that's what you're going to tell us.' Camille nodded, held up her hands, palms out, in supplication. 'Fine, fine,' she said. 'Just sit down.'

Camille looked around the table. 'How do you want to do this?' she asked. 'Should we just start talking, or do you want to ask us questions?' Caleb stated that it would be best if he spoke and then, once he was finished, they could ask questions. Annie shook her head. 'We'll ask questions right now,' she said. 'Fine,' Caleb said, seeming to understand finally that his children had the upper hand.

'Why did you disappear?' Annie asked.

Caleb and Camille looked at each other and smiled. 'Art,' they said in unison. 'Caleb and Camille Fang, our defining work. You know this, don't you? Why else would we disappear? This is all part of something larger, a statement, an event, on such a large scale that it's impossible to deny.'

'How long have you been planning it?' Buster asked.

'Years,' Camille answered. 'Many, many years.'

'We started this once the two of you made it clear that you wanted nothing more to do with our work,' Caleb continued. 'Annie, you left us, and then Buster was gone a few years later. We had worked so hard to make you an integral part of these performances, to turn you into essential elements of our process, and then you left us. So we had to start from scratch, we had to start over.'

'You're blaming this on us?' Annie said.

'We're not blaming you, Annie,' Camille said emphatically, though Caleb's face seemed to suggest otherwise, his eyebrows raised and eyes wide. 'If it wasn't for the two of you, forcing us to rethink how we made art, we never would have come up with this piece.'

'We started with the essential steps,' Caleb said.

'We got new identities, social security numbers, passports, tax history, everything. Jim Baltz and Patricia Howlett.'

'When was this?' Buster asked.

'Soon after you left for college,' Camille responded. 'Ten, eleven years ago.'

'You've had these identities for eleven years? And you only just disappeared last year?' Annie said.

'It was part of the process,' Caleb explained. 'We had to create new characters for when Camille and Caleb died, identities we could easily slip into.'

'There was a woman, Bonnie; you might remember her, actually; she had been an ardent supporter of our work. So we reached out to her. We told her how we wanted to disappear, and she helped us. Her husband, who had no appreciation for art at all, had only recently left her and she had these twins, not even two years old yet, and so your father married her. Jim married her, perfectly legal.'

'I bought a truck and that was my cover, a long-distance trucker. I would spend most of the time with your mother in Tennessee, but every few months, I would drive back here and live with Bonnie and Lucas and Linus for a week or two, before I went back on the road. It worked well enough.'

'What about you?' Annie asked her mother.

'There was a small cabin on a few acres that had been in Bonnie's family for years. I would stay there in the summers, getting to know people in the town, establishing my backstory, so that when I came here for good, people wouldn't be suspicious of this stranger in their midst.'

'You did this for ten years?' Buster asked.

'It wasn't so bad. I like it here. It's quiet; the people are nice. I got used to it.'

'Little by little, we cashed out funds from our bank in Tennessee and then deposited it in the accounts here in North Dakota, building up enough money to live on. So the plan was in place, not quite fully formed but enough of an outline that we knew what would happen when we finally disappeared.'

'And then you two showed up, back in our lives,' Camille said, smiling.

'And we knew we had to take action,' Caleb continued, his voice growing more and more excited. 'We hadn't planned on you two coming back, but we realized it was a sign that we needed to put this thing into motion. If we disappeared, you two would be there to discover us missing. And then our disappearance would have even more meaning. And, if we had done things correctly, we thought you would look for us, and that would add depth to the piece, how our deaths would resonate beyond us.'

'What about all that blood?' Buster asked. 'The police really thought you were dead.'

Camille rolled her eyes. 'That was your father's idea, at the last minute.'

'Bonnie had driven from North Dakota to meet

397

us, and just as we were going to leave, I had the idea of violence, of some signs of struggle. So I took a knife and slashed myself with it. I didn't realize how much blood there would be.'

'Oh god,' Camille said, smiling, remembering the event. 'It was horrible. Your father looked like he was going to bleed to death. Bonnie had to stop at a drugstore and get a first-aid kit. We spread newspaper all over the backseat so he wouldn't bleed all over the upholstery. It was awful.'

'It worked though, didn't it?' he said to his wife.

She laughed. 'You always had a weakness for the grand gesture.'

Annie and Buster watched their parents, obviously in love, appreciating the magnificence of their own handiwork, and felt their power slipping away.

'What about Mom's paintings?' Annie asked. 'What about that?'

Caleb's face darkened and Camille looked away. 'Yes, that was . . . that was well played on your part. After so many years of being the source of unrest, I guess I had forgotten what it felt like to be caught in the middle of the chaos. It was an altogether unpleasant experience. You two almost ruined us.'

'Good,' Annie said.

'Your mother first tried to tell me that it was a hoax, something the two of you had dreamed up. I wanted so badly to come to that opening, to see for myself, but I knew I had to stay focused.

Instead, I went to her cabin when she was away and found more of those . . .' Caleb's face had turned bone-white, flinching as if needles were being inserted under his fingernails, 'more of those paintings.'

'That was a secret,' Camille said to the children, trying to smile. 'I only shared it with you two.'

'But we moved past it,' Caleb continued, though Annie and Buster could see the doubt lingering on his face. 'I do not for a second doubt your mother's devotion to what we have been doing for our entire lives. I love her and she loves me and, most importantly, we love making real, genuine art. We love this thing that we're making.'

'And now what?' Buster said, noticing without surprise, confirming his worst fears, that he and Annie had not been included in the list of things their parents loved.

'Well, we have to be declared dead, and then we come back to life,' Camille answered.

'And all of this?' Annie said, gesturing to the air above them, their lives in North Dakota.

'We leave it behind,' Caleb said.

'Bonnie? Lucas and Linus?'

'We leave it all behind,' Caleb said.

'I talked to them on the phone,' Buster said. 'They called you their dad.'

'I am their dad,' Caleb said. 'But things will have to change.'

'Do they know about all this?' Annie asked.

'God no,' Caleb said, his voice rising. 'Can you

imagine? They aren't like you two. They aren't real artists. They wouldn't know how to handle it. They'd find a way to ruin it. I guess they did ruin it. That fucking song.'

'I told you it was stupid,' Camille pointed out.

'What happened?' Annie asked.

'The twins were always playing with instruments, making this awful racket. So I taught them the song. I had no idea they would become somewhat proficient, would make an album, would sign to a label, would go on tour. How could I have anticipated that? I mean, you've heard them. It was a mistake though. I do take the blame for that. I got lazy and I paid for it.'

'This is insane,' Annie said.

'You're upset,' Camille replied. 'You don't like that we kept you in the dark. But you have to admit this is an amazing piece.'

Annie stared at her parents. Their demeanor had changed since they first entered the food court. They were enjoying the explanation of their grand design. They spoke with reverence about the way they had deformed the lives of those around them so that their idea could take shape, be willed into existence.

'You have never cared for us, for anyone but yourselves,' she began. 'You've done as much as you possibly could to wreck our lives. You made us do everything you wanted, and when we couldn't do it anymore, you left us.'

'You left us,' Caleb said, the anger a heavy thing

in his voice. 'You two left us to pursue inferior forms of art. You disappointed us. You nearly ruined what we'd made. So we moved on without you. And now, we've made something better than anything we've done before, and you two are not a part of it.'

'We are a part of it,' Buster said. 'We're your son and daughter.'

'That doesn't mean anything,' Caleb said.

'Honey,' Camille said. 'That's not true.'

'Okay, fine,' Caleb said, composing himself. 'It means something but it doesn't mean as much as the art.'

'If we didn't make a fuss about you disappearing then no one would notice or care that you had disappeared. Without us, what does your dying mean?' Annie said.

'And we do appreciate that. Like we said, we had hoped that the two of you would add something to the piece, though we had not imagined you would actually find us. You did a little too much, in that respect. What would be great is if you went back to your own lives, forgot about this meeting, and continued to look for us. That way, you would be a genuine element of this piece.'

Annie put up her hand and shook her head. 'We don't want any part of this. In fact, we want this to end. We want to fuck this up so badly.'

'But why?' Camille asked. 'Why would you do that?'

'Because you hurt us,' Annie said.

'You'd ruin more than ten years of difficult artistic work just because your feelings got hurt?' Caleb asked.

'I don't understand,' Camille said. 'You didn't want to be with us anymore. You removed yourselves from our lives.'

'We didn't want to make art anymore,' Buster said. 'Not your kind of art. We still wanted to be with you.'

'You can't separate them,' Caleb replied. 'We are the things that we make. You have to accept that.'

'We did,' Annie said. 'That's why we left.'

'Then why did you come back?' Camille asked. She was beginning to lose her composure, tears welling up in the corners of her eyes.

'We needed help,' Buster said.

'And we helped you, goddamn it,' Caleb responded.

'No, you didn't. You left us,' Annie said.

'Because we had to,' Camille answered.

'This is ridiculous,' Caleb said. 'I'm sixty-five years old. This is it. This is the last big thing I'll ever make. I am begging you not to take that away from me.'

'You're willing to live like this for six more years, until the state declares you legally dead, just to make an artistic statement?'

'Yes,' Caleb said. Annie looked at her mother, who nodded in agreement.

Annie pushed away from the table, and Buster did the same. They stood over their parents, who waited for an answer.

'We won't tell,' Annie said.

'Thank you,' Camille said.

'But we don't ever want to see you again,' Annie replied.

'Okay,' Caleb said. 'We understand. We can agree to that.' Camille hesitated for a few seconds but then nodded. 'If that's what it takes,' she said.

'This is the last time we'll ever see you,' Buster said, emphasizing each word, wondering if his parents understood exactly what this meant. He watched their faces for recognition of the finality of the moment, but there was nothing there but a certainty that they had rescued what was necessary in order to keep living. Buster was about to repeat himself, but he knew that nothing would be changed, and so he simply allowed the moment to pass.

The Fangs looked around the sparsely populated mall.

'All these places are going out of business,' Camille said. 'It's a shame.'

'They were perfect for what we wanted to do,' Caleb said. 'It was like these places were built for our particular kind of art.'

'It was so much fun,' Camille continued. 'We would walk into some mall, fan out, and no one had any idea what we were going to do. It was like nothing I'd ever experienced. I could see each one of you, Annie and Buster, but it was a game. I couldn't even acknowledge you, because it would ruin everything. And I just waited for whatever amazing thing to finally happen, all these people walking past us, movement on all sides of us.'

'It was so wonderful,' Caleb agreed.

'And then it happened, whatever we had made. And no matter what it was, I remember how much I loved the aftermath, the confusion on everyone's faces but ours. We were the only ones in the whole world who knew what was happening. And I couldn't wait for that moment, when we were all together again, just the four of us, and we could finally allow ourselves the satisfaction of having made something beautiful.'

'It was the most incredible feeling,' Caleb replied.

Caleb and Camille, perhaps forgetting their cover, held hands, kissed each other. Buster and Annie began to walk away from their parents, Mr and Mrs Fang. Annie, still holding on to the fantasy of causing unrest, wanted to scream out, to make a huge scene, get the police involved, grind everything that mattered to their parents into dust. Buster, sensing her whirling anger, touched her softly on the shoulder, squeezed, kissed her on her cheek. 'Let's go,' he said. 'Let's get far away.'

Annie, her anger unabated, resisted the urge to do what her parents would have done in the same situation, to cause chaos no matter whom it hurt. This, she finally understood, was not what she and Buster had to be a part of anymore. They had stepped mere inches away from the life their parents had made for them, and all they had to do now was to keep moving. She nodded her assent to her brother and her posture relaxed. As they continued to put distance between themselves and their parents, Annie and Buster resisted the urge to turn around, to change that final image of their parents, embracing, happy, nothing in the world that mattered but the art that was inside of them.

Annie and Buster walked out of the mall. They stepped into their rental car and pulled onto the highway. They did not speak, could not find the words to say what they felt. They had brought their parents back from the dead, some kind of strange magic that only the two of them possessed. Annie held out her hand, and Buster took it, the way their joined hands could steady the rotation of the Earth. They listened to the sound of the car's tires on the road and hoped that wherever they ended up next would be a good place, a place of their own making. And they believed, for the first time in their lives, that it would be.

Favor Fire, 2009
Artist: Annie Fang

Annie sat on the floor in the middle of a cavernous bedroom, a row of tiny beds lining the west wall, as she stared at the four children, two boys and two girls, who surrounded her. 'Your hair is short like a boy's,' the youngest of them, Jake, seven years old, as beautiful as a doll, said. 'It is pretty short,' Annie admitted. 'But it's very pretty on you,' said the oldest, Isabel, a fifteen-year-old girl with huge blue eyes and crooked teeth. The other boy, Thomas, twelve years old and already awkward in his body, said, 'Your hair smells nice, too.' Annie nodded at these children, who seemed to close around her. 'Can I kiss you?' the last child, Caitlin, a ten-year-old girl with a dusting of freckles across her nose, asked Annie. Annie paused, looked down at the floor and then over at the closed door to the bedroom. 'I guess so,' Annie said. 'If she gets to kiss you,' Thomas said, 'we should all get to kiss you.' The children held hands and danced in a circle around Annie, screaming, 'Kiss, kiss, kiss, kiss.' Annie looked at the door one more time and then said, 'Okay. Okay. One at a time.' The children shook their heads. 'All at once,' they shouted. Annie nodded and then closed her eyes. She felt their little mouths, slightly wet, press against her cheeks, her forehead, her own mouth. The children made a single, sustained sound, a humming noise that rumbled in their throats. And then Annie smelled smoke, spiraling around her, emanating from the children, and she pushed them away. 'No, no, no, no,' she whispered to the children, who merely laughed and ran to the far corners of the room, smoke trailing them, kicked into strange shapes by their tiny feet.

'Cut,' Lucy shouted. And then the shapes of nearly a dozen people, who had somehow made themselves invisible up to that point, began to scurry around the room, setting and resetting lights, clearing the smoke-like fog from the room. One of the crew members held out his hand for Annie and she took it, pulling herself up from the floor. 'Looked good,' the man said, and Annie smiled. It was the first day of shooting, but it felt to Annie, who had spent so much time in Lucy's presence leading up to filming, that it had been going on for months. Lucy then walked over to Annie, embraced her, and said, 'You are so fucking good at this.' Annie, still not recovered from the strangeness of the last scene, merely nodded, too confused to disagree.

Before filming that first scene, Lucy had recommended that Annie spend as much time with the children as possible. 'They're supposed to love you. So it would help if you could make them love you for real.' Annie shook her head. 'I don't think that's going to happen.' At the rehearsals, Annie had treated the children as she did all actors, with a polite cautiousness, a respect for their space. But on the final night before shooting, Annie had screwed up her courage, knocked on the door of the children's room, and then walked in to find them playing a video game on their PlayStation. 'What is this game?' she asked the children, who, without looking away from the screen, replied, *Fatal Flying Guillotine III.*' Annie smiled. 'Is there some kind of half-man, half-bear in this game?' she wondered, already knowing the answer. 'Major Ursa,' said Thomas. 'Move over,' Annie said, and proceeded to beat the hell out of these four children for nearly an hour. 'You are so good at this,' Isabel said to Annie, who nodded. 'I am,' Annie said. 'I am so good at this.'

The evening after shooting the first scene, Lucy called Annie's hotel room. 'Do you want to come over?' she asked, and Annie, in her pajamas, walked down the hall to Lucy's room. There was a bank of screens, each showing different angles of the same scene, Annie's body nearly obscured by the children, all in bone-white sleeping gowns

408

that ran from their necks to the floor. She sat next to Lucy, each of them donning headphones, and watched the camera slowly zoom in on Annie's face, her eyes shut, the children leaning closer and closer to place their mouths on her. It was more sensual than Annie had expected, though terrifying as well, how Annie shrank and shrank beneath the children's forms, the creeping, twisting smoke that threatened to swallow all of them. 'It's really great,' Annie told Lucy, whose eyes, unblinking, reflected the final shot of Annie prone on the floor. Over the headphones, they could hear the sound of the children's laughter, echoing against the high ceilings of the bedroom.

Buster had sent Annie the most recent draft of his new novel, which she read at night. One afternoon, Isabel found the pages in Annie's bag during a break in filming and said, 'What is this?' Annie told her that it was a story. 'What's it about?' she asked. 'It's about a bunch of kids who get kidnapped and have to fight each other in order to earn their keep.' All at once, the children lined up in front of Annie. 'We want to hear about that,' Thomas said. 'I don't think it's appropriate for kids,' she told them. 'I hate it when people say that,' Caitlin yelled. 'Why do people write stories about kids if they don't want kids to read them?' They begged her to read some of it, and so she grabbed a random page from somewhere in the middle of the novel and read: 'The children grew restless when they weren't in the pit. They took their frustrations out on their own bodies, pressing lit matches against their skin, rubbing against the sharp edges of the holding pen so that they would not lose the anger that they needed to survive.' Thomas clapped his hands. 'You are so going to read this to us,' he said, and so, when they weren't being tutored, as they waited to walk onto the set and burst into flames, the children listened to Annie tell them about the children in Buster's story, who would do unspeakable acts in order to please the adults who watched over them.

One time, Lucy walked into the room just as Annie was telling the children about another expedition by the child wranglers, who set nightly traps in the outlying towns to capture the children who were brave enough, and foolish enough, to stray from their houses. One girl, wrapped in an ever-tightening net, ripped at the ropes until the skin rubbed off of her hands, kicking and screaming as the wrangler dragged her over the rocky terrain. The children looked horrified, but they kept nodding whenever Annie paused, eager for the next awful thing. Annie could not wait for the chance to talk to her brother, to tell him what an amazing, unusual thing he had created. 'What are you doing to them?' Lucy said to Annie. 'They like it,' Annie said. 'They really like it.'

Annie sat on her bed in her tiny room, nothing but the uncomfortable bed, a small nightstand, a desk, and a cheap, unsteady chair. There was a single window, but it was too high for her to look out of it. She pulled open the nightstand drawer and removed a small packet of wooden matches. Opening the box, retrieving a single, sturdy match, she struck the head of the match against the flint and watched the tiny, flared flame spark into existence. She stared at it until her eye held nothing but the dancing flame, always threatening to drown itself in the cramped air of the room. She held the match even as the flame inched further and further down the wood, leaving a brittle, black ash still struggling to retain its previous shape. The match crept closer to the soft pads of her fingertips until, just as she felt the kiss of the flame, she extinguished the match with her own breath.

'That's great, Annie,' Lucy said. 'I think we got it.'

'One more time,' Annie said. Lucy considered it and then nodded her assent. The crew reset the scene and then Annie performed the same task, another match sizzling awake. Annie let the flame burn down until it was at the same point as the previous take. She did not allow a single spasm within her own body to disrupt the tiny fire that she held in her hand. The heat of the flame bit into her fingertips, the skin turning the softest shade of pink, and then, unable to resist any longer, she extinguished the match.

'That's even better,' Lucy said. 'We'll use that one.'

'One more time,' Annie said. She felt like she could do this forever, inviting the flame closer and closer until it made a home beneath her skin, traveled throughout her entire body, and lit her up from the inside.

Isabel was painting her nails, even though she would have to remove the polish as soon as it dried in order to film the next scene. 'Lucy is in love with you,' she said to Annie, who was sharing a bowl of chocolate-covered pretzels with Jake as they watched a cartoon where aliens had entered a skateboard contest. 'What makes you say that?' Annie asked her. 'I can tell,' she said. 'She's really nice to you.' Annie said, 'But she's nice to everyone. That's just how she is.' Isabel smiled, as though she had already deciphered the code that the adults had constructed to keep her in the dark about important things. 'She is extra, extra nice to you, though,' Isabel said.

'If the two of you get married,' Jake said, his mouth filled with a paste of pretzel, 'you should have four children and name them after us.'

Annie stood at the desk of Mr Marbury, the father of the afflicted children, and stared at the numerous drafts of strange architecture, seemingly unrelated to the laws of physics. He had once been a distinguished architect, had designed this very house, but now he spent hours upon hours in this room conjuring up structures that could only exist in another realm. When Marbury and his wife entered the study, the door slamming shut behind them, Annie stiffened and then quickly backed away from the materials.

'Please sit down, Ms. Wells,' he said to Annie, who obeyed his request. The only other time she had been in this room was when they had interviewed her for the position. Mr Marbury had the same countenance as he did then, the disgusted air of having to deal with such an unbecoming situation and the smug certainty that, even with the utter lowliness of the task, Annie was not worthy of the position. Mrs Marbury, silent as ever, simply stood at her husband's side.

'We no longer require your services,' he informed Annie.

'Why?'

'I'm sure you can imagine. There have been far too many *incidents* in recent months. You have proven incapable of restricting the children's *impulses*.'

'I don't think that's fair,' Annie responded.

'I cannot imagine how that factors into my decision.'

'And the children?'

'We have obtained residence for them at a hospital in Alaska, one that specializes in such unique cases. The children will be separated, to dissuade any collective hysteria, and treated with scientific methods that are beyond your capabilities.'

'But they're children,' Annie said, as if Mr Marbury had forgotten this. 'They are your children.'

'Children are not guaranteed the luxuries of family, Ms. Wells,' he said. 'If people are unable to exist within the parameters that have been created for them, they lose any claim to titles like son and daughter.'

Annie felt the heat radiating within her body, her heart an engine of combustion so powerful that she threatened to crack open and fill the entire house with her fury. Annie, who eschewed using her own personal history to inform her performance, simply allowed her actions to come directly from the material at hand: these parents, so certain of their infallibility, terrified of their children's capabilities, sought to erase any evidence of discord in their lives. These were not her parents; she had no desire to create such a flimsy lie. They were only the people that they were, standing in front of her. And they were deserving of punishment.

Annie's hands curled into fists, her nails digging into her own skin, and she struck out at Mr Marbury, sending him crashing to the floor with the force of her blows. She pounded him into unconsciousness and then, his legs spasming uncontrollably, she ran out of the study, leaving Mrs Marbury frozen to her spot on the floor, unable to step toward her downed husband.

Lucy ended the scene and Annie immediately

ran back into the room to check on Stephen, who played Mr Marbury. 'Did I hurt you?' she asked him and he rose unsteadily to his feet. 'You hurt me just the right amount,' he said, 'but I'd rather not do too many takes of it.'

Lucy beamed, staring directly at Annie. 'That was perfect,' she said. 'That was exactly what I needed from you.'

Annie turned to head back to her dressing room, avoiding Lucy's gaze. As she walked past the crew, she clenched and unclenched her fists, admiring the ease with which her character could welcome disaster into her life.

Annie called Buster. 'How is the movie business?' he asked her. She said it was fine, that she was deep enough into the movie that she was operating on instinct, which was when she knew things were working. 'How is the novel?' she asked. He told her that he had sent it to his agent, who was shocked to find out that he was still alive, still writing. 'He thinks it could be big,' Buster told his sister, and she could hear the excitement in his voice, his desire to show her that he was in a good place, that they had both made it to the other side of their unhappiness.

'I think he's right,' she told him.

'And Suzanne just sold a story to the *Missouri Review*. She wants to frame the acceptance letter.'

It struck Annie that Buster was on such solid ground, having always been the most fragile of the

Fangs, that he had surpassed her. She had always taken care of him, protected him from the worst of the chaos, and now he was happy and in love and she was in a frozen place, still trying to figure out how her own body worked.

'Can I ask you something?' she said. Buster was open to any question from her. 'Do you think you made the right decision with Suzanne?'

'That seems like a strange question to be asking me,' Buster answered.

'I just mean, at first, didn't it seem like a crazy thing to do? Because you hardly knew her? Because you are who you are? Because of just about everything that came before this?'

'Actually, it seemed like a good idea, but I was terrified of it. I feel like I've always done things that were profoundly bad ideas, and it's always ended exactly how you'd expect. That comes from Mom and Dad, I think. With the art, they pushed us into circumstances that we already knew were bad ideas. That was the whole point. So they taught us to walk straight into that bad idea, whether or not you really wanted to do it.'

'You make it seem like, regardless of whether it's a good or bad idea, you'll be terrified when it happens,' Annie said. 'The only difference is what comes after.'

'I guess so,' Buster admitted. 'I don't know what I'm talking about, though. I've written a novel about kids beating each other into comas with the broken-off end of a rake. I have poor instincts.'

'I think Lucy is in love with me,' Annie said.

'I see,' Buster responded and then remained quiet for a few seconds. 'So this is why you asked me about Suzanne? You're interested in a possibly successful case study involving Fang romance?'

'I guess.'

'Are you a lesbian?' Buster asked.

'Maybe. I don't know.' She thought about how she had categorized her experience with Minda Laughton as an unqualified disaster, including the decision to be with another woman. But Minda did not seem like a worthy representative of the lesbian experience. Her psychosis excluded her from the sample study.

'It seems like maybe you should figure that out before you have sex with your director.'

'I guess. I don't know.'

'She is pretty cool though,' Buster admitted. 'And she's pretty.'

'What do you think I'm going to do?' she asked him.

'Whatever it is,' he answered, 'I think you'll be terrified when it happens. Don't let that stop you.'

It was freezing cold, snow swirling in the air, and Annie and the four children stood in front of a space heater in their trailer, holding on to each other for warmth, to prepare themselves for their final, reckless act. 'I really like you, Annie,' Jake said. 'I wish this movie wasn't almost over. I'll have to go back to school and the teachers won't be as much fun as you are.' Isabel was starting to cry, and Annie stroked her hair. 'We're not done yet,' Annie told them. 'We still get to do this scene, and it's going to be amazing.' Isabel rubbed her eyes and considered Annie's statement. 'It is going to be pretty cool,' she admitted.

Because they couldn't actually set the house on fire, not with their meager budget, Lucy and the DP and the set designer and some of the special effects guys had decided that they would simply build a gigantic bonfire, obscure the action behind a dense, wooded area, and allow for the final shot, of Annie striding along the highway with the children in tow, to still maintain that sense of a massive conflagration, everything that these characters were leaving behind.

One of the crew knocked on the door of the trailer and Annie and the children walked outside, the cold instantly sinking under their skin. The children were juggling dozens of heating packets, their bare feet stuffed inside shoes with so much fur lining it seemed like an animal had been turned inside out. Lucy knelt in front of the children and explained how the shot would work, how they would arrange themselves around Annie. 'Remember to stay as close to Annie as you can get,' she told the children. 'She is the only person who really loves you and if she slips away from you, there's nothing else that will save you.' She then leaned against Annie and said, 'You just walk away from that fire and don't look back.'

They could just barely see the pyre from where they were located on the edge of the woods, but Annie and the children strained to watch as the wood, doused in accelerants, was sparked to life, a fireball erupting into the air. They could feel the warmth rush through the trees and blow past them. 'Ahhh,' said Caitlin, 'that's nice.' Someone signaled for Annie and she helped the children shuck off their coats, kick away their boots, and when Lucy shouted 'Action,' Annie, carrying Caitlin in her arms, the other children grabbing onto Annie's clothes, emerged from the dense woods and stepped onto the highway. Annie knew there was a fire behind her; she could hear that popping and sizzling of the wood giving up its shape, burning white-hot, turning to ash. She planted her feet, one in front of the other, Caitlin's arms heavy around her neck, and she guided the children down a road that seemed as though it would go on forever. They walked, staring straight ahead, the wind blowing the snow into their faces, but they did not alter their pace, step by step, away from the fire that threatened to swallow up everything around them.

Over the megaphone, Lucy shouted, 'Cut,' and the children immediately broke from Annie and ran toward the warmth of the trailer. Annie stood in the road and watched as Lucy walked quickly toward her, the light of the fire reflected on her face. She stood absolutely still as Lucy, arms outstretched, came closer and closer. Lucy wrapped Annie in a bug and then turned her around to face the fire burning against the tree line. 'Isn't it beautiful?' Lucy asked, her head resting on Annie's shoulder, and Annie stared at the steady flickering of the flames. She marveled at the chaos that surrounded her, and she did not feel even a second fear the conflagration that threatened to overtake her. It was quite beautiful, she admitted, allowing herself to fully take in the sight, perhaps understanding her parents for the first time. She looked into the distance and smiled, held on to Lucy, and watched the fire, which seemed as though it would last forever, that no amount of effort would ever snuff it out.